Contract with an Angel

Also by Andrew M. Greeley
from Tom Doherty Associates

All About Women
Angel Fire
Angel Light
Faithful Attraction
The Final Planet
God Game
Irish Gold
Irish Lace
Irish Whiskey
Star Bright!
Summer at the Lake
White Smoke

Sacred Visions
(edited with Michael Cassutt)

Contract with
an Angel

Andrew M. Greeley

A Tom Doherty Associates Book
New York

CONTRACT WITH AN ANGEL

Copyright © 1998 by Andrew M. Greeley Enterprises, Ltd.

This book is printed on acid-free paper.

A Forge Book
Published by Tom Doherty Associates, Inc.
175 Fifth Avenue
New York, NY 10010

Forge® is a registered trademark of Tom Doherty Associates,
Inc.

Library of Congress Cataloging-in-Publication Data
Greeley, Andrew M.
    Contract with an angel   /   Andrew M. Greeley. — 1st ed.
       p.   cm.
    "A Tom Doherty Associates book."
    ISBN 0-312-86081-1 (alk. paper)
    1. Michael (Archangel) — Fiction.   I. Title.
    PS3557.R358C6 1998
813'.54 — dc21   98-3036
                                                          CIP

First Edition: June 1998

Printed in the United States of America

0   9   8   7   6   5   4   3   2   1

In memory of Ardis Krainik

Transform yourself: the Kingdom of God is near.
— John the Baptist

(This story is an exercise in speculative religious imagination, not in formal theology. Its premise, like that of my other angel books, is that the works on earth we attribute to angels are in fact the result of the intervention of a much more highly evolved bodily creature from "elsewhere.")

Doctor Faustus signed a contract with the devil.
The consequences were disastrous.
This story is about a man who, without much
choice in the matter, signed a contract with an angel.
It is a risky business to get involved with angels.

Contract with an Angel

1

"The scenario says you don't have much longer to live, Raymond Anthony Neenan," the man in the next seat said to him. "You'd better straighten out the mess you've made of your life."

Neenan hadn't noticed anyone sitting next to him on the Saturday-morning trip from Washington National to Chicago. He glanced at his companion, the only other person in the first-class section of the plane—a large black man in a brown suit, brown shirt, brown tie, brown shoes, and brown homburg. He was perhaps six feet six inches tall and as solid as an apartment building, an NFL linebacker or an NBA power forward. He was wearing a large diamond earring.

Pushy, Neenan thought to himself. Probably some kind of Bible-thumping preacher. He felt a slight jolt in his stomach. He should not have eaten that spicy salad at brunch.

He sipped from his vodka glass. Crummy stuff. Served him right for traveling commercial. His Grumman Gulfstream was out of service for repairs. Should buy another one. His time was too valuable to waste on this commercial junk, particularly in bad weather.

"My name is Michael," said the black man, "not Mike, not Mickey, but Michael. As in Michael Jordan. You got a problem with that?"

Neenan ignored him. Best way to treat pests since the law forbade strangling them.

"I'm a seraph," the black man continued. "In fact, as you will remember from Sister John Mark's class in grammar school, Raymond Anthony Neenan, I am the boss seraph."

Neenan snapped his fingers for the cabin attendant. He had turned on his charming smile for her when he boarded the plane—as he always did for service personnel who might contribute to his comfort. He had long since given up pursuing such women for his own pleasure. However attractive, they were generally empty and uninteresting.

"Yes, Mr. Neenan?"

He was about to ask her if he could change seats because the man next to him was annoying him. He stopped just in time. The seat was vacant. Neenan felt fear stab at him, the kind of fear that assailed him on those rare occasions when he could not escape entering a cemetery.

"Would you mind freshening up my drink?" he asked, smiling again.

"Certainly, Mr. Neenan," she said with a faint blush. Women tended to blush when he smiled at them, flattered and a little frightened.

"She can't see me, Ray," the black man said in a rich baritone voice. "Or hear what you're saying when you talk to me. Very few people are able to see us unless we want them to."

The cabin attendant brought back the replenished vodka. Neenan sipped it. It was terrible, no vodka at all, some kind of rotgut gin.

"Don't like it, huh?" the black man said with a smile that disclosed a mouthful of perfect teeth. "I'll see what I can do. Try it now."

Neenan didn't want to play the game, but he sipped the vodka again. It was the best he'd ever tasted. It reminded him of the body of a beautiful woman — soft, smooth, exciting.

"What brand?" he demanded.

"Something we make ourselves," the other replied with a grin. "You can't buy it, no matter how much money you have."

Lightning crackled near the plane. If it had not been for the stupid delay at Washington National, they would have beat the weather front into Chicago.

"What the hell do you want?" Neenan demanded irritably.

"Your immortal soul," Michael responded promptly. "Well, that's the way you'd describe it. . . . I want to make a deal with you for your immortal soul."

Neenan sipped the vodka again. Absolutely superb.

"I don't believe in souls," Neenan told him. "I don't believe in God or heaven or hell or the devil or angels."

"So I understand," the Michael person said in a slow drawl. "So I understand. . . . What happens to you after you die?"

"We're like flashlight batteries. When we run out of energy, people throw us away and get new ones. There's nothing beyond this life. So we enjoy this one as best we can."

"And develop sophisticated tastes in pleasure."

Neenan shrugged his broad shoulders. "I'm a rich and powerful man. I can have whatever I want and whoever I want."

"A conqueror, just like the Huns or the Viking pirates."

Neenan had often used that image in his mind to describe himself. He had never mentioned it to anyone else.

"You take what you can while you can," he replied.

"Destroy men and conquer women?"

"I never killed or raped anyone." Why did this damn ape make him feel guilty?

"Big deal," Michael scoffed. "Actually you can't have everything you want. You can't have immortality, for example. And not every woman is a pushover for your charm either."

Lightning sizzled again, close to the plane, which rocked uneasily and swayed from side to side.

"I learned how to survive," Neenan continued. "Life is a jungle. You get them before they get you. Most of the men I beat were out to get me."

He recalled with pleasure the battle with Harvey Scott, who had dared to try an unfriendly takeover of his cable company. He had driven Harvey out of the industry and seduced his wife. Amy Scott had been a particularly delicious prize.

"Including your father, your son, the men you cheated out of their pensions, the workers you fired?"

"They were all out to take away what was mine."

"You're going to lose that pension case, you know that."

Why was he wasting his time babbling with this freak? "You're dead wrong. I have the best lawyers in the country. We'll wear them into the ground. Stall the case for years."

"Use the law to cheat them?"

"I didn't make the laws."

"You'll lose, maybe even while you're still alive."

"What the hell do you care?"

"It's my job to salvage your immortal soul."

"I don't have one . . . and why should it matter to you?"

Michael said genially, "As far as I'm concerned, you're a worthless pile of refuse. But the Other wants us to make you a project. We generally do what we're asked to do."

"I don't believe I'm going to die."

"All creatures die."

"I know that. I'm in good health. I'm only fifty-five. I'm not about to die anytime soon."

"Yeah?"

"When am I supposed to die?" Neenan demanded as fear probed again at his gut.

"We don't usually know the exact details. Soon. Maybe before Christmas."

"Look, I don't know who you are or what you want. But whatever it is, leave me alone. I've got a stack of reports to read before we get to Chicago."

"I told you what I want: your immortal soul."

Suddenly the jet careened over on its wingtip in a sickening lurch and plunged out of control toward earth. Trays and dishes ricocheted around the cabin. Men and women screamed. The plane's structure groaned as it tried to tear itself apart. Neenan's body was pinned against his seat belt. His life rushed before his eyes. He didn't give a damn. He clenched his fists and waited for the end. Then he did give a damn.

"Save me!" he shouted.

The plane leveled off and continued on its course to Chicago. He looked around the cabin. Nothing had happened.

"Nice fake," he said as he gasped for breath. "Am I supposed to be frightened by the thought of hell or something like that?"

"It wasn't a fake," Michael said. "Look at the marks your fingernails made in your palms."

"Fake," Neenan repeated. "Good fake, scary fake, but still a fake. Now leave me alone."

"We don't use the hell metaphor much anymore. It's been misused too often."

"What else you got?"

"There's always love."

"That's not worth a damn."

Then time stopped for Ray Neenan. He was filled with love and light and laughter and joy and hope. He knew the whole universe and his place in it. Everything converged around him and absorbed him. He knew that all would be well. He was absorbed in happiness, bathed in wonder and surprise, possessed utterly and completely by love. He floated on waves of ecstasy that seemed endless. He rode the crest of eternity. Later when trying to describe to himself what had happened, he would say that the pleasure made orgasm look like a bite of candy.

Slowly it all faded, yet not completely. An afterglow of love lingered with him, consoling him, reassuring him, caressing him.

"That was a fake too?" Michael demanded.

"Was that supposed to be God?" Neenan gasped.

"It will do as a hint."

"And if I don't shape up, I lose that?"

"Appeal to your gambler's instinct?"

Neenan rubbed his hand across his face. "It was better than the best woman."

"You have a dirty mind," Michael said calmly.

"You know what I mean."

"Yeah. . . . Now, do we have a deal?"

"What's the deal?"

"You agree to sell your soul to me and maybe we save it."

"What do you mean sell my soul to you? Am I supposed to be Faust to your Mephistopheles?"

"You shouldn't take the opera version too seriously. Nor Goethe either. We bailed that idiot out at the last minute, but only because Marguerite wanted us to."

Michael produced a legal-looking document bound in a gold ribbon. He unrolled it and presented it to Neenan.

I the undersigned, Raymond Anthony Neenan, also known as "R. A.," do hereby admit that I am a worthless piece of excrement. Nevertheless, in view of the possibility of saving my immoral soul I do also hereby agree to entrust it to the supervision of Michael, chief of the heavenly hosts. I will follow all the instructions of said Michael to the best of my ability, so help me God.

"You mean *immortal* soul?" Neenan asked.

"Hmnn . . ." The alleged seraph peered over Neenan's shoulder. "Isn't that what we say?"

The letter *t* suddenly inserted itself.

"Better get a new secretary," Neenan murmured.

Michael ignored him. "*Soul* is a word of which we're not particularly fond," Michael said smoothly. "Not *salvation* either, as far as that goes. We're interested in the fulfillment of the total person, as psychologists would say today. However, since you've learned almost nothing about religion since the sixth grade, we felt that these terms would have to do."

"Am I a slave or something?"

"Nonsense! We make suggestions, you consider them and follow them. We'll negotiate the small stuff."

The last sentence was a line that Ray Neenan had often used himself. Those who knew him never trusted him when he said that.

"I'm no mystic," he said, trying to stall, as he often did in negotiations.

"That wasn't the first time," Michael replied.

"What do you mean?"

"You had experiences like that when you were a little boy, before you went to kindergarten. You've never forgotten them. You've resisted similar experiences all through your life."

"Like when?"

"When your son was born."

"That asshole."

"If he's an asshole, you had a lot to do with his becoming an asshole. . . . Now, here's a pen, sign it!"

The pen was apparently of solid gold and thick. Seraphs apparently deserved the best pens.

Neenan hesitated. "How long do I have?"

"Frankly, as I said before, I don't know. Long enough to straighten out enough of your messes."

Frankly was another word that signaled those who knew him to be wary of R. A. Neenan.

"You softened me up with that fake crash and then knocked me over with that ecstasy stuff."

"It wasn't a fake. It's what would have happened if we hadn't intervened. The pilot on this plane didn't make all the checks he should have. More pilot error."

"Do you do these things often?"

"Prevent crashes? Why do you think there are not a lot more of them? Sign it!"

None of this was actually happening, he told himself. It was all a dream, a silly fantasy. There were no angels, much less seraphs. He was not going to die soon. There was no life after death. He was not being asked to turn his soul over to a large, black angel with a jewel in his ear.

There was, Ray Neenan figured, nothing much to lose. It was a win-win situation. Later he would conclude that he had miscalculated.

So he took the fat, gold-and-ivory pen from the alleged seraph and affixed to the document the famous and frightening signature for which he had become famous.

R. A. Neenan

The plane was filled with music and unbearably beautiful song, better music and far better song than he had ever heard in the great opera houses of the world. Neenan didn't understand the words — they were in no language he had ever heard. But he knew that they were songs of celebration, indeed of unspeakable joy.

"What's that?" he demanded.

"Oh, don't pay any attention to them," Michael said, waving a dismissive hand. "Some of my colleagues like to sing."

"When they think they've landed another fish."

"I wouldn't put it that. . . . Now, since we're going to have to circle around Lake Michigan for another hour or so, let's negotiate some of the small stuff."

"The pilot didn't announce that."

"I'm sorry, ladies and gentlemen, we have an air traffic problem at O'Hare due to the thunderstorm which you can see to the north of the city. They're vectoring us over the Lake now. We expect an approach in ten to fifteen minutes."

The damn angelic chorus sang more loudly and more joyfully.

Hell, I must be a really big fish.

2

"First of all," Michael said, relaxing in his seat, "there is the matter of your parents."

"Senile fools," Neenan snorted.

"Ah, ah." Michael waved a warning finger. "We don't like that kind of language."

"It's true."

"It is fair to say your mother suffers from a serious case of Alzheimer's syndrome."

"And has for most of her life."

"Your father, however, is quite sane."

"And as mean and nasty as ever. He resents my success. You'd think he'd be happy that his son is one of the richest and most successful men in the telecommunications industry. Instead he hates me for becoming everything he wanted to be and couldn't because his wife wouldn't let him."

"A fact which you drive home to him on every possible occasion."

"He has it coming."

"I will not try to dispute that. Nonetheless you must try to make peace with him. His reaction to that is his problem."

"I don't want to."

"Might I remind you that you're under contract?"

Laurence and Maude Neenan had married in 1941. He was a corporal in the army, one of the first men drafted as America prepared for war. She had graduated the year before from Immaculata High School. He was four years older than she was. Both of them had grown up in St. Jerome's parish on the north side of the city, not too far from the Lake. He had paid no attention to her until he came home on his leave after his basic training, afraid of death and hungry for the body of a woman. He was overwhelmed by her full-bodied beauty. Who seduced whom was never clear, though in later life they would blame one another. They were married before he left for Hawaii after the bombing of Pearl Harbor, the bride already three months pregnant.

In the wedding photograph, Laurence Neenan, a small, furtive man in a badly fitting uniform, looked like a trapped animal.

Raymond Anthony Neenan was the only child of that shotgun marriage. When his mother was unhappy with him because he did not follow her wishes that he become a priest, she would tell him that he was not good enough for the priesthood because he had been conceived in a rape. Larry Neenan suggested to him that someone else was probably his father because he did not resemble either of his parents. It had been easy to hate both of them all his life.

Larry's father, the original Raymond Anthony Neenan, had survived the Great Depression by operating a small machine shop on Irving Park Road. According to Maude, the elder Ray was a crook who cheated every customer who ever trusted him. The younger Ray never had any reason to doubt this charge.

Nor did he ever have any reason to reject Larry's suspicions about his parentage. A tall, husky, good-looking kid, he resembled neither of his parents. He did not consider his mother's obsessive piety as evidence that she had always been virtuous.

Larry came home from the war in 1945, having never left a supply depot in Hawaii. In early 1946 his father died. Larry inherited the machine shop and a small radio station in Elgin, Illinois, in the Fox River valley, which the elder Ray had picked up as a bargain in 1935. Both possessions were potential gold mines in the immediate postwar years. However, Maude, who had seized control of the inheritance before Larry's return, was certain that the Depression would return and forbade expansion of either enterprise. As it was, the Neenans made a lot of money in the postwar years, but Maude doomed Larry's dreams of becoming rich and famous.

"Just as well she kept him away from the money," R. A. would later remark. "He's a loser. He would have blown it all."

How I hate her, Ray reflected as he paused in his review of his life. Hate, hate, hate. She damn near ruined my life. If she had left me alone, I would have had a normal adolescence. I would have learned more about women. I would never have married my first wife.

Maybe that's unfair.

Then his thoughts turned to his second wife, Anna Maria. She was the kind of woman he would have married in his twenties if his mother had left him alone. His fantasies took over. He recalled the joy of undressing Anna Maria on their wedding night. His sexual hunger, seemingly extinguished by the crash experience, reasserted itself. He longed to caress her. Now. Banish all the fears the damn seraph had created within him.

He would have to wait.

Neenan was a popular student at St. George's High School. His good looks, charm, and athletic ability won him many friends. He played first string on the frosh-soph basketball team and was sophomore class president. However, his mother was convinced that such accomplishments would interfere with his priestly vocation and she forbade him from engaging in sports or running for class office. For reasons that he never fully understood, he complied. His classmates still liked him, but they frequently dismissed him as a pushover for his mother. Neenan withdrew into himself and became a loner. He also gave up on sports until he moved to De Kalb. There he took up golf because he thought he could find financial backers at the country clubs in the Fox River and the Rock River valleys. Golf became his only hobby, if something played with such relentless passion could be considered a hobby.

After he graduated from St. George's High School in 1960, Ray had joined the army to get his military service obligations out of the way and to make some money to pay for college. Since he still refused to consider the priesthood, Maude had decreed that he would have to pay for his education and not "live off your family." Ray despised the military and hated his eighteen months in Alaska. Later he rejoiced that he had escaped the Vietnam War.

At the age of twenty he went to work as an advertising salesman for his father's radio station, WRAN. Although the Chicago suburbs had expanded into the Fox River Valley, the station still served a farming audience with a mix of Glen Miller music, crop reports, commodity news, and advertising for agricultural products. Even within such limitations it was a moneymaker. Ray had no trouble selling time on the station from his apartment in De Kalb, where he attended Northern Illinois University, a safe distance from Maude's pious domination.

After a year as a salesman, Ray knew that the potential of WRAN in the suburban markets was barely being touched. He persuaded

Howard Carlisle, the owner of a small network of farm-oriented stations farther out in the Illinois hinterland, to make Larry an offer that Maude, still convinced of hard times, could not refuse and then to name Ray general manager of the new station.

"You'll run it into the ground," Larry had told Ray on one of the rare occasions they encountered one another. "Howie Carlisle is out of his mind."

"You've been running it into the ground for fifteen years."

He hated his father too, a passive-aggressive weakling, a pint-size ogre, who tried to make up for his surrender to Maude with constant ridicule of his son. Often Ray wanted to beat the mean little man into a pulp. He still wanted to do it.

He was clenching his fists again.

With a new mix of news, rock music, and talk radio—the latter two purchased from syndication—Ray tripled the profits from the station within a year. Carlisle was impressed. Ignoring the complaints of the disappointed farmers, he made Ray general manager of his five-station network. Once again Ray worked his magic and made the new suburban network a huge success. At twenty-five, with a degree from NIU in his pocket and, as he put it, a growing family, he was becoming a name to be reckoned with in the fast-growing radio world of northern Illinois.

His next step was to put together a syndicate of men he had met at the Fox River Valley Country Club who would buy out Carlisle and a minor station in Chicago itself. Carlisle resisted at first but yielded when certain shadowy figures in Chicago to whom he owed large gambling debts leaned on him.

Ray was now the president and general manager and part owner of Chicago Radio Enterprises, a company that the *Chicago Tribune* had called a cash cow. Personally, Ray, already a patron of the Chicago Lyric Opera, hated rock music, but he had known there was a fortune to be made in the youth market, and he made that fortune for himself and his stockholders by the time he was thirty in 1972. He had squeezed out the other owners, one way or another, just as he had dropped his father and Howie Carlisle. He had now become a wealthy and powerful man, but he did not have enough wealth or power yet. He had wanted more of both. He would always want more.

What a lonely time those years in De Kalb had been. Despite his success in business and with the women he had hunted with crafty charm, he felt empty most of the time. He married because he wanted to fill that emptiness, but Donna had only made it worse.

He recalled their wedding night with disgust. Anna Maria had been shy and embarrassed but generous and even playful. Donna, easy with her charms while they were courting, became a irritable prude in their hotel room. She resisted his kisses and caresses, refused to undress or let him undress her, turned out the lights, and snarled, "Let's get this over with."

His powerful passion dismissed as "dirty," he felt like beating her into submission. He restrained himself and never laid a violent hand on her. He told himself often in the early years of their marriage that she would eventually get over her aversion to sex. Then he realized that he was kidding himself.

He hated her too. His fists clenched again, until his nails dug into his palms. So much hatred in his life.

In 1975, Ryan Kane, the wealthy owner of a group of television stations in small Midwestern cities and an endangered cable network lured Ray to turn around his corporation, National Cable, with an offer of a large stock option. Ray did indeed turn around the operation by hiking fees for subscribers every year and cutting the number of free services to an absolute minimum. He also turned Kane out.

By the middle 1980s Ray had become a national figure in entertainment, not as big as Turner or Murdoch perhaps, but big enough to fight off all predators. He had earned his success by shrewdly judging markets, exploiting employees whenever he could, disposing of allies as though they were used paper napkins, and following his instincts each time a new risk appeared.

His father, Carlisle, and Kane all predicted that someday he would encounter someone who was bigger than he was and "would beat him into the ground," as Kane had put it. Ray laughed at them. He had done to them no more than they would have done to him if they had been smart enough to go after him when he was vulnerable. He had merely been more ruthless and much smarter than they were.

"You've been a loser, Dad," he had said to his father. "Always have been since the day you let Mom seduce you. You resent me because I was smart enough to get out of the house when I graduated from St. George's and have been a winner ever since."

At that time, the *Wall Street Journal* had written that he was a "reckless and ruthless — and very lucky — buccaneer." He had told the *Jour-*

nal's reporter that he was not lucky. He had merely been fortunate and his defeated adversaries had lacked "proper caution."

At first he had been baffled by those who trusted him when there was no good reason why they should. Later he realized that all of them, his father alone excepted, had confused his genial Irish charm with honesty and integrity. They were all innocent of integrity themselves. They would have destroyed him if he had not beaten them to it. That's the way the world was. In pursuing money, power, and women, there were no rules. You took what you could get any way you could.

Guilt? He swirled his vodka glass. Not till now. Why was he feeling guilt now?

The damn seraph was messing him up.

When he had succeeded as a film producer with several sentimental celebrations of the 1950s — an era that had been hellish for him — even the *Journal* treated him with respect, quoting one of his rivals who called him "a telecommunications genius." Ray liked the compliment but was not fooled by it. He had seen enough high rollers in the industry go under when they began to believe their own press clippings.

"You're happier than you were in those days when you had WRAN all to yourself?" Michael asked him as the plane circled in the clouds above Lake Michigan.

"What's happiness?" Neenan replied. "I enjoyed that time only because I saw it as a way to something bigger. If I hadn't swept aside all those jerks, starting with my father, someone else would have. None of them are starving. I made them all richer than they would have been if I didn't take over their firms. I don't care whether they like me. I don't even care whether they're grateful. I did them all a big favor. Beyond that I don't give a damn."

"Aren't you afraid that you'll overreach?"

"No way. It's not an ego thing for me like for Murdoch or Turner. I want power, but not so badly that I'm going to risk myself by running up debt like Murdoch or getting involved with those crazies at *Time.* . . . Where are your wings?"

"Wings? Oh, you shouldn't take that art seriously. It's a metaphor for how fast we can move."

"How fast can you move? Speed of light?"

"Faster than that. Not quite the speed of thought."

"Really?"

"Yeah. . . . Your employees don't particularly like you either."

"Why should I care? If they do a good job, they get rewarded. If they don't, they're finished. You can't let your emotions interfere with efficiency. . . . But, look, I'm not a dictator. I don't micromanage. I let the companies and the stations make their own decisions. So long as they show profitability, I leave them alone."

"And if they don't show profitability?"

Neenan snapped his fingers. "They're history."

Why, he wondered, did he feel defensive? He was a businessman. That's what businessmen did, wasn't it?

"All of this makes you happy?"

"What's happiness?"

"And when you die?"

"Then I'll die. . . . What's supposed to kill me?"

"A lot of this stuff is 'need-to-know' and we don't need to know when or why you're going to die."

"And you don't care?"

Was it the vodka or the fake crash or the ecstasy or the feelings of hatred that had followed the ecstasy that was tearing at Neenan's insides? He felt he was coming apart like a house in a hurricane wind. Why had he begun to feel that his life was a waste? Why did it matter whether the angel liked him?

"Another vodka, Mr. Neenan?" the cabin attendant asked, still blushing.

"No, I don't think so. . . . Well, all right, just a small one."

"We're not businessmen," Michael replied. "We care about our clients. We even love them."

"Even if they're a pile of refuse?"

"Do you enjoy making that young woman blush?"

"She doesn't seem to mind."

"She senses you're thinking what she'd be like in bed, and she's both pleased and embarrassed. Later on she'll figure out that you're a tease and won't like it."

"Can't I appreciate an attractive woman?"

"You can appreciate them without the touch of the leer in your charming smile."

"I didn't know I was leering."

The woman returned with the vodka.

"I don't know how you manage to be so polite with this plane racketing around in the clouds," Neenan told her.

This time she grinned and did not blush. "Thank you, Mr. Neenan."

"Better," Michael admitted.

"Is this part of the deal?"

"Reread the contract. . . . Now, about your wife . . ."

"Look, Donna threw me out. After eighteen years. She wanted to be her own person. Was fed up with being a decoration for me. Didn't like the entertainment industry. Didn't like the people I associated with. Should never have married me in the first place. She didn't know I was fooling around and didn't care either. She hated me and wanted to get rid of me. You can't blame me for her."

"I meant your present wife . . . but let's talk about Donna first."

"I don't want to. She was right. We should have never married. She doled out sex like it was a cookie for a kid who had obeyed his mommy. She didn't like it. Didn't want to try to like it. Hated me for wanting it."

"It was more complicated than that," Michael observed.

"I married a woman just like my mother," Neenan protested. "I should have known better."

"I won't argue the first point," Michael sighed.

Neenan was experiencing a nightmare. The seemingly endless circles over Lake Michigan, the bizarre character who claimed to be an angel, the taste of the vodka, the imagined crash, the faint voices singing in the background, the ecstatic experience — all these were the stuff of nightmares. All his previous nightmares had ended. Presumably this one would too. He would play along with the phony seraph until Michael faded back into the murk of his unconscious.

The trouble with this interpretation was that the afterglow of ecstasy seemed all too real.

"You're obsessed with women, aren't you?" Michael said, continuing his cross-examination.

"I'm no Don Giovanni if that's what you mean."

"Oh, no. You're more careful, more discreet, more tasteful, more honest, less promiscuous, less cruel, less stupid."

"I never forced a woman, I've never been charged with sexual harassment, I've never broken anyone's heart, whatever that means."

"You've always been a careful man," Michael agreed. "Both in business and in love, if you want to call what you do love. But you cannot control and will not try to control your hunger for power or for women."

"I have to stop that or I go to hell?"

"I told you that we don't use that metaphor anymore. . . . Naturally you don't have to abandon your appetites. You simply have to retrain them and focus them."

"In a few months?"

"Better that than fighting against them for twenty more years."

This was definitely a nightmare. "I'd rather try the twenty years."

"Twenty years of resisting your quest for what you consider interesting women to seduce? Does this pursuit bring you any fulfillment? Once you've ravaged a woman, you grow weary of her and are doomed to seek another. Is there joy in that?"

"There sure is. . . . Besides, I don't ravage them and I don't drop them immediately — sometimes I don't drop them at all."

"Sometimes they even drop you."

"That's up to them."

"You must also seek pardon from them for using them."

"They don't think there's anything to pardon and they don't think I've used them."

"Are you sure of that?"

Neenan had been initiated into the mysteries of sex as a confused fourteen-year-old by an experienced young woman who was a sophomore in college. She was bored during her summer vacation and found the tall, husky young man, whom she'd encountered on a Lake Michigan beach, an amusing project. She had teased him and tormented him and then led him down the path to some of the outer swamps of pleasure. When she returned to college after dismissing him as a lover, Neenan thought he had learned two lessons: Sex, as he would later say, was a zero-sum game. There was always a winner and a loser. Moreover, women found him a sexually attractive challenge.

He made up his mind that he would never be a loser again and that he would pursue only women who seemed, for one reason or another, "interesting" and prepared for seduction, especially if it was gentle, tender, and respectful. There were, he reasoned, plenty of such women around.

He would make mistakes. His wife was neither interesting or sexually hungry. In that long relationship he was definitely the loser.

He carried on his search for sexual conquests with care and caution. He was, he told himself, too smart to put himself at risk.

Women became for him fascinating, maddening, delicious, intriguing, delectable prizes to be hunted with skill and wit and charm. His next conquest after the woman who found him on the beach was a friend of his mother's, an attractive and restless matron in her early forties, all the more "interesting" because of his delight in deceiving his mother. Just having turned sixteen at the time, he pursued this woman with relentless wariness and finally overcame her resistance in his mother's bedroom while the latter had gone off to the store to purchase cakes for her unexpected tea guest. As soon as she had left, the victim knew she was doomed; but she would not have dropped by the apartment for a surprise visit if she had not wanted to be doomed.

She was a superb prize, a lush taste of forbidden fruit that Neenan had enjoyed intermittently for several years.

This time he was the winner.

From her he had learned that the pursuit and capture of a woman was more fun than the actual possession. Nonetheless, intermittent possession had its rewards too, especially because it involved seduction all over again. He also learned that he had the skills to seduce and satisfy the kind of woman he selected to be a prize — not all the time perhaps, but often enough to make the game interesting. He never felt that he had "used" them as the alleged seraph claimed. They knew there was no long-term future in the relationship. They had enjoyed what there was as much as he had, they had reveled in being pursued as he did in pursuing, hadn't they? What was wrong with that?

Then as the years passed and he became rich and powerful, he came to believe that he had the right to capture women for his pleasure. If they resisted, he continued the pursuit. If they hesitated, he did not give up. If they tried to brush him off, he turned on all his charm. If they told him that they did not want to see him again, he showered them with expensive gifts. The game of chasing a woman commanded at least as much of his attention as National Entertainment. He luxuriated in a long pursuit rather than a short one. Indeed, he avoided quests that threatened to be too easy.

A woman did not have to be young or beautiful to interest him. She had to be intelligent, mature, self-possessed, and, if at all possible, forbidden in one way or another, the sort of woman who would flirt with him discreetly, serene in her confidence that he would not be able to break through her resistance. To be "interesting" a woman had to be a challenge, confident that in any sexual encounter she would be the winner.

In recent years he had chosen for his prey women who were so-phisticated and, if possible, successful in the entertainment world. His last conquest, and he licked his lips whenever he thought of her, had been a brilliant woman film producer. He was currently hunting the president of a regional cable firm, hoping to conquer both her and her company, a mouthwatering prospect — to own the woman both in bed and in the business world. She could hardly claim sexual harassment after he owned both of them. He particularly relished relationships where the woman of her own volition became a temporary slave.

The hunt had gone on for many months. He thought that now he was close to victory.

"Victory" for him was to turn her into the loser and make her enjoy it.

"You're a predator," Michael said. "You hunt women like other men hunt elk or wild boars."

"I'm not going to deny that. I don't kill them though. In fact, I don't even hurt them. What's wrong with that?"

"That's the problem. You don't know what's wrong with that. You're going to have to find out."

"How the hell can I do that?"

"Ask them."

"No way. I won't do it."

Michael slowly withdrew the folded "contract" from his pocket and tapped Neenan's shoulder with it.

"Yes, you will."

"I've been a celibate for long periods of time. Donna wouldn't sleep with me and my adventures often went on for months before I won."

"That should tell you something interesting about yourself."

3

The pilot announced yet another delay. Lightning exploded just beyond the plane's wingtips.

"I don't even have a reputation as a predator," Neenan argued in his own defense. "They don't think of themselves as victims."

"Even though they are?"

"I don't think they are," he said hotly.

"You think they've become temporary slave women. Doesn't that make them victims?"

How does he know what I think? "It's what they want to be"

"Do they?"

"Don't they?"

"You've covered your tracks very cleverly," Michael changed the subject, having created more feelings of guilt.

Neenan finished his vodka. He'd drunk too much. He would not have his wits about him for the meeting at O'Hare.

"You don't want to get a reputation like that," he explained to the pseudo-seraph. "It makes you a sitting duck for sexual harassment charges."

"You were so good at covering up that your wife never raised the issue of infidelity in her divorce suit."

"About the only thing she didn't charge."

"You put a private detective on her and found that she had taken a lover, didn't you?"

"My divorce lawyer suggested it. I told him it was impossible. But her demands were enormous. I offered her a big cash settlement. She wanted more and a share of everything I'd built up. So I told him to do whatever it took. He found out she was sleeping with this doctor from De Kalb she'd gone to high school with."

"So you cut your offer of a cash settlement in half and she took it?"

"You bet."

"Because she was cheating on you?"

"Because she was trying to cheat me. . . . Anyway, she got one of those Catholic divorce things and married the guy and lost a lot of weight and earned her college degree. She is financially comfortable and, I'm told, happier than she's ever been."

"She even produced another daughter, didn't she?"

"That's true," Neenan admitted grudgingly.

"So he must have something you didn't have?"

"We've been given an approach time of thirty-five after the hour," the captain announced tonelessly. "That's forty minutes from now."

Neenan grabbed for the phone in the armrest next to him and impatiently punched in a number. He fumed as he waited for an answer.

"Joe? Neenan here. What the hell took you so long to answer? . . .

"You mean you're not out at the airport? I don't give a damn what time they say the plane is going to land. I told you I wanted you guys there at noon. That meant I wanted you at noon, regardless of the weather. Sometimes these things clear up in a hurry. . . .

"That's no excuse. . . . What's the status of the Gulfstream? . . . It damn well better be ready by Friday. . . . Look, I won't have time to meet you people at the Admiral's Club. You can ride over to Lake Forest in my car. Get in touch with my driver and set it up. Got it?"

Neenan hung up and frowned angrily. "Assholes."

"Nice way to talk to your executive vice president. You have to treat him like an errand boy?"

"Treat him any better and he'll think he has a right to my job."

"I had observed that your wife's second husband must have had something you didn't have."

Neenan gritted his teeth. "It would seem so, wouldn't it?"

Donna O'Connell had been a terrible mistake. When he was a senior, she was a freshman at Northern Illinois, the daughter of a prominent and affluent De Kalb medical family. He had just taken over the farm network and was intoxicated with success and prospects for greater success. The town of De Kalb, if not the university, was still part of the 1950s suburban culture—home, family, two cars, high school football games on the weekend. *The Donna Reed Show*. Donna was intelligent and pretty and quite prepared to participate in every imaginable form of foreplay so long as it did not cross the line into intercourse. Her parents liked him, and astonishingly, his father and mother seemed to like her. She'll make a man of you, they said. So

Neenan had bought into the American dream. It was time, he told himself, that he give up his sexual escapades and settle down with a wife and family, a family that, he told himself, would be as joyous as his own had been devoid of joy.

There had been signs even before the marriage that ought to have warned him. His mother and her mother became friends all too easily. Yet it was unthinkable that Donna could ever become the chronic complainer and nag that his mother had always been. During their honeymoon trip to Ireland, however, she had complained about the food, the weather, the hotels, the service, the poverty, the slovenliness of the people, and the ugliness of the countryside.

Despite her prudery, he had taken her marvelous young body, on which he gorged himself. He had made her undress for him (which she thought was disgusting), insisted that the lights be on when they made love, and forced her to accept his foreplay, which did not seem to arouse her in the slightest. When she protested, he lectured her about a wife's obligation to her husband, exploiting her Catholic education.

He told himself that she would grow in her sexual self-confidence and that all would be well between them.

But it never was. Once their first child, Vincent, named in honor of his maternal grandfather, arrived eighteen months after their wedding, the baby became the focus of her life. Two subsequent children, Jennifer and Leonard, born at two-year intervals, filled her life completely. She was never without help, but the children exhausted her, she had claimed, and she was too tired for sex and too tired to take any interest in his expanding business enterprises.

"I'm sick of hearing how important you are," she had informed him.

She also began to ridicule him in bed when he tried to arouse her, understanding at last his vulnerability to ridicule.

"I hope you're enjoying what you're doing," she had told him one night, "because I'm not getting anything out of it."

She took care of the house and the family, and he took care of the job. They rarely fought because he gave in to almost all of her demands. The children became sullen strangers who looked on him with distaste whenever he came home from a trip to Los Angeles or New York. The boys seemed to him to be effete sissies, and Jennifer hated him, turning away in disgust when he tried to kiss her.

They were all furious at him when he moved the family to Chicago. They dismissed the big house in Evanston across the street from the Lake as "ugly and cold" and promptly hated all their neighbors.

Later when he had purchased a condo on Captiva and an apartment in London, they refused to visit either home because all they wanted was to move back to De Kalb.

Donna also refused to share his interest in opera. "Why should I sit still for four hours and listen to all that shouting? I hate opera and I hate the phonies that don't hate it."

That was pretty definite. Neenan always felt odd when the other major patrons of the Lyric asked him, gently of course, whether his wife was interested in opera. Routinely he would reply that she was still busy with their three children.

Donna had put on at least fifty pounds and seemed to rejoice that she had made herself sexually unappealing. After the birth of Jennifer, Neenan gave up on the suburban domestic dream and carefully began again his sexual adventures.

However, he did not seriously consider divorce. He had long since given up any Catholic faith—though he went to church to give a good example to his children. However, he loved his kids, though they seemed to despise him, and believed that divorce was not good for the children. It did not occur to him that Donna, loyal and faithful Catholic that she was, could ever file a divorce suit against him.

They had been married eighteen years and had three teenage children when she broke the news to him.

"I'm sick and tired of being R. A. Neenan's wife," she said. "I want to be my own person. You've ruined twenty years of my life. I won't let you ruin the next twenty. I want you out of this house tonight. You make me sick, every time I see you."

He felt someone had hit him over the head with a hammer. At first he feared that she had found out about his adventures. But he was never charged with infidelity. Her rationale for the divorce was that she was tired of being an ornament to his career and of being ignored by him as an unimportant nuisance.

A second blow to the head was his discovery that she had taken a lover five years before the divorce, a chubby, bald, little M.D. from De Kalb who had been her high school prom date.

"I don't blame her at all," Jennifer had snarled at him. "A husband like you would drive any woman to adultery."

Neither Jennifer nor Leonard would speak to him. Now, ten years after the divorce, they would not answer his phone calls or respond to his Christmas cards. Leonard, the youngest, was living in San Francisco with a gay roommate. Neenan had learned that Leonard had come out of the closet in a rare phone call from Donna.

"I hope you're happy, you dirty bastard, your younger son is a faggot."

Busy with a major merger, Neenan had had little time to wonder where it had all gone wrong.

Jennifer had declared herself to be an actress, worked as a stage-hand and bit player in an off-Loop company on Lincoln Avenue, and had two years ago moved to Los Angeles to make her way in the world of Hollywood, where pretty young women like her seem to disappear. Anna Maria had insisted that they see her in a play where she had a minor but not totally unimportant role. Jennifer had seen them come in and stormed out from behind the set.

"You and your whore get out of here," she had thundered. "Do you want to ruin my big chance? I won't go onstage as long as you are in the house."

He had tried to reason with her, but Anna Maria dragged him out.

"You were not a very good father to her, were you, Ray?"

"I don't know what I did wrong."

Vincent, who had always seemed timid in his father's presence, had quickly learned to detest his stepfather. When he had graduated from Drake, he came to his father about a job. He had worked for National Entertainment for seven years and, in his father's judgment, was an incompetent weakling, utterly without the killer instinct that the industry required.

Neenan had feared that he too was gay, but he was now apparently happily married to a sensible young assistant state's attorney, named Megan McGrath (pronounced McGraw), and had produced a child whom they had called Ramona.

They apparently wanted to be friends with him, especially since Donna so hated Megan as to refuse to come to the wedding. Somehow they hadn't managed to connect in a relaxed fashion. They both seemed frightened of Neenan and diffident in the presence of Anna Maria. They tried hard to please him, and somehow it never worked out.

"What a lovely young couple," Anna Maria had commented. "They adore you."

"I can't figure out why."

"Neither can I."

Neenan rubbed his hand across his face. Why did he feel guilty about his life? He was not ashamed of himself. Why had he let this damn fool black man upset him?

"You've pretty much made a mess out of your life, haven't you?" Michael observed with apparent satisfaction.

"I don't see it that way," Neenan answered hotly. "I don't believe that there's any reason for me to feel guilty."

Still he felt guilty. And again he had the sensation of being torn apart, like a public-housing high-rise imploding in a demolition explosion.

"What if all the things Sister John Mark told you in grammar school were true?"

"Then I'll go to hell and probably deserve it. But you've told me there isn't any hell."

"I said that we didn't like to use that metaphor much anymore."

"What the hell kind of people are you anyway? You're some kind of angels or something?"

"Let's say that we're responsible for most of the phenomena which your kind attributes to angels."

"You really look like you do now?"

He reached over and touched the black man's arm—firm and solid.

Neenan noticed that the choir was singing softly in the background. Maybe they had been singing all along. He tried to link the music with the conversation. There was some kind of connection all right, but its meaning escaped him, though Michael's words seemed to get the stronger tunes.

"Not ectoplasm?" the alleged seraph said with a vast smile. "Actually, if I should show myself the way I am, it would blind you and scare everyone in three or four states. What you see and what you just touched is a surrogate which interprets us to you in a manner you can understand. It's not me, but it's not not-me either."

"You're pure spirits of some kind?"

"Sister John Mark was wrong on that. We have bodies as you do, though a very different kind of body. We're far more advanced in our evolutionary process than you are in yours. Our bodies have developed in the direction of supporting more profound thought and more intense love and hence are invisible to your eyes, for which you should be grateful."

"You're immortal?"

"Typical human question. If we have bodies, we deteriorate just as you do. It takes a lot longer, but we still die. We believe that we survive death and our evidence is much stronger, but still we do not know for certain."

"How much longer?"

Michael shrugged. "Thousands of years. But it's never enough time."

"You have women?"

"We call them life-bearers. How could a species with bodies survive without procreation? Perhaps you will meet my companion on some occasion."

"I'd like that."

"I doubt it. She's not nearly as patient with human nonsense as I am."

"You, ah, screw?"

"Naturally . . . and to respond to your prurient questions before you ask them, it takes days. . . . Now, to get back to your failures as a human being. Does it not strike you that you are a poor excuse for a husband, a parent, a child, and a friend? Your first wife dumped you, your parents and two of your three children hate you and the third fears you, your employees fear you, your colleagues despise you, and you have almost no friends."

"I'm rich and powerful and I have the women I want."

"That would be true of the silverback in a highland gorilla band or the alpha male in community of chimps or Yellowstone timber wolves."

"That's supposed to make me feel bad?"

"The point is that, whenever you think about your life, you do feel bad."

"I do *not!*"

"And now, when I break through your carefully constructed denial mechanisms, as strong as those business protections against Murdoch or Disney or Turner or Walter Murtaugh, you feel yourself cracking up like an airplane exploding in the sky."

"I don't like that metaphor."

"The question is whether it is accurate. Regardless of Sister John Mark and the Other and your own glorious religious tradition, you have fouled up your life even by the most elementary human standards. I'm not saying that there were not excusing factors, because palpably there were. I am saying that our agreement"—Michael slipped it out of his pocket again—"requires that you admit your failures as a first step."

The background chorus sounded ominous.

"Today? Now?"

"That would be expecting too much. But soon. Especially in your attempts to straighten out as much as you can while you still have time."

"Like in that film Anna Maria and I watched the other night, uh, what was the name of it?"

"*Flatliners?* I trust," the seraph said with what might have been a smirk, "that you don't think we had nothing to do with that choice."

"Anna Maria is an unindicted coconspirator?"

"Not exactly."

"When you started to talk about my wife, you meant her, didn't you? And I thought you meant Donna."

"Obviously Anna Maria is the only wife you have ever had."

Neenan did not get a chance to question that strange observation.

"We've been cleared for landing," the pilot announced suddenly. "Cabin attendants prepare for landing."

The plane nosed forward in a sudden lurch, the landing gears crunched into place, and the plane dove into ever thicker clouds. Lighting sparked again and again at the wingtips. Back in coach, cabin passengers gasped. The two cabin attendants, strapped in and facing backward, were pale and tense.

Michael, for his part, smiled benignly, enjoying every minute of the roller-coaster ride.

"Are you on this plane or somewhere else?" Neenan demanded through clenched teeth.

"Indeed, if I am to bring this plane in safely despite the airhead who is flying it, I must be both places," the seraph said with a light chuckle. "An angel's life is not an easy one." He laughed loudly, a warm, rich, friendly laugh.

"The outcome is in doubt?" Neenan begged as the plane sank lower and lower. Still no sign of Chicago. His headache, which he now noticed for the first time, became worse.

"I don't think so," the seraph said, and laughed again.

Then, without warning it seemed, the landing gear delivered a ferocious blow to the ground. There was still no sign in the fog of the city or even the airport.

The choristers burst into a paean of joy.

The dim outlines of the O'Hare terminal appeared through the gloom.

"Can't you keep those guys quiet?"

"Nope. They like to sing and they have the right to sing. You'd better get used to them. Besides, you're supposed to enjoy classical polyphony."

"Not all the time."

The seraph shrugged indifferently.

"How many wives do you have?"

"You mean companions?"

"All right, companions."

"It has been our experience," the seraph said, arching his thick eyebrows ruefully, "that one is ordinarily more than enough. . . . Now listen carefully to me: You are to be polite and considerate to your colleagues. You are not to treat them like they are, to use your vulgarity, assholes. You are to meet with them in the Admirals' Club so that they can spend some of this glorious autumn afternoon with their families."

"You call this weather glorious?"

"We don't know the future," the seraph said with a frown, "unless we're told on a 'need-to-know' basis. We do pretty well, however, on diagnosing weather fronts. And don't interrupt me when I'm giving advice, understand?"

"OK."

"You will treat them like respected and intelligent colleagues, which in fact they are. You need not fear any of them are planning to usurp your position, because they are too loyal even to think of that. You will in particular be nice to your son, who is a very smart young man, if not as reckless or ruthless as you are."

"I don't want to do anything of those things," Neenan replied with a stubborn grimace.

"Nonetheless, you will do them. You might even find that you enjoy them."

"You don't have to grab for that damn contract of yours. I didn't know I'd have to do these foolish things."

"Small stuff," the seraph replied with a massive show of his perfect white teeth.

The plane caromed across the airport pavement as if it were searching for every bump. Periodically the pilot slammed on the breaks and waited for an agonizing time before inching forward again.

"Can't you stop this idiot?" Neenan demanded. "What's the point of having a guardian angel if he can't do something useful?"

"I have no responsibilities on the ground," Michael said with yet another happy grin. "Not at airports anyway. Others are in charge."

"I bet."

"To continue with my advice . . ."

"Orders."

"Call them what you want. . . . You are not to take out your headache, which comes from too much vodka, on them. Rather you are to do your best to be witty and warm. It may be hard on your facial muscles, but you should try to smile on occasion."

"What about Walter Murtaugh?"

"You don't need my advice to know how to respond to Mr. Murtaugh's offer."

Finally the plane elbowed its way toward the terminal and stopped abruptly a few feet short of the Jetway. Passengers from the coach cabin jumped to their feet, pulled bags from the overhead racks with reckless disregard for life and limb.

"Please remain in your seats till the pilot turns off the fasten-seat-belt sign," the senior cabin attendant vainly pleaded.

Neenan began to leap out of his seat. What was the point in flying first class if you let coach passengers get a jump on you in the rush to desert the plane? Michael reached out a restraining hand.

"The world will wait, Raymond."

"I have work to do!"

"That will wait too."

Before Neenan could dispute the point, the plane pitched forward one last time, throwing a number of passengers off their feet and dumping luggage on their heads.

"See, Raymond?"

The pilot then turned off the seat-belt sign. The cabin attendant rolled her eyes. Neenan grinned at her. Michael nodded his head in approval.

"See how easy it is to be charming without being overtly seductive?"

"When you have a seraph hounding you."

"You wouldn't get to first base with her anyway."

Somehow Neenan's bag was transferred from the luggage compartment to the floor.

"Neat trick."

"Elementary."

Blue sky was sweeping across the airport. The choir greeted it with paroxysms of celebration.

"I hope you're along on our next adventure," Neenan said to the young woman.

"Thank you, Mr. Neenan." She smiled happily. "People like you make this job worthwhile."

"Thank you," Michael said, tipping his hat.

She couldn't see him or hear him, but she stared at the empty space next to Neenan with a puzzled smile.

He tripped as he entered the Jetway and steadied himself, waiting for his balance to return. It didn't.

"See what three vodkas will do?" Michael observed.

"Booze is not one of my problems. It's your fault anyway. You made it too good to resist."

"That's what they all say."

Nonetheless, Michael touched Neenan's arm. The headache and the dizziness and the fear flowed out of Neenan's body, leaving only the still-strong afterglow of his ecstasy and the uncanny sense that he was imploding.

"Now remember," Michael warned him, "you now have no excuse for not smiling at your colleagues."

"If you weren't a seraph, I'd use an obscenity."

Michael laughed again. As they emerged from the Jetway and he saw his anxious team waiting, Neenan realized that he and the so-called seraph had been bantering.

Not a good idea to banter with angels. It was probably one of their tricks. If there were angels and Michael were really one of them and not an undigested green pepper from his dinner the previous night.

The choristers were fading out, a kind of triumphal exit march. A touch of Handel.

Neenan felt a strong jolt of sexual desire race through his body again. What was happening now?

4

The dour expressions on the faces of the three men and one woman suggested that the angelic decision to stop singing might have been the right one. They were not people for whom you would want to sing, even if they probably couldn't hear you.

"Nice trip, R. A.?" asked Joe McMahon, his longtime second-in-command.

"So bad that we wouldn't have made it without the angels," he replied with a grin.

No one laughed. They never laughed at his jokes, because he never joked with them.

"I'll draft a letter of complaint to Bob Crandall first thing in the morning," said Amy Jardine, Neenan's administrative assistant.

"Tell him that I hope he has to fly with that pilot sometime. Without the angels."

Michael, who was tagging along despite the absence of a choral background, was laughing, but no one else did. And of course they couldn't hear his laugh.

"We have another serious offer from Walter Murtaugh, R. A," Norman Stein, Neenan's chief financial officer, said, wanting as always to get down to business without any preliminaries. "It's quite attractive."

"I'm glad I survived the flight. I'd hate to have died without replying to Walter."

"Hi, Dad," said his son Vincent. "Nice to have you back. That was one hell of a storm, wasn't it?"

Trust Vincent to say something idiotic.

"No problem as long as the angels are watching."

Charm came naturally to Neenan. He wasn't quite sure where he had learned it, surely not from his parents. Maybe he had learned charm as a means of survival in the family environment.

However, he suppressed it when he was with his subordinates. Better that they fear you, even Joe, who had been with him from the early days of National Entertainment. If you relaxed with your staff, they might think you were soft, a pushover that they could push over. No way.

"Well," he said, "let's get down to the Admiral's Club and get our work done."

"I thought we were to work in your car. Peter's waiting outside."

"Tell Peter to wait as long as he can and then drive around till we're finished. No point in you wasting this glorious day driving over to Lake Forest."

Dead silence.

"They're going to think you're sick," Michael observed.

"I'm doing what you told me to do."

"And they don't believe it. It's not going to be easy for them to realize that you're treating them like they're human beings. They may never get used to it."

"Are you feeling all right, Dad?" Vincent asked.

"Happy to be alive after that plane trip," he replied. "I want to sign those guardian angels on for our Gulfstream."

Vincent was the exact opposite of Neenan—a short, skinny man with thick glasses, thin hair, and a receding chin, an inoffensive, nondescript, quiet young man from whom you would not buy a used car, a new computer, or a television station. He was, however, totally loyal and worshiped Neenan with an admiration that Neenan found embarrassing.

Joe McMahon was also short, but unlike Vincent he was fat and bald and loud and loved to chomp on an unlit cigar. He perspired at the slightest pretext and wiped his forehead with a handkerchief that he had carried with him all the years he and Neenan had worked together. He was a highly effective administrator. Nothing went on in the far-flung domain of National Entertainment that he did not know about. He was content with his second-in-command role because he did not like to make decisions and because Neenan paid him half a million a year plus bonuses and stock options. He was worth every penny of it.

Amy Jardine was a hawk-nosed, svelte matron in her midforties, supremely efficient and beyond mistakes. She was not unattractive, but her personality was about as warm as that of a polar bear in the middle of winter. The Pope could learn from her when it came to infallibility. She had a husband and children somewhere, but Neenan had never met them and presumed that he never would.

Norman Stein, a handsome, smooth, intense man with silver hair (like Neenan's though not as thick), dark skin, and deep brown eyes, always looked as if he had stepped out of a men's fashion magazine; today he was wearing a dark blue Italian suit with a pinstripe and coordinating light blue shirt with a white collar and a dark blue tie with golden flowers. He always carried a leather briefcase that must have cost at least a thousand dollars.

Vincent didn't matter, but the other three were worth their weight in precious stones, the kind of stones on which Anna Maria doted.

"OK," Neenan said when they had arranged themselves in a conference room in the Admiral's Club executive center and Michael had settled his huge frame into an easy chair away from the table and deposited his homburg on a lamp table. "Let's hear about Walter first. Norman?"

"Basically the offer is for a controlling interest in NE for about one and three-quarters of what our stock is selling for on the market. The stockholders will love it. You would be an extremely wealthy man, R. A. All of us who hold stock in the company would make a lot of money. The contract would guarantee all executive salaries for five years. You would remain as chairman and CEO of NE and report directly to Mr. Murtaugh. It is essentially a better offer than that of Time Warner by about twenty-five percent."

"And Disney?"

"They insist they want a chance to make their last and best offer."

"I see. . . . What do the lawyers say?"

"They say the offer looks ironclad, though we'd want to read the fine print very carefully. They also say that our stockholders would be very upset if we turn down an offer like this. They might go to court to force us to sell."

"Uh-huh. . . . What do you think, Norm?"

The CFO looked surprised. "What do I think, R. A.?"

"Yeah, what do you think?"

"I think you have to weigh the monetary gain against the loss of independence and the possible risk of being sold off when WorldCorp needs liquidity."

"I suppose that's true. . . . Joe?"

"There's a lot of synergy in the deal, R. A. We are in competition with him in only a few major markets. Moreover, the money might give you the opportunity to start your own film production company if you're tired of working for WorldCorp. It might be time to consider consolidating your interests, which are pretty far-flung now. Finally, you know what Walter is like. You turn him down and he'll try to make your life miserable with litigation and competition in our best markets."

"I see. . . . And what do you personally think, Joe?"

McMahon was startled too. "What do I think?"

"Yeah, what do you think?"

"I think Norm's right. You have to think about how you trade off the costs and benefits. You lose some independence, but you make a hell of a lot of money."

"You see," Michael said, resting his chin on a pyramid constructed by his fingers, *"they are all shocked that you asked them what they think."*

"They haven't told me anything I don't know yet. Why should I ask them what they think?"

Apparently there was some angelic arrangement that put his conversations with the self-proclaimed seraph in parentheses that others could not hear.

"Because it is the polite thing to do and because they might just have an insight that you don't have. . . . Why don't you ask your son?"

"It is inconceivable that he would have anything important to say."

"Ask him anyway."

"Vincent?"

His son did not hesitate. "Fuck Walter Murtaugh."

Michael whistled.

"Oh?" Neenan said in total surprise.

"And the horse he came in on. You know what it will be like. He'll move in some vulgar and slimy Brit or Aussie to act as liaison and pretty soon he'll be running NE instead of you. The stockholders can sue you till hell freezes over and it won't do them any good the way you got the company tied up."

"We don't use that metaphor much anymore," Neenan murmured softly.

Vincent ignored him. "Our lawyers are as good as his, maybe better. They can fend off anything he tries in court and make him pay with countersuits. If you can't beat his shit in our locals, then you're getting older than I think you are. Let them all bid each other to the sky. Then say, thanks, but no thanks, we're worth a lot more. Anyone who wants to sell their stock can sell it then. And you look good for facing down the lot of them. It'll be more fun than watching the Bears."

"And possibly less than watching the Bulls," Neenan replied with a slow smile.

His son had delivered his tirade in a calm, matter-of-fact, almost meek voice. The others in the room listened with wide eyes and open mouths.

"Apples," the seraph field marshal observed, *"do not in fact fall very far from the trees."*

"That bastard has run his debt too high anyway," Vincent continued. "Some one of these days his luck is going to run out. He's badly leveraged as it is. If we do let him raise the ante, he may go too far. Then he'll have to sell off NE in little pieces no matter what the contract says. If you're ready to retire, Dad, I'd say take it. Otherwise, let him walk down to Monroe Street and keep going out into the Lake when he comes to the Yacht Club."

"Kid, I don't think your old man is ready to retire yet," Michael said.

Vincent blinked his eyes as though he'd heard a strange voice from a great distance. Then he shook his head to dismiss the illusion.

The three others said nothing. It was astonishing enough that R. A. had asked for their opinion and even more astonishing that Vincent had offered his. They were not going to push their luck, not just yet anyway.

"Good points, Vincent," Neenan said, trying not to sound reluctant in his praise. "I don't think your old man is ready to retire yet."

A puzzled, déjà vu expression appeared on Vincent's youthful face. Michael chuckled.

"OK, what we will do is stall. Tell them we're very flattered and that we're keeping all our options open. We'll say that we're inclined to think that the market undervalues NE because so much of it is closely held. We'll also say that we don't think anyone else can put us into play against our own wishes. That will heighten the excitement and won't hurt us a bit. Can you tell our PR people to get out something like that first thing Monday, Amy?"

"Of *course*, Mr. Neenan."

"I'm not available to return calls from anyone, especially not *Variety* or the *Wall Street Journal*. Tell my counterparts at Time Warner, WorldCorp, and Disney that their offers should be directed to our lawyers and to Mr. Stein."

"Can't go wrong that way," Joe McMahon agreed with an audible sigh of relief.

"Anything else?"

"There's nothing of importance in the mail," Amy Jardine said smugly, "except for a new advertisement from Reverend Wildmon accusing you of being a smut monger."

"Grand," Neenan said with a laugh, "more free publicity."

Again silence around the table. Normally Neenan would have demanded that the ad be checked by the lawyers for possible libel charges.

"Has he mellowed out!" Michael exclaimed. *"Some angel must be feeding him his lines."*

The afterglow from Neenan's ecstatic experience grew warmer and his sexual longings returned.

"Anything else?"

They glanced at one another.

"We're having more trouble with Jerry Carter."

"So what else is new. Do you think we can put out a contract on him?"

Vincent smiled; the others ignored his comment.

"He says he needs two more months to complete the editing on *Rebirth,*" Joe McMahon reported. "That could run us another ten million in expenses and delay release by a couple of months. You know Jerry."

Jerry Carter was a gifted young film director who had already made two TV hits. *Rebirth* was his first venture into feature films and a new experiment for NE. It was a gritty story of an ex-con's attempt to begin his life again. He was successful of course, but only just barely, and the film ended on a note of at best hope but no certainty. It also ended on a note of very convincing torrid middle-aged sex between the convict and his former wife. "Reverend Wildmon will like everything but the end," Neenan had told Carter on the phone, a man still to be treated with charm.

"What do we think?"

They all hesitated.

"He's done good work for us in the past," McMahon began.

"Films get out of hand easily," Stein warned.

"Anna Maria loved the script," Vincent said, "and wife or not, we know she's never wrong."

The room became quiet as a group of nuns would have in the presence of sacrilegious blasphemy. Anna Maria was never mentioned at staff meetings, even though she was perhaps the best script reader in America. One simply did not quote the boss's wife.

"Not much chance, Vincent, of her not being my wife. Not unless I lose my mind. . . . What do you think we should do, give him another ten million? Or sell him to WorldCorp?"

At the mention of Anna Maria's name the choir appeared from nowhere and began a sprightly round. Though he didn't think it fit her at all, Neenan felt again an aching hunger for her. He hoped she would be home when he finally got to Lake Forest. He had never insisted on her coordinating her schedule with his. She wasn't a deep or even an interesting woman, but she was spectacular in bed.

"I say we give him a month. Tell him at the end of the month we will grab the film out of his grubby paws and ship it, regardless."

"OK, let the sin be on your head, Vincent. You fly out there on Tuesday and give him the word."

"OK."

Neenan glanced around the room. He had never given Vincent an assignment like that before. How did the other members of the staff react to it?

No one revealed even a flicker of dissent. They must think more of Vincent than his father did.

"Tell you what, if the lawyer can get out of the courtroom for a day or two, you might take her along. Never hurts to get away from the kid for a bit of breathing space."

Vincent's jaw dropped. "I'm sure she'd love it."

"The Beverly Hills Hotel isn't what it used to be. Try the Four Seasons."

"We certainly will. . . . Maybe you and Anna Maria could join us for supper at our house when we come back?" Vincent sounded pathetically eager.

"You say that you'd be happy to," Michael instructed, *"and you tell Ms. Jardine to set up the day and the time. Got it?"*

"No, I won't do it. I don't want to get involved in a social life with them."

"I don't care whether you want it or not." Michael removed the contract from his pocket.

"When do we negotiate the small stuff?"

"This isn't small stuff. You got a problem with that?"

"I don't believe any of this shit."

A melodic cry of protest erupted from the angelic choir.

"You want to be friends with your son. Are you afraid to try?"

"No!"

"Are you sure?"

"I don't know . . . leave me alone!"

The seraph tapped him with the contract again.

"That'd be a good idea," Neenan said to his son. "You can report on Carter. Amy, will you set it up with Mrs. Neenan?"

"Certainly, Mr. Neenan."

"Both Mss. Neenans," the Angel insisted.

"Both Mss. Neenans."

"Naturally, Mr. Neenan."

"They think I'm out of my mind," Neenan said to the seraph as they walked out to his waiting Mercedes limousine. "Even Vincent."

"Especially Vincent," Michael replied. "He's willing to take a chance on your sanity. The others aren't. They'll be a hard sell."

"How will I sell anyone else?"

"Maybe you won't."

"Then what?"

"The point is that you have to try."

"Yeah."

"Don't you feel happy at the prospect of your son becoming your colleague and friend?"

"If I believe you, I won't have time to enjoy it."

"There's never enough time," the angel replied. "Here's your car."

"I know it's my car, damn it!"

"Good afternoon, Mr. Neenan," Peter said respectfully. "I hope you had a good trip."

"It was all right, Peter. Some strange people on the plane."

"I guess that can't be helped in the world the way it is today, sir, can it?"

Peter opened the car door for Neenan. A distinguished-looking Irish immigrant in his middle forties, he was married to their cook and housekeeper. He sounded and acted like Bertie Wooster's Jeeves with a touch of the brogue. Neenan always suspected that the similarity was deliberate.

"Maeve is free today, is she not, Peter?"

Peter and his wife lived in an apartment above the garage of the Lake Forest home.

"On Saturday and Sunday, sir."

"I won't be needing the car for the rest of the day. If I need a car tomorrow, I'll borrow Mrs. Neenan's Lexus. Why don't the two of you take off for the rest of the weekend."

Neenan had no idea what they would do with a day-and-a-half holiday. Perhaps stay in their apartment. It was none of his business.

In the front of the car Peter seemed dumbstruck.

"That is very kind of you, sir," he said when he had regained his voice.

Neenan closed the window behind the driver's seat as he always did. Peter was a great talker, and in the car Neenan wanted peace and privacy.

"Not bad." Michael relaxed in the seat next to Neenan. "I didn't have to tell you to do it."

"I knew you would, so I beat you to it."

"You're learning quick . . . now let's settle back and talk about your wife."

"We've already talked about Donna."

"I mean Anna Maria."

"I won't discuss her with you."

"The hell you won't," the seraph said with a genial laugh. "You should excuse the expression."

5

"She's not much," Neenan insisted. "Decorative when I need a wife around and great in bed when I need a wife to sleep with. Seems to enjoy sex. But no substance to her. She's a good script reader because she has the taste and the intelligence of the average American woman. But no depth. Not interesting at all."

"Not one of the women you hunt?"

"Not at all. Completely different person. Completely different relationship. She spends her time shopping, buying expensive clothes and jewelry, hanging around church, reading romance novels, watching television, and taking care of her body. Works out every day."

"A body worth pampering, isn't it?"

"I don't deny that. I'm merely saying that she's shallow."

"Which fits your needs in a wife?"

"Exactly."

"We do not normally engage in human vulgarities, Raymond Anthony," the seraph said with a loud sigh. "We find our own much more vivid, but you wouldn't understand them. So I'll have to be content with saying that while you are a monumental asshole, your remarks about Anna Maria mark you as perhaps the greatest all-time asshole of the Western world. You got a problem with that?"

"You're telling me I don't know my own wife?" Neenan fired back, feeling his Irish temper rising.

"You are, as the young people say, totally clueless on the subject of Anna Maria, and that after all the work we did to get her for you."

"Bullshit. I got her myself."

"You are wrong."

"You haven't been around my life that long."

"Again you are wrong."

Hesitantly, warming up for a warm-up, the choir began to hum softly.

Neenan experienced again the cracking-apart sensation, a tree splitting as lightning strikes it.

Had these bastards really been meddling in his life all along?

That was impossible. He had chosen Anna Maria entirely on his own.

Hadn't he?

Donna's divorce and the subsequent revelation of her liaison with the little bald man was a savage blow to Neenan's male ego. He was infuriated by the suggestion, which no one dared to make explicit, that he was a sexual failure. Perhaps he could hunt down attractive and interesting women, but he couldn't keep a wife. Before the divorce, the celibacy required during the hunt was not a great burden. The anticipated prize reduced his daily and weekly sexual impulses. But in the couple of years after the divorce, the delicate balance between celibacy and conquest became unstable. Neenan took some dangerous chances, chances he knew were dangerous.

It was in this troubled time that Anna Maria Allegro arrived on the scene. He had heard of her Hollywood reputation as an infallible judge of scripts, treatments, and series outlines. Moreover he learned that she was a native Chicagoan. He ordered Joe McMahon to offer her a salary in six figures—a lot for a woman not yet thirty—and the title of vice president to return to Chicago and read scripts for National Entertainment. She accepted promptly and thus saved Neenan tens of thousands of dollars more that he would have been willing to pay.

Most people in the industry had no notion of what ordinary folks would like. This young woman apparently did. Therefore she was priceless—until she was wrong a couple of times.

Neenan had been astonished when she came into his office in the Sears Tower. His head pounded with conflicting emotions, all of them desire of one kind or another. Ms. Allegro was petite and slender, a black-haired doll with the face of a pre-Raphaelite Madonna and an exquisite body in a brown suit and sweater that seemed to demand male caresses. Her complexion was flawless, her hair long, her dark, dark brown eyes sparkling, her lips inviting, her every movement rich in sensuality.

And she could pick winners.

She had to be an interesting woman by his definition. He set out in hot pursuit.

He discovered all too quickly that his judgment was wrong. She was not interesting at all, merely a lower-middle-class girl from the old neighborhood on the West Side of Chicago, quite common in her interests. She was good at picking winners only because she was common; she reflected the taste of millions of Americans, especially women, just like herself.

Moreover she was virtuous. She was perfectly willing to eat dinner with her employer and go to the opera and the Bulls games with him — less enthusiastic about the former and more about the latter — but she was not about to go to bed with him.

Old-fashioned too, he told himself.

Yet she was delectable. Moreover she was pleasant, undemanding, witty — and unimpressed by him. Tough, he decided, but sweet. She made him laugh, even when he was not in the mood to laugh, and indeed laugh at himself, which he didn't normally like to do.

In a bikini on a beach, she made his head pound and his hands itch. Not an exciting woman save sexually, and that did not mean she would be a good bed partner. He told himself that he ought to stop dating her.

But he could not — in retrospect perhaps because the seraphs and their crowd would not let him stop.

Even when he was away from Chicago and engaged in one of his pursuits, he could not get her out of his mind. She had become a permanent actor in his fantasy life, as Donna had been almost a quarter century before. Was he falling in love again?

Had he not learned once that was a bad idea?

It wasn't love as most people would have defined love. Rather it was a combination of highly specific desire for her and an instinctive judgment that she would be a useful and decorative and relaxing life companion.

It would not do, he told himself, for someone in his position not to have a wife or a permanent mistress. The latter role was out of the question with Anna Maria. Therefore it would seem logical that he marry her. She did not seem surprised at his proposal and readily accepted it. Nor did she seem to mind the toughly worded prenuptial agreements. Rather, she laughed at them.

She laughed a lot, not a mean or sarcastic laugh but rather the good-humored laugh of someone who thinks life is funny. What more could he want in a wife, especially after Donna?

Anna Maria laughed a lot in bed too. Despite her relative innocence and inexperience, she was an astonishingly satisfying sexual partner, a blend of modesty and abandon, of hesitation and recklessness, of refreshing lasciviousness and uninhibited passion. Moreover, she was not sexually aggressive — Neenan could not stand women who tried to play the aggressive game in bed. When he wanted sex, she was always ready. When he did not want it, she left him alone.

Neenan had been genuinely fond of her and still was as a matter of fact. She was such a tasty prize that he thought of abandoning his pursuits of interesting woman and settling down to a life of agreeable fidelity.

Then a woman came along whom he had to possess.

He did not think that Anna Maria knew of these chases. Such desires were beyond the range of her vision. So he lived, as he thought, in the best possible of both worlds, a compliant wife at home and interesting women away from home. There were costs in such an arrangement, but they did not seem too high. Anna Maria was a handsome consort who lent luster to his presence and was an excellent lover. True, their lives went in opposite directions, she to clothes and jewels and care of her body in their gym and care of her soul in the church, and he to greater power and wealth in National Entertainment and to his temporary handmaids, as he often thought of them.

She had at least come to enjoy opera. Up to Puccini anyway, even if she did not share his taste for more recent composers. She loved to sit next to him at the Lyric and hold his hand and hum softly along with the soprano.

Neenan didn't often feel guilty, but those interludes bothered him a little. The woman was too damn trusting.

It was impossible to make Anna Maria fight. She merely laughed at him when he was irritable. Yet he was never certain what she really thought of him. Behind her bedroom eyes, there might well lurk dangerous ideas. More likely there lurked nothing at all.

They had produced no children. He would not have objected if she wanted to be a mother. But she apparently was infertile, though they had never discussed the subject. Indeed they had rarely discussed the matter seriously. She did not complain about the demands business made on him. He did not complain about her clothes and her jewels and her romance novels and the time she spent in church.

On the whole she was therefore the kind of wife he wanted. He had no idea whether he was the kind of husband she wanted. His only fear was that some night she could become a Sicilian witch and stick a stiletto between his ribs.

Not very likely, he told himself. The prenuptial agreement did not specify a large income for her if he should die. He told himself that he would have to change that as the years went on, but he was in no hurry to do so.

"You didn't mention that she's quite a golfer," Michael said accusingly.

"I guess I forgot. She does win the women's tournament at Lake Forest Country Club almost every year. Good with the short irons and the putter. Plays almost every day during the season."

"Better than you are."

"I wouldn't say that. I don't get as much chance to play as I used to."

"She used to beat you every time you went out on the course with her. Without a handicap. So you quit playing against her. Your male ego couldn't take losing to a woman, not to say a diminutive woman, not to say especially the diminutive woman who is your wife."

"That's not true."

"Come on, R. A., don't try to kid me. She humiliated you and loved it."

"She was a poor winner."

"And you a worse loser. Well, you're going to have to play her tomorrow. She'll probably beat you and you'll be a good sport about it. Got a problem with that?"

"I sure do!"

"Too bad. You're going to do it anyway. And you're going to brag about how good she is when you're eating dinner at the club."

"The weather is terrible."

"Look out the window! There's not a cloud in the sky!"

"It will rain tomorrow."

"I told you we were good on weather fronts. It will be eighty, the last summer day. You'll have a great time on the course."

"I'll have work to do."

"You're going to take your wife to Mass, then you're going out to the club with her and enjoy her skunking you. Got a problem with that?"

"Don't shake that contract at me again!"

Merely talking about Anna Maria in his present state of ecstatic afterglow and sexual hunger tore at Neenan's dubious stability. He twisted uncomfortably in his seat. The damn seraph was playing games with him.

"Haven't you figured it out yet? There's a lot of things you will have to straighten out in the next few months. She's decisive."

"You mean my salvation depends on how I act with Anna Maria?"

"You got it."

"I don't get it at all."

"That's the whole problem."

"What do you mean?"

"To begin with, after eight years of marriage, you don't know who she is. To end with, you don't know how lucky you are."

"I certainly do know who my wife is."

"OK. Let's go down the list. You say she buys expensive clothes and jewelry. How much does she spend?"

"I don't check the bills."

"That's right. You never see them. She buys them with her own money, which is less than the salary to which she is entitled for the work she does. Moreover, she buys the clothes at outlets and discount stores. She looks good in them because she has good taste, and doesn't mind being six months behind the fashions, and she'd look good in anything anyway."

"Oh . . . I don't care how she spends the money."

"Secondly," Michael went on implacably, "if you had any taste at all, you'd be embarrassed at the jewels she wears to your fancy dinners, they're so inexpensive compared to what the wives of other CEOs wear. They look at Anna Maria and hate her for her good looks and then feel sorry for her because she has such a cheapskate husband."

"I'm not a cheapskate."

"Is that so? Tell you what, ask one of your buddies in the industry how much they pay for the jewels they give their wives for Christmas. If you are capable of feeling like a heel—which I very much doubt—they'd make you feel like the lowest of heels."

"I don't believe you."

"We can't lie, R. A.," the seraph said with a benign smile. "We can work truth a little around the edges, but we don't tell outright falsehoods. Not in our nature. You can believe me about the jewels."

"I didn't know . . ."

"You think that is a valid excuse?"

"I guess not."

"Then the matter of her reading. What's she going through now?"

"I don't know . . . some woman romance writer. Huge books."

"Susan Howatch?"

"Something like that."

"You think she's just a romance writer?"

"Isn't she?"

"She's been writing theological novels for a decade. Kind of an Anthony Trollope of the late twentieth century."

"I don't care what the hell she reads. . . . Is this woman commercial?"

"Sells a lot of books."

"Maybe we could do a film . . ."

"Miniseries."

"Yeah, good idea. We'll have to get a writer."

"Got one."

"Not my wife!"

"Yep," the angel chortled gleefully. "Most of the script is done. She's got a dozen or so lying around. You wouldn't know that, of course. You're too dumb to wonder about it."

"Are they good?"

"Every one of them is commercial, as you people say. Too much sex in them for your good friend Reverend Wildmon. But no worse than R."

"I can't believe any of this."

"You don't know anything about what she gives to charity either. Or that she tutors down in Pilsen for the Jesuits at their new high school or that she is one of the principal founders of that school. With her own money, not yours. You're too dumb to know and too insensitive to care."

The angel song was rising in volume, celebrating his wife no doubt.

"It's all impossible."

"So you been chasing around these women executives because you think they make interesting temporary slaves — and thus getting even with your mother — and the most interesting woman you've ever met is the one you sleep with, and not often enough either. You don't even let her in your bed."

Neenan was speechless.

He let pass the comment about his mother. And the one about not sleeping with Anna Maria often enough.

"She likes having a bedroom of her own. Wants privacy."

"If I weren't the head of the heavenly armies, I'd say bullshit. She likes sex, as you know. A lot. But women also like to snuggle and hug. Fat chance of doing that when you're behind a closed door dreaming up new ways of sticking it to Ted Turner and Rupert Murdoch and Walter Murtaugh. You're the one that's afraid of letting a real woman—and she's all of that—intrude into the privacy and secrecy of your life."

"That's not true."

"Yeah? You're beginning to believe that it might be true and you're cracking up like an iceberg in spring. Well, boyo, that's only the beginning."

"So I guess I'd better play golf with her tomorrow, huh?"

"Minimally. And you'll have to invite her because she'd never think of inviting you."

"I don't want to go to church with her."

"You forget who I am? And whom I work for?"

"There's a link between that One and Anna Maria?"

"She's as close as you're likely to get to the Other in this world, not counting me and my companion, if she consents to meet you."

"I don't get it."

"I didn't expect that you would."

"We can't change the habits of eight years of marriage."

"I didn't say it would be easy. None of the changes that you're going to have to make in the next couple of months while you still have time are going to be easy. Still, this one should be more pleasurable than the others. . . . Even now you're caught between hunger and fear as all the defenses you've built up against her start to crumble."

"I don't have any defenses against her!"

"You gotta be kidding!"

"You sound like you're going to enjoy my humiliation."

"Nope. We don't do that kind of thing. I'm going to enjoy your joy . . . if there is any."

6

Neenan's head was whirling as he approached the stately and somewhat static Norman house on the lakeshore. He was breaking apart like a wave crashing on a beach. He could make no sense of anything that had happened since the seraph had announced himself on the MD-80. Could he have been married to a woman for eight years and not know her at all? Could he have been that much of a fool?

Were his days numbered? Would he be dead before Christmas?

He put the key in the front door with a shiver, despite the sultry weather. Had someone just walked over his grave?

He was certain about only one thing: he wanted with an aching hunger this strange woman who was his wife. Let humiliation, disintegration, and death come later. In the moment of love there would be a brief eternity of pleasure. That would be enough. The worries could come later if they wanted to.

Michael had apparently taken his leave, perhaps respecting the intimacy of marital passion. Neenan wasn't sure he could trust him, however. It did not follow that, because he was invisible, the dark-skinned angel was not lurking somewhere judging Neenan's every move and finding him wanting.

He searched through the ground floor of the house and did not find her. Damn! Where had the woman gone? She knew he would be coming home sometime today. Why wasn't she waiting for him?

He didn't need the seraph to tell him how foolish that question was.

Finally he saw her in the garden, now blooming with mums, at the side of the house. She was lying on a wide chaise, her eyes closed and an open book on her belly. Gently he opened the sliding door. His head was thumping, his teeth gritted together, his heart pounding, his finger nails digging into the palms of his hands. The choir began to hum a serenade. So they were still around.

In the garden the scent of mums reminded him briefly of a funeral home, perhaps a funeral home for his wake.

He looked down at her and his whole being filled with tenderness. She was dressed as though she were about to receive guests for a casual Sunday-afternoon cocktail party: neatly pressed designer jeans, a paisley scarf for a belt, expensive sandals, and a gleaming white blouse against which her long hair had fallen in a carefully designed black shower. Two buttons of the blouse were open instead of one, hinting at wonder and mystery. All the requisite jewelry was in place: earrings, necklace, bracelets, rings, even an ankle bracelet.

Had she dressed to welcome him home? Or had flawless dress and grooming become an end in itself?

Was not the extra open button the answer to that dumb question?

Yet he had never returned home from a business trip to seek pleasure in the heat of an afternoon. Perhaps she had dressed for him just in case this return would be different.

It would certainly be that.

She had changed hardly at all in their eight years together. Still unbearably lovely.

He sat on the chaise next to her. Her fragrance was strong enough to blot out the deadly aroma of mums. He drank her in, celebrating her, reveling in her, anticipating his pleasure in her.

She opened her eyes in momentary surprise. Her hand leaped to her throat. Then she relaxed and smiled.

"Raymond!"

"Napping?"

"Partly daydreaming, partly napping," she said, her smile still very much alive.

"Daydreaming about me?"

"Not really," she said, shifting her position on the chaise in a sensuous movement that said that she knew what he wanted. "I daydreamed about you at Mass this morning. I'm afraid I got myself all worked up."

"Dirty thoughts in church? Isn't that a sacrilege?"

"Not if they're about your husband."

"You got yourself all wet in church?"

She lowered her eyes in shy modesty. " 'Fraid so. . . . Rough trip home? There was a big thunderstorm just south of us."

"The angels had to work overtime to bring us through that."

She opened her eyes in astonishment. "Angels?"

"Angels."

Hearing themselves mentioned, the angel choir turned up the volume again on its serenade. Their song was deafening.

Her eyes locked with his. "Out here, Raymond? In the autumn sunshine?"

"Why not?"

"Why not indeed."

He took the book off her belly and placed it on the grass. It was Susan Howatch, as predicted.

"Do you hear someone singing, way far off in the distance?" she asked.

Not far off in the distance but all around us.

"Do you?"

"Not exactly," she said with a frown.

"Maybe it's the same angels that brought us through the storm."

He touched the third button on her blouse.

"Raymond!" she exclaimed.

She squirmed on the chaise, twisted her head to one side, and arched her back.

The angels, anticipating the event perhaps, broke into a triumphant celebration.

The interlude of passion was for Raymond Neenan an exploration of a new and unfamiliar country, dense with thick and blossoming vegetation, filled with mysterious sounds and smells, and alive with wonders that lurked everywhere. He did not know this strange land. Somehow he had missed it in his past travels. But he did realize that he had to treat it with great care, cherish it, reverence it, nourish it, heal it, sustain its fragile brilliance.

Then something or perhaps someone else intervened, not so much to distract him from his exploration as to enhance it. The ecstasy from the plane ride swept back into him, filled him, exalted him. He was swept away on wave after wave of eternity. He no longer feared death, much less Michael's "small stuff." Somehow everything would be all right. He lost all sense of his own selfhood. There was only the presence of the Other and of this human link to the Other that he must protect and hold dear for the eternity of their union.

It seemed that he and his beloved were dancing on the vanilla ice cream clouds above the storm, naked, free, serene, and utterly enveloped now in the Other, who was somehow dancing with them.

In the distance he heard two voices crying out with unbearable pleasure. Eternity was everywhere.

Later, as Anna Maria slept peacefully in his arms, her sweat-drenched body as close to his as another human body could be, he relaxed in serene confidence. The warm sunlight bathed them in tranquillity. The satisfied joy of the moment, he knew, would not last. But it must be savored while it was there. All the other problems in life were far, far away.

"Not bad," Michael remarked, "not bad at all. You're beginning to realize who she is."

He was sitting on one of the lawn chairs, his tie open and his hat and jacket on the table.

Neenan grabbed his wife's blouse from the grass and covered her with it.

"She's gorgeous all right," Michael agreed. "The Other outdid Herself in putting that one together. And it is proper for you to protect her modesty. But we don't react to her beauty the same way another human might."

"You were watching."

"No, I wasn't. I can see the results, however. You've crossed your Rubicon, R. A., no doubt about it."

"Your friends were watching?"

"The singers? Only from a great distance. They're on your side, R. A. Her side too. Don't worry about them. You'll get used to them."

"How come the ecstasy bit?"

"We don't control that. It happens. Not infrequently when people are making love. The Other apparently likes to intrude when passion is intense. Don't ask me why."

Anna Maria stirred in his arms. He caressed her bare shoulder, soothing her. She settled back into peaceful sleep.

"I know what you're up to," Neenan said, jabbing his finger at the seraph.

"Really? What?"

"You're trying to do the Faust scenario in reverse."

"Ah?"

"Yeah. In the story, the devil turns a good man bad with the temptation of illicit love. In this story an angel turns a bad man good with licit love. A nice paradox for the seraphic field marshal!"

"You just figure that out? To quote that great diplomat Oliver North on another subject, it's kind of a neat idea, isn't it?"

"It might make a great premise for a TV film," Neenan said, deflated by the angel's claim.

"Feature film. I wouldn't appear in anything less. And you wouldn't dare do that kind of sex on TV. Maybe not even in a feature film."

"Well . . ."

"Don't get too cocky, R. A., you should excuse the expression. You've got a lot of work here and everyplace else. Don't forget you've lived with this woman for eight years and had no idea who or what she was. You have a lot of catching up to do."

"So far it's been fun."

"Some of it won't be fun at all, like being humiliated on the golf course tomorrow. Well, I'll see you later."

Michael didn't fade out or even disappear. Rather, he was just not there anymore.

Neither were his hat or jacket.

Much later, Neenan and Anna Maria were sitting in robes, hers a glorious peach color, in the garden enjoying the golden glow of the sunset. She had made roast beef sandwiches and opened a bottle of Château Lafitte. Nothing but the best red wine for a picnic in the garden after a romp through eternity.

When she passed to go into the kitchen and then when she returned, she touched his face affectionately. She did not, however, mention their interlude of love, perhaps because it had not seemed to her at all unusual or perhaps because she was afraid to ask what had happened to him.

He filled her Waterford goblet.

"Thank you. . . . You're just trying to get me drunk so you can have your way with me again."

"That's not a bad idea, but you're the one who brought it up."

She sniffed disdainfully, but grinned.

I'm not up to it, he told himself, not twice like that in the same day.

"How much do you hate me, Anna Maria?" he asked suddenly.

"Hate you?" she replied calmly, as if it were a perfectly ordinary and normal question. "Well, sometimes a lot. But usually I don't hate you."

"Ah?"

She pondered the direction of the conversation. "No, I don't hate you all that much. I dislike you intensely much of the time."

"Why?" he said, feeling his stomach tighten.

"You're so much of a little boy, a twelve-year-old boy, who thinks only of himself and his silly little games."

"You mean National Entertainment?"

She bit into her sandwich delicately.

"And your foolish little-boy fights with the other little boys like Eisner and Murtaugh and Turner and Murdoch. As though they were the most important people in the world and the game you all play is the only game in town. Why does everything have to be so secret? Why do you and your friends act like little boys in a tree house, obsessed with what you think are your dirty secrets? Why do you ignore the rest of life when you're babbling about your secrets?"

"You think I should grow up?"

"That would be nice," she said, then sipped from her wineglass. "Mind you, I don't think that will happen."

"Yet you're ready to make love with me whenever I want."

"I suppose I could say that you don't even think that there might be times when I want it and you're not interested."

"You could say that."

"But you probably wonder why I stay with you if I dislike you so much."

"That thought does occur to me."

The moon slipped over the lake side of the garden, a great orange ball, as fresh and alive as the promise of human love. Like an alchemist's miracle in reverse, it replaced the sun's golden sheen with a pale, alluring silver.

"Sometimes twelve-year-old boys can be attractive; perhaps it's their conceited vulnerability."

A spear into his stomach.

"Besides, when you make love, you become a grown-up. I don't know why, but you're gentle and tender and sensitive and concerned about me, as well as demanding. Unlike some of the feminist women, I like demanding men more than wimps. That's more than a lot of women can say about their men. And you're usually thoughtful for a while afterwards, like you are now. Sometimes even as much as another day, sometimes only an hour or two and you're back on your computer planning more tricks for your little-boy games."

"I see," he said, choking on the words.

"You asked me. . . . Do you want me to go on?"

"Certainly."

"You're not the worst of husbands. You're not a drunk; you don't beat me, not that you'd get away with it a second time; you don't fool around, or if you do, you'll never get caught; you let me live my own life; as I say, when you notice I'm around, you're a wonderful lover; and you're not all that bad looking—big, handsome, strong, silver-haired, red-faced Irishman. I had no illusions about you when I married you. I'm a lot better off than most women."

She shrugged. Then she rose from her lawn chair and refilled both his wineglass and hers. Her robe slipped open as she poured the wine. She touched his face affectionately before she tightened the belt on her robe and returned to her chair.

"Why didn't you tell me this before?"

"You never asked. If I had tried to tell you, you wouldn't have heard what I said, you wouldn't even have listened to the words."

Her denunciation, in a calm, dispassionate voice innocent of rancor, hit him just as hard as had Donna's announcement that she wanted a divorce. Anna Maria's assault was all the more devastating because it was so rational, so disciplined, so controlled. He had failed at this marriage too, and for the same reasons presumably that he had failed in the previous one.

"So you don't love me at all?" he asked sadly, realizing that his words were the plaintive cry of a twelve-year-old boy.

"Did I say that I didn't love you?" she demanded impatiently.

"No . . . but you sort of implied it."

"I did *no such thing!* Why is it so hard for you men to realize that logic doesn't apply to emotions. I said I hated you sometimes and disliked you a lot of the time, didn't I?"

"Yes."

"So I didn't say that I didn't love you. I never said that. I would never say it. If I did, it wouldn't be true."

"Oh," he gulped.

"I'm hopelessly in love with you. I have been since the first day I met you, more so probably now. You don't think I'd go through that little romp we had unless I worshiped the ground you walk on, do you?"

"I guess I'm confused."

"Something is happening to you that you won't tell me about, not now, maybe not ever. So far it seems to be for the good. . . . The little romp was wonderful, by the way. Never better."

"We waltzed naked on the top of vanilla ice cream clouds," he murmured.

In the fading light he saw her blush. "Is that what we did?"

"Something like that anyway."

"It isn't a bad metaphor."

"What would yours be?"

"I'll have to think for a moment," she said, her voice amused and playful.

"Well," she continued after a pause, "we were swimming in a crimson ocean filled with beautiful flowers and overwhelming fragrances . . . and you were a gorgeous companion who helped me to swim in places I was afraid to go."

"If I'm as bad a person—"

"I didn't say you were a bad person," she said, displeased again. "I certainly did *not* say you were a bad person."

"OK. . . . Let me try again. A person that it was easy to dislike?"

"That's better."

"Then why didn't you try to change me?"

"No one changes anyone else unless the other person wants to be changed. I pray for you, which is about all I can do. It's a shame because, like I said, you're not a bad man and you deserve a lot more happiness than you permit yourself to enjoy."

Not much time left for the happiness, he thought ruefully.

"You said that I pay more attention to you when we have made love?"

"Some of the time. . . . Well, most of the time. I seem to distract you for a few hours or even a whole day from your little-boy games. As I seem to have now."

"So the solution might be for me to make love with you every day?"

She considered him shrewdly, her face illumined by the spreading moonlight.

"It would be an interesting experience," she said slowly. "But I don't think you're quite man enough to cope with a woman like me at that pace. And you'd lose interest as soon as some new game came along."

Not man enough!

Well, maybe she was right.

"You're willing to try me?"

Again she pondered. "I don't know why not."

"Then I accept the challenge. . . . And I promise that I won't turn it into a twelve-year-old's game."

"That's a twelve-year-old promise. You should promise that you will try not to turn it into a macho game."

"All right. I promise that I will try not to turn your challenge into a twelve-year-old's macho game."

"You realize," she said, shifting in her chair, "that this puts the whole relationship into play."

"To use an expression that is one of my favorites."

She chuckled. "Right!"

"You want to play golf tomorrow, I mean after we go to Mass?"

"Raymond, is there something wrong? What's happened to you?"

In the silver glow of the moon, her face had twisted in a worried frown.

He groped for an answer. He should have had one ready. "It was a very scary plane flight."

"It certainly must have been."

It was his turn to pour the wine. He emptied the bottle, half in her goblet, half in his.

"Do you want some chocolate-chip ice cream?" she asked. "Of course you do. Silly of me to ask. Why not enjoy all the pleasures possible on this warm autumn night?"

She bounded off into the house, peach robe trailing behind, like a jet's trail on a blue sky.

He noticed that the angelic choristers were humming again.

"Not bad," Michael whispered. "You're showing nice progress."

"I'm out of control."

"That's not all bad."

"I suppose that her indictment is the same one that Donna would level."

"Pretty much, with one exception."

"That is?"

"Donna never really loved you. Maybe you could have won her love, but you never tried because, as your woman would put it, you were too busy acting like a twelve-year-old."

"Do your, ah, companions tell you the same thing?"

"The equivalent, I suppose."

"Are you an extraterrestrial?"

"Should E.T. phone home?"

"You know what I mean: Are you from another planet?"

"Let's say we're from another world and leave it at that, shall we?"

"So you leave your home world when you are working one of your jobs for the Other, as you call him?"

Her more often than not. No, not exactly. As I remarked, we move only slightly less rapidly than the speed of thought. . . . Don't worry about it."

Anna Maria bounded back, her robe in becoming and doubtless deliberate disarray.

She stopped for a moment in midflight.

"Did I hear voices, Raymond?"

"I don't think so."

"Maybe I'm the one who is losing my mind. . . . Anyway, is this too much ice cream?"

"There is no such thing as too much ice cream."

She kissed him on the forehead as she gave him the treat, perhaps to make sure that his twelve-year-old ego was not too badly bruised. This time she did not try to tighten the belt on her robe.

"Two treats for the price of one," he said. "Or maybe three."

"Do you really want to play golf tomorrow?" she said, tucking her feet under her on the lawn chair. "They predicted sixty percent chance of rain."

"I have a more accurate weather service at my disposal. It will be another perfect late-summer day."

"I'll beat you."

"Probably. When I get my golf game back in shape, it might be a different story."

"It won't bother you to lose to your wife?"

"It will bother the hell out of me. I don't like to lose to anyone. Wife doesn't add much humiliation to it. Maybe a little. But then I can brag to the other fat cats up there that my wife is a great golfer. As well as great at some other things."

"That would be a terrible twelve-year-old thing to say," she said, then began demolishing her ice cream, which consisted of only two scoops as opposed to the four she had given him.

"No, it wouldn't, not if it is sufficiently, ah, allusive."

She considered that possibility. "No, I suppose it wouldn't."

They were silent as he finished his ice cream. The choir was humming softly.

He lifted his wineglass in a toast. "To the challenge of our future, now that it's in play."

She nodded. "And to more dangerous plane flights, though not too dangerous."

"And to the best possible of guardian angels."

For a moment he was shy about the next step, not that he was not aroused, but that it would probably alter their relationship so that there would be no turning back.

What the hell, he had only a few months to live anyway.

He put the wineglass back on the table, stood up, walked to her chair, took her hands, and lifted her up.

"Raymond," she said dubiously, "it's really too cold out here."

He pulled the robe off her shoulders. She clutched it at her waist and drew her usual deep breath, deeper than usual this time, he thought.

"No, it's not. I loved you earlier in the warm glow of the afternoon sun. Now I propose to love you in the soft shimmer of the moon."

He discarded her robe.

She shivered and huddled behind her arms. "We don't have to do it outside twice in the same day. The moon shines through my bedroom window too."

"Not the same." He lifted her into his arms.

"I suppose not," she sighed.

As he carried her to the chaise, he said, "Anna Maria, you are the most interesting woman I have ever known."

The choristers really liked that line. They went into their celebration songs again, softly however, so as not to waken sleeping children or to disturb young lovers, no matter how old the lovers might be.

"I love you, Raymond," she said, clinging closely to him. "I'll always love you."

Afterward he carried her up to the second floor of the house. She was exhausted and passive in his arms, mostly asleep.

"I think I left my robe and my book in the garden," she murmured. "What if it rains?"

"It won't rain. I told you, I have solid guarantees."

Yet when he entered her room, the book was on the nightstand and the robe neatly folded on a chair.

"Show-offs," he murmured to whatever elements of the angelic hosts were lurking about.

After he had deposited her in her bedroom and returned to his room, Michael appeared, now in jeans and a crimson sport shirt, sitting comfortably by Neenan's computer station.

"You learn quickly."

"I try. . . . Why the change of clothes?"

"We have our own lives to live," the seraph replied enigmatically. "She spoke truth when she said the whole relationship is now in play."

"I understand that."

"It won't always be as easy as today."

"I didn't think it would be."

"Just so long as you understand that." Michael jabbed a finger at Neenan. "We will not take kindly to your breaking her heart."

"Neither would I. . . . What did you mean when you said that Donna never loved me?"

"All you can expect at the beginning of a youthful marriage is the beginnings of love. Donna, poor woman, was in love with the image of herself as a bride and as a suburban homemaker. You didn't help very much. Still you have to try to reconcile with her."

"No!"

The seraph reached into his hip pocket and pulled out the contract, which he waved at Neenan.

"Yes!" he said firmly.

"What's the point in my paying any attention to you, since you tell me there isn't any such thing as hell?"

"I didn't say that at all. I said we didn't use that metaphor too much anymore because it had been so distorted. You still face the risk of loss."

"Meaning?"

"Don't blow it now."

"If you say so."

"Have you ever been as happy in all your life as you are now?"

Neenan pondered. "I suppose I haven't."

"Like I say, don't blow it."

"I don't want to lose her when I die."

"None of us wants to lose those we love. Not to worry, you won't lose her. Not then anyway. It's now that counts."

7

"*I want to tell you a story,*" said the weary-looking, middle-aged priest, "about Patricia the Penny Planter. It's one of John Shea's stories. The kingdom of heaven, you see, is like Patricia the Penny Planter."

That's all I need, Neenan thought, struggling to find a comfortable position in the pew, a story about a penny planter, whatever that might be.

While he had gone to bed the night before with every good intention of attending Mass with his wife and then risking his twelve-year-old male ego on the golf course, he had forgotten to set the alarm.

Not to worry. At seven o'clock, the angel singers had intervened with bright and cheerful wake-up music. Before he opened his eyes, he wondered how large the chorus was. It sounded bigger than the Mormon Tabernacle Choir. On the other hand, a few angels could presumably make a lot of noise.

He had opened his eyes. The sun was shining brightly over the Lake. Why was he so tired? Why did he have to get up? Why did he feel so complacent and yet frightened?

Then it all came back. A black person who claimed to be an angel had pronounced his death sentence, but then beat him over the head with a couple of ecstatic experiences and the best sex of his life. Twice.

It had all been a dream, a nightmare, the result of one too many vodkas. Hadn't it?

Either he was still in a dream or it had all happened. The choir was singing loudly. They had started their caterwauling on the plane when the dream began. The only sensible way to deal with a dream was to go back to sleep.

He had closed his eyes contentedly. The choir, however, refused to accept that decision. It sang more loudly and more insistently.

"Damn," he had said, struggling out of bed and lumbering toward the shower. "Maybe it isn't a dream."

When he emerged from the shower, he found a cup of coffee and a cinnamon roll on his nightstand.

She had never done that before.

"Patricia was ten years old. She lived in a suburban neighborhood where there were only a few children her age, including Morgan, an eleven-year-old boy who was nice but only for a very limited amount of time. Summer was generally a very *boring* period in her life. There were just so many hours a day that you could listen to rock tapes. So she decided to create a treasure hunt.

"How could a ten-year-old girl create a treasure hunt?

"You ask that question only because you don't know Patricia.

"You have to understand, first of all, that right at the corner of her street there was a bus stop to which many, many people came early in the morning to get on a bus, which took them to the train, which took them to the city and their jobs. They were all well-dressed — even on casual Friday — and carried expensive leather briefcases and serious and worried frowns. Then at the end of the day, they came back looking frazzled and wilted and with heavier briefcases and heavier frowns. None of them ever looked up.

"So the first day of her treasure hunt, when it was very hot and no one was on the street, Patricia sneaked out of her house with a large supply of chalk. Looking carefully up and down the street, to make sure the police wouldn't see and arrest her for defacing public property, she scrawled in large red block letters right at the bus stop, **TREASURE NEAR!**→

"Then at strategic intervals along the street, she scrawled other notes:

"THIS WAY TO TREASURE!→

"YOU'RE GETTING CLOSER!→→

"DON'T QUIT NOW!→→

"YOU ALMOST HAVE IT!→→→

"LOOK IN THE TREE!→→→→

"GO FOR IT!→→→→

"Then Patricia found a very bright penny in her large collection of almost a thousand pennies and slipped it into an old notch in the bark of a beautiful oak tree in front of her house. To give her treasure hunters a last bit of reassurance, she wrote on the tree trunk:

"TREASURE HERE!

"Well, at first no one paid any attention to Patricia's signs and the arrows that went with them. You see, while they never looked up when they walked down the street to the bus because their eyes were always downcast, they never paid any attention to what was on the sidewalk. Then the second day it rained and wiped out all her carefully drawn signs.

"This time, she said to herself, I'll do it right!

"So she replaced all her signs, and this time, she did them in psychedelic colors. Sure enough, that night, some people began to notice the signs. Most of them ignored the promise of treasure, but a young woman with an especially heavy briefcase looked at the first sign and her already heavy frown got heavier. Then she saw the second sign and laughed at it, not altogether pleasantly. The third sign caught her attention. Then, when she came to the sign that said, 'Go for it!' she looked both ways to make sure no one was watching her. Then, with a crafty expression, she crept up on the tree, took out the penny, and grinned happily. She put the penny back into the tree for the next customer and strode away with the grin still on her face.

"Not bad for the first one, Patricia chortled to herself.

"The next person was an older man whose walk suggested that all the joy had gone out of his life. He looked like he would hardly be able to make it home each evening, so weary, so discouraged, so beaten, did he seem. He imitated the woman's approach, even to looking in both directions so that no one would think him stupid.

"He laughed and laughed and laughed when he took the penny out of the tree. He kept the penny and put a quarter in its place.

"Patricia wasn't sure that she approved of that. The whole point was the penny. So she found her second—most shiny penny and replaced the quarter. She dropped the quarter in a special place on her dresser. She'd put this extra treasure in the collection in church on Sunday.

"Well, so it went. More and more people found the treasure. It made them all much happier. By the end of the week, Patricia had three dollars and fifty cents to put in the collection on Sunday. She thought about deducting money to pay for the pennies she had lost, but that would have been like totally yucky, wouldn't it, when you had almost a thousand pennies?

"Patricia the Penny Planter decided that this summer was not so boring after all.

"Then late one day, a prim and proper young man, the most prim and proper young man Patricia had ever seen in her long experience of life, saw the sign at the bus stop and begin to follow the other signs. Patricia, who naturally watched all this from the window in her air-conditioned bedroom, could hardly believe it. There must be hope for all the prim and proper young men in the world. He got all the way to the edge of the sidewalk opposite the tree, looked again in both directions, and then turned away and walked briskly down the street.

" 'Oh, drat!' Patricia the Penny Planter said, using her strongest language.

"That night, just before she was going to bed and when the lights in her room were off, Patricia the Penny Planter looked out her bedroom window. There in the gloomy darkness, illumined only by a dim streetlamp, was the prim and proper young man, now in a T-shirt and cutoffs. He left the sidewalk and very cautiously approached the tree.

"Patricia could not contain herself. She threw open the window and shouted at the top of her voice—which was pretty loud, to tell the truth— '*Go for it!*'

"The young man looked up, startled and frightened. Where was this voice in the dark coming from? He turned and ran away as fast as his expensive running shoes could carry him.

"Patricia closed the window. She was laughing.

" 'I'll get him yet,' she told herself. 'He's hooked. I'll get him yet.'

"Now, my friends, the question you will want to ask yourself is how the kingdom of heaven is like Patricia the Penny Planter's treasure hunt."

Neenan looked around. Everyone in church seemed to be smiling. As a matter of fact, he was smiling too.

Someone behind him coughed slightly; Neenan glanced behind him. It was Michael, now in a white summer suit and a white linen shirt. The seraph rolled his eyes and nodded, as if to say, God is exactly like Patricia the Penny Planter.

Neenan wasn't sure that God was really like the little girl who started her own treasure hunt. But it would be nice if He . . . or She . . . were that way.

"That might make a great TV film," he whispered to his wife, who was wearing a thin summer dress, lime in color, that being the current fashion.

"I'll think about it," she said, frowning in pretended disapproval at his interrupting the flow of divine worship with such a distraction.

He wondered how many other men in church were entertaining lascivious images of her. Well, according to her theology, it was all right if he did. So he indulged in them.

"Excellent metaphor, Father," he said with his best smile and a firm shake of the hand after Mass. "Life is a treasure hunt. Could be. But do you think God created us because he was bored?"

The priest grinned back. "More likely because he wanted someone to love."

Anna Maria beamed approvingly.

I had better watch out, Neenan told himself, or I will end up as devout as she is.

Then he remembered that he had only a few months left in his life. His funeral Mass would probably be said at this church. He hoped the priest, whose name he did not remember, would say the Mass. He should tell Anna Maria.

No, that would be stupid and cruel. There would be plenty of time for that toward the end.

Then he wondered, for the first time, what would be the cause of his death. He'd ask Michael, but he was certain that the seraph wouldn't tell him. He might claim that he didn't know. More likely he would simply evade the question. My doctor told me I was in fine shape in August when I had my yearly physical, he reflected. No reason to seek another. Not when it's in the books that my life is going to be short.

"Why so thoughtful?" Anna Maria asked as he opened the door for her to his rarely used Ferrari.

"I'm thinking about my humiliation on the golf course."

"Oh, it won't be too bad." She laughed. "I might just have mercy on you."

"I doubt it."

They both laughed together.

Well, she wouldn't be able to humiliate him next summer because he wouldn't be here to play golf next summer.

He shivered at that thought. Fortunately, Anna Maria did not notice.

Back in their house, he pondered again the lesson of Patricia the Penny Planter.

"Go for it!"

He walked across the hallway to her room. The door was open. Inside she was changing from clothes appropriate for church to clothes appropriate for driving to the golf course and eating dinner afterward. She was not quite naked.

She turned in surprise and covered her chest with her arms.

Some idiot angel pounded a drum.

"Sorry if I frightened you," he said cautiously. "I suppose I should have knocked."

"The door was open," she said tentatively.

"It was indeed. . . . I hope I didn't hurt you yesterday."

"Don't be silly!"

"Come here, Anna Maria."

She lowered her arms and put her hands behind her back. Then she walked to him, a faint smile on her face, her eyes questioning, her breath coming rapidly.

God in heaven, these early moments of love were so wonderfully exciting!

God in heaven? Well, maybe.

"We have an hour and a half before tee time," she said shyly.

"I'm doing what the priest said at Mass," he said, touching her face.

"Going for it, Raymond?"

"An hour and a half ought to do, shouldn't it?"

"I would think so." She was trembling now with anticipation.

"Three times in twenty-four hours is not too much, Anna Maria?"

"It's a record, but I'm not resisting, am I?"

"The open door was an invitation?"

"What do you think?" she replied defiantly.

The caroling angels, who had been silent for a couple of hours, began to sing again. Well they might.

It was just twenty-four hours ago that he had encountered the seraph who claimed his name was Michael.

He wondered as he teased and caressed and fondled his luscious wife whether he was the same man whom Michael had warned about his imminent death.

Later on the golf course, he felt her hands on his hips just as they had been during their lovemaking.

"Are you trying to distract me as I'm about to drive?" he demanded.

"Certainly not," she said. "I'm trying to correct that deplorable slice of yours. Now stay in that position while you swing."

"The pro told me to do it the way I'm doing it now."

"The pro is wrong."

"I feel terribly awkward in this posture." He shifted back to his familiar stance.

"You'll slice every time," she said firmly, once again moving his hips back into the place where she wanted them.

"OK." He swung, sure that he would dub the ball and maybe fall on his face.

Instead the small, white object sped down the fairway, straight as an arrow, for two hundred yards.

"That's better," she said approvingly, and patted his rear end.

She was wearing a blue-and-white-striped halter and white shorts, both tight and both leaving rather little to the imagination.

"Stop thinking dirty thoughts about me," she had said with a deep blush as she emerged from the women's locker room, accompanied by a fanfare of angelic trumpets.

"You're my wife," he had insisted.

"But this is on the golf course, not in the bedroom."

"I can't help that. You look absolutely delectable."

"That's probably a male chauvinist word, but I'll accept it on the condition you don't intend it to be."

"It's only a chauvinist word if it's wrong for a man to admire a beautiful woman and tell her so if she's his wife."

She had blushed again. "Come on! Let's play golf."

"Yes, ma'am."

"Besides," she had said, her back turned to him as she led him out of the clubhouse, "what's the point of all the workouts I do if I can't dress like this occasionally?"

"As often as you want, as far as I'm concerned."

She had sniffed disdainfully.

The angelic fanfare continued as they approached the first tee. Then they had the good taste to stop, perhaps out of respect for the golfer's need to concentrate.

"Why do I keep thinking I hear music?" she asked him as she teed up her ball for the first shot.

"Someone has the stereo on somewhere."

On the golf course she had taken him apart with merciless precision.

Her drives were not long, a hundred and fifty yards at the most. But they were dead straight. Her iron shots went to the green as if a magnet were attracting them, and her putts were miraculous. She was a much better golfer than when he had last played her on their honeymoon.

"You are really good," he had said in unfeigned admiration.

"You mean at golf?" she said with a giggle.

"At the moment that was what I meant, yes."

Then on the eleventh tee she had corrected his shot.

"I might catch up with you," he warned her.

"Not a chance."

He won the hole by a single stroke.

On the twelfth tee he had addressed the ball in his familiar stance.

"Stop that!" she exclaimed, and once more moved his hips into what she deemed was the proper position. Her hands lingered a little longer than necessary.

"Not a bad-looking rear end to tell the truth," she said, and patted him vigorously. "Now swing the club."

He hit another monumental drive. He won that hole, a par five, with a birdie as opposed to her bogey.

"I'll catch you," he warned again.

"Absolutely not. . . . What are you waiting for? You go first! Tee up the ball!"

"I need help getting in the right stance."

She came up from behind him. Instead of arranging his stance, however, she hugged him fiercely and buried her head in his back.

"I love you, Raymond," she whispered. "Hopelessly. Always have, always will."

"You're definitely trying to distract me this time," he said, his voice hoarse with emotion.

"No, I'm not," she said, releasing him. "I'm just trying to encourage you. . . . Now you've got it right. Swing!"

He did. Once more the ball sailed like a guided missile, right down the center of the fairway.

"Not bad," she conceded. "Now, every time you tee up for the rest of your life, remember the way I hugged you and you'll know what to do."

"I'm not likely to forget."

It wouldn't be a long life and he probably wouldn't play golf again.

But if there was an eternity and if he made it into it, he would never forget that hug.

Despite his improved drives, she beat him by nine strokes.

"Next time you'll have to work on my irons and my putting."

"We'll see about that!"

He kissed her in salute of her victory, not intensely enough to embarrass her in sight of the clubhouse, but enough to let her and the busybodies who were watching know that he loved her and that she was his. As well as vice versa.

"Swim?" she said. "Or do you have to get back to your Toshiba."

"I didn't bring a swimsuit."

"I packed one in the car for you."

"You'll be wearing a bikini?"

"What else?"

"Then by all means, let's swim."

After she had produced his swimsuit, the long-silent choristers, now accompanied by a loud wind ensemble, accompanied her to the entrance of the women's locker room.

Later, sitting on a chair at poolside, he found that a large black person in swim trunks, without the diamond earring this time, was sitting next to him in a chair that had not been there a few minutes before.

"You swim in your world?"

"Why wouldn't we?"

"With your companion?"

"Why wouldn't I?"

"Does she turn you on like the woman turns me on?"

"Why wouldn't she?"

He thought about telling Michael that Anna Maria heard the music of the choir and orchestra, though from a great distance. Then he decided that it was the seraph's problem and not his.

"Not too bad for a beginning," Michael said. "You have a lot more to do."

"Three times in twenty-four hours . . . I thought that was pretty good."

"I don't have to tell you that even good sex isn't enough to hold a relationship together."

"Am I not being kind and sensitive and tender and sweet?"

The seraph grunted.

"And appropriately demanding and challenging?"

"So far," the angel admitted grudgingly. "We'll see how you sustain it as the days and weeks go on."

"I don't want to lose her."

"I don't blame you. But like I say, you don't have to lose her ever."

"I'll take your word for it."

"Trying to reconcile with Donna and your parents and your other children won't have any fun in it at all."

"Tell me about it."

"You should also think about giving some of your money away."

"Why?"

"You can't take it with you."

"True. . . . How much?"

The seraph thought about it. "Oh, say five million."

"No problem . . . I'm not greedy."

"Not for money. For power and domination is another matter."

"Do I dominate her?"

"Anna Maria? No, you never have and probably never will and wouldn't be able to even if you wanted to. . . . Didn't I tell you she was the most interesting woman you'd ever meet?"

"You were right."

"We're usually right . . . and you don't really know her yet."

"I'll await eagerly further progress. I hope I'm not *too* demanding sexually with her."

Michael guffawed. "She did leave her bedroom door open after Mass, didn't she?"

"That's true."

"If you ever get too adolescent, she'll tell you."

"Who do I give the five million to?"

"Figure that out for yourself. . . . Now, if I am to judge by the excitement of my singing colleagues, she's emerging from the locker room. Have fun."

The angelic consort went over the top in celebration of Anna Maria's appearance, in a short white robe, open over a blue swimsuit.

Well they might.

"Can I whistle?" he asked her.

She blushed furiously, an attractive color of deep, deep pink, which flowed from her face to her throat to her chest.

"If it makes you feel good."

So he whistled, softly so only she could hear.

"One-track mind," she sniffed, shedding the robe and sitting next to him on the chair that Michael had vacated.

The angel trumpets blasted a long fanfare as she put aside her robe. The music echoed the beat of Neenan's heart.

"When a woman in my house leaves the door to her room open while she undresses, that pushes my mind down that single track."

"Twelve-year-old," she sniffed without much conviction.

"You'd be overdressed in that if you were on a Brazilian beach."

"Remind me then to stay away from Brazil."

"We'll have to go there sometime."

"That might be fun," she agreed. "Thong bikini."

"Can I ask you a personal question on this subject?" he said cautiously.

"Depends on the question," she replied with equal caution.

"It has to do with sex."

"I assumed that it would."

"I don't quite know how to put it . . . you seem to enjoy lovemaking."

"I do. Very much."

"I have the impression that many women do not, at least not with the abandon you do."

She swallowed and nodded her head. "You're right. I'm always astonished in those 'girl talk' situations — at which we tend to act like twelve-year-olds too — how many women don't like sex at all. Those of us who do usually keep our mouths shut, lest the others accuse us of betraying the womanly cause."

"Why don't they like sex?"

She produced a tube of suntan cream and began to coat him with it, in a brisk, businesslike fashion.

"The way they were raised. Bitter mothers. Insensitive fathers. Brutish husbands. Painful experiences."

"Hmm . . ."

"And you have to understand, Raymond Anthony, that when a woman abandons most of her inhibitions, as I did this morning when I left the door to my room open, she becomes totally vulnerable. She depends completely on the sensitivity and, what should I say, the delicacy of the man. It's a big risk to take."

Her cream-covered fingers reached his belly, where they slowed down.

"Very nice flat stomach for a man of your years."

"Thank you, I think. . . . But you take the risk?"

"It seems to me that sex is there to be enjoyed, like food and drink and singing and dancing and reading and laughing. So I take the risk. You may have your limitations as a husband, but you're lacking in neither sensitivity nor delicacy in lovemaking, once you can drag yourself away from your empire long enough to think about it. Sometimes I wonder how, given your experience, you became that way. But I don't worry about it that much."

She wouldn't.

Her fingers lingered on his belly, then tickled him.

"Come on, let's do our swim before we misbehave."

They dove into the pool together. The water did nothing to cool his emotions.

⚜8⚜

"So what did they say about me in the locker room?" she demanded, tapping her finger insistently on the table.

They were sitting in the oak-paneled Old English dining room of the country club, eating supper in dim and what anywhere else would have been considered romantic light. She was wearing a loose-fitting summer print dress. Her hair was pulled back in a long ponytail. She looked as if she might be fifteen or sixteen.

"You're getting awfully pushy in your questions."

"It was you who changed the rules," she said as he consumed a small bit of sea bass.

"I did, didn't I? . . . Well, they said that I was probably the only man in the club whose wife would dare beat on his home course."

"They *did!* And what did you say?"

"I said I didn't mind that you beat me because you had shown me how to straighten out the slice that had tormented me for at least twenty years."

"And *then?*"

"Then they asked whether you were good at anything else, and I said that you were good at everything."

"You did? . . . That was sweet. . . . What tone of voice?"

"A tone which suggested that they could draw their own conclusions."

"*Well,* that wasn't so bad. . . . It shut them up, I bet."

"It did that. Do women say anything about me in the locker room?"

She blushed. "That's not an appropriate question."

"Why not?"

"Because I said so. . . . Some of them have the nerve to ask whether you are any good in bed."

"And you say?"

"I roll my eyes and smile."

"Good response."

"They also ask how often you insist on sex."

He felt his face grow hot. "And you say?"

"I roll my eyes again."

"You might have to change your answer soon."

"I might just . . . all of this change is because of a bumpy ride home from National Airport?"

Neenan thought for a moment about his answer. It had to be true but not the whole truth. Enough of the truth to satisfy her.

"It's true that in situations like that your life rushes before you. I didn't like a lot of what I saw. So I decided to try to change some of the things that need changing."

She nodded as she sipped from a glass of Pinot Grigio.

"I'm not complaining. I hope it lasts."

"So do I."

A loud angelic cymbal crashed in approval. So now they were adding timpani to their combo. Had he decided that his life needed changing or had Michael and the Other decided that?

The question was irrelevant. He was locked into change now. It was only mildly painful these last thirty hours. It could get a lot more painful.

"I think I'm going to give away some money," he continued.

"Oh? How much?"

"Five million."

She raised an eyebrow. "You can afford that. . . . To whom?"

"I thought I'd ask you if you minded if I gave it to Loyola. You went there. You liked it. You said you learned a lot. I don't know whether it helped you in your story reading for us. . . ."

"It did," she said promptly.

He doubted it. Her instinct for stories was almost certainly "natural." But it didn't matter.

"I thought we might give it to Loyola for four or five chairs in the humanities."

"How wonderful!" she said, her eyes glowing with admiration.

"If you don't mind, I thought we'd name the chairs in your honor — the Anna Maria Allegro chairs."

Another woman might have been embarrassed at the prospect of such publicity. He had a hunch she'd love it.

"Raymond," she said, her eyes filling with tears, "I hope this new version of you never changes. But even if it does, I'll treasure these last two days forever."

"You don't mind if we name the chairs after you?"

"Mind? Why should I mind? It's marvelous."

"Still, it was a good thing I asked."

"You'd better believe it. I wouldn't want my name to be used without my permission."

"I thought so. . . . Now tell me about this Susan Howatch person you were reading yesterday when I so rudely interrupted you. She's a kind of romance novelist, isn't she?"

"Well, she is and she isn't. She used to write these long romances about the English country nobility, romances which were far better than anyone else was writing. Then she experienced some kind of religious conversion and turned to writing theological novels. . . . You know who Trollope is?"

"Sure. The Barsetshire saga?"

"Well, I found out about him when someone told me that the six books in her Starbridge saga were something like a twentieth-century version of Barsetshire. Trollope in the twentieth century with more freedom to talk about sex."

"Sounds interesting. Could we make films of any of them?"

"Women would be delighted. She is very popular with us, even when she talks about theology and spirituality with a touch of the occult thrown in. Her men are very attractive."

Neenan eased his plate out of the way and turned to his wineglass.

"Sounds like it couldn't miss."

"The best bet, I think," she said, warming to the subject, "would be an eight-hour miniseries called *Starbridge*."

"I've never known you to be wrong about a story idea. Why don't you find someone to write us a treatment."

"Actually, I think there's someone who has written a script. Let me look into it."

This was the tricky and secretive Sicilian woman who occasionally surfaced. She was not yet ready to tell him that she had written the script. She was, he reflected, particularly entrancing when she played that role. Michael was right: she was the most interesting woman he had ever known.

Or maybe the most interesting woman he had never bothered to know.

"If you think it might be worthwhile, pass it on to me. It sounds like an appealing idea."

"I'll get back to you about it in a couple of days."

Neenan couldn't blame her for the secrecy. She was protecting herself and her work from the possibility of failure. Neenan was willing to bet that it was a script that was ready to go into production and that the series would be a huge success. Probably earn the $5 million he intended to give to her alma mater and a good deal more.

He didn't trust his judgment on her work. He might not be critical enough or he might be too critical.

After he read it, he'd give it to a couple of people at the company — Joe McMahon and Vincent anyway — to get their reaction.

Funny, he wouldn't have thought of giving it to Vincent before his encounter with the seraph.

Back at their home, the songsters having quieted down, he gazed at the computer in his bedroom, thought about turning it on, then decided that was a temptation.

Then another, and much more benign, temptation entered his room — his wife in a white silk robe. She sat on the edge of his bed.

No angelic hoopla this time.

"I want to ask you a question," she said hesitantly, "or maybe make a suggestion."

"Ask away," he said, grateful to the seraph that he had not turned on the machine.

"You have apparently decided to accept my challenge."

"It would certainly seem so."

"Perhaps it would facilitate matters if I slept in your bed every night."

Gulp. Michael had warned him about this issue, and he'd forgotten the warning.

"You'd give up some of your privacy." By that he meant that he would lose some of his privacy. He did not like sexually aggressive women. Now she was being sexually aggressive. Somehow he didn't mind anymore.

"That would not matter."

"You would like it?" he asked her.

"Naturally."

"Why?"

"A woman likes to have a man to cuddle with even if they are not making love, a man beside her when she wakes up, a man who reassures her after nightmares."

He joined her on the bed. "You should have told me that long ago."

"I didn't think you'd listen. I'm not sure you are listening even now."

He eased the robe off her shoulders. It fell back on the bed. She looked delightfully defenseless.

"You realize the risks?" he asked gently as his hand sought her thigh.

"What risks?" she said with a modest laugh.

"A beautiful woman like you might just be assaulted almost every time she appears in a man's bedroom."

"I can live with that," she gasped.

The songsters had not gone to sleep after all. They started up again, this time with an elegiac melody that hinted not at autumn but at spring. And at new life.

9

"It's not a good idea," Neenan insisted in his suite in NE's offices in the Sears Tower as he stood at the windows staring at the deep blue lake, quiet as if it had decided not to wake up this morning. "She hates me too much ever to reconcile."

"Then that's her problem." Michael waved his hand. "You have to try, just like you're going to try this weekend in St. Petersburg with your mother and father."

"I'm not going to Florida this weekend," Neenan thundered.

"Yes, you are. The weather will turn cold in midweek. If you intend to continue your golf lessons, it will have to be at the King's Crown Country Club on Captiva."

"The Gulfstream isn't ready yet."

"It will be."

"How do I know that Anna Maria will want to go?"

"Call her and find out."

So he called her about the change in the weather at midweek, despite the lovely late-summer morning whose high clouds hung like a benign ceiling over the city and the park and the smooth lake in the distance.

"I don't mind a trip to Florida," she said. "But they were saying on TV this morning that the summer weather will hold for another week."

"I've told you that my weather forecasters are unbeatable."

Michael smirked at this comment.

"You should stop at St. Petersburg and say hello to your parents."

"If you insist," Neenan conceded.

Michael rolled his eyes.

"Fine. It sounds like fun. When do we leave?"

"Friday morning from Palwaukee."

"Wasn't that easy?" Michael asked.

"She wanted to go. It won't be easy when I get to St. Petersburg. She'll have to come with me to see Mom and Dad."

"Don't even think about asking her." Michael dismissed that suggestion with a characteristic casual wave of his hand.

What did the seraph mean by that?

The next problem was Neil Higgins, the law partner of Lerner and Locke who earned his living as head of the NE litigation team.

"Thought I'd talk to you about the pension case," Neil began nonchalantly as they seated themselves at a worktable and began to drink their midmorning coffee.

Michael beamed contentedly as he joined them at the table.

"What about it?"

"Are you ready to settle?"

"Why should we settle? We didn't break any law."

Michael frowned.

"We'd probably win the case," Higgins agreed, "though you never can tell in a federal courtroom these days. Every judge wants to become a media celebrity. It's not my field obviously, but there might be a lot of nasty publicity, more than there has been already."

"What do we give them?"

"Their jobs and their pensions back. Maybe with apologies for a regrettable mistake. It would cost less than extended litigation."

"And Tim Walsh?" Neenan asked, referring to the plaintiff's celebrity lawyer.

"He's a kind of friend of yours, R. A., isn't he?"

"Kind of."

"He'll be at the opera Wednesday night. You might off the record suggest that we'd pay his fees, as reasonably calculated. It would be a relief to him. He knows that it will cost hundreds of thousands of dollars to pursue the case, and since he's not likely to win it, that would be money down the drain. He's already won his brownie points as the friend of the oppressed by bringing suit. An equitable settlement will win him some more. You'll still save a lot of money."

Michael nodded his head vigorously.

"Maybe we shouldn't have fired them," Neenan admitted. "Though they were all drones and hadn't earned their salary for years."

Michael waved a warning finger.

"It might have been unwise," Higgins agreed. "Better not to do it again. It's practically impossible these days to prove incompetence."

"But I don't like to cave in."

"I understand that."

"Is there any downside?"

"Some of them won't want to settle. They want a piece of your hide."

"They'd never win punitive damages."

"Early on, Walsh hinted that they might. That was braggadocio and he knew it. Yet some of those folks hate you badly enough to try for punitive."

"Walsh will have to talk them out of it."

"He probably will, but it might take time. Normally, I don't give this kind of advice, but maybe you should talk to him personally to-morrow night. He's afraid of you."

"As well he might be."

Michael shook his head in strong disapproval.

"It's not a hell of a lot of money, R. A., and you can't take it with you."

Michael brightened at that remark.

"Well, that's true, I guess. . . . All right, I'll sound him out tomorrow night."

"Good," Higgins said, emptying his coffee cup. "Tell him to get in touch with me about the small stuff."

"You almost blew that one," Michael said when Higgins left the office.

"We fired only the loafers. To call them loyal executives, like the Chicago papers did, is a farce."

"As you know, the print media hate the visual media, even when they own a lot of visual stuff. Moreover, even drones have some rights. At least to their pension."

"All right, all right."

"Now the next visitor is Bennett Harvey. You remember him, I presume, and his wife?"

"I remember him all right."

Ben Harvey was ten years younger than Neenan. A brilliant entre-preneur and a rotten administrator. Neenan had snatched up his New York cable firm for a song when Harvey had run it on a financial reef. Bennett had no more legal sense than administrative sense and tried to resist the takeover, which made matters worse for him. Neenan had also taken over his wife, Joan, a tall, aristocratic, and sophisticated professor of English literature. At her pleading he had kept Harvey on as president of the firm but under the supervision of NE's financial wizards and with little real power.

"Mr. Harvey to see you, Mr. Neenan," Amy Jardine had announced. "I would remind you that you have to leave for De Kalb at eleven, given the traffic on I-88."

"I'll remember."

"You should offer him a chance to head up your new DTV project," Michael informed him. "It would be a challenge to his innovator's skill and not a threat to his negligible administrative skill."

"Am I the CEO of this firm or are you?"

"Don't push me for an answer on that."

Tall, slim, blond, and handsome, a perpetual youth, Ben Harvey had the knack of entering someone's office as though he were the aloof, powerful boss and everyone else worked for him. Presumably five generations of Yale did that if you were also an Anglican. Neenan had always disliked that style, but this time there was something particularly obnoxious about the man.

Michael continued to watch Neenan carefully. This man is a fool, he felt like saying, why should I worry about him?

Nonetheless they shook hands cordially and sat again at the worktable. Harvey turned down the offer of coffee disdainfully, as though it were a vice beneath his notice.

He had come to Chicago, he explained to Neenan in a tone of voice that said he had no obligation to explain anything, to visit his daughter, who was a student at Northwestern, and to see the Lyric's presentation of *Faust* on Wednesday night. They wanted to compare the Lyric's efforts with that of the Metropolitan. He said the word *Metropolitan* like a devout Catholic might have said the *Vatican*.

"The man acts superior only because he is afraid of you," Michael warned.

"No, he doesn't. He acts superior because he thinks he is superior."

"We'll see you and Joan there on Wednesday night," Neenan said casually. "Why don't you join us for drinks at the first intermission."

He had become accustomed to the reality that when he spoke directly to Michael, no one else heard him, though he wasn't ready to try it yet with Anna Maria because he half-suspected that she might hear him.

"That's very kind of you," Harvey responded in a tone of voice that suggested that Joan and he would be doing Neenan a great favor if they deigned to come to the Graham Room.

"Good. Joan and the children are well?"

"Oh, yes, Joan is publishing a book on Marlowe in which she argues that Shakespeare wrote most of Marlowe's plays. It is very interesting and will no doubt attract much critical acclaim."

Neenan wanted to say that his wife had written a script for the Starbridge saga, but that was still a deep, dark secret.

"Good for her."

"I thought I might mention to you," Harvey said with a mild yawn, "that I have received a very interesting offer from WorldCorp."

"Congratulations."

So they were going after his executives, were they? They were welcome to the weak links like Bennett Harvey.

"*Match it,*" Michael said.

"Almost twice my present salary," Harvey went on in a tone that hinted that the matter was of only minor interest to him.

"*You owe him after what you did to him.*"

"*He's an incompetent jerk.*"

"*Even incompetent jerks have rights.*"

"Might I ask what you will be doing for them?"

"They intend to launch a vast new cable system in this country. I gather they want me to head it up."

Neenan knew that unless he sold out to WorldCorp, they wouldn't have a prayer of launching a cable system.

"It sounds like a great opportunity, Ben. I'm sure you know the risks of working for WorldCorp better than I do. Actually I was planning to offer you the presidency of our DTV effort. It has enormous possibilities as people try to break away from the stranglehold the cable companies have on the market. It seemed to me that it might be the kind of venture you would find exciting."

"Really?"

"*He's interested all right.*"

"*I know the man better than you do.*"

"*Maybe.*"

"I should think we could come pretty close to matching their salary offer."

"That's very interesting indeed. I shall certainly have to think it over and talk to Joan about it of course. I quite agree the DTV has enormous possibilities, especially if it can escape the charges that the cable companies levy on the regular satellite receivers."

Neenan had not been about to discuss the interesting conversation in Washington with the FCC on this subject. Instead he cast out a hint.

"That may not be as impossible as it looks."

"Very, very interesting," Harvey mused. "You had planned this before I told you of WorldCorp's offer?"

"Certainly, though their offer will naturally provide a salary target."

"You are a smooth one all right."

"I'd just as soon he'd go over to WorldCorp. He'll not be an asset to them."

"They assume that he knows more about your operation than he does. Anyway, be sure you give him a fair chance not to mess up his life more than he has. He could be an asset if you treat him wisely."

"All right! All right!"

Harvey muttered that it was quite exciting and that he would have to think through all his options. They promised to meet at the first intermission of *Faust* on Wednesday night.

"You owed him a chance to avoid messing up his life."

"If you say so."

"I say so. Besides, you did take his wife from him."

"He doesn't know that."

"Irrelevant."

Later as his car sped west on I-88, Neenan asked Michael, "How many incompetent goofs will I have to salvage?"

"We will not ask you to endanger your enterprise. Your offer to him was a legitimate offer. He would do very well at it, at least in the short term."

That wasn't really an answer to Neenan's question. The seraph was certainly clever at avoiding answers.

"Why should I rehire the drones?"

"Come on, Ray, you know the answer to that. Pure pragmatism. Get out of that foolish suit you got yourself into."

The car phone rang.

"Ms. Jardine," Peter said.

"Neenan," he said, picking up the phone.

"Ms. Vincent Neenan called about the possibility of dinner a week from tonight. They are leaving for California this afternoon. I checked with Ms. Neenan and she said that it fit with her schedule."

Neenan had never been able to read the implications and the nuances of his administrative assistant's voice. However, he suspected that she disapproved of both Mss. Neenans and of the flight to California and probably of the plan to fly to Florida on Friday. Not that either of these trips was any of her business.

"Fine," he replied, "put it in the book."

Was Amy Jardine another woman he had wronged? Michael said nothing at all so he figured that she wasn't a prime target for his repentance.

As they drove west, across seemingly endless fields, brown and barren after the harvest, and groves of trees that had lost most of their leaves, the sky, a bright blue when they had left Chicago, turned gray and then black. Rain showers appeared on the horizon, misty gray sheets, and raced to meet their Lincoln.

Neenan picked up the phone and punched in Anna Maria's number.

"See what I mean about my weather forecaster?"

"He was way ahead of the United States Weather folks," she said breathlessly. "Excuse me, I was just finishing my workout."

"Sorry to interrupt."

"Not at all. . . . Good day?"

"Unbearably rotten. I'm on my way to De Kalb to try to be nice to Donna."

"That airplane ride really scared you, didn't it?"

"You object?"

"Of course not. Have a nice time."

"Not a chance."

"Bad attitude," Michael said.

"Justified. . . . Don't worry. I'll try. I did treat her shabbily."

"That's progress."

"Did you say earlier that your crowd was responsible for Anna Maria?"

"We were involved."

"That showed excellent taste."

"You bet it did."

Seraphs were apparently not tempted to false humility.

The rain became thicker, the clouds seemed only a few feet above the car. The wipers swished rapidly. Neenan turned gloomy; the dark underside of his personality emerged.

Did he want to spend the rest of his life fighting off WorldCorp or Michael Eisner, worrying about the FCC, trying to settle litigation, and taking care of snobs like Ben Harvey? No way. Yet it was these kinds of problems that bedeviled his daily life. What was the point of it all?

He could not just surrender to WorldCorp, could he? He would earn an immense amount of money and could spend the rest of his days relaxing. But he had forgotten that the rest of his days were not many. Besides, he owed it to his employees to protect them from the devastation WorldCorp would work as soon as they took over.

Maybe he had indeed wasted his life. Well, too late to worry about it now.

"No, you can't quit. NE is your creature and you must protect its life."

"I thought you were not a mind reader."

"We read faces pretty well. You must remember that the kingdom for which Patricia the Penny Planter is a metaphor manifests itself in daily life and its problems and decisions. So the Teacher taught and rightly so."

"The Teacher?"

"The Other's son, obviously."

"Obviously."

The skyscraper buildings of Northern Illinois University broke through the mists. Neenan never felt nostalgic when he returned to De Kalb. It was better than his family and better than the army, but it was not a happy place for him.

There hadn't been any happy places in his life, had there?

"What am I supposed to say to her?"

"You don't need me to answer that question."

"Nothing I can say will work."

"She is a free agent with a free will. Her reaction is her problem. Your problem is to make the offer."

"I'm not sorry that I'm free of her."

"You are sorry for your own mistakes, omissions, and insensitivity in the marriage."

"She won't be sorry for anything."

"At the risk of repeating myself, that's her problem."

"I suppose so."

"It was clever of you to send her flowers this morning."

"I didn't send her flowers."

"Yes, you did."

"You think you have the right to do things like that in my name?"

"Yeah . . . and on your account too."

"And I suppose you didn't bother to send some to Anna Maria."

"Of course we sent them to her. Better ones. Couple of dozen long-stem yellow roses. She hadn't received them yet when you called."

Neenan took out a thin leather notepad from his inside jacket pocket and wrote a couple of words.

"I'll take care of my wife tomorrow, if you don't mind."

Michael merely chuckled

He offered a final warning when Neenan left the car in front of the artsy little restaurant where Donna had finally agreed to meet him.

"Keep your shanty Irish temper under control."

"Yes, boss."

Neenan arrived promptly at twelve. The hostess conducted him to a booth in the corner and gave him a menu. To his horror he discovered that it was a vegetarian restaurant and that, by way of drinks, it served various kinds of herbal ice tea.

Uncharacteristically, Donna was almost on time, only five minutes late.

Michael drifted in with her and joined them at the table.

"Thanks for agreeing to have lunch, Donna."

"Thank you for the flowers, Ray. They were very nice."

Michael rolled his eyes.

"You're looking great, Donna."

Indeed she looked better than she had for many of the years of their marriage She was trim and svelte, her makeup was skillful, and her face had undergone some reconstruction. Moreover she looked content, happy. She was presentable, even appealing.

"Thank you," she said again. "I guess it's because I'm happy."

"I'm glad you are," he said sincerely enough.

They chatted about minor things. He asked her about Susan Howatch's novels. She said they were wonderful and would make a wonderful miniseries.

She ordered a vegetable salad and a bottle of natural water. He ordered pasta with tomato sauce and peppermint ice tea.

Neenan tried to begin his apology.

"I wanted to have lunch with you today," he said somewhat stiffly, "to apologize to you for all the things I did wrong in the marriage. I'm afraid I wasn't a very good husband."

She stiffened. Apparently he had touched the wrong key. Damn, what else was I supposed to say?

"You could spend all your time from now to your deathbed apologizing, and you wouldn't get beyond the first year," she said calmly. "You were a terrible husband."

"I guess I was," he said humbly.

Michael nodded enthusiastic approval.

Then her lips tightened and her brown eyes turned hard.

"Well, if you think I'm going to forgive you and say that we're friends again, you're wrong. I hate you. If I never see you again, it will be too soon."

"I'm sorry you feel that way."

"You're responsible for poor Lenny being a faggot. You're responsible for Jenny wasting her life as an actress when she has no talent. You're responsible for that idiot Vincent thinking that he can be a businessman just like you. But you always favored him, though he was the dumbest of the children."

Neenan recoiled from her wrath.

"I suppose we both made mistakes," he said trying again. "I merely want to say I'm sorry for mine."

"I didn't make any mistakes, except when I married you. That was my only mistake. My friends told me that you were bad news and I didn't believe them. If I had, I wouldn't have wasted twenty years of my life."

He glanced helplessly at Michael. The seraph merely shrugged his shoulders.

"I'm glad that you're happy now," he said, pursuing another tack.

"Certainly I'm happy now. I became happy the day I decided to get rid of you. You get no sympathy from me over your unhappiness. You deserve to be unhappy."

Neenan tried to recall whether he had ever encountered such fierce hatred during their years together. Liberation from him had released her anger, but not healed it.

"I'm not really unhappy," he began.

Michael frowned.

"Well, I won't believe it if you tell me you're happy because of that trashy little Sicilian whore you're living with."

He gritted his teeth and then took a bite of the pasta, which was terrible.

"She's my wife, Donna. We were married in church because of the annulment you were able to get."

"I don't care where you were married. All I have to do is look at her to see that she's a cheap dago whore."

Michael lowered his head.

"We disagree about that," Neenan said mildly, clenching one of his fists.

"I know a whore when I see one," Donna insisted. "I suppose she lets you fuck her whenever you want. That's what whores do. And that's all you were ever interested in from me. My talents, my abilities, my work, nothing I ever did made any difference to you. You barely noticed that I existed. You were not interested in my kiddies either. You let me down and you let them down."

"I'm sorry if I acted that way," he said, biting his tongue. "We're both Catholics. Can we not leave the past behind and begin to forgive?"

Michael smiled his approval.

"You have nothing to forgive. And I won't forgive. You don't deserve forgiveness. You're a vile, rotten, nasty man. All you merit from me is contempt. I have the right to hate you."

"I didn't realize that I was neglecting you and the children and that I was insensitive to you. I was too preoccupied with other things, for which I am very sorry and hope you will forgive me."

Michael nodded his head in approval, almost amazed approval.

"I told you that I would not forgive you. There is no excuse for the way you ruined my life. Then, when I finally wanted freedom to be my own person, you cheated me out of the money to which I was entitled for putting up with you all those years. If I hadn't kept the house together and the kiddies in line, you would never have become the wealthy man that you were. I had every right to half your wealth."

"That would have destroyed the firm."

"Wouldn't that be too bad! You destroyed my life and I destroyed your firm! That's what I wanted to do, you damn fool. And I would have done it if you had not sent your spies snooping into my life. You cheated me out of my revenge."

Neenan had promised himself that he would not mention her infidelity. He was hardly in a position to throw the first stone on that subject.

"I had to protect the jobs of the people who worked for National Entertainment," he said weakly.

"And their jobs were important than my life and the life of the kiddies? I can't believe how vicious you were and are."

Michael lifted his shoulders in frustration.

"I think my efforts to seek your forgiveness for the wrongs that I did are only making matters worse."

Michael again lifted his shoulders.

"Well, your apologies are too late. I don't care about you. I don't think about you. I wouldn't even waste my time hating you. I don't know why I agreed to have lunch with you. I said to myself that I wouldn't let you upset me. But I knew you would."

She pushed aside her half-finished salad, rose from her chair, and stormed out of the restaurant.

"See?" he said to the seraph.

"I saw."

"Let's suppose that I was an extremely sensitive and perceptive young man, the kind of person I'm trying finally to be with Anna Maria. Would it have ended any differently."

"You want to clean your conscience?"

"No . . . well, not exactly. I merely want to know whether if I had been that kind of man, she would be different today from what she is."

"What do you think?"

"I think she would be pretty much the same."

"I can't disagree with you."

"That's the end of it, then?"

"For the moment."

"What do you mean 'for the moment'?"

"You have to keep trying."

"How often?"

The seraph shrugged his board shoulders. "Depends on how much longer you have."

"Did I make her that way?"

"You helped, but, no, you didn't cause it. Likely she'd be the same now, no matter who she married. Still, you have to accept your share for the failure of the marriage."

"I thought I did that."

"You made a good beginning," Michael grudgingly admitted. "I thought for sure that you would lose your temper."

"Let's get out of here. I need some real food. . . . I feel sorry for her wimpy husband."

"After years of therapy she has her fits of rage only when the subject is you. Otherwise she is, how should I say it, tranquil."

"Then why did we come out here and provoke her again?"

"We had to see whether she was willing to forgive you. It would be most helpful to her if she did."

Peter had some real food for Neenan in the car—a Big Mac and a Thirty-One Flavors malted milk.

"I don't know where they came from, Mr. Neenan," the big Irishman said. "I just looked around and there were two orders next to me in the car."

"Wonderful!"

Michael looked like the cat who ate the canary.

Show-off.

On the way back to Chicago, he began to read Anna Maria's script.

"You like it?"

"It seems pretty good to me. I'll have to get the reactions of others. I'm going to stop now. I'm got a splitting headache."

"No problem."

The seraph touched Neenan's head and the pain disappeared. Not bad.

The car phone rang.

"Neenan."

"How did it go?"

"Terrible."

"As you expected?"

"Worse, Anna Maria," he said, "a lot worse."

At the last minute he cut off his flow of anger. No point in making her angry too.

"Well, I just wanted to thank you for the flowers. They are very lovely."

"I'm glad you like them."

"You will be home for supper tonight?"

"I sure will."

"Wonderful! You sound like you'll need a good meal."

"I sure will."

"I'll tell Maeve to cook something special."

"I can hardly wait."

"I'll take that comment on its face value."

Ms. Jardine was waiting for him in the office with more news.

"Ms. Honoria Smythe will be in Chicago tomorrow and wants to have lunch with you to discuss your potential purchase of NorthCal cable."

"Wonderful," he said with notable lack of enthusiasm. At the end of last week he would eagerly have looked forward to a tête-à-tête with that gorgeous woman whom he felt he could buy along with her company. Now neither purchase seemed all that appealing.

He summoned Joe McMahon and Norm Stein and discussed with them his inclination to settle the pension suit, his offer to Bennett Harvey, and the likelihood that Honoria Smythe was ready to sell for the right price.

Joe ran down the list. "It's a good deal to get out of the suit if Timmy Walsh can talk his way out of the mess he got himself into. We shouldn't have tried that in the first place, I guess."

"Not in this day and age anyway," Norm agreed. "Anyway a settlement is the cheapest way out."

"I'm not sure it's a good idea to try to hold on to Ben," Joe continued, "though he probably could do a good job on the DTV project. I don't trust him much. I'd say let WorldCorp have him."

"I wouldn't be unhappy to see him go," Norm said. "WorldCorp is welcome to him."

"Well, we'll have to see what happens," Neenan observed. "I guess his departure wouldn't break my heart either."

However, in his heart he did in fact want to make some kind of restitution to Harvey for having taken his firm away from him.

"Now as to the lovely Honoria," Joe continued, "how much is she worth?"

"Fifty, seventy-five million, a hundred at the most," Norm Stein replied. "She has a nice unit up there in northern California and southern Oregon. Steady moneymaker. Someone is going to gobble her up. And it might as well be us if the price isn't too exorbitant."

Neenan nodded. "I agree."

He wondered to himself what good would come of gobbling up efficient local organizations and merging them with larger and perhaps not so efficient ones. Such thoughts had never occurred to him before. The seraph was probably getting to him. Or the thought that his life would soon be over.

"We keep her on as president with a solid salary?" Joe asked.

"Why not? She'll decorate our offices very nicely when she comes to Chicago."

They all laughed, a mildly chauvinist laugh.

Michael, who had drifted in toward the end of the conversation, frowned disapprovingly at the laugh.

"That part of your life is over, R. A.," he would say as they were working out in the health club later.

The exercise had not improved Neenan's disposition. "You might have waited till after I bought her," he said sadly.

"Don't even think of that. Remember Anna Maria."

"That's right," he agreed reluctantly.

"Finally," Neenan said now to his colleagues, "I think we have to face the fact that WorldCorp is out to get us. They have lots of money even though they are heavily leveraged. Our statement this morning that we are flattered but not interested is hardly likely to keep them off. They want into cable in this country. They'll pay a lot of money for NE and then spin off everything but our cable holdings."

"Eat us alive and then dismember us," McMahon agreed.

"They'll probably go after every executive they think they can buy away from us," Stein warned.

"How can they hope to win?" Neenan asked. "They'd have to buy me out. I control the stock and the board. The company is profitable."

"They will try to harass us to death, steal our executives, buy our directors and producers, dig for dirt about us, sue us for the slightest pretext. They might figure that you'll be so fed up that you'll take their money and run."

"Get our lawyers working on suits we can file against them. Accuse them of trying to steal our executives. Play hardball with their stations in our markets."

"Start our own network to rival WBC?" McMahon suggested.

"I don't think so. We could overextend ourselves that way, which is what they want us to do. If they can harass us, we can harass them."

"What did you find out on Friday at the FCC?" Stein asked.

"They are not likely to oppose our purchase of the station in Topeka, even though we have cable rights in that market."

"Buy some more stations where WBC has a station and go after them?"

"I'm wary of spending too much money in those tactics. We don't need any more stations. We need a hit miniseries."

Neenan asked McMahon to remain in the office for a few minutes and gave him a copy of the Howatch miniseries.

"See what you think of this," he said. "It may be worth a hell of a lot of money."

"Anna Maria like it?"

"She's very positive about it."

Michael waited till McMahon had left the office.

"How is the firm going to resist WorldCorp when you're not here anymore?"

"You had to remind me of that."

"It would be wrong not to plan ahead."

"I understand. . . . How much time do I have?"

"You don't have any time to waste."

Neenan had been afraid of that. Yet he lacked the zest to engage in an all-out battle with WorldCorp. Why put time into a foolish fight when he had so little time?

That night, after he had eaten with great relish a vast Irish beef stew that Maeve had proudly served, he and Anna Maria withdrew early to their joint bedroom.

His wife slowly doffed all her clothes, to the accompaniment of angelic music that seemed rather more lascivious than one would expect from such a choir. Then she spun around a couple of times so he could admire her from every angle. Then she knelt next to him and cuddled him in her arms. She kissed him and caressed him and soothed him and sang lullabies to him.

Not to be outdone, the angelic chorus chimed in with its own exuberant lullabies.

He felt happy for the first time that day.

"You're making me feel like a twelve-year-old," he protested with little conviction as she undressed him.

"Sometimes the poor, battered twelve-year-old in all of us needs soothing," she said.

10

Honoria Smythe was dazzling. Moreover she left no doubt that she was part of the package along with NorthCal. Neenan's hands were wet and his breath was coming rapidly. Worse, Michael had deserted him.

"You're on your own, boyo," the seraph had announced when Neenan was preparing to leave his office for the walk over to the Chicago Club on Michigan Avenue. "If you're going to fight that one off, you'll have to do it on your own."

"Thanks a lot."

Honoria Smythe was in her middle thirties, divorced, tall, blond, and with a model's well-molded body about which there was no doubt because of her form-fitting navy blue knit dress. She had a trick of standing close to him in the elevator, so close that he was absorbed in her fragrance and enchanted by the movements of her breathing.

She was pure California, if the adjective *pure* could be used of her. While there was still a "glass ceiling" above women in the corporate world, some younger women were bright enough and crafty enough to fashion their own companies in small markets and become both successful and wealthy.

When he had walked with her into the grillroom of the club, perhaps the most solemn and pompous eating place in the city, every head had turned to take her in, including the heads of the few women who were present.

Outside, a chill wind from off the lake was blowing curtains of rain against the floor-to-ceiling windows of the club, rattling them in a chorus like the interlude of a Berio opera. Inside, Honoria suggested radiant warmth and bright sunlight.

They chatted aimlessly for a few moments. Her body movements and her flickering blue eyes—a little too icy perhaps—left no doubt about her sexual availability. Indeed they seemed to hint that she was hungry for him.

Her slow, sensuous smile suggested not only longing but admiration. Neenan wasn't sure that she was capable of really desiring a man, yet he was mesmerized by her and was willing to believe that she was obsessed by a craving for him. She was the most seductive of the "interesting" women he had pursued during his life of hunting.

Anna Maria seemed far away. So too did his seraphic majesty.

"Well, what about it, R. A.?" she said with a lazy, inviting smile. "Are you interested in buying me?"

"I assume you mean NorthCal."

"Certainly that."

"It is," he said, shifting in his chair, "an attractive prize. One must, however, consider the cost."

"Not all that much, considering the value of the prize," she said easily. "I should tell you, however, that WorldCorp has offered us a hundred and seventy-five million dollars."

"Have they now?" WorldCorp was everywhere.

She turned on her radiant smile. "I would hardly expect that much from NE, but I think their offer shows what NorthCal is worth in the marketplace."

About twice as much as it was really worth. And maybe fifty million more than WorldCorp would eventually pay. One twenty-five was more like it. Still, WorldCorp was obviously bent on harassment. Their spies were pretty good too, though it was no secret that NE was interested in picking up as many small and successful cable companies as it could, when the market shook itself out.

"What would your bottom line be?" he asked cautiously.

"One and a half. In that area."

"We were willing to go eighty," he said, lifting a piece of calamari to his lips.

They were playing a game of poker, made all the more interesting because the other player was beautiful as well as shrewd.

Not shrewd enough. And today, as opposed to last week, not beautiful enough either.

Or so he uneasily hoped.

Actually as he had said to his staff, he thought NorthCal was worth a hundred at the most. He started out with eighty, hoping that she might be willing to negotiate down to a hundred and ten, which was his absolute high.

"That's less than half, Ray," she said with a small pout as she poured cream and sugar into her coffee, large amounts of both.

"We could begin negotiating the difference."

"I would like to work with you, Ray. You know that. I realize that you can trust WorldCorp just so far. Yet if you consider my position, it doesn't make much difference if they drop me in a year or two. With that kind of money I won't have to worry about money for the rest of my life. I can sit back and relax."

"And surf every day."

"Not in my part of California!"

"You're willing to make a financial sacrifice of twenty-five million to work with NE?"

He waved off the waiter, who was hovering for a possible desert order. The rain continued to slash against the windows.

"To work with you, Ray," she said with, sweet, shy smile, about as persuasive to Neenan as the smile of a woman computer salesperson.

"OK," he said with a deep breath. "We'll make a sacrifice too. A hundred and five."

"Ray" — she shook her head sadly, her blond hair rearranging itself and then falling into place — "that's not enough."

"That's not true," he said, trying to control his temper. "It's an offer which, as it is, overestimates NorthCal's profitability."

"WorldCorp doesn't think so," she said with a sad, vulnerable smile.

"Then they read your numbers differently than we do. Maybe they're right. Or maybe it's worth that kind of money for them to get another foothold in the cable field. They might well figure that if they spin it off in a year or two and take a loss it has been a good investment in opening up the cable market. I don't know how many such losses a company can take, but they've been successful at such tactics in the past."

"That's very cruel, Ray."

Neenan's desire for her had become insistent, demanding. Where is that damn seraph when I really need him?

"Honoria, I congratulate you on the huge financial gain WorldCorp is offering you. However, you should consider all the small print. For example, what will be your annual salary and how long is their contract?"

"I'm afraid," she said, "that's privileged information."

"We'll give you a five-year contract and fifty percent more than they're offering you."

"Only five years?" She leaned close to him. Her fragrance hit him like a mountain avalanche.

"Ten years if you want. You know that I don't dump senior executives of acquired companies."

"You keep them on, like Ben Harvey, in empty jobs."

So Ben Harvey was involved in this, was he? Had he become WorldCorp's point man? Pretty dumb choice. But that's what happened when a company got too big and its CEO was out of touch with the quality of his lower-ranking but important subordinates.

He drew back from her, so he could think more clearly.

"You're a lot brighter than Ben is and a much better administrator. Even if his job doesn't mean much, it pays him a huge salary for very little work."

"I won't be just an ornament for NE, Ray," she begged, her mournful eyes searching his face, "much less a bargain-basement ornament. I've worked too hard and sacrificed too much to let that happen."

She had said earlier that she was staying at the Four Seasons, a short cab ride away up Michigan Avenue. She would be available for lovemaking much of the afternoon. Neenan's lips and throat became dry.

"I have never thought of you, Honoria, as an ornament."

"But you do think of me as a good investment, don't you?"

"I certainly respect you as a businessperson," he said, trying to choose his words carefully, "and I admire you as a human being and a woman. The price is still too high."

"I guess that's all." She gathered her purse and stood up. "I'm really sorry, Ray, and, frankly, disappointed."

Her enticing bodily movements as she rose unleashed a shiver of longing that raced through his body.

He signed the check, with which the waiter had raced up.

"Everything all right, Mr. Neenan?"

"Everything is fine, Cesar."

She had walked out of the grillroom ahead of him, attracting once again every eye in the place.

The word *courtesan* flashed through his mind.

"I so much wanted to work with you, Ray," she said sorrowfully as they rode down on the elevator

"It would have been very nice," he replied, "very nice indeed."

Outside, the wind was blowing the rain sideways, slicing mercilessly into pedestrians.

"I have a car," she said as Neenan helped her into a white leather raincoat. "Can I give you a lift back to Sears Tower?"

Neenan fantasized for a moment about the delights of such a ride.

"I think I'll walk. I need the exercise. . . . Promise me you'll think over the things I've said before you make a final decision."

"I will certainly promise that, Ray. . . . Are you sure you don't want a ride?"

The doorman and the driver of a white stretch limo raced to provide an umbrella to convey her to the car.

"No thanks, I like to walk in the rain."

She laughed at him, mockingly he thought, as she entered the car.

He huddled inside his raincoat and wished he had brought an umbrella.

"Taxi, Mr. Neenan?" the doorman asked.

"No thanks, I like rainstorms."

The doorman did not laugh.

Then someone held an umbrella over his head. The rain rushed all around him, but did not touch him. He was pretty sure who was holding the umbrella.

"You guys really do like to show off, don't you?"

"It's fun," the seraph admitted. "If you got it, flaunt it."

"I'm in a very bad mood," Neenan said grimly.

"Really?" the seraph said. "Because you turned down the ride back to the Four Seasons?"

"How do you know that? I thought you weren't going to listen to the conversation."

"I didn't listen, but I saw the little scene in front of the Chicago Club. I was impressed by your virtuous restraint."

The angel was clad in an enormous black rain cloak that made him look like a huge and healthy Count Dracula, or maybe the Count on *Sesame Street*.

"Shit! I'm worn-out. I feel like I played thirty-six holes on a hot summer day."

"She was determined to seduce you?"

"For maybe fifty million to match WorldCorp's offer."

"Hardly worth it."

"No, but appealing just the same. I'm disgusted with myself for missing such an opportunity and disgusted because I regret the lost opportunity."

"You read Browning?"

"Elizabeth or Robert?"

"Either."

"Neither, except for a poem or two in anthologies when I was in college."

"He wrote an epic poem called *The Ring and the Book,* the first mystery novel ever produced in this solar system. The detective was the bishop of Rome, a certain Innocent, the twelfth of that name."

"Good miniseries?"

The seraph paused and then laughed as they crossed Wabash Avenue. The wind was pushing people all over the street and bending umbrellas. Naturally the two of them were undisturbed.

"You'd have to ask your wife, but it might just make a great feature film. Maybe Derek Jacobi as the pope. . . . Anyway there's a great line in it: 'Why comes temptation, but for man to meet and master and make crouch beneath his foot, and so be pedestaled in triumph?' "

"Good line, but I don't feel very glorious."

"It doesn't matter."

"I can't figure out who was the winner."

"Can't you?"

Neenan ignored that question. "In the other situations I was the seducer, the successful seducer. This time I was the intended seduced."

"Are you sure the other times were all that different?"

Neenan stopped in the middle of State Street and glared at the angel. "Who you trying to kid?"

"Might I suggest we complete our transit of this allegedly great street before I endeavor to explain the obvious. I am permeable: these cars would go right through me. You are, alas, not so blessed."

So they crossed State Street, that great street, still untouched by the rain and the wind.

"You still persist in presuming that in your lengthy seductive adventures, you were the hunter and the woman was the hunted?"

"Of course!"

"You might want to reconsider that presumption and ponder the hypothesis that it was in fact the other way around and that the scene which I assume you played out with the fair but trashy Honoria was in fact paradigmatic. For various reasons we need not consider, the only difference is that now you see what it is for the first time."

"I was the loser?" Neenan said in shocked disbelief.

"If you persist in using that metaphor, which your wife would tell you is appropriate for a twelve-year-old."

"I don't believe it. I chased them."

"So it may have seemed. The next question you should address is what common traits these various women shared."

"So I'm not responsible for what happened?"

Once again Neenan had the sense that he was being torn apart, as boats in a marina are during hurricane tides.

"You are certainly responsible and you must try to apologize to those women, though for various reasons they will not take your apologies seriously. You considered them attractive. You presented yourself to them as a very attractive male. They reacted to you in keeping with their own predisposition. Who is responsible is quite beside the point."

"And what is the point?"

They hurried to catch a green light at Dearborn. Neenan had the distinct impression that the angel had stalled the change to red.

"The point is that the mythology of Raymond Anthony Neenan, all-conquering lover, is a legend that may well satisfy some of your twelve-year-old needs, but hardly accords with reality."

The point was clear enough, all too clear. "You're saying that women are usually the hunters and men are usually the prey?"

"I am saying no such thing. I'm saying in your case you usually pursued women who viewed you as an amusing, if unruly, child on whom it was diverting to prey."

"If that's true, I've been a fool."

"I will not dispute that conclusion. But you were not an innocent fool. You chose women whose needs matched yours. Except, if I may add a remark that is in any case patent, your wife, who is the only wise choice you ever made in women, and you made it for the wrong reasons and then only with our help."

"I don't know whether I believe any of this."

"Think about it," the seraph advised.

Then, too suddenly Neenan felt, they were at Sears Tower. He entered the building miraculously dry.

His first stop was Joe McMahon's office.

"Well," he said, leaning against the doorjamb, precinct-captain style, "I don't think we need to worry about being distracted around here by Honoria Smythe."

"Oh?" Joe looked up from the papers on which he was working and took off his glasses.

"She's asking for a hundred and twenty-five, rock bottom."

"She crazy?"

"Possibly, but she has an offer from WorldCorp for one seventy-five."

"They're crazy."

"Maybe crazy like a fox, you should excuse the expression. It might be worth a loss they'll be able to write off to get their nose into the cable tent — or maybe just to scare us."

"They think that stealing NorthCal will scare you?"

"Probably."

"They're wrong, aren't they?"

"I'll tell you what worries me, Joe: What if something happens to me?"

"God forbid!" Joe said piously. "You're not sick are you?"

"No, I'm not sick at all. I passed my last physical with flying colors. But that airplane ride on Saturday made me think. We all die some-day. A man in my position should get ready, know what I mean?"

"I'm older than you are, R. A."

Michael slipped into the room and arranged himself in an easy chair in the corner. Today he was all in black, including a black shirt with a silver collar and a black-and-silver tie. His cuff links glittered on and off as if a flame were inside them. Had his companion chosen his clothes? Were they like humans in that respect too?

"Impressive."

"I know that, Joe. . . . Still, would you want to take over the firm if anything should happen to me?"

"Hell, no. You know that, R. A. You've offered me top jobs before. They're not my cup of tea. I'm content with where I am."

"Who, then?"

"Why not the kid?"

"What kid?"

"Vinny, who else?"

He had never been "Vinny" to the family. Was this what they called him face-to-face?

"My son?"

"Sure, aren't you grooming him to succeed you eventually?"

"I hadn't thought of it in those terms."

"I've noticed, R. A., that he kind of clams up when you are around."

"Not last Sunday."

"That's true. . . . Normally he's very articulate and very smart. Hardworking, determined. Reminds me a lot of you at that age. Only more . . ."

"Gentle, sympathetic, sensitive?"

"The word I was about to use was *urbane.*"

Neenan threw back his head and laughed. "I don't think I was ever urbane."

"You are now. . . . Anyway, I think he'd be first-rate as vice CEO or something of the sort, if you're looking for someone to fill that kind of a position. A lot of people around here are wondering why you haven't done that already."

"Just goes to show you, doesn't it?"

"You keep out of this."

"I'll get to work on it tomorrow. Have the lawyers rearrange everything. Make an announcement next week."

"You'll have to ask him first," Michael said, raising a warning finger.

"I'll have to ask him first. As soon as he gets back from California."

"Good idea. No doubt about what he'll say."

Back in his own office, Neenan called Lerner and Locke and set up an appointment for the next morning with the team of lawyers that took care of him over there.

"I want to make some adjustments in my will."

"Of course, Mr. Neenan," said the young woman who was a junior partner and the only one of the team that was not still out to lunch. At 3 P.M.

"I'll want to do something about the prenuptial agreement too."

"You'll need Ms. Neenan's consent to modify the conditions."

"To tear it up?"

"It is about time to do that, isn't it, Mr. Neenan?"

"Pushy brat!" he said to the seraph.

"She's right you know."

"All right! All right!"

"You're right about that," Neenan said with a laugh that was not completely forced.

"We'll be looking forward to seeing you tomorrow, Mr. Neenan. At some point we'll need documentation from Ms. Neenan."

"Thank you, Ms. . . ."

"Kim, Mr. Neenan. Lourdes Kim. You know, as in Madonna's daughter."

Even Korean women are pushy these days. Maybe they always have been.

"What a beautiful name!" he exclaimed, and began to hum the refrain from the Lourdes hymn. The young woman, now thoroughly charmed, joined with him.

"One more thing, Lourdes. I will want to found a chair at Loyola in honor of my wife, who went there. Could you provide a draft of a deed of gift tomorrow morning."

"Certainly, Raymond. One chair?"

"Probably something like four or five."

She didn't gasp. Asian-American women rarely admitted that they were surprised by anything. Good for them.

"That's very generous, Raymond."

"An angel made me do it, Lourdes. See you tomorrow."

"Hmf," Michael observed. "You might have said 'seraph.' I'm not just an ordinary angel."

"You guys are vain."

"Practically our only fault. But then we have much to be vain about, don't we?"

"There are seven of you, who stand before the face of God?"

"You have a good memory for what Sister John Mark taught you, good if selective. Actually there are more than seven of us and we stand before the face of God only metaphorically speaking."

"Which reminds me, those singers who work for you . . ."

"They don't work for me, not exactly anyway."

"Are they a few angels singing loudly or a bunch of angels, each one singing softly?"

"Somewhere in between."

"Vain and secretive too."

Amy Jardine buzzed Neenan as soon as he had hung up.

"Ms. Megan Neenan on the phone, sir."

"Hi, Megan. Is everything all right?"

"Everything is wonderful. Vinny wants to talk to you, but I insisted I talk to you first. I want to thank you for these few days out here. We're having a grand time. It was very thoughtful of you to insist he bring me along."

"If I should forget that in the future, you remind me."

"I may just take you up on that. . . . Here's Vinny."

"Hi, Dad. Good news on Jerry Carter. He's promised to deliver the finished print in three weeks. He's agreed that if he doesn't, I can come out here again and take it away from him physically."

"Less than four weeks?"

Michael flashed his "I told you so" smile.

"I started the negotiation at two weeks. . . . I wouldn't mind having to come out here again. Let me second everything that Meg said."

"You're a very fortunate man, Vincent."

"That's what she tells me all the time."

"Amy Jardine has set up a dinner at your house next Monday."

"No one has told me that yet, but if Amy says so, it's written in stone."

"Enjoy the rest of your time out there."

"I intend to. Give my love to Anna Maria."

"I'll certainly do that."

A sudden, unexpected, and loud burst of angelic trumpets was followed by a polyphonic song that sounded remotely like the "Hallelujah Chorus." They were showing off too. The rain had apparently not driven them to silence.

Whence, Neenan wondered, had come all of his son's sudden self-assurance? He had never called Anna Maria by her given name before, had he?

Or had he been confident for a long time and his father had simply not noticed?

"Well," Michael said grudgingly, "I guess you didn't foul up everything with your children."

"If I did well with Vincent, it wasn't because I knew what I was doing."

The seraph shrugged. "When I praise you, accept the praise. It won't happen often."

That night, while they lolled in each other's arms after a deeply satisfying romp of love, Neenan said to his wife, "I'm going to tear up that dumb premarital agreement."

"It's about time," she said with the same laugh as when she had signed the agreement. "It was ridiculous."

"I had a very bad experience," he said defensively.

"I know," she said, kissing his chest. "I didn't blame you. But I thought it was kind of silly to think that, having caught you, I'd ever let you get away."

She kissed his chest to make up for her laughter.

"I'm going to make a few rearrangements in the will. I'll leave most everything to you and Vincent. He'll control the company and you'll get all the real estate and a huge trust fund — regardless of whether you eventually remarry, which I hope you will."

The choir began to sing sweet lullabies.

Anna Maria was silent for a few moments.

"Are you sure you're all right, Raymond?" she asked anxiously.

"I'm fine, Anna Maria. That crazy plane ride last week reminded me of some things I've been planning to do for a long time."

"You don't have any premonitions or anything like that?"

"Premonitions? No, certainly not."

Revelations, of course. But nothing as mild as a premonition.

She relaxed in his arms and went to sleep almost immediately. Her ability to fall asleep easily, especially after lovemaking, astonished him. She was not the unsophisticated peasant he had thought she was. Nonetheless, there was a certain trusting simplicity in her character.

Poor woman, she'd be a widow soon. He was happy that he had thought about telling her that he hoped she would remarry.

The seraph should at least give him credit for thinking about Anna Maria after his death. He had, however, banished that prying angel from their lovemaking sessions. All that meant was that Michael couldn't be seen. It didn't mean he wasn't watching.

Then Neenan began to grieve over his oncoming death. He did not want to die, not now, no that he had found so much for which to live.

Silent tears flowed down his cheeks.

The songsters' lullabies became more sympathetic.

Just now he needed sympathy.

Presumably there would be a lot more grief between now and the end. Well, that happened whenever you died. You had to go through it and get it over with. He'd better get used to it.

Then his thoughts returned to Anna Maria, poor, dear, wonderful woman. She didn't deserve to be widowed before she was forty. Still, she'd find another husband who would be more considerate than he was.

Then he wept for her and for himself, equally he hoped for each.

11

"Wake up, sleepyhead," a woman ordered him.

Neenan rolled over in protest and tried to bury his head in a pillow. He'd experienced a restless, dream-cursed night, filled with terrifying images of dying and death.

"I'm not sure you're up to all this late-night entertainment."

Who was the woman?

He peeked out from his pillow. Ah, it was his wife; who else these days? She was wide-awake and smelled of shower soap and scent. She wore a protective towel and was offering him a cup of coffee and a roll.

The coffee smelled wonderful. Would there be coffee in the hereafter?

"I think I know you, woman," he said as he reached for the coffee cup.

"You'd better hurry," she warned him. "You have a long appointment at Lerner and Locke, then there's an opera tonight, at which I suppose you'll have to do some business."

"Settle the pension strike maybe."

"That's worth doing."

"I guess so." He drank deeply of the coffee.

"I thought we might do it this way. I'll ride down with you and leave my dress at the apartment. Then I'll go over to Christo Rey High School for my tutoring. Then I'll come back to get dressed for the opera. I can send Peter back to Maeve, and you and I can spend the night at the apartment. All right?"

"That sounds like an offer I can't refuse."

"It was meant to be that. . . . Your white-tie outfit is at the office, isn't it?"

"White-tie?"

"Absolutely, you funded part of this production, remember?"

"Yeah, I guess I did."

"So you'd better get up and head for the shower. Like *now!*"

"Alone?"

"We haven't tried that, have we? No time for it now, I'm afraid."

She pulled back the drapes. Sunlight and glare from the lake poured into his room.

He groaned. "Ouch, that hurts my eyes."

"Sunny but cold. Looks like winter is coming early. Am I glad I insisted we go to Captiva for the weekend."

"Yeah."

"If you don't get up this minute, I'll open the window and pull the covers off you and you'll freeze."

"All right, all right, I'll do what I'm told."

"That's better," she said as he struggled out of bed.

She rubbed a hand down his back in a devoted caress, a promise of more later on.

The woman was insatiable.

When they pulled up to the apartment on East Lake Shore Drive, she planted a lingering kiss on his lips, then popped out of the car, dress bag in hand.

Immediately after Peter had closed the door, she pounded on the window.

"Don't forget the Loyola chairs," she shouted.

"I won't. I asked Lourdes Kim to prepare a deed of gift."

"Who?"

"Lourdes Kim, one of the women who does tax things for me. We have women lawyers these days."

She made a face at him and bounded away to the entrance of the apartment building, engulfed for a moment in the radiance of the sun over the Lake. The feeling of peace and ecstasy touched him lightly and slipped away, though with a promise of returning.

"The office, Peter," he said with a sigh.

"Yes, Mr. Neenan."

"I suppose Ms. Neenan has outlined our plans for the rest of the day, Peter."

"Yes, Mr. Neenan. I am to take you to the office and then come back here and drive her over to Christo Rey High School in Pilsen. I pick her up about one o'clock and drive her back to the apartment, and then I head home before the rush hour begins."

"We must always do what they tell us to do, must we not, Peter?"

"Yes, Mr. Neenan, we all know that. . . . If I may say so, sir, Ms. Neenan seems in exceptionally fine spirits these days."

"I've noticed that too."

Neenan settled back in the cushions of the car, trying to relax as they crawled through the Loop's rush-hour traffic.

"We'll take care of her after you're gone," Michael promised as he materialized next to Neenan. "You don't have to worry about her."

"You can stop her grief?"

"I didn't say that. I said we'll take care of her and you don't have to worry about her. Grief comes with being a creature."

"Why will you take care of her? Is that part of the deal?"

"We never lose an account. I repeat, *never.*"

"I'm an account?"

"You and she are part of an account. That's the closest word in your language. We never give up."

"That's reassuring," Neenan said with a tinge of sarcasm in his voice.

If the seraph noticed the sarcasm, he choose to ignore it. "What are you going to do after you come back from the lawyers?"

"Call a meeting of all our executives and outline our plan to resist WorldCorp."

"You don't expect to keep it secret, do you?"

"Hardly. If they are messing with one of my executives, they're after others too. They'll know what I said an hour after the meeting is over."

"You want them to know?"

"I sure do. Give them a bit of a scare."

"The old warrior still lives, huh?"

"For the time being. Anyway, you told me that I should fight them."

"Indeed I did. It should be an interesting meeting."

"You're dressed like it's Friday," Neenan observed. "How come so casual?"

The seraph was wearing designer jeans, a powder blue turtleneck, and a tan windbreaker. He was hatless, but the jewel in his ear was larger than the one he had been wearing yesterday.

"I feel casual. Besides, in our world it is something like Friday."

That seemed to settle the issue. A cymbal clang from the apparently present choir reinforced the definitive nature of Michael's response.

"The guys are still around, I note."

"Sure. They're always around. They especially want to hear Sam Ramey sing tonight, even though they know there's no equivalent in the real world to Mephisto."

"You're sure of that?"

"Of course, I'm sure."

Another clang of cymbals.

"They're showing off."

"I told you that vanity is our worst, indeed practically our only, fault."

Neenan reached over and touched the seraph's arm, just to make sure that he was something more than an optical illusion. Neenan felt solid, very solid, muscle.

"You're really there."

"My surrogate which is part of me is really here. The Loop would just barely contain me if I were all here. And lots of people would temporarily lose their eyesight."

The third clang of cymbals was derisive, a timpani version of the raspberry.

"I hope they don't think they can sing with the Lyric's chorus tonight."

"Hey," Michael said with a distressed frown, "they can do those angel hymns at the end a lot better than Ms. Krainik's crowd. Of course they'll sing. You'll be the only one who can hear it, save for those few other folk who might be able to sense us, and they'll hear it only from a great distance. You'd better enjoy it, incidentally."

"Heaven forbid that I don't."

"You've got to consider their feelings."

"I understand."

They exited the car in front of Sears Tower. Michael ambled along with him.

"Aren't you cold?"

"An angel cold, you gotta be kidding!"

This time the whole timpani section gave him the raspberry.

Unfriendly bunch.

In his office, he returned phone calls, dictated responses to his mail, and told Amy Jardine to summon a staff meeting for two in the afternoon.

"Tell them that it will only take a half hour and that it will concern our response to the naked aggression of WorldCorp against us."

"Yes, Mr. Neenan. . . . You do remember your ten-thirty appointment with your lawyers."

"Thank you for reminding me." Then he realized that he had never responded that way before when she had harassed him about something he would certainly never have forgotten.

She was clearly startled.

Fooled her, he thought to himself.

He spent a few minutes outlining his remarks for the afternoon. He grinned as he did it. WorldCorp would know all the details before the day was out. They would not be certain that he was serious. So they would be deeply worried.

He was in fact serious. Mostly. All the plans he would outline were feasible if expensive. He had thought about some of them for a long time. Most of them would take longer than he would have. But his successors might be just ambitious enough to try them. WorldCorp would have to think twice before they went after NE again.

He put on his coat and left the office.

"I'll be back in time for the meeting," he told Ms. Jardine. "I want you to be there, by the way."

"Yes, Mr. Neenan."

"I'll probably stop in at the Chicago Athletic Club on the way back for some exercise."

"Yes, Mr. Neenan."

"Do you think that altogether wise? In your weakened conditions?"

"I'm not weak. I'm tired. I didn't sleep too well last night, mostly because of you."

"Mostly because of your lack of faith."

Neenan waited for the clang of timpani, but it did not come. Michael may have warned them to shut up.

In the elaborate and stuffy conference room, four lawyers were waiting for Neenan—the managing partner, Sy Renfro; the ponderous tax lawyer, Jim McGlinn; Neil Higgins, the bantamweight litigator in charge of his account; and a lovely young Asian woman, who had to be Lourdes Kim. It was evident after the first few minutes that Ms. Kim would do all the work on his will and that she was far and away the smartest person and the best lawyer in the room.

Michael settled into a vacant chair and closed his eyes.

He outlined what he wanted to do: tear up the prenuptial agreement, rearrange the will so that Vincent would control the company and that there would be a huge trust fund for Anna Maria; and found five chairs at Loyola in honor of her. The other components of the will would remain the same: grants to charities, much smaller trust funds for his two other children, the trust fund to provide for his parents as long as they lived, gifts to Amy and Peter and Maeve and other close aides.

Michael nodded his approval, though Neenan thought none of this was any of his business.

There was considerable heavy debate about the details, about tax problems, about the IRS ("the Service"), which most of them despised and not without reason, about the kinds of investments the funds should make, and about how to avoid as much inheritance tax as possible.

As this nonsense dragged on, Neenan turned to the Asian-American woman.

"What do you think, Lourdes?"

Glancing occasionally at her yellow, legal-size notepad—without which no lawyer can think—she outlined exactly what ought to be done, how it could be done, and how long it would take.

The managing partner looked as if he might object, but instead said, "I think that pretty well sums up our thinking."

She had done no such thing.

"Thank you very much, Lourdes," Neenan said. "How long will it take?"

Michael mimed applause, knowing full well that a few days ago Neenan would have played the male chauvinist role just like everyone else. Is this really me? he wondered. I'm cracking up.

Like the glaciers dissolve into icebergs.

"We will certainly have to check every detail," Sy Renfro said.

"How soon do you want it, Ray?" Lourdes asked, pointedly ignoring her senior partner.

"I'm planning on naming Vincent Neenan president and COO early next week. I'd like to be able to assure him that he's locked into that position no matter what happens to me. Could I have it by Monday?"

"Certainly, Ray, no problem."

The three men gasped with surprise.

"We'll certainly check it all out for you, Ray," the managing partner promised.

Neenan ignored him.

"I have full confidence in you, Lourdes. I'll be out of town for the weekend. Should you need me, Ms. Jardine in my office will have my phone number."

"I'll try not to bother you, Ray."

Virtually a solemn vow from that one.

The meeting broke up, the senior partners with vague feelings that they had been upstaged. Neenan took Neil Higgins aside.

"Neil, can I talk to you for a moment about some potential litigation?"

The little mick's green eyes glowed with excitement, not so much for the billable hours that might be involved, as for the sheer love of battle.

"You bet, R. A.!"

In Neil's office, Neenan came straight to the point.

"I have solid reason to believe that WorldCorp is tampering with some of my officers and interfering in some acquisitions in which we are engaged. Can we get an injunction to stop them?"

Higgins did not hesitate. He never hesitated. "We can ask for one and that will scare them and give them some more bad publicity, which they don't need just now. Whether a court will actually grant an injunction remains to be seen. What are the facts of the case?"

That was one of the things Neenan liked about Neil: facts always came second.

Michael, who had slipped into the office and was relaxing semi-prone on a couch, grinned appreciatively.

Neenan explained the facts.

Neil pursed his lips and raised his red eyebrows. "Borderline at this point. We might prevail, we might not, but they're certainly messing around with more of your executives. Our petition for relief will give them second thoughts."

"Good. That's what I want to hear. Now let me outline some countermeasures that I will propose to my officers this afternoon."

Michael sat up straight and listened intently. When Neenan was finished, the angel threw back his head and laughed. The songsters exploded in an instrumental and vocal fanfare, something like "See the Conquering Hero Comes" from *Judas Maccabaeus*.

Higgins grinned appreciatively. "That's brilliant, R. A. Are these things technically possible?"

"Sure they are. They'd cost a lot of money, but I've been thinking about them for some time. We could do them if we had to. We could do them even if we didn't have to."

"The idea being that when WorldCorp hears about them, they'll take a look at the numbers and figure that you could really do what you threaten, and that will scare the living daylights out of them."

Michael bounded across the room and gave Neenan a high five.

"You are really a dangerous so-and-so," the seraph observed. *"I'm glad you're on my side."*

"I thought it was the other way around."

"You got it, Neil."

"I've never seen you having so much fun over an impending battle, R. A."

"You are having more fun than I."

"Yeah, but I'm a litigator."

"Maybe I've changed. . . . One more thing. Have you had a chance to talk about the pension suit since we discussed it on Monday?"

"Given what we have on most of their work records, R. A., most of them would not prevail. Moreover, they'll never get punitive damages, not those which will be sustainable on appeal."

"The suit will give us a lot of PR problems, especially with this WorldCorp fight."

"I'm sure it would, R. A. . . . Same terms?"

"We give their jobs back and guarantee their pensions."

"And the same offer to Walsh?"

"We'll tell him we'll pay his expenses, as reasonably estimated. After we've negotiated with him over that, he'll still be billing us too high by about ten percent, which should be enough to keep him happy."

"And he knows how much a suit is going to cost him if he goes ahead on a contingency basis," Neil agreed with a nod of his head and a wicked leprechaun grin. "He also knows that he's not going to get punitive damages in the long run. He's looking at a major loss if we go to trial."

"So I'm told. I also hear that some of his clients are so angry at me that they will insist on punitive damages. Probably the ones for whose termination we have the best evidence."

"Then Timmy has himself a problem, doesn't he, R. A.? A pretty big problem. He likes the good press clippings, but he doesn't enjoy losing money."

"Unlike most other lawyers."

Higgins laughed nervously. "Do you want me to contact him?"

"Not yet. As you pointed out the other day, he'll be at the opening of *Faust* tonight. I'll approach him personally, as you suggested. Give him something to think about, and then tell him to get in contact with you."

"You're in such a feisty mood today, R. A., that I have no hesitation in recommending that you take him on."

"An angel suggested this strategy to me," Neenan said with a laugh.

Higgins laughed too, not sure what to make of that remark.

Michael covered his face in mock horror.

"I'll get back to you first thing in the morning about his reaction, though I think it will be pretty predictable."

Outside on La Salle Street, Michael continued to amble along with Neenan.

"You are really one baaad SOB, Raymond Anthony."

"I assume that in the present context that is a compliment?"

"I just want to point out to you that you would not be having as much fun as you are now if you didn't know that you were going to die soon."

Neenan stopped in his tracks.

"I suppose that's true. You approve?"

"You're using your God-given talents the way you should have used them all your life."

"I'm not so sure."

"I am. Why, you didn't even indulge in lewd thoughts about that attractive Korean woman."

"Come to think of it, I didn't. Maybe I am changing. Would a certain amount of erotic appreciation have been inappropriate?"

"You're still a human male, aren't you?"

Again Neenan felt as if he were cracking apart, like the ice floes on Lake Michigan when the first southwest wind of spring blew across the city.

"Hey," Neenan continued, "how did we get to Madison Street?"

"We should have turned the other direction when we came out of that ugly building of theirs."

"Why didn't you stop me?"

"Am I your tour guide for Chicago?"

"You're my guardian angel, aren't you?"

"Only in a very remote sense of that word. . . . Look down Madison, there's St. Peter's Church."

"So what?"

"Wouldn't this be an appropriate time to go to confession?"

"Confession? You gotta be kidding! Are you some kind of Catholic angel or something? I haven't been to confession since the night before I married Anna Maria, and that was a disaster. You don't believe in that stuff, do you?"

"We live in a different economy of salvation, as your theologians say. However, you believe in confession, even if you're not willing to admit it to yourself. Moreover the ritual of reconciliation, which what the sacrament is called these days, is a very useful reminder that you are community-dependent animals, just as we are. Finally, once a Catholic, always a Catholic, as you well know."

"I don't want to go to confession," Neenan said stubbornly.

"Naturally not. Neither would I if I were in your shoes. Nonetheless, you will have to go sometime. Why not do it now and get it out of the way?"

"You deliberately led me in the wrong direction so you could pull this on me, didn't you?"

"We have even arranged to have a most sympathetic and sensitive Franciscan priest, a certain Father Sixtus, in the confessional to which I will direct you."

"You mean that I don't have any choice?"

"Certainly you have a choice. But, since I have been right on every count since I appeared to you, you are quite likely to take my advice. Besides, you will enjoy even more the end of the opera in which the angels sing Marguerite into heaven."

Promptly the angelic choir burst into the song at the end of the opera. Neenan had never heard it sung so well.

"I really don't have a choice, do I?"

"I told you once that wasn't true. You always have a choice, but, as you yourself know, you'd be a fool to pass up this chance."

So, with slow and heavy feet, Neenan turned down Madison Street and against the chill wind sweeping in off the lake.

Inside the vast, mausoleum-like, marble structure that was St. Peter's-in-the-Loop, as it now called itself, Neenan paused. Michael, who had ostentatiously made a giant sign of the cross with holy water, pointed in the direction of a confessional. No one was in line.

They had arranged it very well, hadn't they?

"I can't go in right away," Neenan pleaded. "I have to examine my conscience."

"No way. You just go into the box and tell Father Sixtus that you've been away from the sacrament of reconciliation for a long time and you want to straighten out your life."

So Neenan did just that. Amazingly the priest was kind and helpful. He was more interested in the reasons for the penitent's return than for the detailed listing of his sins.

"I hate to admit it, Father, but I went through a very scary airplane ride last week. I thought I'd better change my life. I haven't been at the new life for long, but I am much happier."

"Remarkable," the priest murmured. "Maybe we should have more such flights."

"I thought I heard angels whispering to me that it was time to change." Neenan assumed that the seraph field marshal was listening.

"Angels are merely God's messengers."

"So I understand, Father."

Neenan was assigned a penance of "one devout Our Father." He decided that he would always come to confession to Father Sixtus.

Assuming that he had another chance.

He did feel a vast sense of elation and relief when he stepped out of the confessional. Michael was busy lighting votive candles.

"For me?"

"It can't hurt. . . . Now, if you're going to get in your swim, you'd better hurry. Can't keep the officers of the company waiting, can we?"

The choir reappeared and reprised the end of *Faust*.

"I've got to say my penance first."

12

"As you doubtless know," Neenan began after the roomful of NE officers had settled into respectful silence, "WorldCorp is trying to buy National Entertainment. I have said privately and publicly that we are not for sale, no matter how high the price. I stand by those statements. Nevertheless WorldCorp is now trying to raid our executives and interfere with some of our acquisitions. I suspect they may have spoken to some of you. If their offer is good enough and you're not afraid to work there, it would be wise to make the change this afternoon because our lawyers are going into federal court tomorrow to obtain a temporary restraining order against WorldCorp.

"We intend to undertake a number of strategies to discourage WorldCorp from this reckless venture. As some of you know, we have considered for some time the possibility of combining our owned and operated stations into a new network, which we will call American Network or Amnet for short. We will now pursue that plan. We have also considered the wisdom of launching our own news network, which we would call American News or Amnews. We now propose to combine the local news capabilities of our stations to provide a comprehensive coverage of news all over the United States. Naturally we will offer this news on all our cable holdings. Eventually we may well make an offer to buy WorldCorp or some of its more substantial holdings. I assume that these remarks will be leaked almost as soon as this meeting is over. We will issue tomorrow morning a statement detailing our plans, the financial incentives and costs, and a time schedule for developing our new ventures."

The choristers were singing martial music. Michael waved a high five and beamed happily.

"Can you please ask those guys to quiet down for a few minutes? They distract me and I need a clear head."

Michael raised a finger. The choir stopped abruptly, perhaps resentfully.

"Are there any questions?" Neenan asked the meeting.

"Might we not be overextending ourselves, R. A.?" someone asked.

"We won't overextend ourselves. You can count on that. We have the capital resources to underwrite expansion. Moreover we will not diminish them substantially in either of these ventures. The beauty of them is that most of the pieces are already in place."

The executives stirred restlessly. Clearly they didn't like the situation.

"Please feel free to ask questions," Neenan said.

Silence.

Neenan frowned. He had expected enthusiasm about the new ventures and about the fight to fend off WorldCorp.

"They're worried about their jobs," Michael informed him. *"They think you're putting their careers at risk."*

"Really?"

"Really! You got security and almost none of them have."

"Perhaps I might add what I should have said initially. I do not intend to put anyone's position in the firm at risk. I guarantee you that no one is going to lose his . . . or her . . . job. If WorldCorp should prevail, many of you would eventually find yourself living off unemployment insurance. I regret the necessity of a fight, but in the jungle in which we work, fights are sometimes necessary."

That seemed to cheer them up a little.

"R. A., that is a firm and solemn promise?"

He grinned. "A vow from which only the Pope can dispense me. I am well aware of my own faults, but among them is not the inability to keep my word."

Michael, who for some reason had doffed his windbreaker, smiled happily.

"You won't sell to WorldCorp."

"Never, not as long as I live."

The words had slipped out. A knife jabbed at his chest. As long as he lived would not be very long. He would have to rely on Vincent's willingness to honor his word.

"What if they back off? Will we still pursue these new ventures?"

"Certainly we will, perhaps more slowly and cautiously. I do not see at the present a need for large administrative staff for either venture. Our major costs will be technical, and even those will not be great. A network, after all, is nothing more than a telephone line or, in our age, many telephone lines."

"That work sometimes," Norm Stein said with a laugh.

The rest of the group joined in the laugh. They had begun to lighten up.

"I can see myself here at midnight managing the switchboard," Neenan said. "It would serve me right, wouldn't it?"

More laughter.

"Better you let Amy do it!"

"That's an excellent idea."

Amy flushed with pleasure.

'Do you think WorldCorp will back off, R. A.?"

"It would be sensible of them to do so. However, the threat of a hostile takeover here is not at all sensible. We'll have to wait and see."

Then technical questions flew thick and fast. The group seemed convinced that he knew what he was talking about. The meeting ended with a standing ovation. Michael appeared next to him with angelic speed for another high five. The choir, their feelings apparently unhurt, broke into happy song. Many of the senior officers rushed up to shake Neenan's hand and congratulate him.

He felt no elation. Rather, a dark pall of weariness and loneliness crept over him. He hardly noticed the sunlight bursting through the window of his southeast corner suite when he returned to his office and slumped into the chair behind his desk.

Stein and McMahon drifted into his office. So did Michael, his windbreaker over his arm.

"Nice going, R. A.," Joe said.

"You wowed them," Norm agreed.

"Totally," Michael said, adding his vote.

"Are you part of my staff now?"

"I kind of thought it was the other way round.... And smile, you won a big one."

"If there's a fight, I won't be around for it."

"I told you we never give up an account."

"The firm is part of your account?"

"Obviously."

"You two tell me the truth most of the time, so I'll believe you."

"Do you want us to start the planning for both ventures?" Norm asked. "Any priorities?"

"If WorldCorp—and I'm sure they're around—finds out that we are not doing that, they'll suspect we're bluffing."

"Are we bluffing, R. A.?" McMahon asked.

"No way. I want to be prepared for them to try to call our bluff. . . . As to priorities, let's do the news network first; that should be easier and quicker to bring on-line. There are a lot of local anchors out there in small towns hungering for fame and possible fortune who are just as good if not better than the talking heads on Fox or CNN or the three networks. They'll love the chance."

"I think WorldCorp will back down," Joe observed. "They'd be crazy if they didn't."

"They'll at least think about it. . . . By the way, Joe, have our PR people work on a statement for tomorrow. I saw Neil Higgins this morning. You might call him to get the details of our petition for a restraining order. We'll want it all on the noon news. As to the news leaks which will be in morning papers, our response will be that we have been planning such ventures for some time and there is nothing new about them."

After Stein and McMahon left his office, Neenan buried his head on his desk. He felt like he wanted to cry, but knew that he would not, could not. All he wanted was to be with Anna Maria.

Michael touched his shoulder. "That was a pretty neat bit of obfuscation."

"Would I lie on the day I reclaimed the state of grace?"

"I didn't say you lied. Rather you told the literal truth: there is nothing new about your plans. You didn't add that you moved them to the front burner because of WorldCorp, but you didn't have to say that, did you?"

"You sound like a Jesuit."

"That charge has been leveled before. . . . Do you actually believe in the state of grace?"

"Hell, you should excuse the expression, how should I know what I believe? Like you said, once a Catholic always a Catholic. When I pray, like I did back there at St. Peter's, I pray 'to whom it may concern.'"

"Or 'occupant?'"

"I take your word for it that someone is listening."

"You can bank on it, you should excuse the expression. . . . Do you pray that you do not die?"

"What good would that do?"

"So what do you say to God?"

"I tell whoever might be listening that it's all up to him."

"Or her?"

"As the case may be."

Amy Jardine buzzed on the phone.

"Ms. Raymond Neenan on the phone, Mr. Neenan."

The choir started in on spring pastoral melodies.

"Thank you, Amy. . . . Hi, Anna Maria."

"You sound tired."

"Hard day. . . . I went to confession, by the way."

"You didn't!"

"I did too. Over at St. Peter's. Nice priest."

"Are you sure you're all right, Raymond?" she asked him nervously.

"Just tired. I didn't sleep so well last night."

"You need a nap."

"Do I ever!"

"Why don't you come over to the apartment and have a nap with me? I don't want you to sleep through the angels', hymn at the end."

The choir immediately returned to the conclusion of *Faust*.

"That's the best offer I've had all day."

"Then we won't have to make love after the opera," she said with a giggle.

"No promises about that. I'll be right over."

"I told you picking her as your wife was a major coup on our part," Michael said.

"I must have had something to do with it."

"I never said you didn't," Michael said, obviously very pleased with himself.

Neenan left in such a rush that he forgot his white-tie suit.

He found his wife lolling in the vast tub that had often seemed the center of the apartment.

"Why don't you take off your clothes and join me?" she said, extending a hand. "I bet you forgot your suit."

"I did," he said, stripping as quickly as he could. "I can go over and get it after our nap and meet you at the opera house."

"You really are an attractive hunk, Mr. Neenan. I think I might just fall in love with you someday."

They played in the tub, he told her the story of his response to WorldCorp, and she nodded her approval as she busily teased him to the point where he shouted with agony and delight.

Then they napped and made love and napped again.

"Let's skip the opera," he said.

The angel songsters cried out in protest.

"Don't be silly, Raymond! We can come back afterward and take up where we left off."

Reluctantly he agreed.

Before he forced himself out of bed, he lay on top of her and devoured her with a fearsome kiss.

"I like it when you lie on top of me that way," she sighed.

"Oh?"

"I feel like I am a powerless captive and you can do to me whatever you want. That's a wonderful feeling."

"You're not a captive. You're my wife."

"I know that, silly. But it's nice sometimes to be captive to your husband. And vice versa."

"You can always say no, if you want."

"Why would I ever want to do that?"

He consumed her again with an equally powerful kiss.

"That was nice," she said dreamily. "Now you'd better hurry. I've got to get dressed too."

As he hailed a cab on Lake Shore Drive, he wondered what had happened to the seraph.

He dressed hurriedly in the small bedroom next to his office and then walked down Wacker Drive briskly to the Opera House.

In the Graham Room, where Lyric supporters ate their precurtain dinners, he discovered what had happened to the seraph.

"You're at that empty table over in the corner," Jim the maître d'said, pointing to a table at which two people were already sitting: Michael, also in white tie and tails, and a breathtaking woman with gray hair and a young face, clad in a shimmering—and tight-fitting—strapless, blue gown.

◣13◢

"Gaby, this is Raymond Neenan. You've seen him before, of course, but this is the first opportunity to formally introduce him to you. Ray, this is Gaby, my companion."

He pronounced the name of the woman seraph as though it were French—*gab*-bee.

She extended her hand and smiled. Neenan melted completely. He bent over the hand and kissed it.

"He has surprisingly good manners for Chicago Irish, doesn't he, Michael?" she said with an impish grin.

"He's learning," Michael replied.

They were at a table in the corner of the long and narrow Graham Room, which overlooked Wacker Drive. Its green walls and lush furnishing were an exercise in understated elegance, a touch of eighteenth-century France tucked away on the fringes of the Chicago Loop.

"Short for Gabriel?" Neenan asked as he sat down at what supposedly his table.

"Those of course are not our real names," she replied. "They are the Hebrew names which describe events in which we participated. We use them when we're in your world."

"So you were the one . . ."

"You don't think the Other would have sent a male angel on such a delicate mission, do you? Your own Catholic tradition often presents the so-called Gabriel in a womanly guise."

The choir was practicing its final scene again. At first he thought it might be the Lyric chorus, singing loudly. But then he realized that they would be saving their voices for later in the evening. It was the angel crowd. He thought it best to ignore them.

"Our names are actually very long," Michael said, "as is proper, I suppose. I'll ask our little friends to chant the first part of my companion's name. It will take about a minute or so."

He held up his finger. They broke off the chorus and chanted an undulating and romantic word, like a stanza of a Hawaiian love song. Gaby smiled and nodded her head in approval.

"Does it translate into our language?" Neenan asked.

"Not really. It is a very intimate name."

Neenan tried to remember the melody, but it had been wiped from his brain. Very clever.

"So you have come to enjoy our *Faust*?"

"And to enjoy our little friends," she replied, "having the time of their young lives singing the final chorus."

"They're young angels!"

"Naturally. Couldn't you tell? Don't they sound like offspring . . . ah, children?"

"Children with perfect pitch."

"Naturally, they are angels, are they not?"

"We can assure you," Michael took up the conversation, "that, despite the snobbery of your friend from New York, this production is much better than anything the Met has ever done with *Faust*."

"We listened in on the rehearsal," Gaby agreed. "They are excellent. You are to be congratulated on supporting it."

The seraphs were very friendly. Had Ms. Michael warned her companion to be on his good behavior?

"You must explain the difference between Mephisto and Satan to me."

The woman seraph across the table glared at Neenan, her lips tight with anger — or was it pain?

"I'm sure," she said, "that my good companion has explained to you that there is no one in creation anywhere that we know of who corresponds with the creature Sam Ramey portrays so well. And as for Satan or the Light Bearer, he was a good angel, a member of the heavenly court, despite all your Christian folktales, borrowed from the worshipers of Mazda."

"You must understand, Ray," Michael said soothingly, "that the Light Bearer was my companion's first companion. We all grew up together and were very close friends. He died young in a massive charge of electromagnetism in another cosmos. She still mourns him, as do I."

"I'm sorry," Neenan stammered, "I didn't know . . ."

"Of course you didn't know." Gaby touched Neenan's face soothingly. "No reason why you should. I'm sorry my grief caused me to be rude. We shall all be together again someday, we shall all be young again, we shall all laugh and sing again."

"So the Other assures us," Michael said with a solemn nod. "It goes without saying that we believe him."

"Her," his companion corrected him, her good humor returning. "But now, Raymond, if you don't mind, I'd like to speak to you about your wife."

"Anna Maria?"

"Certainly, your only wife. You're doing much better in recent days, but we feel you need a few hints and that it would be more acceptable coming from me instead of from him."

"I'm sure it would, certainly more charming."

"Flattery will not distract me," she said severely.

"Not for more than a couple of hours," her companion observed.

They all laughed.

"The first thing you must do tonight," she began, ticking off her instructions on her long, ring-covered fingers, "is give her that lovely necklace you have in your inside jacket pocket."

"I don't have any necklace," Neenan protested.

"Yes, you do," Michael insisted. "Just feel your pocket."

Neenan felt a bulge in his pocket, reached inside, and removed a lacy string of diamonds and rubies.

"Is it not dazzling?" Gaby asked approvingly.

"It sure is, but I didn't buy it."

"Surely you did," the woman seraph replied. "It's charged to your account at Tiffany's."

"I don't have an account at Tiffany's."

"You do now."

"I see."

"Then, secondly, you must touch your wife often, not lewdly, but affectionately. You must hold her hand, you must stroke her wrist and lower arm lightly, you must place your hand on the small of her back as you conduct her around the room and down to theater. Women dote on these simple signs of affection as all men would know if they were not deaf, dumb, and blind."

"Twelve-year-olds," Neenan said.

"Precisely."

"I gotta do all this tonight?"

"Certainly."

"I don't think it's right for a man to slobber over his wife in public."

"It's not exactly slobber that I am prescribing."

"Yeah, but . . ."

"It depends to a considerable extent on the man and on the woman. In your case and at the present time in your love affair with her, she will enjoy such small tokens of affection. More than that, she now expects them and will be disappointed if they are not forthcoming."

Gabriella's deep blue eyes were dancing with amusement. She was loving every second of this advice to a clumsy human husband.

"This necklace is not a small token," Neenan argued.

"Compared to what she is and what you have, it is utterly trivial."

A young woman waiter brought a class of white wine for Neenan.

"Ms. Neenan will be here this evening, Mr. Neenan?"

"Yes, indeed, Barbara, I'm a little early."

Barbara had not noticed the angels. Nonetheless, a glass of white wine materialized in front of each of them.

Michael touched Neenan's glass. "You'll be drinking the same thing we're drinking."

Neenan lifted the wineglass to his lips and sipped. "It's very good."

"The best white wine you've ever tasted," Michael said firmly.

"I won't argue about that."

"Finally," Gabriella continued implacably, "when you are engaged in business here tonight, as you will certainly be, you will be very careful to include her in the conversation, introducing her to whoever approaches you or whomever you approach. Understand?"

"Yes."

"Do you have a problem with it?"

"I have many problems with it, but I've learned to do whatever my guardian angels tell me to do."

"We are not quite guardian angels," she admonished him.

"Guardian seraphs then."

"Michael," Gaby said, suddenly alert, "the woman is here. She is absolutely stunning. I'm sure she sees us. I told you she would. You should have looked into it."

Even among the seraphs, Neenan mused, the male is always responsible for what goes wrong.

"Nothing we can do about it now," Michael replied. "I'm sure she doesn't know what we are."

Neenan was pleased with himself. So seraphs made mistakes now and then.

"She certainly is stunning," Michael said to Gabriella, "for a human."

"For any creature."

"Raymond," Anna Maria said behind him. "The tails still fit you!"

She was indeed stunning. Her hair was piled up on her head, and she was wearing a deep red, miniskirted cocktail dress that hung from her shoulders on precarious, thin straps. There wasn't all that much fabric in the dress. On another woman it would have been vulgar and suggestive. On Anna Maria, however, it seemed tasteful and lovely. No necklace. The seraphs had doubtless thought of that too.

Neenan took her in his arms and held her close, one of his hands on the smooth skin of her back. Following the instructions of his seraphic instructor, he held her for a little longer than the required spousal hug would have demanded and kissed her a little more affectionately than a kiss of greeting in the Graham Room would have required. She caught her breath and then relaxed in his arms.

"Are you going to introduce me to your friends?" she asked, her voice shaky.

"Indeed I am. Anna Maria, these are my two friends Gaby and Michael. They are in the, ah, music business."

He deliberately pronounced the woman seraph's name the way it should be pronounced in Chicago—*gab-ee.*

"Gaby and Michael, this is my wife, Anna Maria Allegro."

"My dear," Gaby said, shaking hands with Anna Maria, "you are absolutely dazzling tonight, stunning, ravishing."

"I don't dare disagree ever with my companion, ah, wife," Michael said as he bent over Anna Maria's hand and kissed it. "Tonight I must say she understates the case."

Anna Maria blushed contentedly. She wasn't sure, women never are, whether she was dressed appropriately. If two such elegant and sophisticated people approved of her, then she must have chosen wisely.

"I'm afraid I can't top those compliments," Neenan said as he extended his arm around her shoulders and eased her into her chair. "So I have to say merely that you quite take away my breath."

"I'm glad you like it, Raymond," she said shyly.

The young woman waiter brought another glass of white wine. Unobtrusively Michael touched it.

"What wonderful wine!" Anna Maria exclaimed as she sipped it. "It must be from Italy."

"In a way," Gaby said, still smiling.

The two couples chatted for a few moments about the opera.

"Their children are singing in the chorus tonight," Neenan explained.

"Really! How wonderful!"

"We're very proud of them," Gaby agreed, not missing a beat, "and like all parents, just a little worried."

Michael just barely contained a laugh.

After a few moments, the two seraphs excused themselves politely and then simply disappeared. Anna Maria did not seem to notice the abruptness of their departure.

"No necklace tonight," Neenan said, his hand under the table touching her knee.

She shifted contentedly in her chair. "You know how I always forget something. So I didn't pack my necklace this morning."

"That's good, because I brought one along that I think you might like."

He removed the diamond and ruby ensemble from his jacket pocket, slipped it around her neck, and fastened it at the back. In doing so, he managed to touch delicately her throat, her chest, and her back. She gasped in surprise.

"Raymond!"

The angel kids took a break from their practice to sing a mighty fanfare. They were obviously little imps, but then what else would angel kids be? Apples don't fall far from their trees.

"You like it?"

"It's absolutely beautiful! I love it! Thank you so much!"

She leaned across the table and brushed his lips with hers.

"I'm glad you like it. I wasn't sure that you would, though I thought it had your name written all over it."

He pretended to adjust it every so slightly and thus found an excuse to touch her lightly again.

"I may cry," she warned him.

"That's all right."

"I feel like saying that you shouldn't have done it. My mom told me never to say anything like that."

"Mom is right. You said thank-you and that's enough."

She lifted the necklace to gaze reverently at it. "Tiffany's?"

"Right. I have an account there now."

"Really! I didn't know that!"

"I didn't used to have one, but I do now."

"How exciting!"

"Shall we have a bite to eat?"

"Let's! I'm starved!"

He helped her out of the chair and, faithful to Gaby's orders, shaped his hand to the small of her back to guide her to their dinner table. Most of his target was bare skin, which made the gesture even more pleasurable. She looked up at him and smiled, surprised but delighted.

"You should drink your soup," she said when they were seated at the table, "and not stare at me like that."

"I'm admiring my good taste."

"In women or jewels."

"Jewels of course."

She slapped his hand lightly. "I don't believe that."

The slap became a caress.

That necklace will touch her skin long after I am unable to touch her, he thought sadly to himself. Well, I may as well enjoy our love while I can.

Tears were about to sting his eyes when Timmy Walsh passed their table.

"Hi, R. A.," he said genially.

"Hi, Timmy. Got a second?"

"For you, R. A., always."

"Anna Maria, this handsome giant is Timothy Walsh, the famous public interest lawyer. He has managed to win more than a few cases against the big corporate giants. . . . Tim, this is my wife, Anna Maria Allegro."

"Good evening, Mr. Walsh."

"Good evening, Ms. Allegro. I must say that your necklace is lovely, as indeed are you."

"I'm used to quick-tongued Irishmen, Mr. Walsh, but thank you. My husband bought the necklace for me."

"Always a man of excellent taste in all things." Irish blarney.

"Timmy, let's settle this pension case."

A quick look of enormous relief raced across Walsh's face. He covered it up, but too late.

Got him, Neenan decided.

"I'll have to talk to my clients," Walsh said guardedly, "but I'd be interested in your general outline of a settlement."

"Sure. You can negotiate the small stuff with Neil Higgins tomorrow. I propose that we do something like restore all of them to their jobs and their pensions."

"With back pay?"

"Naturally."

"I see. . . . And what about us?"

"We would of course negotiate with you on a fair price for your expenses."

That was code for probably a third more than their real expenses.

"I see. . . . Some of my clients want punitive damages."

"They'll never get them, as you well know, Tim. In fact with the materials we have on their work performance, most of them will not prevail in a trial for compensatory damages."

"We think they will."

"It will cost a lot of money and a lot of time to find out. Better that they have jobs."

Neenan watched the thoughts flit across Walsh's face. Walsh knew he had to settle. He would lose hundreds of thousands of dollars in a suit and appeals. There was little likelihood of his recouping much from his share of whatever awards there might be. His pockets were pretty big, but not as big as NE's.

"That's certainly true," Walsh mused thoughtfully. "I'm surprised that you are eager to settle, R. A., I thought you had dug in your heels."

"It's a waste of time and money, Tim. For all concerned. We shouldn't have tried it in the first place, even if most of your clients were loafers. Even a loafer has a right to a pension."

The angelic offspring found time for a single desultory clash of cymbals. They obviously had other things on their mind as they prepared to sing Marguerite off to heaven.

"I may have a hard time persuading some of them to settle. They may want a piece of your hide."

"That's not negotiable," Neenan replied briskly. "You're the lawyer, Tim. You have the obligation to give them responsible advice. I'm sure they'll go along."

"Well, we'll see."

"Talk to Neil tomorrow morning."

"I will certainly do that. . . . A very real pleasure to meet you, Ms. Neenan."

Anna Maria smiled back.

"Slick shyster," she said after Walsh had gone to his table. "He'd fit perfectly in a couple of dozen scripts I've had to read."

"You got him."

"But it is time you got that case off your back."

"I agree."

"He's not sure that you're leveling with him."

"He'll probably wonder about the other leopards changing their spots."

"Like all of us."

"I figured I didn't have to tell him about my plane ride last Saturday."

"He wouldn't believe that any more than anyone else does."

He ignored that thrust. Instead he moved his knee against her knee under the table and rubbed back and forth.

"You seemed determined to keep me in a state of semipermanent sexual arousal," she said with a slight gasp.

"All you have to say is 'Stop it!' "

"Why should I say that? . . . This is absolutely the best red wine I've ever tasted! Lyric is buying wonderful wines these days. What's the label?"

Neenan picked up the bottle. The label said "Seraphic Vineyards" and the locale was alleged to be "Heavenly Valley." Triple wings served as a logo.

Show-offs!

"It's a very high quality California wine. Heavenly Valley."

Anna Maria was not a wine phony. If there were a valley in California with that name, she would know about it. She glanced at the label, frowned, then put it aside as though someone had wiped the question from her mind. Forgetfulness dust. Seraphs undoubtedly carried that along as a matter of course.

He had to agree with her, it was the best red wine he'd ever tasted.

A couple of thousand dollars a bottle—if you could buy it, which you certainly could not. Still, if he was real good to the angels and praised their kids' singing, maybe they'd provide him a supply.

Not that he would be around long enough to enjoy it.

"We'll have to find out later from the management," she said dreamily.

Don't bet on it, my love. You'll have forgotten it by the time we leave the table.

They spoke briefly with Ardis Krainik, the administrative genius who had made the Lyric great, as she walked by the table.

"Marvelous wine," Neenan said. "Absolutely superior."

"Thank you very much, Ray," she replied. "We try to keep our customers happy."

Anna Maria blinked her eyes as though she wanted to say something but couldn't quite remember what it was. She settled for, "Quite wonderful, Ardis."

Pretty effective stuff, that forgetfulness dust. I wonder how often they've used it on me.

After they had finished dinner, he guided her through the dining room and down the stairs to the theater and their seats. Neenan did not believe in boxes, because they were too far away from the stage. So their seats were on the aisle ten rows back. He assisted her into her seat and then captured her hand.

She glanced at him with a quizzical smile, but said nothing.

This is Wednesday, he told himself. Last Saturday seems a lifetime ago.

The lights went down, a hush settled on the audience, and Bruno Bartoletti, now celebrating his fortieth year with the Lyric, emerged to tumultuous applause. He raised his baton and the music began.

Poor old Faust, the dried-up scholar, lamented in his attic study the effect of age on his life. Outside, the chorus sang of life, a powerful and vigorous chorus, as it should be. Faust's problem was age and, by implication, Neenan thought, death.

Was he like Faust, trying to recapture his youth with a younger woman?

Then Mephistopheles appeared at Faust's call and promised him youth and a woman. Faust signed the fateful document, just as Neenan had signed Michael's. What was the difference between the two of them? Both he and Faust feared death. Both knew they would die.

Both wanted a little life and a little pleasure before the day of death came.

Neenan caressed his wife's lower arm throughout the first act. She sighed a couple of times, but hardly in protest.

We can't keep this up indefinitely, he thought. Maybe it's a good thing I won't be around long.

He quickly dismissed that thought.

He made two observations during the act. First of all, Sam Ramey had never been in better voice, and secondly, the angel kids were participating with enormous vigor in all the choral parts.

"Isn't the chorus wonderful tonight?" Anna Maria whispered in his ear.

"They sure are."

She heard them of course, if not quite as clearly as he did. He wondered how many others in the audience also heard them. The seraphic parents, of whom many were presumably hanging around, might well be playing games with the sound waves so lots of people might hear their kids.

Sure enough, when the curtain came down on the first act, the crowd streaming out of the theater spoke only of how wonderful the chorus had been.

They bumped into Michael and Gaby in the lobby.

"The chorus was wonderful," Anna Maria exclaimed. "How proud you must feel!"

"Their performance was adequate," the woman seraph said with a maternal smile.

"They did OK," Michael agreed.

"Can you join us upstairs?" Neenan asked mischievously.

"Thank you, but we already have a date with some friends."

Then they were simply not there anymore. Anna Maria apparently did not notice, nor did she wonder why children would be singing in the chorus in the first act when there were no children's roles. The forgetfulness dust apparently worked well indeed.

"Joan and Ben Harvey will join us for a drink in the Graham Room," he whispered.

"Do I know them?"

"He presides over a cable company for us in upstate New York. He was a pioneer innovator but ran his company into the ground. We picked it up for small change, though it was worth less than that. I

146 Andrew M. Greeley

retained him as president under strict financial supervision. World-
Corp is trying to lure him away from us."

"Do we want to keep him?"

"I had intended to offer him and in fact did so our new direct-TV
venture. It's the kind of innovation at which he'd be very good. I think
he's tempted, but he still resents me. No great loss if he leaves."

"Still, we will be nice to him, if only to spite WorldCorp, right?"

"Got it."

In the Graham Room Neenan introduced Anna Maria to the Harveys. Joan spared his wife one quick glance and then dismissed her.
Ben's eyes, however, constantly drifted back to her.

Joan was a handsome woman, slender, full-breasted, regal. Her
black hair was almost certainly dyed, though by an expert. Her face
had also received some careful and highly skilled attention. But in her
long black dress, she was still luscious. Neenan's imagination undressed her swiftly as his hands once had. She noted his inspection
and smiled aloofly.

Neenan ordered a second bottle of red wine. It was another cabernet from Seraphic Vineyards.

"It is really a wonderful production," Ben began the conversation
in his usual persnickety tone. "Ramey is truly wonderful as Mephisto,
and the chorus is outstanding. The Met had better look to its laurels
if it wishes to keep its lead."

"The Lyric has come a long way," Joan agreed. "You Chicagoans
should certainly be proud of that."

Her eyes were now locked with Neenan's. She was signaling that
she was still available anytime he wanted her.

His reaction, he told himself, was unbridled lust. He did not love
her. He loved his wife, who was more beautiful, easier to get along
with, and a better lover. Joan Harvey, however, had been one of his
great conquests, and in some fashion she still belonged to him.

"This is a pleasant little wine," Ben said with a sniff. "Better than
what the Lyric used to serve."

"Still a bit pretentious," Joan observed.

Never in their stupid lives would they ever drink better.

On the other side of the room Michael and Gabriella were sitting
with a younger and equally handsome couple, a tall, blond Viking type
and a black-haired woman who looked as if she were cast from the

same mold as Gabriella. They watched Neenan with languid amusement.

Don't worry, guys, I'm not going to act out. He raised his glass of the cabernet from the Seraphic Vineyards to them in a quick salute. They returned the toast.

"I'm told that the *New York Times* has sent its regular opera reviewer here tonight," Anna Maria informed them. "He's been very favorable to the Lyric in the last couple of years."

Neither Harvey paid any attention to her. Snobs.

Nonetheless he could not banish his desire for Joan, who, in his imagination, was now totally naked and completely at his disposal.

"Well, we still have the Bulls," he said with a laugh. "The Knicks will never catch up with them. . . . Have you had a chance, Ben, to consider my offer?"

Harvey sighed softly, like a man about to decline a woman's invitation to dance with her.

"It's a challenging venture, R. A.; ten years ago I might have jumped at it. But I've been with NE for a long time now and I feel that this is the time for an, ah, change of venue, if you know what I mean, for a new start. If I wait too many more years, I won't have the energy, I fear, to make a new start."

Neenan had torn his eyes away from Joan, but out of the corner of his right eye, he noticed her smiling triumphantly. For reasons of her own she had shot his offer down.

Interesting.

"I'm sorry to hear that, Ben. There will always be a place for you at NE if you want to come back. Moreover, I would suggest that you communicate your decision to WorldCorp first thing in the morning. We're going into court before noon with a petition for a restraining order against them for tampering with our executives and our potential acquisitions."

"Really?" Harvey said as if he were astonished. "I'm surprised to hear that. May I ask why?"

"It's part of their standard harassing tactics when they want to take someone over. They're wasting their time with us. We want to signal them of that fact early."

"I'm sure," Joan cut in, "that their decision to offer a major position to Bennett has nothing to do with such a scheme."

"I'm sure of that too," Neenan said with little regard for the truth. "However, I don't want him to get tripped up in the litigation."

"How you men love litigation and conflict," Joan said, her eyes wide open with invitation.

Thanks but no thanks, Joan, he told her mentally. He wondered whether Michael and his crowd would expect him to apologize to her. Alone in a room with her, he might have a hard time with the firm purpose of amendment he had promised to Father Sixtus earlier in the day.

"Sometimes you have to fight off barbarian invaders," Anna Maria replied. "Litigation is not less harmful than broadswords and pikes."

"And more expensive too," Neenan said with a smile. "But we don't end up with a lot of captive women and children."

That put out the fire of longing in Joan's eyes.

Not a peep from the angel brats, who could not this time spare him even a single cymbal clash.

His comment had been a decisive ending to the relationship, not a happy ending, but an ending nonetheless. What would Michael think? To hell with what he thought. You survive any way you can.

They chatted amiably for a few more minutes, wished each the best in work and life, and bid good-bye. The Harveys barely noticed Anna Maria in their leave-taking.

How could they not notice her?

As they left, Neenan realized that Joan was a perfectly ordinary woman, with a strong streak of nastiness in her personality. How had he ever been obsessed by her?

"Small loss," Anna Maria said as he guided her back to their seats. "He might have some talent. She's a terrible snob. He'd like to work for you, but she won't let him."

"You're right on both counts. We won't miss him. The fire's long since gone. And she's the one who told him what to do."

"Do you find her attractive?" Anna Maria asked casually.

A booby trap.

"Not anymore," he replied. "Once I thought her rather striking. Now I think she's ordinary as well as unpleasant."

"I think she'd like to sleep with you."

"Not a chance," he replied, discreetly hugging her as he assisted her into her seat. "I already have a perfectly satisfactory bed partner."

"I didn't feel threatened," Anna Maria said softly. "I'm not the jealous type."

"No reason you should be."

"None at all."

"I'm sorry they were rude to you."

"I kept my Sicilian temper under control only because I didn't want to embarrass you."

He had never seen her alleged temper. It might be interesting, but he was not eager to observe it.

The second act was even more triumphant than the first. The audience gave it a standing ovation.

"I never noticed before," Anna Maria said as they stood, "how Catholic this story is."

"Charles François-Gounod was a devout, even mystical Catholic. He considered being a priest and went to the seminary for a while. That's why it seems so strange that he would make Mephisto almost a gentleman."

"Evil sometimes is very attractive," Anna Maria observed. "I wonder what an opera about an angel would be like."

"I suspect that angels are pretty creepy characters."

"I think they'd be slick and funny and charming. And maybe just a little tricky. They would, naturally, be very bright and very passionate."

Close enough. "You ever met one?"

"No . . ." she said slowly. "But sometimes I sense they're lurking around and loving us and maybe laughing at us a lot."

"An interesting possibility."

"I think it would be nice if someone did a script about such angels. They'd be much more attractive than the angels in the cults everyone is crazy about these days."

"That is not a bad idea."

In the Graham Room before the final act they encountered Honoria Smythe with a handsome, balding psychiatrist in tow. Her gown, unlike Anna Maria's, was intolerably vulgar. Neenan had only minor trouble fighting off fantasies about her.

As ordered by the ineffable Gabriella, Neenan dutifully introduced his wife to both of them. She rated one dismissive glance from Honoria, but constant visual attention from the shrink.

"Have you had an opportunity to reconsider my offer, Honoria?" Neenan asked casually, not ready to invite her to his table for a drink.

"Yes, Ray," she said sorrowfully, "I have. I'd love to work for NE, but I simply can't turn down the opportunities WorldCorp has offered me."

"I'm sorry to hear that, Honoria," he said. "I'm sure you and NorthCal would be wonderful assets for the firm. But I have to respect your decision. I wish you all possible good fortune. Incidentally, you might want to, ah, consummate the deal as soon as you can. We're going into federal court for the Northern District of Illinois tomorrow morning to seek a restraining order against WorldCorp for tampering with our executives and our potential acquisitions. It won't be a retroactive order, so it's not aimed at you."

"You really wouldn't do that, would you, Ray? It would certainly make things difficult for NorthCal."

"I don't think it would, Honoria. I sincerely hope not. However, I must protect NE from more harassment by those barbarian invaders."

She shook her head in sorrow and turned away, her built-in shrink right behind her.

Neenan conducted his wife to their table and discovered a half-full bottle of the Heavenly Valley wine waiting for them. The bossy seraphs did not want either of them to drink too much.

"Strumpet," Anna Maria said curtly.

"An attractive strumpet, however."

"They often are," she said, filling both their wineglasses. "I'm afraid we'll sleep through the final act."

"I doubt it."

"WorldCorp: two," she said, lifting her glass to him, "NE: zero."

"I'm afraid so."

"Did you really want either of them?"

His knee found her thigh and moved gently back and forth.

"Losing them doesn't cause me any deep sorrow, if that's what you mean. Ben Harvey was creative once, possibly could be again, but Joan dominates him completely. Honoria has been very successful, but I think she'd be a dangerous person to have around."

"Too true," Anna Maria said with a quick gasp of pleasure.

"I'd like to win the first two battles with WorldCorp, but they might be costly victories in the long run. I thought I owed poor Ben another chance after what I did to him. I guess that debt is discharged."

"And Honoria?"

"I don't owe her anything."

"She wanted to sleep with you too."

"The problem with her is that she wants to sleep with everyone who might help her career."

"You see things very clearly, my husband."

"Sometimes more clearly than other times."

The seraphic couples were nowhere to be seen. Probably backstage calming down their brats. Except what was backstage in their world? Was it even in this universe?

Ms. Krainik walked by beaming at everyone.

"Congratulations, Ray," she said. "You're backing a winner. The *Times* man has been telling people that it is the best *Faust* he has ever seen."

People whom Ms. Krainik had undoubtedly assigned to listen to his reaction. No bets were missed in this very Chicago enterprise.

"The chorus is simply divine," Anna Maria enthused. "I've never heard them so good."

"Me, neither," Ardis said with a chuckle.

"I'd say they were more angelic," Neenan commented.

Someone pounded angrily on a drum.

Too bad, brats, I'm entitled to have my fun.

Had the whole thing been set up as a seraphic favor because he had supported the production?

What a dumb question!

Of course it had.

"Did you hear a drum, dear?"

"A drum?" he replied. "We're a long way from the timpani section."

"I suppose so. . . . Are we going down for the third act or are you going to try to seduce me up here?"

"Do I have to choose?"

"Come on." She dragged him to his feet. "You've had far too much wine."

"So have you."

Nonetheless they were capable of wending a straight path back to their seats, his hand always guarding and protecting her back. No one looked at him with surprise during this exercise. Apparently that's what a certain kind of gentleman was supposed to do.

I keep learning.

"Those women are terrible," she said when he more or less tucked her into her seat.

"Gaby?"

"Oh, no, not her. She's sweet. I know I've seem them around somewhere. Probably back in Lake Forest. Can't quite remember where. Are they neighbors?"

"I don't think so."

"I meant the other two. They are mean and nasty and vindictive, like your mother was before she got sick and like Donna was at Vincent's wedding. Different veneers maybe, but the same kind of person."

"I suppose you're right."

The lance plunged into Neenan's chest again. He sank back into his seat as the curtain rose on the finale, feeling that he was mortally wounded.

Then he once more had the sensation that he was collapsing, coming apart, breaking up—like the voice of a soprano who had tried to sing one year too many.

14

He did not, indeed could not, challenge Anna Maria's assertion about his former lover and his almost lover. They were indeed cruel and angry women. It was obvious, though he had never seen it before. Both were more attractive than his mother and his first wife, but they had similar personalities. Indeed his first wife was very much like his mother when he reflected on their similarities.

He felt he was sinking into a swamp like bits of a shattered airplane after a crash. He had pursued women all his life who were carbons of his punitive, mean-spirited, grudging mother. He had thought that he was conquering them when, in fact, they had conquered him.

He was a fool, an idiot, a clown, a hapless loser.

Anna Maria took his hand in hers. Damn! He'd forgotten Gaby's stern mandates. Then she rested her knee against his thigh. She at least did not fit the pattern. The only reason for that, however, was that the seraphs were meddling in his life even then.

"Fresh!" he murmured.

"Shush," she whispered back.

He had wasted his life. He had tried time after time to screw his mother. He had taken delight in seeming to punish women who reminded him of her. That they had in fact seduced him instead of the other way around made him even more the fool, a stupid, ineffectual fool. Small wonder that he quickly lost interest in his conquests, though they continued to remain physically appealing to him.

That was what the seraph had meant.

Did the women know what was happening? Probably not. How could they? They knew only that he was a desirable male they wanted to drag into their bed. No reason to blame them. He was the villain of the stories.

He went through them in his head. Indeed they all fit the pattern, one way or another, some more than others.

Was that the way all women are?

Probably, he decided. They intuit our weaknesses and then exploit them.

Anna Maria withdrew her knee from his thigh and placed her hand on it instead, complacently claiming what was hers as a matter of right. He rested his hand on top of hers so that she couldn't move it away.

She was different from the others. She candidly and frankly enjoyed him. Indeed she reveled in him. Most women were unlike those he had thought he was hunting, but he had hardly noticed, so determined was he to conquer and punish his mother.

He was a sickie, a weirdo, a pervert.

No, not completely. Otherwise his wife would not dote on him.

What did it all mean?

Had his ambition for money and power been driven by his twisted sexual desires?

That was absurd.

Or was it?

A psychiatrist would certainly think so. He had spent his whole life attempting to escape from his mother and had failed. In fact, while he was piling up power and money to complete his escape, he was in fact pursuing her. How he hated that terrible woman!

But that was probably not fair either. She had been pursued by her own past, her own unhappiness, her own demons, about all of which he knew nothing.

His stomach turned in self-disgust. He was afraid that he would have to run from the theater to vomit.

Anna Maria moved her hand gently and tenderly on his thigh. His stomach calmed. Did she know what was happening?

That was unthinkable. She was too healthy a person to think of such things. She merely wanted her man. Her sexual hungers were open and straightforward and honest. No wonder he had avoided her for most of their marriage.

The good news was that he could still fall completely under her spell and luxuriate in her passion. The bad news was that he had so little time left.

He shivered.

"Are you all right, dear?" she whispered. "Are you sick?"

"Hungry."

"For food?"

"No."

Slowly he climbed back from the canyon rim of despair. He would not fall into the abyss, not as long as this marvelous wife was near him. Life had humiliated him, disgraced him, turned him into a big, silly clown. Nonetheless, and for reasons that utterly escaped him, someone found him lovable.

Maybe that was what the seraph had been trying to tell him all along about the link between the delicious Anna Maria and whoever lurked in his experiences of ecstasy.

It was too confusing to think out tonight. He wanted only to lose himself in Anna Maria and forget everything else.

The opera continued. He tried to focus on it. Who needed Mephistopheles when blind human idiocy tricked humans into evil? Poor Marguerite, the innocent victim of Faust's lust and the demon's villainy, had murdered her child. She was in prison awaiting her execution. With Faust as his agent, Mephistopheles made one last desperate, nearly successful attempt to carry her off to hell.

"Damnation!" the demon exclaimed; it was the cue for the angels to exult in their own conclusion to the story.

"Salvation!"

The walls of the prison collapsed. Marguerite was transported to heaven.

Anna Maria's hand moved again, exploring, probing, arousing. It was his turn to gasp. Next to him she chuckled softly.

Brazen hussy.

The chorus went wild with joy, indeed with a glee that Gounod had probably not intended. The angel brats were having the time of their life.

> *Sauvée! Christ est ressuscité!*
> *Christ vient de renaître!*
> *Paix et félicité!*
> *Aux disciples du Maître!*
> *Christ vient de renaître.*
> *Christ est ressuscité!*

Maybe that's how it all does end, Neenan told himself. Maybe even poor Faust, kneeling there in desperate prayer, would also be reborn because of Marguerite's prayers. Maybe.

So the seraph had said.

The audience rose for another standing ovation. They clapped and cheered and shouted "Bravo!" repeatedly in loud voices. The opera was a complete triumph. His wife kissed him in congratulation. People shook his hand as they walked out. He smiled and thanked them and responded with his left and his right hands, as if he were a precinct captain. Or maybe even a ward committeeman. Beside him, Anna Maria was accepting congratulations too, a grand duchess hailed by her people.

In the lobby he saw Michael and his companions at a distance. He gave them the thumbs-up signal and they responded. What were they really up to? How many birds were they killing with the same stone? No point in trying to figure out that either.

As they strolled out of the theater to Wacker Drive, he heard a man tell the *Tribune* music critic, "It's the best *Faust* I have ever seen, and I've never heard a chorus like that, never."

By the looks of him he had to be the critic from the *New York Times*.

Neenan hoped that the Harveys would read the paper the next morning.

In the limo he had ordered to pick them up, Anna Maria cuddled with him.

"A triumph, dear," she sighed. "A very important night."

"It's not finished yet."

"Really?"

"Really."

"What did you have in mind?"

"There's a woman I intend to rape in the very near future."

She laughed. "Dearest Raymond, you respect women too much ever to force them."

That was true too. Contradictory evidence. He was a tender and sensitive lover. How did that ever happen?

It was too late in the evening to ask that question. He was too intoxicated by heavenly music, heavenly wine, and a heavenly woman to think anymore.

Instead, in the privacy of the backseat, separated from the driver by thick, transparent plastic, he went to work on her thighs, both of them, a task greatly facilitated by the shortness of her skirt.

She groaned softly.

She wanted him more than he wanted her. As long as he lived, there would be no exits for him, no chance of going back to his pattern of indifference punctuated by occasional outbursts of passion.

As they rode up in the elevator to their apartment, he helped her off with her coat, draped it over his arm, and then, with quick and deft movements, removed her dress. As he had expected, there was not much beneath it.

She stiffened, arched her back, and turned her head away.

"You're embarrassing me, Raymond."

"I know that."

"What if someone sees us?"

"In this place at this hour?"

"Don't spoil my dress."

"You can always tell me to stop."

"Why should I do that?"

By the time they had reached the door to their apartment, she wore only the barest minimum of garments — and her necklace.

He fiddled with the door key, distracted by the garments on his arm.

"Are we going to make it into the apartment in time?" she asked with a giggle.

"I hope so."

"All we need is the security guard to pop out of the elevator just now. . . . Hurry! It's cold!"

"I'm trying!"

Finally the door sprang opened and they slipped into the apartment. He reached out to crush her in his arms. She ducked away.

"Not so fast, my darling one. Turnabout is fair play. You look awesomely handsome in that suit, but you'll look even better out of it. I'm going to undress you too and I'm going to take my sweet time about it."

She teased him for what seemed an eternity, suspending him on a tightrope between agony and pleasure.

"Not so fast, my darling," she said again when she was finished stripping him. "I want to admire you for a moment or two. . . . I wonder if there is anything better in life for a woman than having a man like you."

"You make me sound like a slave."

"Isn't that what men are?"

"I thought they were at best amusing twelve-year-olds."

"Amusing twelve-year-old slaves, who have some very bad habits," she said as she embraced him and kissed him with wild abandon.

Much later, while Anna Maria slept in the disarray of their bed, he opened the drapes and glanced at the moon as it turned the smooth waters of the lake into shimmering silver.

"You seemed to like the opera," Michael said. The seraph was standing in the dark beside him.

"Your angel brats were wonderful."

Michael chuckled contentedly. "They are very proud of themselves. They figured they wanted to do something to help our project."

"All of you guys are imps."

"Why would you expect anything else?"

"What will the *Times* say tomorrow?"

"How many times do I have to tell you, R. A., that we do not know the future."

"Michael, don't try to bullshit a bullshitter. The review is already written and you certainly had one of your crowd peering over his head while he was putting it down, maybe even feeding him words."

"We absolutely did not do that . . . at least we didn't feed him any words."

"Only because you didn't have to."

"Actually Ariel, Rafaella's companion, monitored the writing of the article."

"The blond linebacker type?"

"Naturally. Rafe is Gaby's offspring by our lamented friend Lucifer."

"I would have thought as much. . . . And the review?"

"The headline will say, 'Another Important Triumph for Lyric.' It will praise every aspect of the production, an unheard of event at the *NYT*. The chorus is mentioned in the second sentence."

"I trust the Harveys will read it."

"They will, I guarantee you. They will also see the photo of yourself and your companion as you walk into the lobby that the *Times* photographer snapped. I must acknowledge that it concentrates more on her than on you."

"That shows good taste."

"Indeed yes."

"They didn't happen to get a picture of you and your companion did they?"

"Hardly. Though sometimes certain kinds of cameras with the right kind of film do pick us up. Usually we manage to erase the traces before anyone sees them."

"Isn't it kind of unfair to provide, ah, extraterrestrial help to the Lyric?"

"Not really. The only ones who heard our offspring in full voice were you and your companion and a few other highly sensitive people. The rest heard only a faint background tone. What the offspring did was inspire the human chorus to sing at the maximum of their talents. That was enough."

"I bet that tomorrow they won't be able to figure out what happened, even if you don't use your forgetfulness dust."

Michael was amused. "Is that what you call it? Well, I suppose it's as good a name as any. . . . The point is that the Lyric chorus will be much better for their experience because they will have more confidence in their natural talent. That's basically what we do, you know."

"So you're merely enhancing my natural talents by giving me more confidence in them?"

"Judging by the depth and happiness of your companion's sleep, I would say your talents in that area at any rate are improving."

"She makes life worth living."

"That's what companions do to one another."

They were silent for a moment, contemplating the chill mystery of Lake Michigan.

"So, your companion's insight was a savage blow to you?"

"You were watching?"

"From a distance, yes."

"She's right of course?"

"Dead-on."

"I don't know why I didn't see it before. I have been chasing women like my mother all my life, trying to punish her by capturing them."

"There is wisdom in that insight, but it is not perfectly accurate."

"What's missing?"

"Ah, that is not for me to say. You must figure this out by yourself if you are to really believe it. You will see it all eventually, of that I have no doubt."

"I don't want to think about it anymore tonight."

"I would advise you not to try."

"I've been such a fool."

"All creatures are fools in one way or another. As the good priest at your parish said, we don't fully understand the implications that the Other is near, indeed at hand."

"I suppose so."

"You seem sad on this night of multiple triumphs."

"Omnis animal tristis est post coitum."

"That is less true of reflective animals. . . . You are unhappy now about what you see as a waste of most of your life and the brief time ahead of you?"

"You got it."

"Yet should you not be happy that you have been granted time to reverse that waste and enjoy happiness more intense than most humans know?"

"So many mistakes to straighten out."

"And so much joy in improved relationships."

"Like which ones?"

"Your wife and your son, so far."

"Do I have to apologize to all those women?"

"It would not be wise to pursue that as a project. Many of them would not understand. It would not be wise to be alone with some of them. Should you by chance encounter one of the more perceptive of them in a safe public place, you might make an effort. We would expect no more from you. Neither, it is safe to say, would the Other."

"I'm glad to hear that."

"There are your parents and your other children and Donna."

"I don't need you to remind me about them. I'm going to try day after tomorrow, am I not?"

"You must not expect to be successful with any of them, not immediately anyway."

"Should I leave them more money?"

"We are not displeased with your new arrangements. More money at the present would only increase their hatred for you."

"I guess you're right. Those two women tonight were horrible."

"I will not dispute that either. Yet if one views the relationship from their perspective, you did appear to betray them."

"Betray them? That's nonsense!"

"Is it?"

"Maybe not. It's all too complicated for me to understand."

"You will understand more of it on reflection. You must at least forgive them."

"You're right, as usual. A person who needs so much forgiveness needs to be generous in forgiving others."

"Did not the Teacher himself say the same thing?"

"Not in so many words."

"In those very words. Unfortunately, no one bothered to write them down when they got to that stage. . . . I must say, Raymond Anthony, that you are showing considerable progress."

"Am I? I don't know about that. I don't know about anything. Except Anna Maria."

"That should be more than enough."

"For the present."

"Forever," Michael insisted. "Now you should join her in your bed of love and sleep."

"I can't sleep."

"We should be able to help in that direction."

The lance plunged into Neenan's chest again. He sank back into his seat as the curtain rose on the finale, feeling that he was mortally wounded.

Then he once more had the sensation that he was collapsing, coming apart, breaking up—like the voice of a soprano who had tried to sing one year too many.

Michael touched Neenan's head.

Instantly, Neenan was drowsy. He stumbled toward the bed and fell into it.

Before he went completely under, he had time to say, "Have a good time with Gaby tonight."

"Insolent human," Michael said with a complacent laugh.

☙ 15 ☙

Look, occupant, or Occupant if you prefer, I am now prepared to believe that there is someone or Someone out there who is remotely interested in us and listens to us on occasion. I have no idea what you're like. Nor am I sure that your little friends are all that clear either, despite their pose of superiority. I am, however, prepared to believe that You had something to do with putting them on my case. So on the premise that you might be listening and might even care—though on the face of it that seems unlikely—I am going to try to talk to You. You can call it prayer if You like. I don't much care what it's called.

There is some remote possibility that you are linked to these feelings of ecstasy that I have been experiencing lately, especially when I'm with Anna Maria. Which reminds me, you were apparently there again last night, three of us instead of two in bed together. I want to thank You for that—what should I call it? will interlude do? Insofar as you were responsible for it. It was unbearably good.

If You are what some teachers claim You are, I suppose You are present in any act of love which is really love. I can understand that, I think. But it still seems strange.

You seem to want me to think that You touch me and I touch You through her. If that is true, it is a very clever scheme and I certainly won't complain.

If You are really the Third that explodes into my life through my wife, then You are not only the Other, but Something Else Altogether and I'm afraid of You and deeply in love with You. I'm not sure I can separate You from my wife or that I should even try. If You are that Someone Else Altogether, it is a privilege to get to know You. I hope I don't say anything to offend You. However, it might turn out that You are beyond being offended after the long centuries and millennia of dealing with our kind.

I'm not sure what I'm doing here at Old St. Patrick's Church. It could get to be a bad habit.

But I need to talk to You.

Only I'm not sure why. Maybe I feel the need to go to the top instead of *communicating through that damn imp of an angel. Or seraph. Or whatever. I accept his word that there is no devil, but they are so tricky and so vain and such incorrigible show-offs that I can understand why some people might have been confused.*

I am thankful you sent the whole crowd of them to me, even though they think they can take over my life completely.

What I'm trying to say, not very clearly I admit, is that I am grateful to You for everything that has happened to me during the last couple of days, even if the price I have to pay is an early death. I am not going to ask you to change that. Such a prayer would be intolerably churlish. I only ask that You help me through the days ahead and take care of Anna Maria after I'm gone. Michael and his bunch promise me that they will take care of her and I believe them, but it still seems to be better that someone at the top also look after her.

Mind you, I don't want to die. I'm afraid to die. But I accept it. I will have to die eventually anyway, and I may as well die now and get it over with.

Right?

As I ramble on, I want to ask You about what happened yesterday. My wife undressed me twice. In the afternoon she turned on the energies of ecstasy, You maybe, as she stripped me physically. At the theater she tore me apart with her insight into the women I have pursued all my life, thus stripping me spiritually. I felt like I was a wave breaking up into tiny drops of foam as it crashes on the beach.

Michael thinks that this experience of coming apart is good for me. Maybe it is. But it's terrifying. Is it part of coming to terms with death? Or merely coming to terms with life, my life to be specific? Or maybe both?

I'm sure that I'll have to undergo it many more times before I find out what You're really like. I want to go on the record now as saying that I'll be terribly disappointed if You're not like that experience of love and laughter and joy and peace and the coming together of everything that I now seem to encounter often.

You might well say in response that You offered that touch of Yourself often before and I shied away from it. You might even add that I'm still very frightened by it. Especially here in this church where I expect you're lurking everywhere.

In a way, both experiences of nakedness were similar. While I like it when Anna Maria strips me, I am also mortified. Her desire for my body, her admiration of its nakedness, is, like everything else about sex with her, open and frank and consuming. That is the way men act with women. They should not act that way with us. Usually they don't, probably because they are afraid to abandon all inhibitions lest they be totally unprotected. For me it's a completely new experience and I'm not used to it yet. I'm glad I'm in pretty good shape.

I guess I'll have to get used to it, won't I? By the time I do, it will probably be too late.

But that's the way of things, isn't it?

Well, it's Communion time. So I'm going to go up and receive for the first time in many years. Don't be surprised if I come back.

One more thing as I go up the aisle. It's implicit in what I've been saying. But, knowing what lovers are like, I'd better be explicit:

I don't know who You are or what You are really like. I'm not even absolutely convinced that You are there or that, if You are, You give a damn about me. Nonetheless, I must say what I must say.

I love You.

16

"I am of course delighted," Neenan began his preliminary statement at the press conference, "to hear that World-Corp has denied that it has any interest in acquiring National Entertainment, in either a friendly or an unfriendly takeover. I must add two qualifications. The first is that they'd better not try it and the second is I almost believe them."

There was a rustle in the large crowd of reporters who had crowded into the NE auditorium. Neenan, who was wearing a lavalier mike, stood in front of the podium. Next to him on a table were copies of a half dozen papers. On the cover of every one but the *Wall Street Journal* there was the picture of him and Anna Maria at the opera. It was probably on the front page of most papers in the country.

He had called her earlier in the morning.

"Good morning," she had said sleepily.

"Still in bed."

"You bet. I'm tired."

"I don't know why."

"Too much wine maybe. Or maybe too much man."

"Possibly both. . . . Have you seen the papers?"

"You mean with the picture? Sure I've seen it. What do you think?"

"I wonder how that grumpy old man found such a gorgeous and smiling young wife. At least he's in the background and she occupies most of the frame."

"You're being obnoxious, Ray. It's a splendid picture of you and you don't look grumpy. You have a perfectly marvelous smile. And as for the young woman, she doesn't have nearly enough clothes on."

"Matter of opinion. I hope you realize that you're radiantly lovely in that picture."

"If you say so, I suppose I have to agree. But I don't see it myself."

"Women claim that they never do."

She had snorted.

"Will it help or hurt in your fight with WorldCorp?"

"My PR adviser, May Rosen, says it's the best possible press. A man with a wife like her who supports great opera can't be all bad."

She had snorted again, but she was obviously pleased.

"A handsome and smiling man like that who is being so gentle with his wife can't be all bad either. . . . Are you having that press conference this morning?"

"In fifteen minutes. WorldCorp has issued a statement saying they have no designs on us."

"Do you believe them?"

"Not for a minute. Not yet. When their boss calls me and tells me personally, I'll sort of half-believe. Do you want to come over?"

"I'd love to . . . but I must get myself in order and go home to get ready for tomorrow."

"Tomorrow?"

"You may have forgotten it, but you have a golf lesson scheduled on Captiva Island.

"Oh, yeah. And one last thing, lover boy, WorldCorp may not have any designs on you, but I do."

She had then hung up.

See what I mean, he had said to the Occupant, just in case She was listening.

Why *She*?

If the Someone Else Altogether was like his wife, then She was definitely womanly, whatever else She might also be.

Michael had then materialized in Neenan's office. "About ready for your press conference?"

"Just about. I'm busy now. What can I do for you?"

"Raymond Anthony, need I remind you that I am the boss seraph and not one of your underlings?"

"I am well aware of your rank, though I note you're wearing a three-piece lawyer's suit and not the dress of a field marshal."

"Smart ass. . . . In any event in response to your rudely phrased question, I want to know when you intend to call your son and inform him of your plans."

"Damn! . . . Ms. Jardine, will you see if you can get Vincent Neenan on the phone, please?"

"Well," Michael had observed, "you're at least saying *please.*"

"Ms. Megan Neenan on the phone, Mr. Neenan."

"Hi, Megan," he had said genially, "how is the mini-vacation going?"

"Wonderful, Ray. Hey, that's a bitchin' picture of you two guys on the front page of the *Los Angeles Times.*"

"Bitchin' " he understood was high praise from those who were part of Megan's generation — Valley Girls in their late twenties.

"Even out there? Neither Anna Maria nor I was aware that the picture was being taken."

"She is like totally gorgeous!"

"Funny thing, Meg, I've noticed that too."

"The opera was a huge success?"

"Totally. The chorus has never been better."

Michael had rolled his eyes.

"You want to talk to himself? I think he's half-awake. . . . Hey, lover, your old fella is on the line."

"Dad?"

"Sorry to disturb your sleep, Vincent."

"I was mostly awake, Dad. Time to get up anyway."

"I'm having a press conference this morning to announce our response to WorldCorp. I thought I'd fill you in before the fact."

"Great!"

So easy was it to please this bright and able young man.

"They've issued a denial."

"They would. Do you believe them?"

"Hardly. It's merely a preparation for a redeployment out of the battlefield, if they decide they can't win."

"Figures."

"I suppose the *L.A. Times* had an account of the rumors we unleashed yesterday?"

"Pretty garbled, but I thought I saw your hand in them. Sounds like fun."

"I'm sorry that I didn't get in touch with you before now."

"Hey, Dad, not to worry. You had a few things on your mind yesterday and last night."

Neenan outlined the strategy.

"You're serious about the two new ventures?"

"I'm serious about taking a much more serious look at them than we have before."

"I think they're great ideas."

You'd better think that, kid, because you're going to have charge of them.

"If our preliminary analysis shows by the end of next week that they'll fly, I'd be inclined to move to the pilot-project level, regardless of what WorldCorp ends up doing."

"What's to lose?"

"At this point, as far as I can see, not much."

"And a lot of potential gain. . . . The opera was a great success last night?"

"As your good wife might say, like totally super!"

Vincent laughed heartily. "Speaking of good wives, yours looked scrumptious in that photo."

"Funny thing, I thought so too. Positively angelic."

Michael had smirked.

"We'll see you both at supper on Monday?"

"Yes. She's giving me some golf lessons down on Captiva over the weekend. I think she might have eliminated my slice."

"Thanks for calling me, Dad. I totally appreciate it."

"Only sorry it was so late."

"Enjoy the golf, Dad."

Now what did he mean by that?

It was pretty obvious, wasn't it?

"Thanks," Neenan had said to Michael.

"Don't mention it. We have our uses, don't we?"

"I'd never deny that."

"Noticed that you went to church this morning."

"Another bad habit."

When Neenan finished his brief opening statement at the press conference, almost every hand in the room went up. This was the part he hated. The vultures could twist everything he said out of context and make him say what he had not said. Moreover, under pressure he could flub an answer and set off a firestorm of controversy. Even presidents did that. Some of the vultures even worked for him, but that did not make any difference.

"R. A., what's the point in another news network? Don't we have enough already?"

"I'm glad you asked that question, as a CEO of a much higher rank than mine might say. The concept behind Amnews is that it would focus entirely on news and features that are American and would be reported by local newspeople. This country stretches three thousand miles across a continent. It has many distinctive regions and subcultures. We don't know much about the other subcultures, except for the stereotypes. I think it would be fascinating to have reports from inside them."

"R. A., do you think that the local newspeople around the country are capable of doing national news?"

A booby trap!

"I think there's a lot of talent out there and a lot of ambition. I also think that men and women who have been reporting, let us say, Oklahoma news for years might understand that state a little better than brief visitors from the Beltway or Midtown — or Lake Forest, as far as that goes."

"Why another network?"

"There are a lot of TV outlets who are not affiliated with one of the four major networks, including some we own. Our investigations lead us to believe that there is a real possibility that many if not most of these stations would be interested in Amnet, or perhaps AMN, especially if it offered a richer, family-oriented service as opposed to sex and violence, which seem to obsess certain other networks, whose names I won't mention."

Laughter.

"This would be a somewhat more complicated task, but we would probably proceed incrementally by starting with a small number of network-programmed hours and increasing them each year."

"Are you going to try for NFL football, R. A.?"

"Why not? If we go ahead with AMN, we are prepared to try for anything and everything. I think everyone here at NE would welcome the challenge and excitement of filling two previously unperceived niches in the American entertainment industry."

"Are these nothing more than ploys to fend off WorldCorp?"

"We don't need ploys."

"You own a controlling interest in NE, don't you?"

"That's what my lawyers tell me."

"So no proxy battle is likely?"

"I don't see how there could be."

"How high would WorldCorp have to go to buy your control in NE?"

"NE is not for sale at any price."

"Not at twice market value?"

"Not at ten times market value."

The questions went on; Neenan handled them deftly, surprising himself at his control over his anger. The boss seraph nodded occasionally in approval. Finally the PR person called a halt.

"Thank you, Mr. Neenan."

Wearily, he retreated to his suite.

"Ms. Jardine, hold the calls . . . please."

"Certainly, Mr. Neenan."

That was like thirty-six holes of golf, he thought. I'm exhausted. Am I getting sick or coming down with something? Is this the beginning of a fatal illness?

"Michael?" he said, looking around. "Where the hell are you? Why aren't you here when I need to ask you a question?"

Instead of Michael, Gaby appeared in a perfectly fitting and perfectly pressed dark gray business suit.

"Something wrong?" she asked sweetly.

"Where's Michael?"

"He's temporarily engaged elsewhere. He asked me to take charge of you for a while. What's the matter?"

"I'm exhausted."

"Too much sex?" she asked with a sly smile.

"I don't think so. . . . Do you know whether I'm supposed to die from a fatal disease?"

"We have not been told."

"Maybe I should see a doctor?"

"Let me check you out?"

She put her hand on Neenan's forehead and gazed into his eyes, a deep and prolonged probe. It was an intensely soothing experience, like taking a strong dose of Valium.

"Nope, you check out fine. Nothing wrong with you except nervous exhaustion from the various excitements of the last few days. Especially that press conference. You will need those two days off. They should relax you."

She withdrew her hand from his forehead.

"Do you honestly think I will ever be able to relax again in this life?"

She pondered that question for a moment.

"I can understand why you would not, though I think it will grow easier as you gradually let go and trust us—and of course the Other."

"You expect me to let go of Anna Maria?"

She laughed softly. "Have we ever said that?"

"I certainly won't let her go!"

"You'd better not! . . . You will be separated for a time, Ray, but even then you won't ever let each other go, and then you will be together forever, more deeply in love than you were last night."

"Are you sure?"

"As sure as I am that I will meet my first companion again."

"That's only because this Other entity—"

"Person. Most definitely a person."

"—has told you so."

"We have every reason to trust the Other. She is often tricky, but that comes with the job," Gaby said, shrugging her wonderful shoulders. "She is never dishonest."

"Tell me more about the Other."

"What is to tell? You know us to be creatures of great knowledge and deep love, do you not?"

"Yes." It was obvious enough, though, that he had not thought of them that way before.

"Compared to the Other, our light is darkness, our knowledge is ignorance, our love is unreliable."

"A great and overwhelming force?"

"Perhaps that too, but we experience as your kind does—a tender lover, for me not unlike my Michael and for you not unlike your Anna Maria. Note my words: I do not say 'like' because that might be blasphemous. I merely said 'not unlike.' "

"And you're His . . . Her messengers?"

Gaby smiled affectionately. "Are you planning on doing a TV program on us, Ray?"

"It would be a good idea, but I don't think you'd cooperate and I'll be dead anyway."

She winced in pain and her eyes filled with tears. "To answer your questions, the word *angel* is the translation of our name in Hebrew—Malek. We are the Malek Yahweh, the messengers of the Lord. That only refers to one of our tasks. We call ourselves merely 'people.' "

Like the Inuit. "Are you, ah, in contact with the Light Bearer?"

"In a certain sense we feel him very close to us. He is always near."

"So there's an angel heaven where there are millions of you distinct from your own world."

"Something like that except that there are certainly not millions. There have never been many of us. We're a very small species."

"What do you do with your spare time?"

"You must not look at me with so much desire. We are different species and you already have a satisfying companion of your own species."

"Sorry, I was just thinking how beautiful you are."

"If I should take off my clothes?"

"Er, well, I mean . . ."

"Do not turn red with embarrassment, Ray. I am merely joking with you. Michael has already told you that we are vain beings, not that we don't have much to be vain about."

"I repeat the question: What do you people do when you're not out on assignment?"

"We like the work which the Other gives us, but to tell the truth we are very lazy creatures. What we like to do most is to sit around and talk and sing and tell stories and argue and engage in athletic games—and of course love. Very decadent lifestyle by your human standards, but it is our way."

She was telling him a lot. It was probably part of their plan.

"Do you just patrol our world, earth I mean?"

She laughed and then quickly apologized. "I'm sorry, Ray, for laughing, but you humans are so terracentric. The correct answer is that we are responsible for this cosmos and several others besides, though we have reason to believe that there are other cosmoses about which we know practically nothing."

"So Earth is not all that special?"

She sighed patiently. "Every world that the Other has created is special—that should be evident. To be fair to you humans, we take a special delight in your kind. You really are so much like us. You have a passion for knowledge and love that is not unlike ours. We admire greatly how much your kind has done with the talents you were given."

"Kind of like humans admire smart chimps?"

She chuckled gently. "Certainly not. . . . I must leave you now. The good Amy has many calls that you must answer. First you must call your splendid wife, who has just arrived home, and report on your press conference."

"Thank you for holding my hand and for telling me so much about your kind. I'd much rather deal with you than that Michael fellow."

"I should hope so."

Then she abruptly disappeared.

"One more question?"

She reappeared even more abruptly.

"Why all the changes in clothes?"

"Our clothes?"

"Yes."

"You know that we are very vain. I wore this suit partly to show off, partly because it fits your office, and partly because we also have our world of business where we engage in activities not unlike your business, though far more interesting. It is fitting that I appear in my business garb."

She disappeared again.

Uh-huh, Neenan thought to himself. They tell you a lot and they tell you nothing. Jealous of their private lives.

Or maybe afraid that we'd be terrified if we knew what they did with their time.

I'd sooner have a mother angel than a father angel.

Somehow that thought seemed filled with profound meaning that he could not comprehend.

"Amy, would you please get my wife on the line? Then I'll take the calls. Thank you."

"How did it go, Raymond?" Anna Maria said as she picked up the phone. "I've been praying for you."

"I need the prayers. . . . It seemed to go well. Our media people were pleased. They say that our ideas are appealing. Heaven knows how the reporters and the news editors will play it."

"I'm sure you were wonderful. . . . And, Raymond?"

"Yes?"

"I love you—wildly, desperately, passionately!"

"I've noticed!"

"And?"

"Um, I reciprocate in kind."

"I worry about you," she said, suddenly sad.

"I worry about you too. But neither of us should worry. God will take care of both of us, one way or another."

"I know that."

Who am I, he asked himself, after a day in the state of grace, to be talking about God to her?

Then he took the calls. Most of them were calling about the press conference. They thought he had pretty well scared WorldCorp off. He wished he could be so sure.

Then he ate a salad from the firm's dining room, called Vincent and left a voice mail for him about the press conference, and went over to the club for a swim. Tired or not, he needed the exercise.

On the way back, he turned right on Madison Street and walked by St. Peter's.

I was here yesterday. I went to St. Pat's today to see how they have rehabilitated it. I don't want to become a religious fanatic. I'm not going in.

However, he did enter the church and lit two votive candles, one for him and one for Anna Maria.

You'll get tired of me showing up here. I know even less about who I am than I did this morning. I have been run ragged. Or maybe I have run myself ragged. I still feel I am being torn apart or maybe tearing myself apart. I feel like I am a beach swept away by a storm. Maybe I'll never know who I am. Maybe I am being eroded away as I prepare for death. Maybe none of that matters.

However, I stopped by to thank You for Your goodness, whoever or whatever You are, for sending Your angels and one special human to take care of me. I don't deserve such affection, but I am sure going to sop it up.

After he had left the church, he was astonished at what he had said. The seraphs had brainwashed him!

⟎17⟐

ANCHORPERSON: Mr. Neenan, we hear that you could probably make three times the value of your present holdings in National Entertainment if you sold your interest to WorldCorp. Is that correct?

NEENAN: More than that most likely.

ANCHORPERSON: Do you think your stock is worth that kind of money?

NEENAN: It seems that they estimate that to be a fair market price for NE's worth to them.

ANCHORPERSON: And you expect us to believe that you're not going to sell?

NEENAN: I don't know whether you will believe it or not. I know only that I will not sell.

ANCHORPERSON: Do you mind telling us why not?

NEENAN: No, I don't mind at all. Why did coach Gary Barnett refuse to go to Notre Dame?

ANCHORPERSON: Because he didn't want to go there.

NEENAN: Same thing. I don't want to sell. I like being CEO of National Entertainment.

(Michael, dressed now in a navy blazer and gray slacks, but not wearing a tie, is seated at the anchor desk. The anchorperson cannot see him. Intermittently, Gaby flits in and out of sight. She's wearing a gray sweater and jeans. They both nod vigorous approval of Neenan's responses. Since TV cameras cannot pick up angel surrogates, it is reasonable to assume that no one in the watching audience can see them. Still, you never can tell about seraphs.)

ANCHORPERSON: Would you not continue in that role according to rumors about the offer?

NEENAN: (dismissively) Figurehead.

ANCHORPERSON: You don't want the money?

NEENAN: What would I do with it?

ANCHORPERSON: You think you have enough money already.

NEENAN: What's enough? Money you can't take with you.

ANCHORPERSON: What can you take with you?

(Michael and Gaby frown, fearful that Neenan will spill the beans.)

NEENAN: Self-respect, some shreds of integrity, a sense that you didn't betray your colleagues.

(The seraphs relax.)

ANCHORPERSON: Have you always felt this way?

NEENAN: I don't think so. I experienced a very rough airplane flight recently and I had to make explicit some of the assumptions that have been influential in my life. The prime one is a gut feeling that you don't let down people from your neighborhood—like Marty Scorsese said in *Mean Streets*.

ANCHORPERSON: I don't believe I saw that film.

NEENAN: Probably too young.

ANCHORPERSON: And you intend to go ahead with your news channel—AMN as you call it?

NEENAN: We're doing intensive studies of that venture at the present. We expect to have a decision by the end of next week.

ANCHORPERSON: You believe that this news channel will eliminate the need for programs like this?

NEENAN: I'm sure that it won't.

ANCHORPERSON: Thank you, Mr. Neenan. . . . We have just talked to Mr. Raymond Anthony Neenan, chairman, president, and CEO of National Entertainment. He vigorously denied that his corporation is for sale, no matter how many hundreds of millions of dollars he might make on such a deal. He also insisted that his company intends to continue with their new project of a twenty-four-hour news station which will concentrate on regional news from all around the country. This channel could well revolutionize coverage of news in this country.

NEENAN: One more word, ma'am?

ANCHORPERSON: We're running out of time.

NEENAN: *(genially)* I'm chairperson of NE, not chairman.

(Scene dissolves into a commerical. Michael and Gaby exchange high fives with each other and with Neenan. The choristers, their days off apparently over, sing something that sounds very much like a hosanna.)

18

Both Neenan and his wife were in a sleepy, grumpy mode when they woke up late.

"We'll miss the plane, Raymond."

"It's my plane. We can't miss it."

"A lot you know."

They stumbled and bumbled though their showers and dressing and last-minute packing. Wisely they stayed out of each other's way.

"There's rain and fog, Raymond," she protested as she pulled a Loyola sweatshirt over her head. "Surely we are not going to fly today."

"The pilot says there'll be no trouble."

"A lot he knows," she said with a derisive sniff as she drew on her jeans. "What if we crash?"

That was a possibility that he had not considered: the two of them might die at the same time. Not very likely, however. "Then we both go to heaven together."

"Hmmf."

He had never seen this aspect of Anna Maria's character before. So she had moods? Perhaps he had never noticed because he had never lived so intimately with her.

Maeve, believing that they both drank too much coffee, had prepared two thermos jugs of hot chocolate for them and two bags of her best cinnamon-raisin rolls.

"That woman," Anna Maria complained, "will never give up on her anticaffeine crusade."

Anna Maria sat on the backseat of the car as far away as possible from Neenan as she could be and still be in the same car. Thus he had to reach long when he nudged her.

"Sorry, Peter," she said contritely to the driver, whose plastic separator from the back of the car had not been closed.

"Not at all, ma'am," he replied cheerfully. "Haven't I been telling her that for years?"

"The hot chocolate is wonderful," Anna Maria said, trying to make up for her gaffe.

"Isn't it always? . . . I tell her that chocolate is as addictive as caffeine. Doesn't she say that it's good for your heart?"

"Especially, Peter," Anna Maria responded, "if you drink it with red wine."

"Sicilian red wine," Neenan said softly.

They all laughed. Peter closed the screen between the back and the front seat. Anna Maria reached over and took Neenan's hand.

"Sorry, love," she said softly. "Really sorry. Now you know what a bitch I can be when I wake up late in the morning. It's one of the risks of our sharing the same bed."

"I'll gladly take that risk."

Somehow she had managed to move next to him and lean on his shoulder. "I promise I won't be this way in Florida."

"I'd worry about improving my golf game if you are."

"We can't permit anything to interfere with that, can we?"

He put his arm around her. "No way."

"I have a rotten Sicilian temper. I'm sorry."

"I wasn't exactly lively this morning either."

"This last week has been wonderful, Raymond," she said, snuggling closer to him. "It has also been very difficult."

"I'm sorry," he said, wondering to himself where all his patience and sensitivity had come from and feeling once again as if he were disintegrating, melting as the fog would when the sun's heat burned it away.

"It's not your fault," she said, patting his arm. "I like you much better this new way, though I'm not sure about this airplane ride explanation. But I have to study you very carefully, so I can understand what to expect from you, almost as though you were a different person. That's hard work."

Neenan pondered her words. He had not believed that his explanation had persuaded her. Now he knew it hadn't.

"It's fun too," she continued. "I don't mind it, except sometimes I get a little stressed." She slipped her hand under his sweater and caressed his belly.

"Do you plan to seduce me on the plane?"

"I kind of wish that cabin attendant wasn't with us, even if she is a nice young woman who needs the job. So I guess I'll have to wait till we arrive in Captiva."

"You know what I'm thinking?" he asked. "I'm remembering that, when I was at DeKalb and didn't have a car, I had to ride in on Greyhound to Chicago. I hated the trip so much I almost gave up on Chicago. It will take me less time to fly to Florida."

"That means you're a success?"

"No, that isn't what I was trying to say. It means only that my life has changed, though perhaps it really hasn't. Though I can get to the airport at Fort Myers quicker, I don't know that I'm better off. I go to Captiva much less often than I used to ride into Chicago."

"We'll have to go there more often in the years ahead," she said as her fingers rested lightly on his stomach.

"That's for sure."

That exchange made him feel sad. This would almost certainly be his last trip to Florida. How much more time he might have spent there with his wife, enjoying both the town house and her. Yet he had wasted the opportunity, just as he had wasted so many other opportunities.

So I must enjoy this one as best I can to make up for all I've missed.

He sighed, felt sorry for himself, and then ate another of Maeve's cinnamon-raisin buns.

"More hot chocolate?"

"Why not?" he said.

He had never, come to think of it, enjoyed hot chocolate or cinnamon buns enough.

The rain and the mists were thick at Palwaukee airport.

"The planes are landing and taking off on time from O'Hare," the pilot of the G-5 said to him. "Ceiling and visibility are notably above the minimum. It clears off at two thousand feet. Your call, Mr. Neenan."

"Anna Maria?"

"If we crash we'll all go to heaven together," she said with a brave laugh.

"You sure?"

"Certainly! Let's get on the plane. I'm sure Linda has come with coffee for us."

Linda was the name of the cabin attendant. He could never remember. Trust Anna Maria to remember.

"I'll bring the rolls along," he said.

"You better. The crew will like some too. Also some of Maeve's hot chocolate."

Peter and the pilot and the copilot helped them to load their baggage and golf clubs into the plane.

"You packed light for us," Neenan told his wife. "I hope you didn't forget swimsuits."

"Certainly not. I packed two."

Then she whispered in his ear, "Both for me, none for you."

"Why not?" he asked as he felt his face turn hot.

"You won't need one."

They took off without delay. Anna Maria clung to his hand until they broke through the clouds.

"That's much better," she informed him, "sunlight and blue sky. Almost in Florida already. . . . No thanks, Linda, enough coffee for now. I intend to catch up on my sleep."

She curled up on her plush seat that Grumman provided for moguls and their wives and promptly went to sleep.

Neenan took a stack of reports out of his briefcase and began to study them.

Michael appeared in the empty seat ahead across from his and smiled benignly.

"You're coming with us?" Neenan asked as he took off his reading glasses.

"We like weekends in Florida," the seraph replied with a mischievous grin. "Did you think we were about to let you face your parents without our supervision?"

"I'm almost happy you will be there."

Michael was wearing a white ensemble, suit, shirt, tie, shoes, socks, and homburg. He looked a little like pictures Neenan had seen of high-ranking voodoo priests.

"Aren't you afraid she'll hear you?"

"Nope, she's a sound sleeper."

"She said she was suspicious about my pretext for changing."

"I heard. She did not ask for an explanation, however. So don't worry about it till she does, which I don't think she will."

"I'm sad. My last trip to Florida."

"Should have enjoyed it long ago," Michael replied without a touch of sympathy. "Thank the Other that you at least will enjoy this one . . . if you don't blow it."

"Yeah," said Neenan sourly.

Gaby materialized next to her companion. She was wearing white shorts and a red tank top and was devastatingly attractive.

"I want to know," Neenan told her, "whether you look as gorgeous in your real form."

She blushed and laughed. "This fellow is very fresh, Michael."

"The straight answer," said the boss seraph, "is that she is much more beautiful."

Gaby dissolved into a cloud of multicolored lights that danced and spun and whirled and then filled the whole cabin of the plane, before bursting through the fuselage and escaping into the sky.

It was the most beautiful vision Neenan had ever seen. As it grew ever brighter, he had to close his eyes against the blinding radiance of the light.

"Small hint," she said calmly.

He opened his eyes. The striking woman with the gray hair and the youthful face and luscious body was sitting across from him again.

"Can I get away, boss seraph, with saying that I am dazzled, but I like her better this way?"

"You'd better say that," Michael said, "or you would be in the deepest of deep trouble. . . . Now, about your parents . . ."

"What about my parents?"

Michael kicked off his shoes and relaxed in his seat. Gaby picked up the latest issue of *U.S. News and World Report* and began to thumb through it. Could there be anything there that she didn't already know?

"It is very easy to hate those who have given us life but have not given us the freedom to be ourselves instead of what they wanted us to be, is it not?"

"I suppose so."

"It is much more difficult to stop feeling residual attachment to them, a feeling that might even be called love, though love contorted by powerful ambivalence, is it not?"

"I would not deny that either, though I have never looked at it that way."

"One of the reasons for our being here," Gaby said, not looking up from her magazine, "is to suggest that you look at the obvious from a slightly different perspective. . . . Incidentally, put those papers back in your briefcase. You ought to be ashamed of yourself for bringing them along. That's contemptuous of the lovely woman we have given you."

He wanted to argue that no one had given Anna Maria to him and that he had rather won her himself. It would have been a losing argument.

"Yes, ma'am," he said, complying with her instructions and putting the reports away.

"To return to your parents: they are elderly now and very angry. They feel they have been dealt an unfair hand."

"I've bought them a home, provided them with servants, made their days better than they possibly could have been . . ."

Michael held up his hand.

"I understand these things. They are, however, irrelevant. Your mother and father are angry at what life has done to them. They are unforgiving. They blame each other and you for what has happened to them, instead of assuming, each of them, their own personal responsibility. They are too old to change. You must therefore not expect gratitude, much less love. Do not enter their apartment with any expectations that you will be able to resolve anything, because, I assure you, that you will not. All that matters is your own willingness to put aside your resentments and forgive them, despite how they behave."

"That's asking a lot."

"That's asking for the bare minimum."

"I understand," Neenan said with a sigh.

"You must also understand that while you are the occasion of the anger and to some extent its target, they are really angry at themselves and one another."

Gaby produced from somewhere a notebook computer, flipped it open, and began to type. In the meantime, the choir manifested itself again and returned to some of its favorite lullabies. Michael glanced up and frowned.

"Let them sing," Gaby said, her eyes still glued to the screen. "They adore the human woman and want to sing for her. The song will make her sleep more peacefully. She needs the sleep."

Michael shrugged as if he knew that he had lost the argument before it started.

"They sing very well," Neenan said.

Gaby smiled and nodded, but did not take her eyes off the monitor.

Neenan noted that the computer seemed both smaller and far more advanced than any machine he'd ever seen. Still, why did they need it? Or was it merely part of the act?

"Your challenge, Raymond Anthony," the male seraph continued implacably, "is to respond to them with charm and grace, no matter what they say and no matter how angry they are. You gotta problem with that?"

"Yes, I have a problem with that, but I'll try."

"You must do more than try."

"The lovely one is waking, Michael," his companion said firmly. "It is necessary for us to appear to take our leave. The offspring may continue to sing, but very softly so that she is not aware that she is hearing them."

"OK," the alleged boss seraph agreed.

Gaby stood up, touched Anna Maria's face with her fingers, and then kissed her on the forehead. Anna Maria smiled contentedly.

Then Gaby kissed Neenan's forehead and filled him with warmth and peace.

Both seraphs then dematerialized. Where they had been, there was nothing. Neenan was not at all sure, however, that they were not still on the plane.

Anna Maria opened her eyes, glanced around as she tried to figure out where she was. Then her eyes found him.

"Who are you, strange man?" she said.

"One of your worshipers."

"That's what they all say," she said as she stretched. "I think I'll change my clothes so I'll be ready for Florida."

These two angels, if that was what they really were, had become substitute parents for him. They were the kind of parents that he had always wished he had. Undoubtedly they knew that. But, he thought, grinning to himself, they didn't know that he knew. He was one up on them again, just as he had been when he had figured out that Anna Maria could see them, before they did.

They were pretty good parents. This seraphic mother could kiss his forehead anytime she wanted.

Anna Maria emerged from the other room. "Florida clothes. We Sicilians like warm weather."

She was wearing terry-cloth shorts, held together by a drawstring, and a cropped tank top and an unbuttoned white shirt.

"I don't think you'd dare wear that outfit in Sicily," he said approvingly.

"I'm not in Sicily."

"True . . . What if it's not warm?"

"High today in Fort Myers," she said, reclining in her chair, "will be in the mid-eighties—and through the weekend. This was a good idea of mine. How far are we from Tampa?"

"Half hour out of St. Petersburg; we'll land at the airfield by the bay."

She hesitated. "If you want me to come with you, I'll change into something more appropriate."

"I would like to have you along as a reinforcement; yet I'd better try to do it by myself. It's my problem, not yours."

"I'd probably make things worse anyway."

"If you did, it wouldn't be your fault. My parents are acutely unhappy people. Always have been. They look for people to blame instead of assuming personal responsibility. Most of us do the same thing, but not with such intensity."

"How did you ever survive, love?" She leaned across the aisle and kissed his forehead just as Gaby had done. Once more Neenan was filled with peace and reassurance and warmth.

"Thank you . . . I'm not sure that I have."

"You have to straighten everything out, don't you? Like you think you're going to die?"

"I'm afraid they're not going to last much longer. It's probably now or never with them."

She didn't contest his evasion, but it did not follow that he had convinced her. Whenever the end came, she would look back and understand.

That thought saddened him, more this time for her loss than his.

"They've been unhappy all their lives?"

"As long as I've known them. They had to get married, you know. I'm sure they did not want to and blamed each other for what happened. It was probably hate from day one."

"She was pregnant?"

"Yes."

"With you?"

"Who else?"

Anna Maria sighed. "No wonder they are angry at you, even if you were the innocent."

"I think Mom wanted me to be a priest so I would atone for their sin."

"Do you think it was sinful?"

"Young people in wartime when the man is home for his final leave and both their bodies are stewing with hormones? I won't throw the first stone."

Anna Maria nodded, but with a puzzled frown.

I would never have said that before, Neenan thought. I'm changing too fast to keep up with myself. I'm breaking up, just like this jet would break up if it crashed into the bay.

"Fasten your seat belts please," the captain announced. "We'll be landing at St. Petersburg shortly. The temperature is seventy-eight degrees. The high is expected to be in the middle eighties this afternoon."

They flew in off the Gulf, over St. Petersburg, which glittered in the clear sunlight, circled above the azure bay, and then descended toward the bayside airport. Anna Maria clutched his hand.

"I love you," she said.

"Even after a safe landing?"

"More then."

The plane landed smoothly and taxied to the small terminal. A stretch Cadillac limo waited for them in front of the terminal. Anna Maria released his hand.

"Can I walk along the bayside?" she asked as she buttoned her shirt.

"Sure. Turn left and you'll walk down to the St. Petersburg campus of the University of South Florida. There's a nice marina there too."

"How long will you be?"

"I don't know. Probably less than an hour. Their apartment is only ten minutes from here."

She kissed him briefly on his lips. "Good luck."

"I'll need every bit of it. . . . Don't forget to put on some suntan lotion. The sunlight is intense."

"Sicilians don't sunburn. . . . Don't look so serious. Of course, I'll put on suntan cream. It's too bad you won't be here to do it for me."

The limo driver had turned on the air-conditioning. The car was cool and relaxing. Neenan, however, became more tense with each succeeding moment.

His parents' condo was in a tall building facing the bay, with a spectacular view of the bay, the bridges, downtown St. Petersburg, and Tampa in the distance. It was probably the most expensive dwelling place in the city. They hated everything about it.

The doorman rang them for almost a minute before anyone answered.

"Mr. Neenan, your son, to see you, Mrs. Neenan."

The doorman turned to Neenan and said, "Your mother is very forgetful, Mr. Neenan. She says she doesn't have a son. I believe your father has pushed the buzzer, however, so you can go right up."

"Great beginning," he whispered to himself in the elevator.

He knocked repeatedly at the door. Finally, his father, a small man, gray and grizzled and wearing wrinkled tan slacks and a tattered, plain white T-shirt, opened the door.

"What do you want?" he snarled.

"I was in the area and thought I'd stop in to say hello."

"You did, eh? What made you think we'd want to see you?"

Despite the hostility, his father stepped aside to permit him to enter. The apartment was permeated by a foul smell and a mess — newspapers, potato-chip and popcorn bags. An elderly Cuban woman came in every day to clean and cook for them, but apparently she could not stay ahead of the mess. The forty-five-inch television he had bought for them was blaring, but the picture was blurred.

"Look who's here," his father said to the woman who was crouched low in a chair by the window, staring, malignly Neenan thought, at the bay.

Where the hell are my seraphs? I thought they'd be in the car with me.

"Who's that?" the bent old woman said with total disinterest.

"Says he's our son, pays the bills here in this dump, so maybe he's your son anyway."

"The only son I had was a priest and he's dead now."

She began to wail softly, a tuneless cry of grief and despair.

"Shut up, old woman," his father ordered. "You're as crazy as a loon. . . . Well, what do you want?"

Uninvited, Neenan sat down.

Michael and Gaby materialized, apparently through the window overlooking the bay. Gaby put her arm around his mother. Gradually the wailing ceased.

" 'Bout time that old fool shut up," his father snarled, sinking into a dirty easy chair. "Someday I'm going to strangle her and throw her out that window. . . . Now, what do you want?"

Michael touched the TV and the picture—of a daytime soap—went into instant focus. He touched it again and the volume diminished to a whisper. Neither his father nor his mother noticed the change.

Michael—now in white shorts and a black T-shirt that announced in golden letters "Seraphic Vineyards"—sat on the windowsill. The smell that had permeated the apartment yielded to a flower-garden aroma.

Show-offs.

"I wanted to see how you were doing."

"How the hell do you think we're doing? Aren't we locked up in this ugly dump? Doesn't that bossy nigger you hired to keep an eye on us try to run our lives? Isn't the food terrible? Aren't the neighbors bums? With all the money you have you could have done better by us, especially since you euchred us out of all our money."

Euchre was his father's favorite word. Gaby bounced out to the kitchen.

"This is the best condo in St. Petersburg, Dad," Neenan tried to respond.

"It's pure shit and you know it."

Gaby returned with a bottle of white wine, Seraphic Vineyards chenin blanc, according to the label, and three glasses. She poured a generous portion of the wine into each glass and gave one to him and one to her companion. Then she resumed her place at his mother's feet, put her arm around her, and began to sip from her own glass.

"I can move you somewhere else, Dad."

"Into worse shit. . . . I know you came here to lord it over us again. You want to rub it in that you euchred me out of my business. If I wasn't saddled with a crooked son, who really wasn't my son at all, I'd be richer than you are."

In fact, his father lacked all the abilities that would have been required to move beyond his small station and his little machine shop. But his conviction that he had been cheated by his son was unshakable.

"I've been wondering whether we could forget the past and try to be friends again," Neenan said, trying to get down to business.

"Again?" his father sneered. "When were we ever friends? I tried to be a good father to you, even though one look at you was enough to see that you were no son of mine. You hated me before you could talk."

Neenan sipped the wine. It was pure delight. If he could import enough Seraphic Vineyards, he would double his holdings. Shouldn't be thinking about such things.

"I don't think that's true, Dad. But that's all behind us. I'd like to forget the past and try to be friends in the present."

Michael was watching Neenan intently, doubtless waiting to see if he'd lose his temper.

"I ought to throw you and that whore who deceived me out that window right now."

"Would that make you happy, Dad?"

"It would make me the happiest man in the world. I'd get even with you for euchring me out of my fortune."

His father struggled to rise from his chair, then sank back into it.

"You goddamn son of a bitch," the old man snarled.

"Would you like a glass of wine, Dad?"

"If you got any, that shit-faced nigger won't let us have any."

Gaby cocked an eye in Neenan's direction and smiled.

"She's Cuban, Dad."

"A nigger is a nigger. This one sticks pins in little dolls."

From somewhere, the womanly seraph produced a fourth wineglass and filled it with the remains of the chenin blanc.

"She's a registered nurse."

"Registered witch doctor, if you ask me."

The wineglass appeared in his father's hand. Gingerly he sipped. Then he spat it out in disgust.

"You trying to poison me with this goddamn cow piss?"

"I'm sorry, Dad. It's the best chenin blanc in the world."

"I said that it's cow piss, and cow piss it is. I wouldn't put it past you to try to kill us. Someday someone's going to investigate you and give us all our money back. You'll go to jail where you belong. I'll have the last laugh."

The wineglass disappeared from his father's hand. Michael watched implacably.

"How much money do you want, Dad?"

"Every fucking penny, every cent you got, all the property and the stations and whatever else, every bit of it. Then maybe I won't tell the truth to the reporters when they come around."

"Is there nothing I can do to persuade you to forgive me?"

"*Forgive* you? Why the hell should I forgive you, asshole? I won't be happy till I see you rotting in jail where you belong. I wouldn't forgive you to save my immortal soul!"

Neenan winced. Michael looked somber. Gaby shifted from her position next to Mom and reached her arm around Neenan's father.

"Those are pretty strong words, Dad."

"I thought that after the war was over, I'd come home and have a great life. Build my machine shop into a chain, turn my station into a big network, make a lot of money, marry a good woman who liked sex, and have a bunch of nice, respectful kids. Instead, look what happened. That crazy old coot seduced me and then tricked me into thinking you were my son. I never had a happy day since then . . . I hope both of you rot in hell!"

Gaby's embrace had no effect on his father. She returned to his mother, who had begun to wail again, and soothed her.

Neenan glanced at the boss seraph. Michael shrugged his broad shoulders.

"Enough?"

"One more try," Michael replied, *"then we're out of here."*

"I'm sorry, Dad, truly sorry. I wish you would find it in your heart to reconcile with me."

"Get the fuck out of my house."

Anger swelled inside Neenan. It was after all his house. This man was old and bitter, but he was not crazy. He knew what he was saying. He had deliberately said and done everything he could to hurt and offend his son. Words surged to Neenan's lips to give it back to him in kind, to tell him that he was a miserable failure who would have lost his radio station anyway and for a lot less money than Neenan had insisted he be given.

With an enormous effort, he stifled his anger.

"Don't ever come back here again," his father said, rising unsteadily to his feet. "And I hope that cheap little dago slut you go around with sticks a knife in your gut some one of these nights after you've fucked her."

Neenan stood stone still, his face hot with anger, his heart pumping, his fists clenched. The seraphs watched, anxiously it seemed.

"Good-bye, Dad."

Neenan went over to the window and kissed his mother on the forehead.

"Good-bye, Mom."

He left the apartment abruptly, this time the angels trailing him.

In the elevator, he said to Michael, "Do you happen to know whether I'm really his son?"

"Of course we know and of course you are. You're the spitting image of his father."

"I see," Neenan said, and slumped against the elevator wall.

"You did pretty good," Michael admitted grudgingly. "Almost lost it a couple of times, but didn't."

"Can't you two do anything for either of them?"

"You saw how he turned me off," Gaby replied. "Most humans don't do that. I'm a pretty soothing being when I want to be."

"We can help her, calm her down" Michael admitted. One or the other of us will stop by occasionally and do that."

"She'll be at peace for a while, Ray," Gaby added.

"If she weren't out of it, she'd be as bad as he is."

"Nowhere near as bad," Michael replied. "Nowhere near. She didn't ruin his life. He ruined hers. There's not much we can do for him, I'm afraid. He's the Other's problem now. The Other dislikes losing even more than we do."

Neenan felt as if the elevator were plunging out of control toward the ground. He was being spun off into tiny pieces by a centrifugal force that was tearing apart what little was left of his selfhood.

He felt Gaby's arm around him.

"You all right?" Michael said with apparent sincere concern.

The elevator landed safely and Neenan staggered out into the lobby, supported by the woman seraph's strong arm. He had enough presence of mind to give the doorman two twenty-dollar bills and thank him for taking care of his parents.

The angels helped him into his limo and arranged themselves one on either side of him.

"What happened to you?" Michael demanded.

"I saw it all. Everything!"

"What did you see?"

"That I went after all those women who were like my mother to take them away from my father."

The seraphs exchanged high fives.

"You're not so bad after all," Michael observed.

"We've saved you a lot of money and a lot of time on therapy," Gaby informed him.

"The time I don't have," he said, tears welling up in his eyes. "I wish I had figured it out a long time ago."

"Better late than never," Michael said philosophically.

Neenan leaned into Gaby's peaceful embrace and wept bitter tears of frustration and rage.

"We'd better get you back into Anna Maria's arms," she said.

Then, quite suddenly, they were at St. Petersburg Municipal Airport, his tears had stopped, and his wife embraced him tenderly and led him into the plane.

"I need a drink," he murmured to Linda.

"We have some totally excellent white wine on board today, Mr. Neenan. Would you like some?"

"I sure would."

He assumed that it would be the Seraphic chenin blanc. It totally was.

"It must have been terrible, Raymond," Anna Maria said as they finished the wine just before the plane had taxied into a takeoff position. "You look like you've been kicked in the stomach."

He sighed and tried to pull himself together. In a world with so many good things, such as a woman's love and delicious white wine and even concerned seraphs to take care of you, how could there be so much hatred?

Anyway, he had tried.

And not lost his temper.

"He said you were a bastard?" Anna Maria asked. "I mean an illegitimate child?"

"That among other things. . . . And I look just like his own father, whom I suppose he hated too."

So perhaps there was some grace even for Dad, some explanation of why he had become what he was.

"You lose your temper?"

"Nope."

The plane soared above St. Petersburg and then out over the Gulf.

"Bravo!" she said softly.

One advantage of an early death, he told himself, was that he would never have to return to this place.

"Maybe."

Linda refilled his wineglass.

"You want to take a nap, Raymond?"

"Not now. Maybe when we get to the island."

"We can nap and swim and lie in the sun and forget about the golf lessons today."

"And maybe engage in other healing experiences?"

"We'll have to see about that," she said, raising her glass in an admiring salute. "Linda dear, I think we need our lunch. My husband has been drinking a lot of wine."

"Certainly, Ms. Neenan."

"Tomorrow we start the lessons bright and early, do you hear, my love?"

Neenan felt his personhood slowly come back together again.

What an idiot he had been not to have figured all of this out long ago.

19

"Why do Italians always make too much pasta?"

"Sicilians," Anna Maria replied primly. "We're not really Italians at all."

Neenan drank her in with his eyes, every wondrous, lovable inch of her. Even if he had just possessed her, he still wanted her. Never enough, never enough. And so little time. Thank God . . . or Occupant . . . or Whomever . . . that he had straightened out his relationship with her and with Vincent. If he lost either of them, his life would lose all meaning. That would not happen. He would not lose them till he died, which could be almost any day, could it not?

Fear sank its cold, mummy's fingers into his heart. What if he did lose one or the other of them? What if he did something incredibly stupid and drove them both away. He shivered.

"Cold?" Anna Maria asked.

"A draft somewhere."

"It's still seventy; how could there be a draft?"

"So, all right, why do you Sicilians always make too much pasta?"

"Because," she said as she poured her special sauce on the noodles she had already prepared, "we're afraid to take a risk that anyone will leave the table hungry. Besides, we can always warm up what's left over for lunch the next day."

Dressed in T-shirts and shorts, they were in the kitchen of their town house on the Gulf of Mexico. The sliding doors were open all around them, and a soft breeze off the water was caressing them. They had relaxed in the sun, swum till they were exhausted, and then made slow, leisurely, exquisite love. Knowing what he needed, Anna Maria had been a shy, sweet, and deeply sensuous partner.

She is much more perceptive with me than I am with her.

"Stop leering at me that way," she insisted, blushing.

"Can't help it."

"It embarrasses me," she said as she stirred the fettuccine and the sauce.

"Good."

She was a fine one to talk. Her vast brown eyes often caressed him with admiration, even adoration. He didn't deserve it. No other woman had ever looked at him that way.

"I am not," she said firmly, "going to take off my T-shirt while we're eating supper. So stop looking at me like you want me to."

She then scooped the pasta out of the large bowl in which she had stirred it with the sauce and filled both their plates with it.

"I might just take it off anyway."

"Don't even think of that."

He poured the Chianti into their tumblers. Seraphic Vineyards, it turned out, also produced Chianti. Moreover, a couple of dozen bottles of it were stashed in the kitchen. Still showing off. Anna Maria, probably blinded by angel dust, did not seem to notice it or reflect on how unusual it was.

He caught her in flight, kissed her, and explored the wonders beneath her shirt. She did not try to fight him off.

"Dirty man," she sighed.

"Besotted man."

"Same thing."

"Tell you what, you can keep the T-shirt on till dessert."

"You'll have a fight on your hands."

"You can ogle me in the nude and there's nothing wrong with that."

"It's entirely different," she said, sitting in her chair. "Now, if you can dismiss your dirty thoughts for a minute, let's say grace."

"All right."

So they held hands and prayed to the Other to bless them and their food. Neenan added an extra and silent prayer of gratitude for his incredible lover.

"It was bad, wasn't it, Raymond?" she asked as her fingers lingered briefly on his.

"In a way it wasn't as bad as when I was younger. Mom is out of it, so she's not snapping at me and at Dad. It's a two-cornered fight and not a three-cornered one. Still it seemed worse today, maybe because we are all so much older, or maybe because I understand it better now or maybe because I am more aware of how their never-ending war shaped what I am."

"Tell me about it."

So he reported in detail his encounter with his parents, leaving out only the seraphic interventions.

"I don't know how you survived the horror, Raymond," she said when he was finished, her eyes filling with tears.

"I'm not sure that I did."

"That's silly! Of course you did! Or we wouldn't be here and wouldn't love each other so much."

"It took so long . . ."

"It's worth waiting for," she said as she wolfed down a large fork-load of fettucine.

"So much of what I am and what I have done is the result of my fighting with my parents and their fighting with one another. Donna, the kids, the people I work with —"

"You're not to blame for all that," she cut in.

"That's too easy, Anna Maria," Neenan said, misery in his voice. "I knew what I was doing, not completely, sure, but enough to be responsible."

"You knew all along that you were fighting with your father?"

He winced. Naturally she had perceived that long before he did.

"Not exactly. . . . You knew it all along?"

"Certainly, from day one. It seemed like a silly fight. Now I understand that it wasn't."

"I always thought Mom was the problem. Now I know I wanted to take her away from Dad."

She nodded vigorously. "Eat your pasta, it's good for you. You've had a hard day. Lots of exercise."

In the background the angel brats began to hum softly. Their song sounded like variations on "Red Sails in the Sunset."

"That's true."

"Is there anything you can do about your parents now, Raymond?"

"Not much. Continue to take care of them. Visit them occasionally. See that they're taken care of. Try to forgive them. Understand how much they have made me what I am. . . . Incidentally, I am his son, despite his pretense that I am not."

"Of course. You look just like his father in the pictures. I bet that was not a good relationship either. Great big handsome father, pint-sized, ugly son. . . . Do you think you can really forgive them?"

"That's not a problem. They're so sad. I can't be mad at them anymore. I didn't lose my temper today. Almost, but I didn't."

If the seraphic bunch hadn't been there, it might have been a different story.

"You're a very generous man, husband mine. Your story makes me love you even more. . . . Am I imagining it or do I hear music in the background?"

He pretended to listen. Sure, Wife, you hear the angel brats, who are singing too loud. If they were around, the older seraphs were doubtless present. Protect us from all evil, he begged them, don't let me mess up with her.

Aloud he said, "What kind of music?"

"Vocal. Maybe."

"It's probably coming from the house next door. Despite the high walls and the trees, we do have neighbors."

"They can't see us, can they?" she asked in a burst of nervous modesty.

"No way."

"*Well,* I hope *not.*"

She refilled his wine tumbler.

"Good Chianti," he said.

"Astonishing! A lot better than the dago red with which I grew up."

"I'd never use that word."

"We used it."

"That's different. Anyway, you're not a dago, you're a Sicilian."

"True!" she said with a laugh. "Now eat your fettuccine! It's good for you."

He obeyed. What other choice? "It astonishes me how well you have me figured out, especially when I compare it to my dumb perceptions about you."

"Well," she said, shifting in her chair as she prepared to deliver a lecture, "it's not all that difficult. Women are better, nicer, more perceptive, and more sensitive than men, but we have to be because you're stronger and because you have what we want."

"Easy to figure out twelve-year-old boys?"

"Sure. Sometimes twelve-year-old boys can be amusing, so we're careful to understand them. It makes it easier for them to amuse us."

"I don't understand you at all."

"Naturally not, Raymond dear. I'll always be a mystery to you. But that's all right. It makes for fun for both of us. Anyway, you certainly understand me sexually."

"Do I?"

"Do you ever!"

"I did not realize that women could be so . . . so candidly abandoned."

"A lot of us can't. And the rest of us can only when we are with a man we totally trust. A man like you. So keep that in mind the next time you feel worthless."

"I'm a worthless but amusing twelve-year-old who is useful sometimes as a lover."

She threw back her head and laughed, loud and long. "Fair description. Correct 'sometimes' to 'always.' "

"I'm glad."

"And add 'remarkably sensitive—for a man.' "

They had both become giddy, laughing and drinking wine and eating fettuccine and enjoying their own silliness.

She went off to the fridge to dish the ice cream for dessert.

Behind her in the sliding door, Michael appeared in white swim trunks. He nodded in something like approval.

"You've learned a lot today," the seraph said. *"Not enough, but not bad for a human."*

"Promise you'll take care of her after I'm gone."

"I've already promised that. Take care of her while you still are with her. Don't blow it."

"I won't."

"Better not."

"Did I hear voices?" Anna Maria said as she returned to the table with two huge dishes of ice cream.

"Neighbors," he suggested.

"I don't think there's anyone in either house now."

"Passing cars, maybe. We're near the road."

He rose from the table and approached her.

"No!" she squealed, and ran away from him.

She ran into the front room of the house, where he cornered her—only because she wanted to be cornered. She pretended to fight him off, but not even half-seriously.

"Beast! Monster! Brute! Savage!" she bellowed.

But she did not resist the removal of her T-shirt.

"Satisfied?" she said with a sigh.

"Momentarily. It's easier to leer at you this way."

"Hmf!... Let's go eat our ice cream before it gets cold."

"Before it gets cold?"

"See what you've done to me? I can't even think straight—Before it melts, you hungry idiot!"

Nonetheless, she snuggled close to him.

Back at the table, she drew her chair to his side of the table and curled up as she dug into her ice cream.

"You have your choice," she said. "You can ogle me or eat your ice cream."

"I can do both," he said, kissing her lips firmly.

"I see that you can."

"Do you still think I'm not enough of a man to keep up with you?"

"Well, the jury is still out on that. Just because you can make me topless at the supper table doesn't prove all that much."

"You are so beautiful that you take my breath away," he said, realizing it was a cliché and meaning it just the same.

"Thank you, lover." She sighed contentedly. "You'll do until a better one comes along."

She rested her head against his chest so he could fondle her as she ate her ice cream.

"Nice," she cooed. "Totally decadent but nice. . . . No, don't stop doing that!"

He turned to his own ice cream. "I like being decadent."

Then fear of losing her hit him like a tidal wave.

"I hope I didn't offend your modesty," he said cautiously.

"Don't be silly. You might have offended it slightly if you wanted me for the pasta course, but certainly not for dessert."

They finished the ice cream and nestled in one another's arms as the sun sank into the Gulf and the dark clouds of night ran quickly across the sky. Then the clouds followed the setting sun—the three-quarter moon having long since disappeared over the horizon—and a circus canopy of stars illumined the warm darkness.

Having placed their empty ice cream dishes on the floor, they continued to cuddle in each other's arms—happy, content, and deeply in love.

Neenan felt again the tsunami of terror charge through his body. He shivered, this time far too obviously to escape a satisfactory explanation.

"What *is* the matter with you?" his wife demanded. "You've been shivering all evening. It's warm and there's no breeze!"

"Occasionally I am afraid of losing you."

"Why would you lose me?" she said with an annoyed frown. "You're older than I am; you're likely to die before I do. I'm the one who should be afraid of being a widow."

"I don't mean through death."

"Well, then, what *do* you mean?" she asked impatiently, removing her head from his chest.

"That I'll mess up some way, make a mistake, act like an incorrigible twelve-year-old, and do irreparable harm."

"That's impossible," she snapped. "I may have a terrible Sicilian temper, but I don't hold grudges. Besides, I've never blown up at you. Why should I do it now?"

He hesitated and then spoke cautiously. "Because there is so much more of each of us involved in our intimacy. It is easier to hurt one another."

Michael and Gaby appeared at the sliding door behind her, the latter in a flattering two-piece swimsuit, and both of them frowning.

"That's the craziest thing I've ever heard!" she said, now obviously angry at him. "I've forgiven you for your idiocies a thousand times; now when I'm crazy in love with you, I won't forgive you?"

The two seraphs shook their heads more vigorously.

"Now you're the one who is hearing what I say instead of what I mean."

She bit her lip to contain her rage and nodded.

"All right, lover," she said with forced calm. "What do you mean?"

He folded her in his arms. She accepted the embrace, at first reluctantly and then eagerly.

"I mean that I don't trust myself in this intricate, delightful, miraculous relationship. I'm not worried about you. I'm worried about me fouling up."

The angels nodded in approval.

"Why didn't you say that in the first place?" she said with a sigh, and nuzzled closer to him.

Desire surged again in Neenan's body. He forced it back under control.

"I was trying to."

"I understand what you're saying, lover. I even understand why. Now that we're so much closer together, we are both likely to be clumsy on occasion—you more than me because you are a man and men tend to be clumsy. I must say, though, that, since whatever really happened to you on that plane, you haven't been clumsy at all in any aspect of our relationship."

She pulled off his T-shirt and pressed her chest against his. "You really are developing into something of a model husband. I have nothing to complain about."

He pressed her even closer to him. "I'm glad of that."

The two seraphs dematerialized. Does a night like this do the same thing to them that it does to us?

"I promise you that nothing, nothing at all, will alienate me from you, or at least, given my temper, not for long."

"Wonderful."

But it really wasn't wonderful, not at all. Desire for her deadened his fears, but he was sure they would return. If he should lose her and Vincent, there would be nothing left in his life.

"Why don't you make love to me," she said, mounting him, "then we can so swimming in the gulf under the stars. Without any swimsuits. I've never done it and I think it would be neat."

"If I swim, I have no choice about a swimsuit. You refused to pack one for me."

"That's true. . . . You could always pack yourself, you know. . . . Hold still, you're not being very cooperative."

"I think someone is trying to rape me!"

"You got it, buster," she said with a groan.

"I'll get even after our skinny-dip."

"You won't be able to," she replied triumphantly. "Now hold still, amusing twelve-year-old slave; I propose to divert myself with you for the next half hour or so."

"Hey, stop tickling! You're driving me berserk!"

"I'm the berserker this time! And I will not stop tickling."

Neenan enjoyed the romp. Yet the fear that clutched at his heart would not go away. She was pretending to be the attacker to reassure him that he would never lose her.

But, even during the height of his agony of pleasure, he was certain that he would and it would be his fault.

"Wake up," she said later, "time for your starlight swim."

"I was just getting comfortable in my bed."

"You're on the carpet, silly! Come on! Don't be a tired old man!"

She threw a blue terry-cloth robe at him and slipped a similar robe on herself.

"Last one to the beach is ancient!" she shouted, and dashed toward the beach.

Neenan, who was still exhausted, didn't contest the prize.

As she hit the beach, she tossed off her robe and dashed into the Gulf without a pause. Shrieking with delight, she dove into smooth water and swam her swift, competent crawl as though water were as much her natural habitat as it was for a small, neatly packed dolphin.

She is truly too young for me, Neenan told himself. She's a better lover and a better athlete. She was right when she said I couldn't cope with her.

He touched the water with his toes, discovered that it was a good deal warmer than Lake Michigan was even in the summer, and gingerly eased into it. Before he could dive into the star-drenched Gulf, his submerged wife tackled him and pulled his head underwater.

"Isn't it great!" she exulted when she let him breathe again. "I've never done this before! I knew I'd love it! . . . Did you think I was going to drown you?"

Before he could answer, she pulled him under again.

Sputtering as he surfaced, Neenan said, "Yes, I was sure —"

She cut him off with a wild, passionate embrace.

"I'm a sea nymph or maybe a mermaid and I've found a human male with whom I am insanely in love."

"Funny thing," Neenan replied as he crushed her in a return embrace, "I seem to have fallen in love with this wild sea creature."

She pulled him underwater again, kissed him underwater, then permitted him to bob back to the surface.

"Do you like me naked under the stars?" she asked, leaning against him, her long, wet hair sticking to his chest.

"I can't believe my good fortune to have been found by a sea nymph innocent of inhibitions."

She giggled and then nibbled at his chest. "You were absolutely wonderful inside, my twelve-year-old friend . . . do you mind my being so abandoned?"

"This last week has been the best honeymoon of my life . . . so far!"

"Let's do some serious swimming," she commanded, and pushed off him and dove into the calm Gulf, a deft sea creature triumphant in her skills.

Docilely he swam after her. Despite possessing and being possessed by a bride who deliberately played to his hungriest male fantasies, he continued to feel morose because of the time he had wasted and the little time he had left. She was not merely the best lover he had ever known, she was light-years better than any of the others. He had missed what she was and what she could be because he had been trapped in the blindness and stupidity of his parents.

He told himself that he should enjoy what he had if only for a few weeks because that was more than most men ever had.

"We're on a sandbar," she informed him. "Go on, if I can stand on it without going under, so can you."

Sure enough he could.

"Do you think heaven is like this?" she asked him.

"Like what?"

"Warm water, a ceiling of stars, and a good man to love?"

"Anna Maria! That's a pagan fantasy!"

"More like Islamic. . . . Well, we Sicilians are only one step away from pagans. I wouldn't want to go to a heaven where I couldn't screw you every day!"

"Anna Maria!" he exclaimed again, this time really shocked. "That's a terrible thing to say."

"You've ruined my morals," she giggled.

"People don't screw in heaven."

"Yes, they do! I know they do! Differently from here on earth, but better. You just wait and see. . . . We better swim back now. We have a busy day at golf tomorrow."

"Okay."

I'll have to ask God that, he told himself. If I get a chance to say a word.

Then something strange happened. It was an ecstatic experience but not one at all like the invasion of light and fire and love on the flight from Washington to Chicago and after some of his romps with his sex-crazed wife. Rather it was like a ride through a mind-bending computer game or an LSD trip, with which he had once experimented back in the sixties at the university.

Anna Maria and he were skipping over the water, almost skating on it. The angel choristers were singing psychedelic songs. Gaby and Michael were dancing with them, both also unclad. Gaby was even more devastating than he had imagined her, but Neenan felt no desire for her or for his wife. There was longing, however, enormous longing. For what? Good question. Then they slipped under the water and into the world of the sea, near a reef somewhere and a dark blue lagoon in which weirdly shaped, multicolored fish swam peacefully, untroubled, it seemed, by their human visitors. Human and seraphic to be more precise.

Then a mammoth shark rubbed his snout against Neenan's face in a gesture of friendship it seemed. It seemed to grin at him, and then, with a flip of its huge tail, it swam away. Two dolphins made themselves steeds under him and Anna Maria and carried them to the surface and far beyond in a mighty leap. Anna Maria screamed in hysterical delight as the dolphins arched over the water and began a manic roller-coaster dive back into the water. They entered it with a huge splash and sent their two passengers on a plunge deep into the darkness far beneath the surface.

They breathed under the water without difficulty. Their plunge into the darkness had been a pleasant ride, not the battering and dangerous collision it ought to have been. This had to be some sort of dream, induced by seraphic dust or maybe a delayed effect of the Seraphic Vineyards Chianti.

Then they were in a glowing underwater cave, lolling it seemed on a comfortable ledge. Gaby drew both Neenan and Anna Maria into her arms. She sang to them wondrous lullabies, accompanied by the soft humming of the angel brats.

Neenan knew peace, not the peace of his other ecstasy but the peace of happiness without worry. Maybe the seraphs were doing all this to reassure him. That thought did not, however, take peace away from him.

Michael appeared with a purple-colored, subterranean fruit, shaped like a long, thin pear. Its taste was heavenly or perhaps more properly seraphic. Then Gaby provided a cup of auburn-colored liquid that tasted like highly spiced fire. Anna Maria seemed relaxed and happy, smiling often and enjoying the whole experience.

Neenan realized that no one was talking. People didn't talk in dreams, did they?

Their journey continued through dark canyons deep in the sea, across vast sapphire lagoons, into deep red forests, down to the very bottoms of the oceans where inky darkness turned into light, then under unbearably bright icebergs that rumbled noisily above them. The choir continued to sing, now softly, now at the top of their powerful lungs. Gaby produced from behind an ocean rock an instrument that looked like a cross between a trumpet and a French horn and played melodies on it that were so sweet they almost broke your heart. She was the one who was supposed to sound the horn on judgment day, was she not? Was this the music that all would hear on that day of wrath? How come it was so gentle and loving? Another one of God's tricks?

Then they surfed on the waves of an Atlantic storm, riding up and down on monumental waves, glorying in the foam and the swirling, dark green waters and screaming with joy as they rose and fell on the best ride in the whole amusement park. How did he know they were screaming, since he heard no sounds? How did he know there was music? And why did he seem to hear the rumble of the icebergs?

Stupid questions. Enjoy the fun while it lasts.

Their cruise through all the oceans of the world continued. They met giant and friendly whales, skittery sea lions, curious pelicans, playful seals, unfriendly octopuses who would have nothing to do with them, and sleek sea otters. Many other animals, most of them friendly and none threatening, Neenan was unable to name.

They swam up the Mississippi as far as New Orleans and the St. Lawrence as far as Montreal and then returned to a warm and rapid ocean current that had to be the Gulf Stream. In the distance Neenan thought he saw the green shores of Ireland. In the Mediterranean they explored sunken Greek triremes, Spanish galleys, French frigates, and Italian battle cruisers. Their dance went on and one, seemingly for years, a time of almost but not quite unalloyed joy. The seraphs had deceived him, he had much more time than three months to live.

Then the dance through the oceans slowed down gently and stopped. The fun was over. He and his wife, both still naked, were on the beach in front of their town house on Captiva Island, he standing over her and she, leaning on an elbow, her face toward the sand, both of them breathing heavily as though they had come through great physical exertion.

He devoured her perfection—white skin, long, black hair flattened against her shapely back, and flanks, hips, and legs arranged in flawless symmetry. Her skin was still wet, a protective sheen in the starlight. He was filled with a thirst for her that demanded to be quenched. His heart beat more rapidly, his brain seemed to spin with insane desire, his fists tightened in determination, his lips pressed together.

I will have her now like I've never had her before. I will teach her what a totally aroused male animal wants.

She rolled over, half sat up, both her elbows supporting her. She was vulnerable, defenseless, frightened by his grim visage, and marvelously alluring.

"What do you want?" she demanded nervously.

"You."

"It's much too late," she said, but she made no move to escape.

"I've have been dared, challenged, ridiculed," he said grimly. "It has been said that I cannot cope with a much younger woman."

"I never said 'much younger,' " she pleaded. "Don't look at me that way."

"I'll look at you any way I want."

He stood over her.

She lowered her eyes. "Don't hurt me," she begged.

"Have I ever hurt you?" he demanded as he fell upon her and pinned her against the beach.

Her "no" was drowned out by an all-consuming kiss.

"You win," she said weakly when he was finished. "You can cope with me."

"You better believe I win."

He picked her up, slung her over his shoulder, and carried her up to the town house, where he tenderly laid her on their bed and slipped in next to her. He felt her take his hand as he sank into a deep and peaceful sleep.

❊　❊　❊

"Golf," she said the next morning. "Then more golf. We gotta be serious today."

"Right," he agreed, refusing to open his eyes.

"Come on. Three more strokes off your score this morning."

"Right," he said, sipping the coffee with his eyes still closed.

She pulled him out of bed.

Later, as they drove to the Captiva Island country club, she spoke for the first time since she had wakened him.

"I was drunk last night."

"We had only one bottle of wine."

"You drank only one glass."

"Two."

"Only one!"

"There are two options, Anna Maria, my darling. One is that you weren't drunk. The second is that you're the shortest short hitter in the whole Sicilian tribe. I prefer the first."

"Was I terrible?"

"That's not the word I'd use."

"It's all a blur, like a dream. . . . Did I act like a savage?"

"Like a good wife."

She sighed softly. "There were wonderful dreams. I can't remember some of them and I don't how much with you was a dream too."

"Very little."

His left hand on the wheel of the car, he stroked her long hair with his right hand.

"Did I really say that if I couldn't screw with you in heaven, I didn't want to go there?"

"You did."

"Is God mad at me?" she asked, worry in her voice.

He stopped the car for a red light. Gaby was on the corner, glistening white in tennis clothes. She shook her head in a vigorous negative.

Neenan scowled at her, as if to say, I don't need your help to deal with her. Not now anyway. Even when we can't see them, they still know what we're doing. But angels would, wouldn't they?

"Do I love you, Anna Maria?"

"You'd better."

"My love for you ends where God's begins. God is even more crazy for you than I am. I don't think you have any reason to be afraid of God. He understands what you mean."

That was pretty good, he told himself. I'm even beginning to sound like a seraph.

Gaby smiled, waved her racket, and dematerialized. What did the tennis racket mean? Were they showing off, as they often did — doing something because they could do it? Or did they really have a game that was something like tennis — balls of plasma light bounding across several cosmoses?

The light changed and he slipped the gear into drive.

"Do you mean we will make love in heaven?"

"Something like it, only better. . . . You said 'screw' last night." He continued to stroke her hair.

"I was drunk."

His next words slipped out before he reflected on them. "I hope I didn't hurt you on the beach."

"Will you please stop that!" she shouted. "How many times do I have to tell you that you never hurt me. If you ever do, I'll tell you, but I know you won't."

"OK."

"And I didn't mean that you should stop playing with my hair. . . . That's better. . . . I was terrified on the beach. Great big male ravisher hulking over me. But it was nice terror, if you know what I mean. He wants to get even with me for what I did earlier. How sweet."

She kissed him lightly. "I'm dizzy in love with you, Raymond," she whispered in his ear. "I didn't know lovers like you existed. You can do anything you want with me."

"I probably will," he said, his eyes glued to the road.

"I think I've figured out something that puzzled me about you."

"Oh?"

"I told you not to stop stroking my hair, didn't I?" She rested her hand on his knee.

"What have you figured out?"

"Why you're so gentle and tender. You never had any example when you were growing up. But you did learn to be sensitive to others in intimate situations because you suffered so much in them at home, poor dear."

"I messed up with Donna and the kids and in that crazy pension mess."

"The pension foolishness was not intimate. You had problems with your first wife and your children, not because you were insensitive to how they felt but because you could not do anything about their feelings and backed off from them."

He thought about that as they turned into the pine-shaded drive that led to the King's Crown Country Club. "I think you're being too kind to me. I'm not sure the women who were my mistresses would agree."

It was the first time he had admitted to her that such women existed.

She seemed unconcerned, as if she took them for granted. "They might be disappointed that you didn't remain with them. I could understand that. I'd feel the same way. But none of them would say that you deliberately hurt them, much less that you weren't sweet and gentle in bed. Absolutely not."

She squeezed his thigh to emphasize "absolutely."

"Maybe," was all he could manage. He'd have to think about it.

These days he had to think about a lot of things.

There were, no flirtations on the course. Anna Maria was dead serious about cutting three strokes off his game. Although he felt clumsy every time he swung the club the way she ordered, in fact he cut his score by four strokes.

"You're improving," she said with an air of clinical detachment as they headed for the clubhouse. "You're still not concentrating enough. You're letting yourself be distracted."

"My instructor is too pretty," he pleaded.

"I wish that was all that was distracting you. I wish I knew what you were worrying about."

He did not reply because his answer would be one word.

Death.

⚛20⚛

"What was that all about last night?" he asked Michael when the massive black angel, wearing purple undershorts, materialized next to him in the locker room. "Were you guys just showing off? Seraphic vanity again?"

"More like seraphic playfulness," the boss angel replied. "We are also very playful beings, as you no doubt have noticed."

"It was quite a show . . . mostly illusion, none of it real?"

"It was real in a certain sense. We wanted to show you that we were quite capable of taking care of your companion when you take your temporary leave of her."

"You will find her, uh, someone else?"

"Jealousy is not one of your faults, is it, Raymond Anthony? I will not comment on that question, though I would imagine that she will be able to find one for herself when she wants to without our help."

"That's true. Speaking of such matters, I hope you're not offended when I say that your companion is devastating when she takes off her clothes."

"You mean of course," the angel said, drawing on purple socks, "her surrogate. Believe me, Raymond Anthony, she would be offended if you did not say her surrogate was devastating. We are vain creatures, and that is not wrong because we have much to be vain about, as I have told you so often. Our life-bearers are far more vain than we life-givers. My companion, since she is the most beautiful of all, is the most vain of all. Or so I tell her."

"Do you wear clothes in your, what should call it, ordinary forms?"

"Naturally." Michael pulled a purple knit shirt over his massive shoulders. "Raymond Anthony," he continued solemnly, "you have reduced your own companion to a condition of nearly total vulnerability. We will be seriously displeased if you hurt her while she is in that condition."

"She says I can't hurt her."

"We hope that she is correct. However, that remains to be seen."

With those ominous words, Michael dematerialized.

On the way back to their town house, Anna Maria yawned, nodded, and then fell asleep. He woke her when they arrived at the house.

"Sorry, Raymond. I'm tired."

"I can't imagine why."

She stumbled into the house. "Can I take a long nap?"

"Certainly. We're going out to dinner tonight."

"I think I remember that. . . . Oh, I have to go into town to buy more suntan cream."

"I can buy it for you."

"You would buy the wrong kind." She yawned.

"Same as this on the table?"

"No wonder you're such a success in life."

He helped her into bed and drove back to the town. He found a drugstore in a tiny mall. Michael was browsing the shelves in his distinctive purple costume. What was up? Why was the seraph waiting for him?

Neenan found the approved brand and carried two large tubes to the checkout line.

Then he discovered why the purple crusader was lurking.

"Ray boy," said a sultry voice. "Returned to the scene of the crime, huh?"

It could only be Estelle Sloane, whom he had captured in the Captiva house in the days between Donna and Anna Maria. Or, in his new perspective, they had culminated their mutual seduction in the town house on the Gulf.

"Was it a crime?" he asked.

She kissed him with something much more than mere affection. Instantly he wanted her just one more time.

"You tell me. Buy me a drink, a quick one."

She had been one of his more spectacular prizes, or so he thought. A model turned public relations woman, she was tall, slender, with short brown hair and a model's perfect body. She had been funny, reckless, blunt, and delightful in bed.

Standing behind him in the line, she was if anything more attractive in the same uniform of strapless top and short jeans that Anna Maria had worn on the golf course. A certain wisdom that comes with experiences that are assimilated into one's character appeared to have modified the coltish enthusiasms of a decade ago. She was more "interesting" than before.

Should he try to ask her forgiveness? What good would it do? On the other hand, the seraph gang had undoubtedly set up this encounter to test him, perhaps with one of the most likable of his "prizes."

He glanced at Michael. The seraph shrugged his shoulders indifferently. That meant he'd better give it a try.

"It will have to be quick," he said in reply to her request for a drink. "My wife and I have an early dinner reservation."

"Your wife is here, huh?" she said as they went out of the pharmacy and into the piercing sunlight. "Worse luck for my plans to take you to bed tonight. I heard you had married again."

She was dressed like Anna Maria had been on the golf course with a single exception: Anna Maria, modest woman that she was, usually, had in public worn a bra. Estelle had disdained such modesty. Her breasts, he remembered, were the prettiest he had ever touched. Desperately he wanted to play with them just once more.

"I have indeed. It's worked out very well." He did not add, "For the last week."

"She any good in bed?"

"Very," he said firmly.

"Too bad for my scheme to seduce you. Still I'll give it a try. . . . Wait a second till I get a shirt out of my car. There's a lounge down at the end of the street. It'll be cool inside."

Cool and dark and intimate as it turned out. Michael ambled in after them and sat at a table across from the booth that Estelle had chosen.

They ordered a dry martini for her and a diet Coke for him. She had put on her shirt but had not bothered to button it, which heightened her appeal.

"What do you think of me after all these years?" she asked.

Neenan chose his words carefully. "I think you're more beautiful than you were then. You have acquired a sheen of wisdom and experience that cancels out the effects of time and makes you more fascinating. To be totally candid, I worry about the edge of cynicism I see around your eyes and sometimes around your smile."

When Neenan said that he was about to be totally candid, it was a sure sign that he was about to offer a highly stylized version of the truth. In fact, Estelle was only one step away from falling into a pit of bitterness from which it would be hard to escape.

She shut her eyes, gritted her teeth, and caught her breath. "Damn you."

"Sorry if I am wrong."

"No, you're perfectly right. You didn't used to be able to see through me. I don't like to have my emotional clothes taken away. . . . But I don't want to talk about me. Tell me about this woman you've married."

"She's a script reader for NE. Makes decisions about possible films and miniseries for us. Best in the business. That's why I hired her. Then fell in love with her. Sicilian American from Chicago. Wonderful woman."

"You're in love with her still?"

"More than ever."

"Really settled down, huh?"

"Getting old."

She examined him critically. "Sexier than ever, if you ask me."

Estelle Sloane's moves were far more subtle than those of Honoria Smythe. Someone at a nearby table would not notice she was trying to seduce him—unless that someone happened to be the boss of all the seraphs.

"And your husband?"

She shrugged indifferently. "Banker. Nice guy. Irish Catholic like you. Crazy about me, which shows he has good taste. Cute. Adequate lover. I kind of love him, you know what I mean. He'll never walk out on me, heaven knows. I'm faithful to him, more or less. I won't walk out on him either."

"I see."

"He's in Paris now. Gets back on Monday. So I have time on my hands."

"Too bad."

"Maybe not," she said with an inviting sigh. "That depends on you." Her soft, cool hand found his thigh.

He swallowed and clenched one of his fists. "Thanks, Estelle, but no thanks. It would be very nice. But I love my wife."

"And I love my husband, but what harm would it do if we spent an hour or so together?" She squeezed his thigh.

"I'd hate myself afterward. So would you."

She removed her hand and began to work on her drink. "You're right, Ray. I would too. . . . What do you remember most about me from the old days?"

"Most wonderful breasts in the world."

She smiled, then laughed. "But you don't want to play with them one final time?"

"Sure I do. But I won't."

"OK, Ray, I'll turn off the steam. No hard feelings?"

"Not at all. I'm flattered that you would still want me."

"Who wouldn't? Your wife is a lucky woman. Does she know that?"

"She claims that she does."

They both laughed, uneasily lurching out of the seduction mode.

"Are you going to tell her you ran into me?"

Michael rolled his eyes. "I think so."

"I would if I were you. She'd know how important she is to you."

Michael nodded in agreement.

"Maybe. . . . Estelle, there's something I want to say to you."

"Say away. By the way, could I have another drink? I promise it's my last of the day."

He ordered the second martini.

"I am sorry that I hurt you during our time together."

"What do you mean hurt?" she said with a puzzled frown. "You're the most gentle lover I've ever known. It took you long enough to get around to taking me to bed after I'd been sending signals for months. But I never had any complaints about you when we were together."

"I kind of felt that I used you."

She thought about that. "No more than I used you, Ray. Both of us were consenting adults. We knew what we were doing."

"Yet," he persisted, "I thought you were angry at me when we broke up."

She lowered her head into her hands. "I don't want to talk about that," she said curtly. "Too much pain. Years of pain. I won't talk about it."

"I'm sorry, Stelle, terribly, terribly sorry."

She looked up at him and reached out and touched his hand gently. "It wasn't your fault, Ray. . . . Well, it was your fault, but it was mostly my fault."

"You don't want to talk about it?"

"Hell no. But I have to talk about it. OK?"

"OK."

Michael leaned forward with obvious interest. This part was apparently not in his script.

"Will you hold my hand please? I'm not trying to seduce you now, honest."

Michael nodded approval, so Neenan took her hand.

"You remember what I was like in those days? Bossy, bitchy, domineering woman. Tough, hard, brittle. Dumb. I could have anything and anyone I wanted. And then throw them away. Mean. Stupid."

"Those aren't the words I would use."

"Come on, Ray, you know better. You once told me I was imperious. Have you forgotten that?"

"I remember it now."

"I did act like I was an empress. So you came along, a great big, handsome Irish Catholic hunk. He'll be fun. I'll enjoy him for a while and send him on his way."

"We told each other that it was only a temporary affair, Stelle."

"You believed it, Ray. I found out quickly that I didn't believe it."

"Oh."

"You were this luscious, macho male. Perfect target. If that's all you were, I would have tired of you in a couple of weeks. Do you know the effect you have on people, Ray? No, I'm sure you don't. You're strong and powerful and demanding and charming. People fall in love with you easily. You're irresistible."

The angel brats began to hum softly, reassuringly.

"Oh," he said again—and held her hand more tightly.

"I'm sure you've been that way all your life. Women just automatically get a crush on you. I figured the charm would wear thin pretty quickly. Well"—she began to weep—"it didn't."

"I'm sorry."

"Stop saying that! . . . Are they playing Muzak in here? Or am I imagining I hear it?"

"Something kind of soft, maybe."

"It's beautiful. It helps what I'm trying to say. . . . Do I imagine a purple color somewhere in this room? I must be losing my mind."

Michael grinned.

"Anyway," she went on, "I found out that when we were intimate, not just in bed, but certainly there, that you were as kind and sweet as a mother with her newborn baby. I know the feeling because I have a couple of kids."

"Oh," he said, falling back on his standard reply.

"Then I went head over heels for you. I was in love like I'd never been before. I belonged to you completely. Then you lost interest and broke my heart. . . . And don't say again that you're sorry. It was all my fault."

"No, it wasn't, Stelle. It was my fault as much as yours. We deceived ourselves because we wanted pleasure. Then we got caught up in something else."

She reached for a tissue and dabbed at her eyes with a tissue. "I ached for you for years, loved you, hated you, and then finally realized that it was all an illusion. Neither of us were ready for marriage. You were still getting over your wife and I was a flake. So I stopped hating you. Then I realized what I had learned about myself and I was grateful to you."

"I said to my wife recently that every woman is at heart a mother and every man is at heart a bachelor. She replied that, no, every man is at heart a twelve-year-old."

Estelle laughed sadly. "Wise woman, your wife."

"I think so."

"I'd like to meet her sometime. Not today, not after what I tried. I'm sorry about that too." She began to cry again. "You're right about my getting brittle around the edges. After I figured out what happened with us, I really did try to change. I married, I settled down, I had kids. I told myself that I was happy. Maybe I was, but in the last year, after my son was born, I don't know what happened to me. I do know that whatever it is turned me into a bitch again and I made a fool out of myself a few minutes ago when I tried to seduce you."

She rested her head on the table and sobbed. Neenan, not knowing what else to do, continued to hold her hand. Michael watched, sympathy for the weeping woman in his deep brown eyes.

"You're doing all right," the seraph whispered. *"Now don't blow it."*

"What should I say?"

"Figure that out for yourself."

"Great!"

Her head still on the table, Estelle reached in her purse and pulled out a wallet. She flipped it open to a picture of two children, a girl about four and a boy perhaps a little older than one.

"Neat kids."

"I love them both. I love their dad too. Maybe he doesn't demand enough of me, but I love him a whole lot. I'm not the wife I should be. I don't do nearly enough for him. It would be so easy to be a better wife, but the last couple of years all the fun went out of it."

She began to sob again.

What the hell am I doing? Neenan demanded of himself. I'm supposed to be a counselor to a woman who was once my lover?

He stroked her hair lightly. "The challenge is not to avoid growing old," he said far more confidently than he felt. "Rather it is to grow old gracefully, that is, showering grace on those we love. We must bathe them in grace not as those would who are afraid the supply will run out but like those who believe that grace is limitless."

Now how did I come up with that? Must have read it in a screenplay somewhere. Maybe one of the clerical characters in Anna Maria's screenplays.

Estelle stopped sobbing and sat up straight, her face with its tears and its flowing makeup almost unbearably beautiful.

"You sound like a priest."

"I don't mean to preach, Stelle."

"You mean I should shower my husband and kids and anyone else I meet with more affection than they would expect, more than they have any right to, more than I have ever given anyone ever in my life?"

Michael nodded his head briskly.

"Something like that."

"Do you live that way?"

"I've tried recently. I don't do a very good job at it. I kind of think that trying is what counts."

"How does your wife react?"

"With surprise and delight."

"Doesn't it seem unfair that you have do all the work?"

Now what am I supposed to say?

Michael shrugged his shoulders.

"It's fun," was the best Neenan could manage.

She nodded slowly. "I can see that it might be. Will Terry ever be surprised when he comes back from Paris!"

Then Gaby, in a purple beach outfit that matched the color of her husband's array, materialized behind Estelle and caressed her neck and face.

Estelle put her wallet back into her purse, dried her tears, redid her makeup, and pushed aside her half-empty drink.

Gaby smiled down at her with maternal love.

Neenan decided to push his luck. "You should realize that Terry is a gift you have been given for a time and that you should treat that gift with abundant gratitude while you still have time."

Gaby stopped her massage and stared at Neenan in astonishment. Behind her, Michael seemed equally surprised.

"I'll drown him with grace, you just watch!" Estelle smiled happily, the brittle edge of cynicism at least temporarily banished.

"It won't be easy all the time."

Gaby continued to stare.

"Finish your work, woman," Neenan said to her.

The woman seraph, presumably the angel of Nazareth, snorted but returned to her healing ministration.

"May I call you when I need a kick in the ass?"

"You sure can."

You'll have to find the phone number of heaven.

She seemed an empty shell as he helped her out to her car, a woman who had been drained however transiently of her lifeblood.

Ray felt powerful love for her, a love from which desire was absent.

"I'm wiped out, Ray," she said, leaning against his arm.

"You'll be all right."

"I think you just saved my soul."

"God and her angels do that."

She hugged him as he took the keys and opened the car door for her.

"Someday I want to meet your wife. The next time Terry and I come to Chicago."

"Grand!"

He was not altogether sure he wanted Anna Maria to meet this former lover of his.

"One of you guys go with her," he commanded the two seraphs. "She's in no shape to drive."

"I'll do it," Gaby said, and leaped into the car, without the formality of opening the door. "See you two later."

"Ordering around seraphs?" Michael asked. "Just because you've been an instrument of amazing grace?"

"Put her on my account."

"What do you mean?" Michael asked, unable to hide his smile.

"You told me that you never give up an account. I want Stelle on my account. She's part of the contract from now on."

"Even if I didn't find her charming—which I do—my companion would give me no choice."

In Neenan's Lexus, Michael returned to his "head coach" style. "That success gives you no reason for overconfidence, Raymond Anthony."

"Who's overconfident? I feel like I've been run over by a semi."

"You must also," the seraph boss continued implacably, "learn about yourself from what she said to you."

"You mean that I get seduced by women who are like my mother? I know that already."

"No, that's less important than the other truth."

"Which is?"

"You know it. You tell me."

Neenan sighed. You can't escape from the head coach, especially when he is a seraph.

"That I have a personality which both men and women find attractive, especially women. Somehow I combine strength and tenderness, which is a kind of magic. I don't believe any of it."

"You'd better believe it. It's the reason why the Other told us to bother with you."

Neenan felt as if he were a piece of fruit, a pear perhaps, that had been left to rot in the sun. There was nothing left to him except the deteriorating skin of what he had been. Or of what he thought he was. No illusions left.

"If you're right," he told Michael, "I don't know what to do about it."

"What you did for that poor child this afternoon. You healed her by your word and example. Surprised even me and my companion, which is hard to do, especially her."

Oh.

"You going to tell your companion about the incident?"

"I think I'd better."

"I think so too."

Neenan's companion was sitting in the cabana by the pool, clad in her underwear, reading a script and sipping red wine. Normally he would have teased her about working on a vacation weekend. Now he was too empty to play the game.

"It took a long time to buy that suntan cream," she said without glancing up. "You missed an important phone call. . . . Good heavens, Raymond, you look terrible. What happened?"

"I met an old lover in the drugstore."

Anna Maria's lips tightened in a thin line. "Is she more attractive than I am?"

"No."

"Was she better in bed than I am?"

"Nowhere near as good."

"Her breasts better than mine?"

"Different."

Pause. "I'm sorry Ray for sounding like a Sicilian bitch, a jealous Sicilian bitch at that. Tell me about her."

He told her the story, omitting only the seraphic interventions. Midway though his story, Anna Maria put on a thin kimono—as though the story required a more careful modesty—and curled up at his feet, her head resting against his knee.

"So I didn't sleep with her," he said at the end of his story.

She tapped his thigh vigorously. "Who ever said, even hinted, that you did!"

"No one," he said sheepishly.

"I would certainly like to meet her, poor dear woman."

With any luck I'll be dead by then. "The two of you will bond against me."

"Naturally. That's what women do. . . . You were surprised that she made a pitch for you?"

"No . . . I had to try to put closure to the relationship."

"Who ever said, even hinted, that you shouldn't?"

"No one."

"Were you surprised that you were able to turn her life around in a few minutes?"

"Did I do that?"

"You sure did."

"Well, whatever I did, I was astonished."

"I'm not. It's the kind of man you are or can be when you put your mind to it."

"I can't see myself that way."

"Work on it, lover. That's who you are."

She stood up, tossed aside her kimono, kissed him, and headed for their bedroom.

"Hurry up!" she ordered. "We'll be late for our dinner reservation. I've already changed it once. . . . Oh, damn! I forgot the phone call."

"Who called?"

"Jenny?"

"Jenny who?"

"Your daughter Jenny," she said impatiently. "She said she'd call back. Maybe. We had a very nice conversation. She is a sweet and confused young woman. More sweet than confused."

"What did she want?" Ice once more stabbed at his heart. Another opportunity. He could hear Michael saying, "Don't blow this one."

"To quote her verbatim, she is reconsidering her options in regard to her relationship with you. I gather she wondered whether there were any options left. She wanted to know if you hated her a whole lot. I told her that I didn't think you hated her at all, at which she started to cry. She wants to make friends but isn't sure she can."

"I see," he said uneasily. Was this another setup by the seraphs?

The phone rang.

"You get it," he snapped at Anna Maria.

She raised an eyebrow.

"Please," he added quickly.

She grinned as she picked up the phone. "Neenan residence."

"Hi, Jenny. The old man is here now. It's up to you whether you want to talk to him. I'm sure he wants to talk to you."

She handed Neenan the phone and wrapped her arms around his waist, her head resting against his back, as if she were propping him up.

"Hi, Jennifer," he said, trying to sound as if he were the charming male that people had lately been alleging that he was. "Good to hear from you."

"Your wife is, like, totally cool, Daddy," she blurted. "I really like her."

"I do too, Jennifer. We're very happy."

"She says she's improving your golf game!"

"I haven't beaten her yet. I don't think she'll permit that."

"Daddy, I have been trying to reconceptualize my relationship with you."

"Totally cool" and "reconceptualize"—half teen and half would-be intellectual.

"I'm glad to hear that, Jennifer."

"I mean, I go, like, I don't know who my father really is. Mom tells me one thing and Vinny tells me another thing, and I don't know which one is right. Then I talk to Annie and she confuses me all the more."

"Annie?"

"Your wife, Daddy!"

"That Annie."

Jennifer giggled. He had never once heard her giggle.

"So I'm like totally bummed out, you know. . . . What I wanted to ask you, Daddy, is, well, whether if I, like, you know, want to rec- oncile with you, you'll take me back. I'm not saying that I will want to. I'm, like, just trying to find out whether if I do, there is any point in trying, you know . . ."

Her voice trailed off in tears. Neenan was crying too.

"Now there's two of us crying, Jennifer. . . . To answer your ques- tion, anytime, anyplace, in a minute—if you want to take the risk."

"Bye, Daddy," she said in a gurgle of tears.

"Bye, Jennifer."

He thought she had hung up. Then he heard her last, almost in- audible words: "Give my love to Annie."

They both hung up.

"She said to give her love to you, Annie."

He was as tight as steel fence, stiff with emotion in every cell of his body.

"Poor kid," he said as the tension flowed out of his body. "What do you think, Annie?"

His wife continued to cling to him, her head still propping him up.

"In the long run, sure. In the short run, toss-up. Depends on whether she talks to Donna again."

"I'm sure she will."

"Better that way. She has to break that chain."

"Did I do good, Anna Maria?"

"You did real good. You did perfect. Like totally. And you can call me Annie sometimes. Pretend I'm Irish."

"Should I do anything?"

"Like call her back? Don't even think of that. Give her time. . . . By the way, she had a small part in a film. One of yours, I think. Doesn't want you to know which one. Thinks she might get a much bigger part soon. Maybe then she'll call you again."

He nodded dully. "Maybe."

Somehow this was the worst experience yet. Anna Maria, Vincent, his parents, Honoria, Ben and Joan Harvey, Estelle—all wrenching experiences. But this poor child, messed up by her mother's hatred and her father's neglect. All he could do was speak cordially with her on the phone and pray.

"Is she seeing a psychiatrist?"

"I think so, Raymond. . . . If you want, we can forget about dancing at Captain Al's tonight."

"No reason to do that. It wouldn't help poor Jennifer."

He did not want to dance. Not at all. Yet the chances of Jennifer returning to him while there was yet time were thin. Maybe he would never dance with Anna Maria again.

"Are you sure?"

"If you don't get a dress on right away, woman, I'll drag you off the way you are."

He spun her around and began to dance with her, suddenly more light-footed than he had ever been.

"You frighten me," she said as she wiggled free, then dashed into the bedroom and slipped on a lime-colored sheath.

"Come on, Raymond, change your clothes, we have to eat tapas and then dance the night away."

So they did dance the night away, the kind of activity that Neenan had never liked before, but which, with his boundlessly energetic wife, he thought he might learn to enjoy.

Back at their town house, they agreed that they were too exhausted for lovemaking, sank into their bed, and went instantly to sleep.

When he wakened in the middle of the night, he found his wife sleeping peacefully in his arms. He understood that in some circumstances holding a beautiful woman in your arms with no intention of making love can be a most pleasurable activity. He sighed contentedly, drew her closer, and went back to sleep.

He was dragged out of bed early in the morning for Mass before golf.

Look, Occupant, he prayed, *or someone else altogether, if you prefer, I don't know what to make of all of this. Your seraphs keep hitting me over the head with situations they've set up and for which I am totally unprepared. I don't know what I'm doing or where I'm going. Like I thought yesterday, I feel like a rotting pear at the side of a road, mostly corruption and rot. About all I can do this morning is thank you for my wife, who just now is so gorgeous that she is distracting me in my prayers. I hope you don't mind if I devote my full attention to those distractions and to my fantasies about what I'm going to do to her—oops, with her—back at our house.*

Since the Occupant did not offer any objections, Neenan directed has full devotion to his wife.

As soon as they were inside the door of the town house, he set about converting his fantasies into reality, first by unzipping the back of her white dress and summarily removing it from her body.

"Hey! We're supposed to play golf!"

"Later."

"Do I get a choice?"

"Only by a very loud protest. Now."

No protest was forthcoming.

They played golf (taking two more strokes off his score), swam, played tennis, swam some more, and then packed their luggage and drove back to the airport. They took off just as darkness had settled on the island below them.

Pity the poor older man who marries a young bride, he told himself. Still, it was the young bride who was asleep, was it not?

He had given up trying to figure out what the weekend meant.

He knew only that a weekend with Anna Maria was worth many extra years of life. He figured that so far he was a winner in his bargain with death and the pushy black seraph.

What, however, if he should lose Anna Maria? And Vincent? And Jennifer, whom he had yet to win back?

He shivered at the fantasy of total desolation.

Fortunately, his wife was not awake to notice.

21

Neenan had resolved that he must concentrate on his work. He was the CEO of a major entertainment company. He was responsible for thousands of jobs, tens of millions of dollars in cash flow, potentially billions of dollars of capital, and resistance to corporate raiders. He could not let a little slip of a Sicilian girl so bewitch him that he was useless at his job. Anna Maria in the evening and on weekends. NE during the day. That's the way life must be, right?

So he was going to die soon, perhaps very soon. He would do the best he could to put his life in order. The seraphs would continue to set up encounters for him. He would continue to do his best. But he could not let NE drift, not when it was under attack. God, he imagined, wouldn't like that.

While Peter drove him into the Loop, he worked over a stack of legal documents that Neil Higgins had left at the house in Lake Forest on Sunday evening—along with a note that said, "The judge is going to give us a temporary restraining order Tuesday morning and we'll go in with a motion that WorldCorp show cause why it should not be made permanent."

Preliminary legal maneuvering that meant little or nothing. Neenan doubted that their injunction would stand up, not unless WorldCorp did something really stupid, which they might very well do.

However, the papers kept his mind off his wife for the ride into the Loop. He banished lecherous fantasies about her during Mass at Old St. Patrick's at Adams and Desplaines, whose renewed interior made him feel that he had walked into the Book of Kells. He must remember to make a substantial contribution to the parish before he died.

Died?

Yes, he was going to die and soon. So was everyone else, if not quite so soon.

So what. There was work to be done first.

Imaginings about his vest-pocket Sicilian Venus had no place in such a solemn Celtic setting, did they?

Alas for his restraint, on his desk when he entered his office was the script of *Starbridge* with a note from Joe McMahon:

"This is a sure winner. We gotta do it. Four parts I think, just like it is written. Finance it internally so no one can interfere with our production. When they hear about it, the networks will come running. We'll have a bidding war."

Joe had the hardest head of anyone in the business. His enthusiasm never rose above mild. If he thought that Anna Maria's script was a winner, then it certainly was. He'd give it to Vincent later in the day and get his reaction. Then he'd tell Anna Maria the good news.

At that thought, the images of her delicate delights that he had been repressing all morning flooded back to his consciousness.

He picked up the phone and dialed her private number.

"Anne Allegro," she said primly.

"Hi."

"Raymond?"

"Who else?"

"What do you want?"

"I wanted to tell you that I love you."

"I know *that*."

"I wanted to make sure."

"Really, Raymond, I'm trying to read a treatment."

"Sorry to have bothered you. . . . Oh, by the way, do you remember the script we turned down a year or two ago about the woman who died and went to heaven?"

"Sure. You turned it down despite my strong recommendation, if I remember."

"I must have been wrong. What was it called?"

"*Light in the Tunnel.* First thing that has to be changed is the title."

"I'll look into it. I'm sure we have a copy around here someplace."

"Do me a favor, Raymond?"

"Sure . . . don't call you when you're working?"

"No, silly, read the script yourself."

"That would be a pretty radical departure."

"I know."

"OK, I'll get it and read it."

"And, Raymond . . ."

"Yes?"

"I love you too."

His delight at those final words made him feel silly. He was acting like an adolescent male with his first crush.

"Mr. McMahon and Mr. Stein to see you, Mr. Neenan."

"Thank you, Amy. Would you see if we have a script in the files for a film called *Light in the Tunnel.*"

"Certainly, Mr. Neenan."

"Thank you."

"What's the news this morning, gentlemen?" he asked his two senior colleagues.

They were both taken aback by the enthusiasm of his greeting.

I guess I must not have smiled too often around here.

"I guess the first news," Joe said with a cautious laugh, "is that the boss had a good weekend at the golf course."

"Down to the low eighties anyway."

They would not have dared to say that the boss had a good weekend in bed too. They would never have thought of it.

"Where do we stand with WorldCorp?"

"Despite your press conference and despite our legal actions and despite their denials," Norm said grimly, "they're acquiring as much of our preferred stock as they can through various fronts they have set up. No voting rights, but they could always go to court with a plea that we are not considering the advantage of our stockholders."

"How can they make a case out of that?"

"It's just harassment," Joe suggested. "They're also going after our executives. We've had five reports since Friday morning of indirect, one might say sneaky, approaches to our people and our clients. I've passed it on to Neil. It will be useful evidence when we seek to make the restraining order permanent — not that they'll give up just because of an injunction, which they will appeal, though it will remain in effect until it is overturned."

"It makes no sense to me," Neenan said. "What do they know that we don't know?"

"They're spreading the rumor," McMahon said carefully, "that you're going to sell out. Take the money and run."

"I'm not going to do that," Neenan said bluntly. "You know that."

"There are stories going around about your health, physical and mental," Norm said softly, "that your behavior has been, uh, odd for the last two weeks."

Just at that moment, Michael, dressed in a dark gray banker's suit with a flower in his lapel, materialized in the office.

Neenan considered the situation before replying to his colleagues.

"Because I take a Friday off to play golf with my wife, I'm a sick and maybe dying man?"

"Someone somewhere leaked the changes you're making in your will," Norm Stein observed, his voice steady and neutral.

"Aren't they perfectly rational in the circumstances? If I should not have made it back from Florida, would not the company have been in terrible shape to resist a hostile takeover? It only makes sense to think about an heir."

Michael nodded, which was a big help. Get lost, seraph, if you can't help me now.

"You never did before."

"Then I was a fool."

"We believe you, R. A.," Joe said reassuringly. "All we're suggesting is that you permit us to release your medical records."

"Am I the president of the United States? Is there some thought that I might have AIDS? Or be addicted to drugs?"

Michael frowned and shook his head.

"Of course not, R. A.," Norm said. "Not in the least."

"Release them if you want," Neenan said, giving up. "And add that I have no intention of selling out. If I knew I were going to die next week, I wouldn't sell out!"

Michael grinned and gave him the A-OK sign.

"You'll have young Vinny in place before the week is over?"

"If he wants the job, sure. Then stories about my being sick because I go off to Florida for golf lessons from my wife won't make any difference."

Come to think of it, it did sound a little weird.

"Something else we can do," Joe took up the conversation, "is announce that we're going to make that miniseries. Solemn high announcement. Finance it internally. It's an absolute sure winner—a mix of Jane Austen and Anthony Trollope in modern dress and without the sex taboos. Just enough of the occult and nostalgia. That we're taking a risk like that should send a signal."

"It's that good?" Neenan asked.

"It's that good," McMahon said, his enthusiasm rising. "We announce it at a press conference with this woman who wrote the novels—what's her name?"

"Susan Howatch."

"And the scriptwriter, this Marianne Swift, who's she anyway?"

"I'm not sure."

"We tell the world that we're going to have a contest for the principal roles and that the two authors will choose them."

I'd better be dead when that happens, Neenan thought. There are some advantages, are there not, in slipping out of sight permanently? Damn good thing these guys don't know any Italian.

"Do we have the rights to the novel or the script as far as that goes?" Stein inquired.

"I think we might," Neenan replied.

This Marianne Swift person would hardly have written a script for a miniseries without getting the rights and, probably, without charming the author. Wonder what she would have done with it, if I hadn't . . . well, done whatever I've been doing.

Michael confirmed that hunch with a broad grin.

"I'll give it to Vincent at lunch and get his reaction. Then I'll see what I can find out about the rights."

"You've got an exclusive on this, R. A.?" Stein wondered with a worried frown.

"Next best thing."

Michael grinned again.

Might Marianne Swift have gone elsewhere with her script? Might she still? She did have some obligation to the author. Count on it, if Marianne Swift didn't have a scheme, than there was no football at the toe of Italy. He would have to obtain closure on this whole thing before the week was out.

"I'll give it to Vincent to read at lunch today," Neenan continued. "We should have him on board before we make the decision definitively."

"Vinny will love it!" McMahon insisted.

"What about the pension suit?"

"Walsh is still dragging his feet," Norm Stein said with a note of contempt in his voice. "Says that some of his people still want a pound of your flesh."

"Tell him for me that he has till Wednesday or we will announce our settlement offer and say it is on the table for two weeks and then we will withdraw it. Most of his clients will be all over him to accept it."

"That threat should do it," Stein agreed.

"He'll want to save face, so when he comes back on Wednesday and says that he needs more time, give till Friday and not one day more. He'll cave in. Pension stuff was foolishness to begin with. And you don't have to tell me it was my idea. I know it was. I must have been sick in the head then and not when I went off to play golf."

"Annie's a good teacher?" Stein inquired.

Michael nodded his head.

"The best, knocked eight, nine strokes off my game, eliminated my slice. Now if she'll teach me how to putt, I'll be as good at the game as she is."

Michael applauded.

McMahon and Stein left the office, wondering if Neenan had indeed lost his mind. Did he really go to Florida with Anna Maria just for golf? Let them wonder.

Ms. Jardine put a copy of *Light in the Tunnel* on his desk.

"Thank you, Amy."

"You're welcome."

Neenan glanced at it and then picked up the phone again. He dialed his wife's private number again, not without some trepidation. Michael watched blandly.

"Anne Allegro."

"Your husband."

"I'm so glad you called, Raymond. I've been sitting here all morning feeling guilty about brushing you off. Don't go looking for another wife, will you?"

"Not hardly. . . . I'm sorry for bothering you again. Do you like to be called Annie?"

She giggled. "It's my name, dear. All through school. The only ones who use the Sicilian version — which is very lovely by the way — are my parents and grandparents. And you. Either one is fine with me, especially on your warm, wonderful lips."

The conversation lifted his spirits. What would he do if he lost her? Dear God, don't let that happen.

He turned to the script.

"Are you reading that," Michael demanded, "because you think you made a mistake when you vetoed it or because you want to find out what awaits you?"

"I didn't veto it," Neenan insisted.

"Yes, you did. You said that no one would believe that the woman gave up the happiness of heaven to go back to earth to take care of her stupid husband and ungrateful children. In fact, thoughts of heaven, as you humans call it, scared you."

"I can't quite remember that reaction."

"I suppose not. Nonetheless, you were wrong. It would have been a huge success. The good Annie was right, as always. It still would be."

"I thought you didn't know the future."

"We don't, but we're pretty good at guessing the market. Your wife's script, by the way, will become the most successful miniseries ever and a classic in the form which, as you doubtless know, has produced very few classics. If you don't blow it."

"Do you want a job?"

"I have one already, as you may have noticed."

"True."

"As for the depiction of what happens at the end of human life, the woman's story is based on the testimony of those who return for one reason or another. I have had some experience in such matters, and I can testify to the general accuracy of the literature, which by the way, goes back at least to the Middle Ages as Professor Carol Zaleski has wisely observed in her excellent volume *Otherworld Journeys*."

"Those people weren't really dead."

"Yes, they were, Raymond Anthony, yes, they were. Quite dead."

"They did not, however, get beyond the figure in light."

"That is true. We surmise that in certain extraordinary cases for reasons of Her own the Other gives people the option of returning for a time. My kind have charge of this process."

"I see."

"So they don't really know what life after death is like."

"That does not seem probable. Why would the Other fool them or us or anyone? Still, uncertainty remains. Necessarily. No cheap grace, you see."

"I wasn't asking for any—though I'd take some if it came."

Later in the grillroom of the Chicago Club, Raymond Neenan began his crucial conversation with his firstborn, as the Irish always do, by talking about other matters.

Michael, still dressed as a banker and still with the fresh flower in his lapel, made himself comfortable at the table.

"I had a phone call from Jenny down at Captiva on Saturday."

"Really?"

"I wondered who gave her my phone number."

"Megan," Vinny replied promptly. "Who else? . . . Did it go well?"

"I don't know. We both wept. In effect she asked me whether, if she decided on a reconciliation, I would be prepared to accept it."

"That was a matter of great concern to her," his son said guardedly. "You must remember, Dad, how Mom tried to fill us with the image of you as a cruel and inhuman man. Which of course you aren't and never were. Overinvolved maybe, but never deliberately cruel."

"I was out buying suntan oil when she called the first time, so she talked to Annie. I guess they hit it off pretty well."

"That does not surprise me."

"I did what I could, at least I think I did."

"Annie thought so too?" his son asked, a bit too casually.

"Yeah, she approved."

"I think it will work out, Dad. It will take time. She still feels great loyalty to Mom. She's unwilling to say you're basically a good guy without Mom agreeing. As you know well, that will never happen this side of paradise."

I don't have time. "We'll have to see what happens. . . . Should Annie stay in touch with her?"

"I'll have to see what Megan thinks. My guess is that she will think it's a great idea."

Would he and Donna be together in paradise — if there was such a place? That would not be easy.

"On another subject, this is a script for a miniseries. It's based on the novels of an English writer who apparently has done a series about a mythical place called Starbridge."

"Actually it's Winchester. Meg has read them all. I've read a couple. They're very good. It would be difficult to do a good miniseries, but if someone wrote it right, it would be a huge success. There are millions of dedicated readers."

"Let me know what you think."

"Sure will. . . . Has Annie read it?"

"Naturally."

"She likes it, if that's a fair question?"

"She does, but if I were you, I'd read it before you talked to her."

"I get it," Vinny said with a grin.

"*No, kid, you don't get it at all,*" Michael interjected. "*It's a good thing your old man warned you or there would be chaos tonight if you started talking about the script.*"

"Now to get down to the real business, Vinny." Neenan took a deep breath and plunged into the unknown. "I've made some changes in my personal and professional position in the last week or so. First of all, I am stepping down as president of NE. I will retain my position as chairman and CEO. With your permission, I will recommend you to the board to succeed me. I have talked informally with most of them, and I'm sure the votes are there . . . if you want the job. Secondly, I am making some modifications in my will. I'm going to establish five chairs at Loyola in honor of Annie. We will call them the Anna Maria Allegro chairs of humanistic studies."

"Hey, Dad, great idea. Does she know?"

"Indeed she does and accepts it as her due."

"She would," his son said with a merry grin. "Great idea."

"There will be other charitable gifts, to Old St. Patrick's Church where I attend Mass every morning, to the Lyric, that sort of thing."

"Every morning?"

"I told you that the flight from Washington scared me. I'm going to establish a large trust fund for Annie, whether she remarries or not."

"Dad!"

"Come on, Vinny, I'm seventeen years older than she is. I'll make bequests in trust funds for your mother and for Jenny and Leonard. I intend through various mechanisms to leave NE in effect to you."

His son turned pale. "I don't know that I'm ready for that kind of responsibility yet, Dad."

Michael raised his seraphic eyebrows, as if to say, "You didn't expect that, did you?"

"For which?"

"For both, for all of them. I'm not sure I can do COO at my age or that I could take over the company if I had to."

"That's up to you, Vincent. It's a free choice. The directors agree on your promotion. I don't know who else I could leave control of the company to. As you know, I've been skeptical about your abilities for some time. I now realize that I was mistaken. I don't know whether it makes any difference to you, but you've convinced me. I'm sorry it took so long."

Vincent nodded thoughtfully, perhaps weighing the arguments pro and con that tore at his soul and fighting with his demons. Michael watched him intently.

"Who are the other candidates?" Vincent finally asked.

"There aren't any. The board couldn't think of anyone as new president of the firm. I can't think of anyone else to turn the business over to if I should die."

"What are you going to do with your time?"

Actually what I'm going to do is die, but don't tell anyone that.

"Hang around the office. Answer questions. Offer advice. Stick my nose in, perhaps when it isn't wanted. Fight with you sometimes, which we both should learn how to do. Travel a lot. Become involved in pro bono stuff. Spend a lot of time with Anna Maria."

"It took you a long time to really fall for her, didn't it, Dad, but you're as bad now as a teenager in his first love. Your eyes glow when you mention her name."

Neenan felt his face grow warm and his body suddenly pulse with passion. "I won't deny that."

"Megan says we should enjoy our spouses while we still have them."

"Megan, as usual, is right."

"I can fight constructively with her."

"And she always wins."

Vinny laughed. "Let's say we clarify matters. I'd like to be able to fight with you. It'd be a hell of a lot of fun."

"When you get good at it, I probably lose most of the arguments."

"Majority, like I do to Megan. . . . I've always wanted the job, Dad. Now that I can have it, I'm afraid of it."

"I can understand that. Take your time. I'm in no rush."

In fact I am. I am rushing against death.

The seraph was shifting his eyes back and forth between father and son, enjoying the interchange.

"No way! If I take time, you'll change your mind. Dad, you've got a deal!"

Vincent grinned broadly, stuck out his hand, and shook Neenan's vigorously.

Michael smiled broadly in approval.

"We can celebrate it at your house tonight."

"Megan loves celebrations," Vincent said, his eyes wide and filled with stars.

They walked back to the Sears Tower almost unaware of the vigorous rainstorm that was beating against their faces, chatting about the enterprise that they were about to share as partners. Michael prudently disappeared. The angel choir had weighed in again and were softly humming Christmas carols, a little ahead of the season.

Exhausted and for some reason shaken, Neenan returned to his office and took up the script for *Light in the Tunnel*.

"You surprise me sometimes," Michael said as he materialized in the office, with what looked like a new flower in his lapel.

"I scare myself," Neenan said, conscious that his fingers were trembling. "It as though someone else is operating within me. You're not whispering in my ear, are you?"

The seraph shook his head. "We're capable of it, but we haven't had to do it. You seem to know what to say before there's any need for us to whisper."

"Ten days ago I would have made a mess out of that lunch with Vinny."

"Ten days ago you wouldn't have had lunch with Vinny."

"I feel like I'm possessed."

"We're not into that," Michael said, perhaps a little defensively. "Those people are all mentally ill."

"How do you account for what's happening then? I feel like I'm out of control, a runaway car careening through heavy traffic."

"Bad metaphor. You're not banging anyone up. Most likely the previously repressed goodness and skill in dealing with human beings is bursting out on you. I suspect your passion for your wife is partially responsible."

"Couldn't that become dangerous? I don't mean the way I feel about Annie, I mean this repressed goodness stuff."

"Everything could be potentially dangerous," Michael said enigmatically. "We don't know how this scenario is going to end, and we don't know what you are going to do next."

"I don't find that reassuring."

"I suppose you don't. Incidentally, the only thing you didn't tell Vinny this afternoon that he ought to hear was that the employees want him to take the job."

"I think I did."

"Nope. You said the directors."

"Does it make a difference?"

"It might."

"I'll tell him tonight."

"Might be a good idea."

Then Michael dematerialized.

Big help he is.

Neenan returned to the script. He'd been an idiot to turn it down, especially since everyone else liked it. Life after death had always been marketable in the human condition and always would be.

The film even had a skeptical scientist who explained the near-death experiences as a function of brain chemistry. Perhaps it was, but that was an explanation that would convince few people, especially since it was speculation.

Do I believe that it's like this immediately after death? Neenan asked himself as he finished the script. Maybe. I'll know for sure soon enough anyway.

He sighed. Maybe the trick for the next couple of weeks was not to be cautious. The angels were no longer reminding him that he had to change his life. If anything they seemed a little uneasy about the pace of change. It would be ironic if he blew it all toward the end by some sudden burst of goodness.

He laughed to himself. How could R. A. Neenan ever do that?

He penciled a note at the top of the script:

"Whoever decided not to do this film was a jerk. *Let's get it out for next Xmas. R.A.N.*"

Was there really a God? Was He really like the figure in light in the story? If there were, there was no possibility of being too good, was there?

His phone buzzed.

"Mr. Higgins from Lerner and Locke, Mr. Neenan."

Neenan picked up the phone. "We got it?"

"We did. Immediately we entered a plea that they show cause why the injunction shouldn't be made permanent. WorldCorp lawyers asked for a delay in the temporary injunction so they could appeal. The judge laughed at them and told them to respond to the plea to show cause first. They're still going to appeal, which is a waste of their time and money."

"Ours too," Neenan said thoughtfully. "Can they continue to try to raid us till the injunction becomes permanent?"

"They can do it even after the injunction if they're shrewd enough in the way they do it. We'll drag them into court and seek a contempt citation. Their lawyers will make a lot of money."

"And you guys won't bill us because you're such nice guys?"

"You got it!" Neil Higgins said with a laugh. "Next thing you know there'll be editorials in the *Wall Street Journal* calling on us to compromise."

"To hell with the *Journal*."

"Also, we've given Walsh the ultimatum about the pension suit. He tells us that all but one or two of his clients will come around in a day or two. He says that if the others don't take his advice, he'll advise them to get another attorney."

"Who will bleed them to death."

"Right."

"If that happens, can we ask for a summary judgment?"

"If it's the one I think it is, I'm sure we can. The Human Resources people have a huge file on him."

"Good, we'll do that if we have to."

After Neenan hung up, he thought about the potential lone holdout: he had used his position in the firm to live the good life in Los Angeles—booze, women, gambling over in Vegas. Talked big but hardly did any work from one end of the week to the other. A jerk. Yet he had a family . . . and who am I to judge anyone else?

Well, if the man wouldn't take the compromise, there wasn't much choice, was there?

The world was unpleasantly gray.

He put the screenplay in his out basket and glanced at his watch. Anna Maria was in Pilsen this afternoon. Peter would bring her to the apartment and then pick up the two of them for the ride up to Wrigleyville and dinner and then take them home to Lake Forest. It was almost four. They would leave for supper at six-thirty.

It would be a shame to waste those two hours.

"You're supposed to be working," she said when he ambled into the apartment fifteen minutes later. "I have to finish reading this script."

She was wearing a gray skirt and a blouse, her uniform in Pilsen, and looked very much like a young and attractive mother superior, her face innocent of makeup, her hair tied in a severe knot.

Something clicked in the back of his head about a script. But then it clicked off.

"I don't have to work anymore," he said. "I appointed Vincent president of the firm this afternoon and told him that I was leaving it to him in my will."

"I know all about it." She continued to work on the script, jotting neat little notes in the margin.

"Meg called you?"

"Of course. You made them both very happy." She looked up from the script and smiled at him.

"I'm sorry I didn't fill you in on all the details."

"Oh, Raymond, you don't have to fill me in on the details. I knew in general what you were going to do. That's enough. I'm not the kind of person who sulks because you don't tell me everything, am I?"

"No," he said, towering over her. "Still I should keep you informed."

"Well, I knew what was happening and I'm delighted that you did it so quickly and so sweetly. We'll have a grand celebration tonight."

The choristers, perhaps somewhere over Lake Michigan, were suddenly singing a variant of "Gaudeamus Igitur."

She looked back at the script, avoiding his eyes.

"We'll see the president of Loyola tomorrow just before lunch."

"Fine."

If he had only a few weeks of life left, he should enjoy every moment of pleasure that was possible. Why waste this moment?

He took the script out of her hand and lifted her to her feet.

"I have work to do," she protested. "Can't we wait till tonight?"

"No," he said, consuming her with an insanely passionate kiss.

"Raymond!" she gasped.

He kissed her again.

She melted into his arms. "Each time . . . each time you take me," she sighed, "I become more completely yours. It is as if I have no mind or will of my own anymore, no reality distinct from you. I just want to please you, satisfy you, make you happy. Always and forever. Nothing else matters."

"Always and forever," he echoed her words, knowing that at most that meant another month or two.

Then neither of them could say anything at all. For a time Neenan did not think about death.

22

The champagne at the younger Neenans' house was, needless to say, from the Seraphic Vineyards. As was the chardonnay and the new Beaujolais. Even the Irish cream displayed the three pairs of wings that were the seraphic logo. Oddly, or perhaps not so oddly, Neenan was the only one of the four humans around the table who noticed the label. He kept his mouth shut. He also did not mention that the music, playing on the elaborate stereo system and filling the old house a block off Irving Park Road, was something more elaborate than the polyphony of Giovanni Pierluigi da Palestrina.

The Palestrina Mass was playing because Neenan had brought a collection of such music for the woman of the house because he had remembered her love of classic polyphony. He remembered because Gaby had materialized in the bedroom of the apartment, while Anna Maria was still sleeping, with the discs and a strong warning that Neenan not forget to bring the present to his daughter-in-law.

"You're the new, considerate, sensitive Ray Neenan tonight," Gaby had said.

"Yes, ma'am," he had sighed as he tried to wake up.

"She looks happy," the seraph had said, glancing at Neenan's naked wife, sound asleep with her head on his chest.

"I try."

"Keep trying," Gaby said briskly, then vanished.

There was much to celebrate at the party — Vinny's new role in National Entertainment, the promised advent of a second child to the younger Neenans, the decision to go ahead with the script of *Light in the Tunnel*, the good news of Jenny's possible reconciliation with her father.

"I didn't look for her in Los Angeles," Vinny said. "I thought I might give her a ring if we had time. Then she shows up for dinner with Jerry Carter, whom, it turns out, she's dating. I didn't even recognize her as the daughter in *Rebirth* because she's a blonde in the

film. Jerry didn't know she was my sister because she's Jenny
O'Connell professionally. She didn't know that they would meet the
boss's son at dinner."

"Didn't even recognize his own sister in the film," Megan continued, "although she almost stole it—and did steal the director, though
from no one in particular."

Meg was the sort of Irish Catholic young woman whom Neenan
would have dated when he was at St. George's High School had he
been able to work up the nerve to invite her out. She was tall, willowy,
with black hair, dancing blue eyes, freckled face, and enormous energy
and enthusiasm—and a quick tongue to go with the energy and enthusiasm. She might occasionally be in error but never in doubt.

"I stress that she's dating Carter, not sleeping with him," Vinny
continued. "He's hopelessly in love with her, even accompanies her to
Blessed Sacrament Church on Sunday mornings."

"We argued with her that she ought to give you a second chance,"
Megan, an assistant state's attorney, took up the narrative. "I think
she's willing to do it, Ray, especially now that she's made it professionally without being known as your daughter. She has to work
through her relationship with Donna, however. And that won't be
easy."

"I'm glad she's in touch with you, Annie," Vinny said. "Did she
talk to you again today?"

Neenan's wife and daughter-in-law must have been in communi-
cation during the day about Jenny. Women were conspiring all
around him.

"She called me at the apartment just after I got back from Pilsen.
I think she'll come around sometime, but she still feels an enormous
loyalty to her mother. She hates Donna but loves her and can't break
away from Donna's version of things. At least she doesn't hate me. In
fact, she's kind of curious about her stepmother, as she doesn't call
me."

"Are you going to ask Carter to direct *Light in the Tunnel*, Ray?"
Meg asked. "He would give her a big role, maybe the lead."

"We have a number of possibilities for him." Neenan evaded the
question since he had Carter in mind to direct *Starbridge*, but he did
not want to say anything about that prospect until a decision had been
made. "We certainly don't intend to let him sleep away. I'll be eager
to see Jenny in *Rebirth*."

"I'm not sure you'll like to see your daughter in a torrid love scene," Vinny told him.

"I'll probably be furious," Neenan said, laughing.

"Do I hear a noise from herself?" Megan raised her finger.

Astonishingly, the choir paused in its singing so they could listen for sounds from two-year-old Rae Neenan.

Nothing.

The angel brats began singing again.

"She is not only lovely," Anna Maria observed, "she's a sweetheart at bedtime."

"She gets her good manners and her even disposition from her father," Megan observed, "not from me and I don't think from her paternal grandfather either."

Everyone laughed, the seraphic wine having taken effect.

Rae had spent most of her lap time with Anna Maria instead of her grandfather. Neenan, whose emotions were bittersweet at this family festival, was moved by the longing in his wife's eyes as she held the pretty little tyke. We should have done something years ago about having children, he thought. Now it's too late.

"If you really are stepping back from the firm," Meg informed him, "it's time you take your wife to London and Paris and Dublin."

"I agree," Vinny chimed in.

"It should be Palermo first," Neenan suggested.

"London will be just fine," Anna Maria announced. "A weekend before Christmas."

More giddy laughter.

"Long weekend," Neenan agreed. "As soon as we get this business with WorldCorp lined up."

"Did you see the closing numbers on our stock today, Dad?"

"I didn't have a chance this afternoon."

Anna Maria blushed. Meg noticed. Naturally. She noticed everything.

"Our common stock is up another eight points. It's doubled since rumors of a WorldCorp takeover surfaced. You are twice as rich as you were two weeks ago."

"Who's buying it?" Meg asked.

"WorldCorp is trying to create a momentum," Vinny explained. "So they're bidding it up. Speculators are riding along in the expectation that there eventually will be a sale or a stock trade or something like that. They also might think that there'll be pressure, even a suit, from some of the speculators to force a sale. They won't win, but it would cause more trouble."

"Vinny, Anna Maria and I will be seeing the Loyola president tomorrow morning about our Allegro chairs. Would you see that we get out a press release in which we say that we are confident of the profitability of our company and that speculators must weigh that profitability against the current price of the stock and make their own decisions. Add that we are not and will not be for sale to WorldCorp or anyone else."

"Wow! Sure will, Dad! That's tough talk."

"Are you overvalued?" Megan asked.

"We were probably undervalued by maybe ten percent," Vinny replied to his wife. "That's because we are a closely held corporation. Now I think we're overvalued. Dad's statement will be an appropriate warning, especially to the retirement fund managers who are taking a big chance with their clients' money."

"Ray, Annie"—Megan raised her glass of the Seraphic Irish cream—"I'd like to propose a toast to the two of you. When I married this guy I thought I wouldn't have to worry about his family because he really didn't have one. Now I find that he does and that it's a wonderful family. So I drink to your long lives and good health."

"Slainte!" her husband echoed the toast.

They wept like sentimental Irishmen who had consumed a lot of wonderful wine. Well, like three sentimental Irishmen and one sentimental Sicilian woman.

Neenan had his own special reasons for weeping. This tight and loving family of his would soon be struck down. At least he had created some relationships that would last after he was gone.

He raised his own glass of Seraphic cream in a toast that he would never have expected to cross his lips. "To my family," he said hoarsely.

Gaby and Michael materialized briefly behind Anna Maria's back to join in the toast.

"Cheers!" his wife and son and daughter-in-law said in unison.

"*Cheers,*" the two smiling seraphs joined in.

Later that night with his naked wife again resting her head on his chest as she slept, he tried to puzzle out everything that had happened to him in the last ten days. It made little sense, but it had been wonderful. What a shame it would not last, he thought sadly.

In life, he reminded himself, nothing ever lasts.

The next day in the office of the president of Loyola, overlooking the Water Tower, he was trying, more than anything else, to leave a memorial of his love for his wife — who sat demurely on a chair across from the president, like a pious novice.

"My wife, Anna Maria Allegro, was a student here, Father," he said to the young and charming Jesuit, "not too many years ago. She seems to have received a superb education at Loyola."

"We keep track of our alumni, Mr. Neenan," the priest said. "We know that she has extraordinary good taste in popular entertainment, perhaps the best in America. I'm not sure how much contribution we really made to that taste, but we're happy to claim some share of the credit."

Anna Maria blushed modestly. "A lot, Father," she said in her shy voice.

"We're both grateful," Neenan continued, savoring every moment of the conversation, in both the professional and personal sense. "We'd like to express our gratitude in a concrete form."

He opened his briefcase and removed the deed of gift.

"I hope my eyes are not glittering too brightly," the president said with an easy smile.

"I have a deed of gift here which my lawyers over at Lerner and Locke have put together. You will want to have your lawyers look over it."

"Loyola is very grateful, Mr. Neenan, Ms. Neenan."

"It is for the Anna Maria Allegro chairs of humanistic studies."

"Chairs?" the president gasped.

"I hope that five won't be too many?"

"Five?"

"Five. Six million dollars or so."

The president nodded. "I'm sure my eyes are glittering eagerly now, Mr. Neenan. I think we can absorb the money without any trouble." He laughed again. "Without any trouble at all! Thank you! As long as this university exists, you and your wife will be remembered with affection and gratitude. I'll be telling the story of my astonishment for the rest of my life."

"It's my wife who should be remembered, Father. She's the alum. Incidentally, my lawyers suggested that the first ones to occupy the chairs should be chosen at the discretion of the president, so that the appointments will not be mired in faculty politics."

"A very wise suggestion. We will find the most distinguished men and women to fill the chairs."

"I hope," Anna Maria said timidly, "that you'll have one teacher who specializes in popular culture."

"I was thinking the same thing myself, Ms. Allegro. Students will flock to such classes."

"You certainly made that man's day," Anna Maria said as they left Loyola and walked across Water Tower Park. "Let's go back and buy me a Loyola jacket. Or two."

They heard trumpet music in the background, a couple of spectacular fanfares.

"A band is practicing somewhere," she said. "Funny, they didn't used to have a band down here."

"Yeah, it is kind of odd."

The entered the bookstore across the street from the park. As Anna Maria found a winter jacket and two sweatshirts, he thought about his own future. He would be dead before the chairs were filled, perhaps even before the gift was announced.

What difference did that make?

Perhaps it was better that he die now. Anna Maria would be a widow eventually anyway. With him dead, she would be able to remarry someone more her own age. That morose self-pity made him feel better.

He felt no delight in his generosity and no grief in having spent so much money in a few moments. His own sensation was a dull ache at the time that was so quickly running out.

~23~

Before Friday night it had been a good week. Tim Walsh had accepted settlements for all but one of his clients. The pension case, for which Neenan now had deep regrets, was virtually over. The directors of NE had unanimously approved the appointment of Vincent Neenan as president and chief operating officer. Neenan and his son enjoyed ten minutes of friendly conversation before Norm and Joe joined them. Neenan felt that the new partnership between Vinny and himself was working far better than he might have expected. Plans for the production of *Light in the Tunnel* were going ahead rapidly; ABC and CBS were both bidding for it. Jerry Carter was tentatively scheduled to direct *Starbridge*, which Vinny was reading with delight. WorldCorp had filed a motion in the federal court for the Northern District of Illinois seeking to vacate the state court's temporary injunction — a strategy that NE's lawyers thought was foolish, though, as they quickly added, you couldn't tell what some federal judges would do these days.

Neenan had also watched the penultimate version of *Rebirth*. It was a brilliant film, far better than he had expected. Jenny was wonderful as the daughter who hated her criminal father and became sexually involved with a younger criminal to punish her father. The love scene was not exactly torrid. Neenan, however, had pushed the fast-forward button.

Jenny was a superb actress nonetheless. He was both proud of her and shocked at her behavior. He'd better accustom himself to such mixed emotions.

No, that wouldn't be necessary. He would certainly never see another film with her in it.

Unless they had movies in heaven.

Most important of all, his "honeymoon" romance with Anna Maria had become more intense, more satisfying, and more challenging than he had thought could possibly exist between a man and a woman.

Neenan was still not certain who he was or where he was going.

He was still afflicted by interludes of devastating self-pity, but he usually drove off such emotions before they could cause any harm to others.

The angels, perhaps convinced that he had reformed his life, appeared infrequently.

On Friday night, a bitter cold evening, he and Anna Maria were sitting in front of the fireplace in their Lake Forest home sipping port and reading. They were going to try for Paris on the following weekend. The scene that night was one of comfortable domesticity at the end of a busy week before they went upstairs for another exploration of the outer fringes of human passion.

It was as good a time as any, Neenan figured, to report the good news about *Starbridge*.

He removed the manuscript from his briefcase, which leaned against his chair.

"Good news, Anna Maria. We're going to produce *Starbridge*."

"Produce it?" she said, suddenly furious. "You didn't dare give it to other people to read, did you?"

"Well," he said apologetically, "I can't make the decision by myself. I showed it to Joe and Vinny."

"You had no right to do that," she shouted. "None at all. I gave it to you to read. I did not grant permission for you to pass it on to others."

"I thought you wanted us to consider it for production."

"Did I say that?"

"Well, no, you didn't, but I presumed . . ."

"You had no right to presume. You should have asked me. If you had, I would have forbidden it."

"Then why give it to me?"

"Because I thought I could trust you to treat it as a private document. It was wrong, terribly wrong of you to violate my confidence."

"We all loved it," he said, trying to be reasonable.

"That is totally irrelevant. It was for your eyes only."

"You didn't tell me that."

"I shouldn't have had to tell you that."

"You've never given me a manuscript before in such confidence."

She rose from her chair, snatched the thick manuscript from him, and waved it at him as if it were a weapon.

"I never gave you a manuscript before that I had written."

"You didn't tell me that you wrote it."

"Who did you think Marianne Swift was?"

"I thought it might be you."

"*Might!* . . . Who the fuck are you trying to kid! You knew it was mine and you still showed it to others without asking my permission. How typically arrogant and oppressive!"

Neenan knew that there was no point in arguing. He had lost the case. Still he tried to reason instead of listening, not that listening would have changed the situation in the slightest.

"When you have given me a manuscript before," he pleaded, "you've always wanted to find out whether we agreed with your judgment on whether we should produce it. I had no reason to think that this was a different situation."

"No *reason*! Didn't the fact that it was a very personal and private document of mine suggest it was different? How did you dare to violate my privacy? I feel like you've raped me!"

She strode across the room and threw the screenplay into the fire. It flamed up immediately, spreading a cloud of smoke in the room. Anna Maria poked at it furiously with a poker.

The fire alarm system screamed in protest.

"Shut that damn thing off!" she shouted at him.

Obediently, Neenan turned off the alarm and called the Lake Forest emergency number to head off the fire department.

"I'm sorry," he said when he returned to the smoke-filled parlor. "I thought you wanted a dispassionate, objective view of it from people who didn't know that it was written by the boss's wife. If you had told me that it was yours and that you didn't want me to pass it around, I would not have shown it to anyone."

"Sorry won't do!"

"What else can I say?"

"You can't say anything! You betrayed me! If I wanted an objective opinion I would have asked for it. You are not going to make a film out of this script. Not ever."

"That's clear enough," he said sadly.

"I hate you!" she cried. "I hate your stupid male arrogance. I don't want to live with you anymore."

She stormed out of the parlor and up the stairs to the second floor.

Somehow she had missed the point, Neenan told himself. It was a great screenplay; she had enormous talent not only as a script reader but as a scriptwriter. Why put all the time and energy into composing such a work only to throw it into the fire because his procedure had been clumsy?

What was he supposed to do now?

Nothing until her Sicilian temper cooled.

"You really blew that one." Michael, in jogging clothes, materialized in the chair Anna Maria had vacated.

"Apparently I did," he replied ruefully.

"You know how writers feel about their first work. You should have proceeded much more cautiously."

"So I gather . . . though I don't think it would make any difference."

"Regardless."

"Is this a black mark on my record?"

"You should follow her upstairs and beg for forgiveness," the seraph insisted.

"Not now, not tonight."

"Her anger will only increase."

"Look, Michael, she's my wife. She'll have to calm down before she'll listen to me."

"This is a totally unique situation for her. You are too insensitive to realize how closely she has identified her core self with that screenplay."

"Are you invoking the contract?"

"Contract? Oh, *that* contract. No, not yet anyway. Play it however you want. Only remember that you don't have all that much time to effect a reconciliation."

"I know," Neenan said sadly.

"You should also realize that if you die without a reconciliation, she'll feel guilty for the rest of her life. Do you want to be responsible for that?"

"I didn't start the fight," he said defensively.

"That's hardly the issue, is it?"

Then Michael vanished. Neenan was patently on his own.

All right, I was dumb. I didn't mean to offend her. I thought I was bringing home a pleasant surprise. He felt sorry for himself. Then he realized that was no help.

He decided that he would go upstairs and see if she had calmed down.

He found that she had cleared all her things out of what had become their room and shut the door to her own room. Their marital bedroom was now his again.

He put on a sweater and a jacket and went for a long walk along the lakeshore. It didn't help.

She avoided him throughout the rest of the weekend.

Well, there was surely a copy of the screenplay on her computer. Even if she should delete it, there were also two copies in his office.

Monday morning she had disappeared from the house. Ms. Neenan had gone to the apartment on East Lake Shore Drive, Maeve told him as he drank his coffee.

Bad news waited him at the office. A federal judge had vacated the temporary injunction against WorldCorp. They were free to raid his executives, his clients, and his potential acquisitions. Tim Walsh's recalcitrant client had hired another lawyer, a notorious manipulator who would destroy the poor man, not that he didn't deserve destruction.

Neenan's phone buzzed.

"Ms. O'Connell on the line, Mr. Neenan."

"O'Connell?"

"Ms. *Jennifer* O'Connell."

"Hi, Jenny," he said brightly.

"You miserable bastard."

"Huh?"

"How dare you try to trick me into a reconciliation after the terrible things you've done to my mother through the years!"

"I wasn't trying to trick you into anything, Jennifer. You called me first."

"Only because you sent your weak little stooge out here to trick me."

"I didn't know he was going to see you. I don't think he knew either."

"I'll never turn my back on Mom, never! Never! You may have fooled poor Vinny, but you'll never fool me. I know what you are!"

"What am I, Jennifer?"

"You're a bastard, a fucking asshole, a creep, a genuinely evil man! I will never speak to you again!"

She slammed down her phone. Neenan replaced his slowly.

"That one's not really your fault." Michael, in jeans and a University of Chicago sweatshirt, was sitting across from him. "Not in the present context anyway. You should have paid more attention to her when she was a kid."

"Would it have done any good?"

The angel lifted his massive shoulders. "Who knows? Maybe. As it is, now she must choose between what her brother says about you and what her sainted and martyred mother has to say. In such a contest, you don't have a chance. When you're dead, she'll blame herself. You'll leave a lot of guilt feelings behind."

"Will I be in trouble if I say I don't give a damn?"

Michael burst out in a noisy, seraphic laugh. "You want to argue," he said when he recovered from his outburst, "that you've done your best and that's that?"

Neenan became crafty; after all, he'd been dealing with angels for what seemed to have been an eternity.

"Who does their best?"

The seraph laughed again. "The Other loves you or we wouldn't be here," he said enigmatically.

"Mr. Vincent Neenan to see you, sir."

A warning bell went off inside Neenan's head. Vincent had barged in all last week without waiting to be announced. He was, after all, the COO and heir apparent. Why was he asking permission this time?

"Thank you, Amy. Send him in."

His son was pale and anxious. "I'll be up front about it, Dad. I'm resigning my position with National Entertainment to take a high-level position at WorldCorp America."

Neenan drew a deep breath. "Well," he said slowly, "there is a family tradition of breaking away from the father. I'm in no position to be critical. It's your call, Vinny. Best of luck in the job."

Michael gasped in surprise.

Well, just once, I've surprised a seraph.

Vincent plunged ahead with his explanation, almost as though he had not heard Neenan's initial reaction.

"Everyone around here thinks that the only reason I got the job is that I'm your son. I'd have to live with that for the rest of my life. At WorldCorp America I will have to survive on my own skills and talent. That will be better for me and better for National Entertainment."

In fact, if he were not Vincent Neenan, WorldCorp would not have given him a second thought. Vincent, however, could not permit himself to consider that possibility because then his behavior would be seen as treason.

"You have to follow your own instincts, Vinny."

"If I can't cut it there, Dad, they won't hesitate a moment to get rid of me. Here I'd have a lifetime job no matter how bad I was. You'd better change your will again. I don't want to inherit the firm either."

So WorldCorp knew about the new will. If anything should happen to Neenan—and, though WorldCorp didn't know it, something would happen—a senior executive of WorldCorp would own National Entertainment.

"If you don't mind, I'll hold off on that for a while."

"I can't stand," Vincent exploded, "the look of hatred on people's faces around here when they see me. I'm the great man's son and I'll never be anything else."

"I have no doubt some people feel that way. However, Joe and Norm polled all the senior people with an open-end question about a president and COO. You won in a landslide. I would not have voted for you, but virtually everyone else did."

"You should have told him that last week," Michael insisted. *"Remember that I told you to."*

"I am not likely to forget."

"You'll excuse me, Dad, if I don't believe that story."

"Don't believe?"

"Not its implications anyway. . . . I suppose you want me to leave right away? With the federal court order, they are free to sign me."

"Take your time," Neenan sighed. "We'd hardly bring action to prevent you from starting a new career."

"I can never be sure, Dad, what you will do."

Before his son left the office, Neenan almost asked whether Megan knew of the decision. That bright young litigator would not trust WorldCorp any farther than Irving Park Road. He thought better of it and settled for a handshake, strong on his part, limp on Vinny's.

"The tragedy of this," Neenan said to Michael, "is that he would have been a great success here where everyone knows him and likes him and now he'll be a failure at WorldCorp."

"Doubtless. He'll also have guilt feelings for the rest of his life."

"Nothing I can do about that."

"You have to try just the same."

"Why?"

"Because in a certain sense all of these problems are your fault. If you had been more sensitive to Annie and Vinny last week, these situations might not have occurred. Worse still, you created an atmosphere for most of your life in which neither of them—nor Jenny for that matter—were really capable of trusting you under pressure."

"It's all my fault?"

"I'm not excusing them," Michael said solemnly. "Still, you must assume your own responsibility and strive to change the situation."

"I don't want to."

For the first time in what seemed like ages, the seraph boss produced the contract.

"I won't change either of their minds."

"Probably not. You have to try, however."

"All right," Neenan sighed. "In my own way and in my own time and when my instincts say I should."

Michael nodded impassively. "I don't propose to dictate either strategy or tactics."

"That's generous of you," Neenan said ironically. "There's not much hope of success."

"In the condition of your species there rarely is."

Great.

"You let yourself be deceived by your early successes," the angel continued grimly. "Your charm and passion and apparent generosity covered up temporarily their memories of your past failings. . . . Incidentally, if I were in your position, I would be wary of the possibility of your wife and your son taking *Starbridge* to WorldCorp."

"If they want to, let them," Neenan said sadly. "If it makes them happy, it's fine with me."

"More guilt feelings for them if they do," Michael warned.

"They'll probably outgrow them," Neenan said bitterly, "since they'll figure they got their revenge on me. . . . What about Leonard, by the way?"

"That situation is not sufficiently mature at the present time. However, for your wife and your daughter and your older son, the situation is critical. Their future depends on the skill of your efforts."

And with that solemn warning, the seraph was not there anymore.

"And their own free will," Neenan shouted after Michael. "I can't force them to do anything."

The seraph boss, however, was certainly right. Neenan knew that he had to do something. But he had no idea what. He ought not to panic. Rather he ought to bide his time, wait for the golden opportunity, and then follow his instincts, as flawed as they might be. This was the way he had worked all his life. It was too late to change.

He assembled his senior executives and announced that he was reassuming his post as president of the company because his son had resigned and would be taking a senior post at WorldCorp America. Their parting had been amiable and he wished Vincent success and happiness in his new job. He instructed the PR people to get out an appropriate statement, to which they should add his firm statement that National Entertainment was not for sale and never would be.

There were only a few questions, each delicately worded.

What about the injunction?

It is currently vacated by order of the United States Court for the Northern District of Illinois. There is nothing to stop WorldCorp from recruiting any and all of you, if you think the ship is sinking. It's not, but that's up to you to judge for yourself.

Are we going ahead with *Light in the Tunnel*?

We certainly are.

Will Jerry Carter accompany Vinny to WorldCorp?

He hadn't thought of that possibility. His response was that Mr. Carter would have to make his own decisions. He is an extremely talented young man, but by no means the only gifted young director in Hollywood.

Are the rumors about the miniseries true?

One is pending, yes.

Is there any hope that Vinny might change his mind?

While there is life, there is always hope.

Joe McMahon remained in the conference room after the others had silently filed out.

"What the hell got into the kid, R. A.?"

"Fear, I suppose. Hell, I broke with my own dad. I have no cause for complaint."

"Do you want me to hunt down the agent for Ms. Howatch and

see who has the film rights? They may be floating around out there. Do you know whether the scriptwriter had an option?"

"No, I don't."

Anna Maria might have written the script on spec. Cautious peasant that she was, that was not unlikely. If NE could get the film rights, that would at least prevent *Starbridge* being taken over to WorldCorp.

Would that be a cheap trick of which he ought to be ashamed?

He thought about it. If it came to a battle with his wife and son over the series, they would never forgive him. On the other hand he had an obligation to protect the company, did he not?

"Find out," he told Joe McMahon, "and if there are no options out there, get one for us. Be generous with the price. I want to do that film."

"Mr. Jerry Carter on the line, Mr. Neenan."

Fine. Another one leaving the ship.

"Hi, Ray."

"Hi, Jerry."

"What the hell happened to Vinny?"

"He wants to be his own man. I understand the feeling, God knows."

"Yeah, but it's crazy. They'll exploit him over there and then cut off his balls, you should excuse the expression. Doesn't he know that?"

"I don't think so."

"Did you tell him?"

"No, Jerry, I didn't. Think about it. If you had a son who wanted to break away, would you tell him that?"

Jerry hesitated. "Probably I would, but only because I'm not as smart and as generous a man as you are."

"Thanks, Jerry." Neenan grinned in spite of himself.

"I like the guy a lot," the director went on. "I'm in love with his sister, whom I'll marry if she'll have me, but I don't think the ship is sinking, and anyway I'm not a rat. Count on me, Ray."

"Thank you, Jerry. . . . Incidentally, did Vinny try to win you over to WorldCorp?"

"Yeah. I told him that just because he was a bastard, it didn't make me one."

"Jenny?"

"She agrees completely."

Still uncertain whose side she was on.

"Thank you again."

"See you at the premier of *Rebirth.*"

Neenan picked up the phone to call Anna Maria and tell her about all the developments. Then he remembered that she had walked out on him, perhaps permanently. He hesitated. Maybe if he made an overture now, pretending that the quarrel had never happened, he might effect a quick reconciliation.

He put the phone down. It was too soon.

Ꙩ 24 Ꙩ

Neenan bumbled and stumbled through the rest of the week. Vincent's defection was headline news on every business page in the country. So was Jerry Carter's refusal to defect. Vincent's public image was at rock bottom. He looked like a traitor, which in a way he was, though no worse a traitor perhaps than Neenan had been to his father. WorldCorp took a terrible beating because it looked like a slippery, crooked operation. Their stock plummeted and NE's held steady. The Seventh Circuit rebuked the judge who had vacated the state court's injunction and reinstated the injunction. No one else left NE in the brief window of opportunity the courts had created.

He heard not a word from his estranged wife. He thought about calling her to ask about their trip to Paris and decided that it would be too risky. Michael pushed him to do something about a reconciliation.

"Next week," he argued, "when she's calmed down. You know what Sicilian tempers are like."

"Maybe she's already calmed down and is too ashamed to call you."

"Maybe."

Nonetheless he did not call her. Rather he canceled the reservations for the Paris trip, after he had thought briefly of going himself, an idea he did not share with the seraph.

Joe McMahon was able to buy the film rights to the whole Star-bridge cycle for a hundred thousand pounds.

"Bargain," Neenan murmured.

"I could have got it for fifty. I told the agent it was worth more than that."

"Thank heaven we're not a ruthless outfit."

He and Joe laughed mirthlessly at that line.

Michael did not intervene to advise against the purchase of film rights, to which, presumably, he did not object.

A woman reporter from the *Journal* called to ask if he was angry at his son. Michael appeared for that conversation.

"I can hardly be angry at him," Neenan said urbanely. "I did the same thing myself when I was a young man. Every male in the species has to satisfy himself that he can make it on his own. I wish Vinny all the luck in the world in his new job, except when he's competing with National Entertainment."

"Would you take him back?"

Neenan searched for the right words. "We hired him here because the directors and the staff thought he was the man for the job and despite reservations I had about the appearance of nepotism. If they would make the same decision again, I could hardly object, could I?"

"That doesn't sound like the public image of R. A. Neenan," the woman said crisply.

Neenan laughed genially. "Sorry to disappoint you."

"On the contrary, I am impressed."

He almost invited her to lunch. Michael would have had a fit.

Thank goodness the media had not learned that his wife had also left him.

Neenan had worried every morning as the week went on that during the day he would hear from a divorce lawyer.

"Mr. Len Neenan on the phone, Mr. Neenan."

"Len, it's good to hear from you."

"We're not in the same business, Dad," his gay son began, "not even in the same world. If we were, I hope I wouldn't do to you what Vinny did."

"I appreciate that, Len. He's got to prove himself to me, just like I did to my father."

"No, he doesn't, Dad. It's completely different. Your father wouldn't let you do anything. You let him do almost everything he wanted in the firm."

"I suppose that is a difference, but I figure I should let my children be who they are."

"Unlike Mom."

"I suppose so."

"You ever get to San Francisco, Dad?"

"Sure."

"Can we have lunch next time?"

"You bet."

"Would you mind meeting Johnny, my, uh, partner?"

"Not at all."

Michael was present again, wearing a gray ensemble that was in all respects but color like the one he had worn on the flight to Chicago, a century or two ago.

"Aren't we getting tolerant," he said.

"You said the situation wasn't mature."

"If I've told you once, I've told you a thousand times, Raymond Anthony, that I do not know the future. You consistently underestimate the appeal you exercise on those who are close to you. Clearly, Leonard was looking for an opportunity to effect a reconciliation."

"So the situation is mature now?"

"Patently," the angel said without blinking an eye. "However, it is not as critical as that with your wife."

"I agree. First thing next week."

"Time is precious, Raymond Anthony."

"You don't have to remind me of that."

He slipped out of his habit of attending Mass every morning and of exercising every day. On Thursday, however, he realized that he had to swim if only to exorcise all the tensions from his body. He walked up Wacker Drive to the East Bank Club.

As he fought the water with a determined Australian crawl, he noticed a shapely woman in a gray maillot who was swimming much faster than he was.

No, he told himself, I don't need another problem.

When the woman pulled up alongside him, he realized that she was not likely to be a problem.

"You're the good cop," he said to Gaby, "and your companion is the bad cop."

"We have our ways," she said with a devastating smile.

"I need to give her time."

"And Vinny too."

"How is she?"

"Annie? How would you think she is? Heartbroken of course."

"What should I do?"

"No more questions about her. I won't violate her privacy."

"Fair enough."

"You have not read that Polish poet who won the Nobel Prize?"

"No. Is there a film possibility in her work?"

They continued to swim side by side.

"You should read and find out. I want to cite one of her best poems,

'Nothing Twice.' She says that we arrive here impoverished and leave without a chance to practice."

"So we make mistakes."

"And she adds that you can't repeat the class in the summer because the course is only offered once."

"Yeah. . . . Is that supposed to encourage or discourage me?"

"What do you think?"

Then the beautiful woman disappeared in a burst of multicolored light that no one else in the pool noticed.

"No naked dance on the water today?" he asked.

No reply.

He pondered the quote as he dressed and decided that it was probably meant to encourage him. He bought a copy of the book of poems on the way back to his office.

"Today is always gone tomorrow" was, he thought, the key line in the poem. You could build a film around that.

Did the lovely seraph intend to tell him that he should lighten up?

Well, maybe he should, except he didn't know how.

The next day something happened to him that seemed to occur in another world, one that looked like Chicago and yet was subtly different, a mirror world perhaps, but not one that reflected this world so much as altered it, a world in which strange things seemed to happen as a matter of course, a world where boundaries between levels of existence were perilously—or perhaps wondrously—thin.

25

Neenan was walking back to the Sears Tower on Adams Street from the noon Mass at Old St. Patrick's — so called not because the saint is old, but because the church is old. Later he would distinctly remember that he was still in the ordinary world when he crossed the South Branch of the Chicago River. It was when he passed the Starbucks coffee shop on the east bank of the river that he seemed to spin off into another layer of reality — or so he thought after the fact.

A young woman, sitting at the window of the coffee shop, smiled at him, waved, and then motioned him to come in. At first her short black hair, olive skin, and dark, dancing brown eyes made him think she was a Palestinian, and a very young Palestinian at that, still in her teens. She was short and pretty and was wearing a blue suit and a light blue blouse. Her smile was contagious and her laugher, when she waved him to her table, made Neenan smile, something he had not done all week.

He sat down across the table from her and noticed that her eyes, for all their suggestion of mischievous fun, were wise far beyond their years.

Then he knew who she was. Palestinian indeed.

"They've sent in the first team," he said, wondering whether charm would work with such a woman.

She clapped her hands in delight. "I don't think of myself that way, but if you want to, it's all right."

Her complexion was flawless. She wore no makeup and only a gold wedding band and a pendant with a fish on it.

"You don't look like your pictures."

"All those Italian women are quite lovely, aren't they?" she whispered, as if sharing a great secret with him. "But they're not me, if you know what I mean? A little too bland, you know?"

"Not enough vitality and mischief?"

"What other kind of woman would get the job?"

That was an interesting point, perhaps an indisputable one. Why had nobody ever thought of it?

She poured him some tea, Earl Grey. Starbucks didn't do tea, but in this world nothing was quite the same. He began to work on a plate of chocolate chip cookies, the most delicious chocolate chip cookies he had ever tasted. Even the Seraphic Bakeries, should such exist, would never produce such cookies.

"My little playmates are giving you a hard time, aren't they?"

Neenan didn't believe what was happening. It was an illusion, a dream, a hallucination. Yet it all seemed genuine enough. The vivacious teen across from him seemed like a very real woman, though hardly what one would have expected.

"You should know, you're supposed to be their queen."

She waved that title aside with a brisk and playful gesture. "Oh, that's only a metaphor. I wouldn't want to be responsible for that bunch, not at all."

Her gestures and facial expressions were Semitic, which is what they ought to be. She also spoke with a touch of New York Jewish accent, which was doubtless added for effect.

"I see."

"The angels," she continued as though she were explaining the rationale for an important bargain that was available for today only, "are darling creatures, brilliant, intense, passionate, brave . . ."

"A little vain."

She clapped her hands again. "As they'd be the first to tell you, they have a lot to be vain about. I love them all very much, but, you know, Ray, there's one thing wrong with them." She grinned happily as though she were about to deliver a wonderful punch line.

Considering the nature of the company, Neenan was willing to play along. "They're too pushy?"

"Close," she giggled, "but not quite on target."

"I give up."

"They're not human!" She clapped her hands again and laughed happily.

"Not like you and I."

"No way, Ray, no way."

"What do I call you?"

She shrugged as though it were a matter of complete indifference. "*Well*, my real name is Miriam. Is that OK?"

"That's fine, Miriam. You've been called a lot of other things."

She waved her dismissive hand again. "A lot of metaphors."

"Like what all generations will call you?"

"I totally did *not* write that Magnificat hymn. Some of the early folks made it up for their Christmas plays and that's how it got into the Bible. It really is very lovely, but I would never dare say anything like that. Then or now. And while we're at it, do I look like the kind of woman who would be involved in those creepy apparitions?"

"Now that you mention it, Miriam, no."

"Not that they do any great harm, but they're not me, you know?"

"Do you do this sort of thing often?"

"What sort of thing?" she said, hunching her shoulders in gleeful anticipation of another riposte.

"Meet troubled people for a cup of tea in a café that doesn't do tea?"

For just a moment she was serious. "More often than most people realize. Those with whom I have these little chats know that it's not wise to talk about them, which is fine with me. Otherwise folks would start making up more silly stories."

"Unbelievable stories, Miriam?"

She waved that away too. "I don't mind unbelievable. I do mind just plain silly."

She refilled his cup of tea and shoved a plate of oatmeal raisin cookies in his direction.

A few moments ago they had been chocolate chip cookies.

"I see."

"You like my cookies?"

"Scrumptious. You make them yourself?"

"Of *course* I did. You don't think I'd buy them in a store, do you?"

"Best I've ever eaten."

"What else would you expect?" she said proudly. "I'll see that you get some occasionally, just to remind you that I am not an illusion."

"Maybe you are, Miriam, but right now you don't seem like an illusion. But aren't oatmeal raisin and chocolate chip cookies after your time?"

"You gotta keep up," she said with an artificial sigh. "Now I suppose you wonder why I dragged you in here as you were walking down Adams Street?"

"To feed me the best cookies ever made."

She flushed with pleasure. "Well, that too. But we've been a little worried about you."

Neenan was not inclined to ask who "we" were. He did not have a map to explain what the world was like beyond the thin boundaries of ordinary life.

"I'm glad someone is worried, to tell you the truth."

"Michael and Gaby are worried too, terribly worried, but you see they don't know the future."

"You do?"

"Naturally."

"When will I—"

"No questions." She held up a hand that was gentle and maternal but that could become imperious if necessary. "I give the answers only to the questions I intend to answer."

"Fair enough, Miriam, you hold all the cards."

She giggled again. "I do, don't I? I usually do. Anyway, my answer is simple. It will be all right."

"What will be all right?"

"Everything. What else?"

"Oh."

"You know, everyone really loves you, Ray. You're a very special human. God loves you, my boy loves you, I love you, your family and friends love you. Even your enemies love you, kind of anyway."

My boy. But what else would she call him?

"The seraph crowd are pushing me to take what I think are desperate measures."

"Don't," she said firmly. "Don't do a thing. Everything will be all right. It always is in God's time anyway. Right now I'm talking about human time."

"I should follow my instincts?"

"Absolutely. And don't tell the seraphs about our little chat, promise? It will hurt their feelings, the poor dears."

"Heaven forbid."

She giggled again. "Aren't they attractive?"

"Very, but those are only surrogates I see."

"Well, they give pretty good hints, Ray."

"The other day Gaby turned into a burst of light in the East Bank pool."

"Yesterday," Miriam reminded him. "She was just showing off. No harm in that. But I really don't want to hurt their feelings. You should be gentle with them too, even if they do push you too hard. They are very sensitive."

"I would never have guessed it."

"Believe me, they are."

"I'll get my wife back?"

"Isn't she the dearest, sweetest woman?"

She didn't answer his question, which meant she wouldn't. He'd have to make do with the promise that everything would be all right.

"Sicilian temper."

"That makes her even more attractive."

"You sound like you're on her side."

"*Well,* you haven't been the world's most sensitive man, you know that. But I do think she overreacted a tad this time. However, don't worry about it. Just wait. Like Advent, a time of waiting."

"You were involved in that too, weren't you?"

She smiled, this time a smile of a woman of immense wisdom. "Just a little."

"Thank you for the cookies and the tea," he said, sensing that this most remarkable tête-à-tête was coming to an end. "And the message of hope."

"Hope is my business. Now before you walk back out on Adams Street, I want to sing you my favorite lullaby—if you don't mind?"

"I need to hear a lullaby, Miriam."

"Later you will wonder if any of this ever happened. Then you'll hear the song in your head and know that something very important did happen, even if you don't quite understand what it was."

The song, in a language Neenan did not understand (Aramaic, maybe), was unbearably sweet, tender, loving—and hopeful. Much better than anything the noisy seraph brats had ever done. But they were not human, were they?

He realized that he was back on Adams in the ordinary world, but he was still hearing the lovely song.

Naturally she would be good at lullabies.

Later he entered his office, content, happy, and ready. For whatever would happen next.

He phoned Leonard at his office in San Francisco and said he would be flying out to Sacramento the next day and could hop over to San Francisco for brunch on Sunday. Leonard seemed delighted.

"How's the market out there?" Neenan asked.

"Same as in New York, Dad. You're up a bit, WorldCorp is down. You're not going to sell to them, are you?"

"Not a chance."

"Well," Michael observed, "that was decisive activity, wasn't it?"

"I felt that I might as well handle an easy one over the weekend while I get ready for the big ones next week."

"You think Lenny will be easy?"

"Compared to the others, sure."

"Maybe you're right," Michael agreed, bemused perhaps by his charge's newfound confidence.

Then Neenan remembered that he was supposed to be careful of seraphic sensitivity. "It will be all right, Michael. Don't worry about me. It will be all right. I promise."

The seraph's massive face widened in a benign smile. "First time I've heard you sound confident since the flight to O'Hare."

"I'm going to reclaim my wife and my son, Michael, that I promise you. This time I won't blow it."

"If you say so, Ray. You're beginning to talk like one of us."

"It rubs off."

The trip to Sacramento was something he had to do sometime, if only to fend off potential raids on his cable company out there from Honoria Smythe who with WorldCorp money behind her might become a dangerous predator.

More dangerous, that is.

On the other hand, if WorldCorp gave up the battle for NE, NorthCal might be vulnerable for a takeover. Neenan did not want to get directly involved in such a fight. Leave it to the Californians.

He spoke with his Sacramento people at the airport. They seemed delighted by his energy and his confidence that they would drub WorldCorp.

Back in the Gulfstream, the pilot told him that fog was closing in at SFO.

"Typical," Neenan said. "What do we do?"

"We're cleared to take off. SFO says the fog may blow off and then again it may not. We'll circle around and see what happens."

It would be a nice irony, he thought, if he was killed out here. But he had been told on the highest authority—well, almost the highest—that everything would be all right.

"OK," he said. "I know we'll be careful."

He called Leonard, spoke to Johnny, and said, "I hear you guys have some fog over there."

"Out beyond Twin Peaks, sir."

"I still plan to land at SFO sometime today and put up at the Fairmont. We still on for brunch there tomorrow?"

"We're looking forward to it."

Sounded like a nice kid. Thank God I never said anything nasty about gays to Leonard. Unlike his mother.

Michael was seated in the cabin of the plane. This time he was wearing a Forty-Niners warm-up suit.

"Where's the companion?" Neenan began aggressively. "She'd do better in that getup than you do."

"She couldn't fit in it," Michael replied nonchalantly. "She is in Chicago taking care of some problems there."

Neenan knew that he was supposed to ask what problems, so he deliberately did not. "You guys can move almost as fast as the speed of thought."

"My job is to see that we don't have any accidents up in that fog."

The plane took off and climbed rapidly to get over the mountains. The sky was blue and the valleys below were sharply outlined in winter shadows.

"It's snowing in the mountains behind San Francisco," the pilot announced. "The fog may lift, however. They're giving us an hour-and-a-half estimate for touchdown, but I wouldn't believe that."

Gaby did appear, wearing a form-fitting Chicago Bulls warm-up suit.

"You look gorgeous," Neenan told her as the Gulfstream took off.

"I'm not sure, Michael," she replied with a blush, "that it is appropriate for a human creature to leer at me in such a fashion."

"He's not leering, dear one," the boss seraph replied gently, "he's only admiring. He's given up leering. It is impossible not to admire you in whatever form you take on."

Gaby blushed again, this time with pleasure, as, come to think of it, she had the previous time.

"Associating with these quick-tongued Irish humans, dear one, may have a permanent effect on you."

Preliminary love signals between the two companions, doubtless displayed for his admiration and instruction. These superbeings for all their power and wisdom had to be tender with one another too.

Interesting.

"Since I'm the only one in the pool when you swim with me, Gaby, you really don't need your swimsuit. We can pretend it is Captiva again."

This time she didn't pretend to be embarrassed. "I'll try to remember. Perhaps for a moment before I spin off in light, though only with your companion present."

"I find the light more interesting myself," Michael admitted, "but that's because I'm a seraph."

All very domestic. They were up to something. They were always up to something. It was in their nature to be up to something. Were they sometimes too clever by half? Did some of their convoluted schemes have no impact at all because they were too twisted for their human "accounts" to understand?

I wouldn't bet against it.

"I better get back to work," Gaby said as she kissed her husband on his cheek and then Neenan on his forehead. "See you both soon."

I've never been kissed by a seraph before, he thought.

He realized that he was supposed to ask questions about the seraphic family life, but ignored the obligation. Instead he shut his eyes and curled up for a nap.

"Keep us away from the mountains," he said to Michael.

"It's the humans flying around in these things that I have to watch out for."

"You guys should have a team looking after airports."

"We have six monitors at SFO. Two dozen at ORD."

"Just ordinary, commonplace angels?"

"Some archangels actually."

They were two hours late landing at SFO. One runway glowed in bright sunshine, the other was still shrouded in fog.

"Do you really have a crowd of your folk at O'Hare?"

"Working overtime. They love the job. Kind of like your chess."

The choristers returned to action, humming soft songs of praise.

"What's that about?"

"The choir? They're singing one of our hymns of praise for the work angels do. You've never seen the hymns, have you?"

"*Seen* them?"

"Certainly. Our singing has color as well as sound. Let me see . . . Ah, that will do."

The cabin filled with a gently changing colored glow that matched the colors of the rainbow to the musical scale. The effect was breathtaking.

"Naturally your human eyes are not capable of detecting all the nuances, nor the colors beyond ultraviolet or infrared."

"Naturally."

"Would you like something to drink, Mr. Neenan?" the cabin attendant asked.

"Do we have any Irish whiskey?"

"I think so. I'll check."

She looked around the cabin for a moment and shook her head, as if she had a vague sensation of sights and sounds.

"We do have a bottle," she said when she returned, "of Seraphic Single Malt. Would that be all right?"

"As long as you don't have anything else."

Michael snorted derisively.

Neenan sipped the amber brew and coughed. Seraphic Irish whiskey, Neenan thought, might also be marketed as a cure for postnasal drip.

He shut his eyes and drifted in and out of sleep as the symphony of sound and colors lulled him into peacefulness — helped now by the water of life.

"We've been cleared to land, Mr. Neenan," the pilot reported. "Please make sure your seat belt is fastened."

It was.

Neenan looked out the window. He saw nothing but fog so thick that the wingtips of the Grumman were invisible.

"Does he know what he's doing?" he asked the boss seraph.

"He's a good pilot," Michael said, not opening his eyes. "But, even if he doesn't know what he's doing, I do."

"The view on landing, Mr. Neenan," the pilot said, "will be spectacular. We're landing on the east runway, which is cleared of fog. The west runway is still closed down."

"Great," Neenan murmured.

"We like to keep our accounts entertained," Michael commented.

The scene was indeed spectacular. On the right the sky was blue, the sun was shining brightly, the Berkeley Hills were gloriously green, the Bay glittered as if it were the Mediterranean. On the left ominous masses of fog shifted in and out, sometime revealing the other runway and sometimes concealing it.

"Which is life and which is death?" Neenan reflected.

"If you can understand something," Michael mused, "it's no longer a mystery and hence no longer a surprise."

Doubtless that was true.

He called Leonard on the plane's phone.

"I was worried about you, Dad."

"Not to worry, Leonard. My guardian angel takes good care of me." Michael scoffed.

"I'm glad to hear that, Dad. . . . You're checking into the Fairmont?"

"And sleeping nine or ten hours. I'll see you and Johnny at ten-thirty at brunch."

"We'd sooner take you to brunch at the Oak Court. It's San Francisco's most famous brunch."

"Great," Neenan said, wondering whether it would be a gay scene where he would be out of place and then dismissing the idea.

"Same time?"

"Sure."

"No hanging around at the bar after you check in," Michael warned.

"I have enough problems as it is," Neenan insisted, even though the idea of a drink in the bar had occurred to him.

Michael dematerialized as Neenan climbed into the limo that was waiting for him. Automatically Neenan reached for the phone in the car and then realized that there was no one to call.

He was greeted like a long-lost friend at the Fairmont and conducted to an elegant suite, the kind he told himself that one should not occupy unless there was a woman with one. He hung up his suit bag and then rode down the elevator to buy the Bay Area papers. He glanced into the oak-paneled bar. An attractive woman sat by herself at the bar, nursing a glass of white wine. She looked intelligent, lonely, and unhappy.

Without any prompting from the seraph, he rode back up to his suite.

What has happened to me? he wondered.

I signed that damn contract.

Impulsively he reached for the phone and punched in the number of the house in Lake Forest. No answer.

He then called Anna Maria's private line there. Still no answer.

Finally, throwing caution to the winds, he pressed 312 and 642, then hung up the phone before he could punch the final four numbers of their East Lake Shore Drive apartment.

Was he more afraid that she would answer or that she would not?

He found two glasses of Baileys in the minibar, poured them into a tumbler, glanced at the local papers as he drained the tumbler, far too rapidly, and then, lonely and discouraged, collapsed into bed, hoping that sleep would come quickly.

In his last few conscious moments, he thought he heard again the Aramaic lullaby.

☙26☙

After Mass at the Paulist Church in Chinatown, Neenan arrived early at the Oak Court. He waited anxiously in the lobby for Leonard and his partner and asked himself what he thought about having a gay son. Politically and socially he was a pragmatist. He usually voted Democratic out of heritage and habit and the conviction that conservative Republicans were more of a threat to the entertainment industry than were "tax-and-spend" Democrats. Though he had been raised to think that homosexuals were queers who could be like the rest of humans if they only tried harder, he had learned early in his business career that talent was more important than skin color, gender, and sexual orientation.

He figured that if they were good at what they did, he did not care what kind of sexual acts they preferred. He also saw that minority rights were a fashion that was too strong to fight and that there was no point in fighting them anyway. He was tolerant because it was good business to be tolerant.

He had learned three years before that Leonard had "come out of the closet" only when Donna screamed at him in one of her more hysterical phone calls that it was all his fault.

He had shouted back that everyone knew that castrating mothers were responsible for gay sons. He had heard that or read it somewhere and didn't particularly believe it. It was, however, a way of getting her off the phone.

Nonetheless he was shocked and angry. What the hell was wrong with Leonard, he wondered. Then he asked himself again if he should have tried to break through the wall of hatred that Donna had built up between him and his children.

There had never been enough time.

He tried to forget about Leonard, a tall, handsome black Irishman rather like himself. Sometimes he was able to pretend that Leonard did not exist. Other times he was haunted by his neglect.

Finally Vincent had told him cautiously that Len had graduated

from Berkeley and was working at a brokerage and that his partner
was a sergeant in the San Francisco police force. Impulsively Neenan
sent a quick note wishing his son success and happiness in his work
and life.

He did not expect an answer and did not receive one—until the
out-of-the-blue phone call a few days before.

I messed it up, he told himself, like everything else.

"Hi, Dad, I hope we haven't kept you waiting?"

The past rolled over Neenan like a tidal wave, pride at this son's
good looks and athletic ability, his quick wit, his easygoing disposition.
Leonard had always been his favorite. Why had he felt no sense of
loss when Leonard apparently cut him off?

Because he had become numb to all personal relationships. No wonder the angels were on him.

"I got here early," Neenan said easily, and then added with all his
Irish charm, "Happy to meet you, Johnny."

Another tall, dark, handsome Irishman. "I feel that I've known you
for a long time. Lenny talks so much about you and is so proud of
you."

Michael, seraph boss, where are you when I really need you?

"We both hope you beat that bastard Murtaugh into the ground,"
Leonard said. "How's it going? . . . Let's go get some breakfast."

Neither of them looked or acted gay. But then how does a gay man
look or act?

"I don't see why anyone thinks we can lose. I own or control the
majority of the stock, I'm not going to sell. Therefore Walter Murtaugh loses. It's that simple."

They were conducted to the table Leonard had reserved and then
began to collect food from the buffet.

"Champagne?" a waiter asked when they returned to the table.

Neenan nodded. The young men declined.

"We don't drink," Len explained.

Oh.

"So why did poor Vinny sell you out?" Leonard asked.

"I wouldn't call it that," Neenan said as he dug into his eggs Ben-
edict. "He's actually taken a lesser job at WorldCorp, though they're
probably paying him a lot more. Moreover he was going to inherit
the company."

"Don't go leaving it to me," Len said with an easy laugh. "Selling stocks is a breeze in comparison . . . and by the way, yours is still strong."

"It's about where it belongs. . . . I think Vincent wanted to get out from under my shadow. Can't say that I blame him. I did the same thing."

"The hell you did," Len insisted. "But that's not the point. He had everything he always wanted and, poor guy lost his nerve."

"Maybe."

"Does Meg know?"

"Probably."

"She'll give him the hell he richly deserves."

"I know it's not a fair comparison," Johnny chimed in, "but my dad's a captain in the police. I have to keep ducking out of his shadow, and it's a big one."

What does an Irish San Francisco cop think about having a gay son on the force?

"I polled the top executives and the senior staff about who to make second-in-command. They all voted for Vincent. I should have told him that."

"Wouldn't have made a bit of difference, Dad. It's the old lady of whom he's afraid. He imagines her hovering around and whispering that he's not good enough. What difference do all the executives of NE make when your mom is always telling you that you are no good?"

"She meant well, Lenny."

"The hell she did. Anyway, let's not talk about her. I hear nothing but good things about your new wife. I'd like to meet her sometime."

So would I.

"She would like to meet you too, Len, both of you. I didn't deserve to be so lucky."

"Yes, you did. After your bad luck the first time. But we weren't going to talk any more about that subject, were we? Do you think the Bulls will win again?"

It turned out that both young men were Bulls fans. Neenan knew enough about the team to carry on a conversation. He also accepted a second glass of champagne. Maybe it would help him to sleep on the long ride back to his empty home in Chicago.

It also emerged that they were active members of the Paulist parish where he had attended Mass — or "participated in the Eucharist," as Len reminded him were the proper words "these days."

The meal passed quickly. Neenan enjoyed himself. He liked his rediscovered son and his austere partner. Thank God he had made peace with them before the end came.

"So what's with Jenny?" Len asked as they walked to the limo that would bring Neenan back to SFO.

"Apparently making it as an actress and dating Jerry Carter, the director."

"A very gifted guy," Johnny said firmly. "Genius."

"We're signing him up for a miniseries," Neenan said. "*Starbridge*, we're calling it."

"Susan Howatch?" they both said together.

"Neat," Johnny added.

"Johnny is studying theology over at Berkeley," Len explained. "He's sky-high on her."

"We have the rights and hopefully the screenplay. I'm going to read it on the way home."

"It'll take a great writer to pull that all together," Johnny said reverently.

"I think we have one."

"I don't know that Jenny will ever break away from Mom. A lot of womanly loyalty there."

"My guess," Neenan said, relying on the Jewish teenager he had met in Starbucks, "is that in time she will."

They shook hands and Neenan entered the limo. Both young men waved at him as the car pulled away.

"You really are the smooth one," Michael commented. He was wearing, for Sunday morning in San Francisco, the appropriate garb — jeans, a blue turtleneck sweater, and a vest that matched the jeans.

Did they go to church on Sunday?

"It was easy, maybe too easy. Why didn't I do it long ago?"

"You tell me."

Neenan sighed. "I was too busy using my charm on power and women."

"Well, you're honest enough."

"I'm glad I had a chance to work things out with Len while I still have time."

"That's the whole idea, Raymond Anthony."

"Where's herself this morning?"

"Busy elsewhere," the seraph said in a tone that indicated the issue was not appropriate for discussion. "You also did well last night with the woman in the bar."

"I didn't do anything."

"That's what you did well. She needs someone to help her, but not you. Not now."

"I take your point."

"Maybe some other time," the angel said enigmatically. "As it is, we'll arrange some other help for her."

"If there's going to be another time, it will have to happen soon. It's not likely I'll be back here, is it?"

"Probably not enough time," Michael agreed somewhat enigmatically. "But then you can't tell about time as the Other sees it. Sometimes He takes a much longer view of time than you do. Or than we do for that matter."

The Jewish teenager had promised him that everything would be all right. He had to ride with that hope.

"Do you guys go to church on Sunday?"

Michael didn't bat an eye. "In all rational species there is a need for rest and for worship.

On the way back, Neenan opened Annie's manuscript and began to read it carefully. Since he had not read any of the six books, he did not know what to expect. The story moved with dramatic speed through a half century. The characters were clearly drawn, the conflicts sharp, the theology remarkably interesting, and the conclusion triumphant.

The 3,600 pages of novel were reduced to twelve hours of brilliant programming. It would be the television event of the year, indeed of the decade.

"Not bad, huh?" Michael reappeared as the Gulfstream vectored over Lake Michigan for its final approach to O'Hare. The city stretched out in front of them, a checkerboard of twinkling orange lights on a cloudless, moonless night, caught between the deep dark of the lake and the straggling paths of light on the prairies beyond.

"Dazzling. Someone has to talk her into letting us use the script, even if I'm not the one."

"Tomorrow is Monday," the seraph reminded him. "I start invoking the contract."

"We'll see what tomorrow brings."

Caught between the seraph's insistence and the advice of the young woman in the blue suit, he had no doubt which way he would go.

He simply must not worry.

It was Peter's day off, so a hired limo awaited him at the airport. As it spend north on the toll road toward the Lake Forest exit, Neenan felt lonely and alone. We come into the world sobbing, he thought, and that's the way we depart.

Well, no one ever promised anyone that everything would work out. At least it had worked out with Len. No fuss and bother. Moreover, that relationship was now, astonishingly, solid. Not many guilt feelings there when he died.

His tentative conviction that everything would be all right seemed shaky. He shifted uneasily in his seat, dreading the empty house that awaited him. His knee encountered a small box. He picked it up, held it to the light. No label.

A bomb?

Maybe.

He shook it.

Cookies!

Carefully he opened the wrapping. Oatmeal raisin this time.

The first team was active. Everything would be all right.

He ate every one of the cookies. Long swim tomorrow.

But his morale faded as they pulled up to his house. Eleven o'clock. Two long, tiring days. He'd have to cut back on these kinds of trips.

He thanked the driver, who opened the door for him, signed the bill and added his usual 25 percent tip, and carried his bags up to the house.

It was completely dark inside.

He opened the door and trudged up the stairs to his room. He turned the light on in his bedroom and dropped his bags on the floor. Home is the hunter, home from the hill.

Then he noticed that someone was in his bed. He quickly dimmed the light he had turned on and tiptoed over to the bed. Sure enough, she had come home.

She looked like a peacefully sleeping child, her body flat on her back, her limbs neatly arranged, her face serene, her hair done up behind her head, one strap on her pink nightgown hanging off her shoulder. He leaned over her and gently caressed her face with the back of his fingers.

She sighed contentedly.

"Don't you dare hurt her!" a voice hissed nearby.

Gaby, in an elaborate off-white gown and negligee.

"Why in the world would I hurt her?" he asked. "She's my wife and I love her and I'm happy to have her back."

"You're furious at her."

"Nope. That's the first mistake I've ever caught you guys in. I'll be as gentle as a mother with a little child."

"Don't you dare wake her up," Gaby replied, somewhat mollified.

"I wasn't planning on waking her up."

He touched her shoulder tenderly, moving the strap farther down her arm, so he could see the top of a lovely breast.

"She's terribly fragile," Gaby insisted. "She knows she's made a fool out of herself and is terribly sorry. All she needs is you lording it over her and she'll break down completely."

"Do I look like I'm about to punish her?"

"No."

"Or lord it over her?"

"No."

"Or even tell her 'I told you so'?"

"No." ·

"Then why are you hassling me?"

"Just to make sure," she said with a giggle. "All right, I guess you won't hurt her. It's going to take time for her to get over what she did to you."

"Not because I am going to be angry at her."

"I guess not. But she'll be angry at herself."

"Gabriella, ma'am, I love her. I intend to love her for however many days or weeks I might have. I won't hurt her."

"All right. I believe you."

"Good. Now if you will kindly remove yourself in that very sexy outfit and go fight with your companion, I intend to take off my clothes and slip into bed with my wife. I'll wait till tomorrow morning to make love, as badly as I want to."

"Don't wait too long in the morning," she warned him, and dematerialized.

"Bossy," he sighed.

Anna Maria sighed softly when he stretched out next to her. Almost immediately he went to sleep, perhaps aided by some angel dust. Or by the ancient lullaby that was playing in his head again.

"Thank you for the cookies," he murmured.

He woke up once in the night to discover his wife's head on his chest where it belonged. He eased the other strap of her gown off her shoulder and went back to sleep.

27

Neenan awoke to the smell of coffee, fresh cinnamon-raisin rolls, and the soap of a wife fresh from the shower. He opened his eyes. She was sitting on the edge of the bed, pale and grim in a lime-colored terry-cloth robe. She offered him a tray with a mug of coffee and three buttered rolls. He took the tray, put it on the table next to the bed, and took her hand. She lowered her eyes and murmured, "Sorry."

She was a step away from hysterical sobs.

He caressed her arm with one hand and raised a finger to her lips. "That's all you need to say. It's over."

With his fingers he forced her lips into a smile. Then he withdrew his fingers. The smile remained.

"I was worried about you when I came home last night . . . ," she said. "You're taking off my robe." She looked away in embarrassment.

"I want you in bed with me while I eat my breakfast."

"All right," she said as she discarded the robe and snuggled in next to him, her eyes still downcast, her body stiff.

"I flew to Paris."

"You did not," she giggled. "I canceled the reservations."

"I had an assignation with another woman."

"No, you didn't," she said laughing. "Megan said she thought maybe you went to California to see Jenny."

"No, Len."

"How did it work out?"

"Fine. He and his partner, who is a very nice boy, are active in the Paulist parish in San Francisco."

"I didn't go to church this weekend."

"Shame."

"You should be angry at me and I should be sobbing my regrets."

"Not in this house."

"Love means you don't have to say you're sorry?"

"You did say you were sorry."

"Not very forcefully. . . . What are you doing to me?"

"What do you think I'm doing to you?"

The stiffness went out of her body and she clung to him. "Are you going to make love with me?"

"Eventually; when I've finished with my breakfast. I may just kiss every inch of you to show how happy I am to have you back."

"I missed having you inside of me," she said with a sigh. "I've become a wanton woman."

"I missed you too."

"I knew by Monday morning that I had been a stupid fool. Especially after all I had said with my loud Sicilian mouth about your not having to clear things with me. I was afraid to call you. I thought you'd be furious at me."

She rested her hand on his chest.

"Like I've been furious with you before."

"I never did anything that dumb before. . . . Promise me something?"

"Sure."

"If I ever do anything that dumb again, give me twenty-four hours, forty-eight at the most, and then come and drag me back. I promise I'll come without protest."

"Fair enough," he sighed. "I thought about that, but wasn't sure." He put aside the coffee mug.

"Don't think about it again," she said as she rested her lips against his. "I feel I shouldn't be forgiven this easily."

"I was never angry at you, Anna Maria." His fingers captured one of her graceful little breasts and teased it.

"Really?"

"I was angry at myself for being clumsy. A person doesn't have to earn forgiveness from a lover. It's a given. It's always there."

How the hell did I ever come up with that line? Is Gaby around here whispering in my ear?

"How beautiful. . . . I'm sorry I burned the script . . . please don't stop that."

"You know and I know that it's still on your hard disk and I made copies of it at the office."

She sat up straight, dislodging the sheet and blanket that had protected her.

"Really!"

"Of course, really." He kissed her smooth, cool belly.

"You really are going to make love to me?"

"After I have caressed and kissed you at great length."

"How do you know I need a lot of caressing and kissing? . . . I suppose that's a silly question. . . . You'll be late for work."

"I own the company." He threw the covers off the bed and thus exposed her pliant body.

"That's true. . . . Are you really going to make the miniseries? I don't own the rights to the novels."

"I do."

She threw back her head and laughed. "My husband never misses a trick. . . . Stop tickling me!"

"You'd better get a lawyer."

She stopped giggling and restrained his marauding hands. "A divorce lawyer!"

"Of course not! A lawyer who can negotiate with our people about the script. They don't have to know who Marianne Swift is. For all concerned it might be better that you be anonymous till the critics go wild."

"We tell them that Marianne is your wife only when the series is a success? If it fails, none of us know who the author is, right? See, I can be reasonable on occasion."

"It won't fail."

"You can go back to tickling me now. . . . How much is it worth?"

"Whatever you can get from us. I'll stay out of the bargaining."

"I'm such a stupid idiot," she sighed. "I don't deserve all this loving."

And I don't believe I'm as patient and forgiving as I am.

"You're going to get it anyway."

"I was terrified when I came home last night that you wouldn't let me in the house."

"Or maybe that I would beat you unmercifully."

"No," she said with another giggle, "I knew you wouldn't do that. . . . I thought you were going to cover me with kisses."

"In due course."

The phone rang. Neenan directed one of his wandering hands to pick it up.

"Neenan."

"Mr. Neenan, we're wondering if you will be in today."

"Before noon, Amy. I'm heavily engaged in difficult work just now."

"I see."

Did she have any idea what he meant?

"Mr. Vincent Neenan is most eager to talk to you."

Another victim of the Palestinian woman named Miriam. It will be all right, she had said. It would be, at least until he died. Then others would have to take over.

"Tell him I'll be in around twelve or so."

"Yes, Mr. Neenan."

"What are you going to do for the next three hours?" Anna Maria asked.

"Fool around with my wife. I have to make up for lost opportunities."

"You punish her by driving her crazy with desire?"

"Seems the most useful way of doing it."

"Vinny wants to see you?" she said, squirming now as her hormones drove to the far edge of desire.

"So she says."

"He is such an asshole. Not that I'm anyone to talk. . . . Oh, Ray, please . . . I can't stand it anymore."

"I'm only working up steam. . . . You've talked to Meg?"

"She thinks that he's an asshole and I am too. She just about ordered me to come back . . ." Her voice trailed off in a groan.

"How did she predict I would react?"

Anna Maria struggled to find her voice, "Just about the way you are. . . . Please . . ."

His lips began their promised assault. She screamed with pleasure and joy for the rest of their romp. The choir hummed softly and the colors of the room modulated, not that his wife was in any condition to notice these sideshows.

In the shower afterward she murmured, "I think I'll lose my temper and run off every week if this is what happens as a result."

"You don't have to do that," he said.

"By the way, I changed the reservations for our Paris trip to this coming weekend."

"When did you do that?"

"Last Monday when I knew what an asshole I was."

"Did Megan predict all of the details of how I punished you?"

"Megan is too young to know that such things are possible between people desperately in love with one another. She'll learn."

"With your subtle advice?"

"Maybe not too subtle."

The angelic trumpets struck up an intricate fanfare.

"I keep imagining I hear music," Anna Maria said.

"Maybe Maeve has the radio on too loud."

Later when Anna Maria was sleeping and he was dressing for work, Gaby appeared, still in the gown and negligee.

"You really did astonishingly well," she said. "For a human male."

"Thanks a lot," he replied as he tied his tie.

"It's still going to be awkward for her for a time. She continues to be quite vulnerable . . . but I don't have to tell you that, do I?"

"I never ignore useful advice."

She laughed. "That's not altogether true, but we'll let it pass. . . . You understand that the problem with your son will be the opposite? You had to restore Annie's faith in her womanliness. You must rebuild his confidence in his manliness."

"Good point. . . . It's useful to have guardian angels around, especially when they are as pretty as you are in that bedtime outfit."

"You are as bad as my companion," she snorted as she faded into whatever sixth or seventh dimension of space-time her kind lived in.

"Do you two," he asked the empty room, "ever do things analogous to what we did this morning?"

She reappeared briefly. "All the time."

So there too, earthling.

Vincent was waiting in Neenan's office, along with Michael, today in a dark blue three-piece suit with a carnation in his lapel.

"Hi, Vinny," Neenan said. "Sorry to keep you waiting. I was in Sacramento over the weekend, improving the fortifications. I went over to San Francisco to have brunch with Len and his partner."

"How's Len?"

"Seems fine. Very active in his parish."

"He always was the most religious one in the family."

They were beating around the bush. What should he say? Nothing till Vinny made the first move.

"Megan won't talk to me."

"That makes for a lot of silence."

"No, it doesn't." Vinny shifted uneasily. "She shouts at me and won't let me answer."

What the hell do I say to that?

So he said nothing.

"She says I am a coward, a traitor, and an asshole."

Neenan's mind went blank. The conversation was not going well. "I knew a lot of young women like her when I was at St. George's. Kids from Immaculata mostly. Often in error, never in doubt." Dumb comment, albeit true.

"She's not in error this time. I am all of those things and maybe more."

Michael shook his head in disbelief. Neenan was blowing the conversation.

"She says she'll divorce me if I go to work for WorldCorp."

"That's a little harsh."

Michael winced.

"I wouldn't blame her if she did," Vinny said dolefully.

Not having anything to say, Neenan figured he'd better keep his mouth shut.

"So I'm wondering if maybe I can return to NE."

"You tell him that will get you off the hook. Everyone in the firm is blaming you for losing him. That's true, by the way, only they are afraid to tell you."

"Wow! Does that get me off the hook! I'm getting blamed on all sides for losing you. As I told you, they wanted you and they figure the only reason for losing you is your old man."

Michael nodded patiently.

"That's not true, Dad. You know that."

"Regardless. They don't."

"Tell him that he can withdraw the resignation, which hasn't been passed on to the board yet. Then give it back to him and let him tear it up."

"Right."

"Simple matter. The board has not met since you gave me your formal resignation. I'll give it to you and you can tear it up. . . . It's around here somewhere." He rummaged through his file drawers.

"Fourth drawer on your left, blue folder."

"Right! Here it is!" He passed the letter over to his son.

"You sure you want me back, Dad?"

"Me personally? Sure I want you back, but what I think hardly matters. The team wants you back."

Michael nodded, as if to say, you're finally pitching strikes again.

With a broad grin on his face, Vinny tore the resignation into little pieces.

They grinned and shook hands with each other.

"Now get down to business."

"We're definitely going ahead with *Starbridge*. We have the rights already. We have to purchase the script. Has that Irish goddess to whom you're married read it?"

Vinny nodded. "She loves it, naturally."

"And she's figured out who wrote the screenplay?"

"The nom de plume didn't fool her for a second."

"That presents a bit of a problem for us. Annie wants to remain out of the picture for the present, which is a good idea. If the media make it look like a vanity project for me, they'll destroy it before it's off the ground."

"Compare you to William Randolph Hearst?"

"Or worse. So we're going to have to negotiate indirectly with a lawyer she'll choose. Change her name again so that other people as smart as Meg won't figure it out. I'll find out who she's chosen as a lawyer and pass it on to you. You can pass it on to Joe and let him handle all the negotiations. It wouldn't do for us to get involved."

"Deniability?"

"I don't want to let there be any appearance of conflict of interest."

"I'll take care of it, Dad. Don't worry at all."

"You want to tell the others or should I?"

Michael smiled happily. "Let me tell them, Dad. I'll make a joke out of it."

"Big joke," Michael sneered.

"Shut up, I carried it off."

"With my help."

"I don't deny that."

"May I make a suggestion," Neenan said, "about your wife?"

"Sure. I'm still in deep trouble."

"Stop by Tiffany's and buy her something truly gorgeous."

"Hey, great idea!"

"I have an account there."

"Really? I'll use my Visa card, but thanks anyway."

❄ ❄ ❄

In the days after his double victory, Neenan discovered that nothing in real life is ever quite "happily ever after." Anna Maria and Vincent were both a bit unstable in their relationship with him, shaken in their confidence. Moreover, the launching of *Starbridge* became bogged down as they tried to prepare for the press conference to announce it. Lawyers and agents got in the way.

Sex between Neenan and his wife became "spousal," satisfying and frequent, but the ecstasy had faded. Anna Maria was not yet quite ready to forgive herself.

Or maybe their delayed honeymoon was now over.

Vincent regained his composure with the rest of the firm, but was still uneasy with his father. He had not regained the relaxed and witty camaraderie of his first few days as president of NE.

"It'll take time," Michael had argued.

"Time?"

"As I have said before, the Other has different perceptions of time than we do."

Tim Walsh had settled the pension suit for all but one of his clients. The court threw out the suit of the remaining plaintiff. Neenan offered to restore his pension if he dropped the appeal. When his new lawyer deserted him, he accepted.

Neenan did not hear the Palestinian lullaby anymore and no special cookies appeared.

He talked to Len on the phone several times a week.

Anna Maria and he had canceled two weekends in Paris because of the distractions of lining up the tin soldiers for *Starbridge*.

Neenan felt again the sensation that he was falling apart, that what he had been he wasn't anymore and that what he had become wasn't really him. Melting ice, he thought. An ice floe becoming a puddle of water.

He knew his time was running out. So, he was convinced, did the seraphs, who were remarkably solicitous toward him, as if they wanted to make his final days easy.

Nothing is ever easy.

Finally everything was in place for *Starbridge*. NE staged a solemn high press conference at the Four Seasons Hotel in which Neenan appeared on the platform with Jerry Carter and Ms. Howatch.

Carter seemed as nice a young man as one could want for a son-in-law. He did not mention Jennifer and neither did Neenan.

The press conference was a huge success. The three participants might have made a wonderful comedy act.

The networks began a bidding war. The first one to call was Walter Murtaugh himself, the boss of WorldCorp.

"Would twenty million be a good basement, Ray?" the Scotsman asked genially.

"First one in, so it will have to do, Wally."

"Would you grant us the right of final refusal after all the other bids are in?"

"In return for?"

"For my calling off this bloody, stupid war?"

"I guess that's a reasonable offer."

"Deal, Ray?"

"Deal, Wally."

"Gentleman's agreement?"

"Why not?"

"He's no gentleman," Michael observed.

"Let him think that I think he is."

Finally, the weekend before Thanksgiving, Neenan and Anna Maria flew to Paris.

"I want you all to myself for a couple of days," she said wearily.

"Funny, I was thinking the same thing."

☙28❧

The Paris weekend died the first day.

Neenan and his wife chatted and joked as the American Airlines MD-11 (Flight 42) hurtled across the Atlantic. There had been few moments of peace, little time to talk after their reconciliation. Perhaps he was slipping back into his old ways. The few days in Paris might turn that around.

When they finally arrived at the Athène Palais after a tedious ride in from de Gaulle, they sank into their bed and slept for several hours, heedless of the Arab children who were running up and down the corridors of the hotel.

Then they showered and went out for supper. They walked along the Left Bank part of the way back to the hotel and admired Notre-Dame, an illuminated ship drifting down the Seine. They made love gently—a prelude to more serious love the next day—and slipped into grateful sleep.

The phone rang from a long distance away. Neenan wondered where he was and why the phone was ringing. He grabbed for it so that Anna Maria could continue to sleep.

"Neenan," he murmured in a groggy voice.

"Dad?"

"Yes, Vince, what's up?"

"I'm sorry to disturb you at this hour. It's three o'clock in Paris, isn't it?"

Paris, that's where I am.

"I think so."

"Grandpa Neenan has died, Dad. He had put a padlock on the door to his apartment so the nurse's aide could not get in for the last few days. The management finally forced the door. They found him dead of a stroke. Grandma is still alive, but out of her mind."

"She's been that way for some time," Neenan said automatically.

The old man had done himself in out of his own malice.

"I took care of matters because you are so far away. We have flown

Grandma to Chicago and have her in a nursing home in Lake Bluff. Grandpa's body will come in late tomorrow, that's Saturday here. We have scheduled a one-day wake on Sunday afternoon and a funeral at your parish on Monday morning. Burial at Calvary. I hope this all meets with your approval."

Neenan's head was reeling. Thank God Vinny had taken charge.

"It certainly does, Vincent," he mumbled. "Thank you for taking over."

"You will be coming home for the wake and funeral?"

"Yes, of course."

"I have tentatively scheduled you on AA 41 from de Gaulle to Chicago at one twenty-five tomorrow afternoon, that's today your time. You will arrive in Chicago about four. Will Annie be coming home with you?"

He glanced at his wife, now wide-awake. Somehow she had understood the conversation. She nodded her head.

"Yes, she will."

"Actually I have made reservations for both of you. They will revalidate your ticket at the Admiral's Club. An American agent will meet you at noon at their check-in counter at the airport. I'm sorry, Dad, to bring you bad news."

The old man had his last revenge. Neenan knew that he and his wife would never return to Paris.

"Thank you, Vincent. And thank you for taking care of everything so smoothly."

"I'm sorry your trip has been ruined. . . . Peter and I will meet you at Terminal 5 tomorrow, which is today where you are."

"Your mom?" Anna Maria asked when he had hung up the phone.

"Dad."

"I am so sorry, dear."

"I find that I am too," he said slowly. "I hated him, yet somehow I mourn him."

"I understand."

How could she?

There was grief inside him, sorrow for what might have been. But the mourning was locked up, perhaps never to emerge.

In a way the wake on Sunday would be his wake while he was still alive.

He shivered.

Anna Maria drew him into her arms. "Try to get some sleep, dear," she said. "We will have a long couple of days ahead of us."

She went back to sleep promptly. In the straightforward family life that had nurtured her, there was no understanding of the possibilities of ambivalence with which his family had drained each other's life-blood.

Would he and his father meet in whatever awaited them both?

Would he be able to smother his hatred for the old man? Or express his love?

"Sorry," a voice said.

"Huh?"

"Michael here."

"Oh. . . . Thank you."

"We didn't know."

"I understand. You folks don't know the future."

"We knew he would die soon. We did not know when or how."

"No problem, Michael. . . . I will be following him shortly."

"These matters are in the hands of the Almighty, whose time frames are not ours. . . . May I help you sleep?"

"That would be great."

The angel touched his forehead and Neenan slept almost immediately.

The wake on Sunday afternoon was sparse. A couple of old friends from the World War II years, senior executives from National Entertainment and their spouses, Michael and Gaby in solemn black, visible only to Neenan and his wife, the priests from the parish, Amy Jardine, her hair down, her dress attractive. She hugged Neenan and introduced him to her handsome husband.

At the end of the day, Jerry Carter and Jennifer walked in. "My sympathies, sir," Carter said respectfully, perhaps knowing some of the strange story of Neenan and his family.

Jenny fell into his arms and sobbed, not for the loss of a grandfather who had ignored her, but for the pain she and her father had suffered through the years.

"I love you, Daddy," she said over and over again as they hugged one another and wept together. "I'll never leave you again, never."

"I won't let you go again, Jennifer, never."

So his father had indirectly provided the unexpected gift of his daughter's love. Donna had finally been routed. Not a bad trade. A lot less guilt feelings.

They went out for supper together—Neenan, Anna Maria, his daughter and her young man, his son and his wife. An almost complete family reunion. Neenan was quiet and thoughtful through the meal as he pondered his own wake, which would certainly happen in a couple of weeks. The women, however, were lighthearted, rejoicing as women do in restored bonds. Vincent and Carter watched Neenan closely, perhaps trying to figure out what kind of a man he was.

Lost cause.

The priest who had told the story about Patricia the Penny Planter said the Mass and preached about the infinite grace and mercy of God's love.

When they returned from Calvary cemetery the next day, there was a message that his mother had died at the nursing home. Neenan reacted numbly. He sank into a chair in the drawing room of his house, Annie's arm around him, and let his children make the arrangements.

Because it was Thanksgiving week, the wake would be postponed till Friday evening and the Mass would be on Saturday morning. Len and Johnny would be able to fly in and spend Thanksgiving with them.

A final gift from his mother, a last reunion with all his family. At Anna Maria's insistence, they would all stay here and she would preside over the meal with Megan's help.

Neenan accepted these arrangements without comment. What would be, would be.

Yet on Thanksgiving Day he played the paterfamilias role with wit and charm and vitality.

Later, as he stood at the window of his bedroom and stared somberly at the lawn under the bitter cold starlight, he tried to make sense of it all.

Who was his mother? Had he ever really known her? What had destroyed her life? What point did life have for someone like her? How had it all turned bad?

He thought of her in her high school graduation picture, a bright, lively, pretty young woman with her whole life ahead of her. The hopes had all turned to nightmares. Why?

No answer, he thought grimly.

"You were wonderful today, my darling," his wife told him. "Perfectly splendid."

"Thank you, Annie. It was mostly an act."

"I know that, but it was a marvelous act. You bound the family together."

"I'm afraid I haven't been much for you the last couple of days, Anna Maria."

"You've been a wonderful example of how a man deals with complicated tragedy."

"Have I?" he said absently.

"Come to bed now and let me hold you in my arms."

"All right," he said dully.

The seraphs came to the second wake, but they and their chorus were retreating into the background. Perhaps they knew that their assignment with him was coming to an end.

"Tear up the contract yet?" Neenan asked Michael at the cemetery.

"I did that a long time ago."

☙29❧

When death came for Raymond Anthony
Neenan, it came suddenly and violently.

On Tuesday the week after the two funerals, he and Peter had
driven Anna Maria to her work in Pilsen. She and Neenan had hugged
each other, as though they would see each other again at supper. They
spoke about a trip to Paris, this time for a week of Christmas shopping. Neenan half-believed that it might happen. He thought he had
a little more time. Perhaps till after Christmas.

There was a traffic jam on Halstead. Peter turned off on a side
street just north of the Burlington tracks. He turned another corner.
Suddenly they were in a scene out of a Scorsese film. On both sides
of the street, black cars were lined up. Men, some black, some brown,
dressed in dark clothes were pointing guns at one another. Two terrified little Mexican kids, a boy and a girl, maybe four or five years
old, clung to each other in the middle of the street. A drug deal going
wrong, Neenan thought, fear clutching at his heart.

This was probably the end. Why had he not told Anna Maria one
more time that he loved her?

Automatic weapons began to pop on either side of the street.

They'll kill those kids, Neenan thought. I can't let them do that.

He bounded out of his car, rushed out into the fire zone and
scooped up the two children. He had almost made it back to his car
when he felt a massive blow to his back. He dumped the kids in the
open door and then fell to the street.

He felt blood pumping from his body. The world was turning dark
and cold.

All around him there were explosions of fire and light. Members of
the two gangs were shooting at each other. Guns were exploding in
their hands. Bodies everywhere.

The seraphs were restoring order.

A little too late but effective. At least they would save the kids and
Peter.

Then it was quiet. Gaby and Michael, wavering figures of light, were standing over him. So was Peter. All three were sobbing.

"Too late," Michael choked.

"We didn't know," Gaby murmured.

"It's all right," Neenan said. Or thought he said. He tried to smile and give the thumbs-up sign.

He didn't mind dying. Rather, he felt relieved. All the problems were over, all the mistakes irrelevant, all the complexities gone. He closed his eyes.

He tried to say, "I love you," but he didn't know whether words came out.

There was darkness.

Then nothing at all.

⋆30⋆

Raymond Anthony Neenan lingered for some time, he did not know how long, between life and death. He knew that his family and friends were in his death room because occasionally he heard voices. He could identify only Anna Maria's voice and pick out some of her words. Over and over she said, "I love you, Raymond. I love you so much. Please don't leave us."

He tried on occasion to squeeze her hand, but was unsure that he had succeeded.

There was also a woman doctor who said often, "He's going to make it. We're going to pull him through. He's a strong man in good health. If we avoid infection, he'll be fine."

Neenan knew better. His life was over. Soon he would know whether the seraphs were telling the truth about the Other. He was mildly curious. If there were no Other, no Occupant, no Someone-Else-Altogether, then he would never know.

All he really cared about was getting it over with. Leave me alone and let me die, he tried to say, but naturally no one heard him.

Then, finally, he died.

He felt a gentle twist out of his body and then floated to the top of the room, just as *Light in the Tunnel* said he would. Interesting he thought.

"We're losing him," the woman doctor screamed. "Damn it, he's going!"

He observed pandemonium in the intensive care room as doctors and nurses worked frantically over his body. Bells rang, electronic warnings beeped menacingly. Anna Maria was leading people in prayer. She and Jenny were clinging to one another, as were Vinny and Meg and Len. Norm and Joe were weeping behind them. In one corner, Michael and Gabriella watched with somber expressions. It's all right, guys, he wanted to say; not your fault. Was that other couple Estelle and her husband? Odd that they should come. Behind Anna

Maria were two lovely young women, early teens perhaps. Their faces were expressionless. Who were they?

Don't weep, guys. Don't worry. I'll be all right. I'm not afraid. I think I'm headed for the long tunnel and the figure in white. Occupant!

"Gone!" the woman doctor said despairingly. "We've lost him."

That's all right, Neenan tried to tell them, but they could not hear him. Then he floated out of the room, up through St. Luke–Presbyterian Hospital and out over the city of Chicago. Christmas tree lights already, red and green panels on the John Hancock observatory, the star suspended from the twin aerials. He must have hovered between life and death for a long time. For a moment he regretted all the Christmases he had wasted. Then he realized that the time for regrets was over.

Chicago slipped away beneath him and he was in the long tunnel of the screenplay. Maybe they should have made the film after all. Well, too late now. No, that was wrong. They would make it.

The tunnel seemed transparent. Outside he saw a vast and busy city, its people engaged in intense activity. The city was radiant in colors that seemed to fade periodically from red to violet and back again. Choirs sang (though not, he thought, the angel brats), musicians played, fountains and waterfalls sparkled and glowed. This city was like a city on earth but richer, fuller, more beautiful. If this indeed were heaven, was life in heaven like life on earth, only better?

We might do worse, he thought, and wished that Anna Maria was with him to share his surprise. Foolish thought.

Everyone was young and apparently happy. He drifted by GIs he had known in Alaska who had been killed later in Nam. They waved enthusiastically. Then a handsome young couple with broad grins who seemed to be cheering him. Who were they?

Mom and Dad! Looking like they did in their wedding picture. Maybe now they could straighten things out. He had never seen the two of them grinning at the same time.

The inhabitants of the city wore loose robes of many different colors and designs, robes that did not obscure the beauty of the bodies of both genders. Women were more attractive in heaven than on earth. Thank goodness, admiring attractive women still seemed possible.

He glanced at his own body, now young and strong again. He was wearing a light black robe with gold zigzag stripes. Did the design mean anything? he wondered. Did it mark him as some sort of problem case who had to be watched carefully before he was let out of the tunnel and into the crowd in the city?

He felt the need to exercise, to discharge the energy that was pent up in his apparently brand-new body. It had to be new, didn't it? His old body was back in the intensive care room or probably on its way to the morgue by now. Maybe not all of it. The priest had suggested that some of the human body remained with the spirit when it departed, perhaps that slight twist he had experienced when he had left his body was the breaking free of something that the people here could turn into a new body.

How *did* they figure out what kind of robe a new arrival should wear? They had a made good choice in his case. Did they have a file on him? Was he an entry in a massive database?

Did they play basketball up here, if *up* was the right word? He would have to find out.

What about human love? Anna Maria had said that she didn't want to go to heaven if she could not make love with him. No, she had been more colloquial—she had said "screw." He'd have to find out about that.

As he walked down the tunnel, Neenan felt a surge of happiness. Peace, joy, laughter, took possession of his being. He had never known so much happiness. It was deeper, broader, higher than the emotions in the ecstatic experiences that had started so long ago on the flight from Washington to Chicago and had continued during his love affair with his wife. Yet it was neither abrupt nor fleeting and certainly not intrusive as had been his previous ecstasy. Rather he felt that joy, smooth and natural, had taken permanent possession of whatever of his mortal self that remained.

No more worries, no more stress, no more fear. Maybe, he thought, this is the way we are supposed to live. Or the way we can live when we know that death is not the end.

I'll never go back to the old way of living, not even if I'm given a chance. The terrors of life are stupid. Why endure them? Anna Maria? The seraphs would take care of her. She would be with him soon and they would be happy together.

Wouldn't they?

Were not his mother and father together?

And were not many of the men and women who are strolling together through the sweet-smelling parks and gardens or rushing down
the broad streets holding hands or walking arm in arm? Did not his
parents have their arms around one another's waists?

Whatever form it took, human love certainly existed here and
seemed to be intense. For now it was enough that he know that.

Then the tunnel came to an end and the vast and dazzling globe of
light waited for him, the light that the script they had rejected said ought
to be here. The light was bright enough to be blinding, but it did not
hurt his eyes. Inside the light, waves of radiant energy swirled around
like the storms of light he had seen in pictures of the planet Jupiter. As
if from the center of the light there blazed streams of passionate love
that made the most powerful love he had ever known—the love between him and Anna Maria—seem weak and unimportant.

"Occupant," he whispered.

"Someone-Else-Altogether. . . . Welcome, Raymond Anthony," a
rich alto voice said with an amused laugh. "You never thought you
would enter this place as a hero, even as a martyr, did you?"

"I'm not a martyr."

The Voice laughed again in gentle amusement. "Perhaps not by the
Church's definition, but here I make the rules."

The Voice was thunder, but tender thunder; roaring waves, but
waves that touched the beach softly; wild waterfalls, but falls that also
bubbled like a brook; screaming winds, but winds that were as light
as the first zephyr of spring.

"Are you really a woman?" he asked.

The fragrance around the Voice combined every garden in the
world, but did not overwhelm. The music that accompanied her words
sounded like Mozart, not Beethoven, played on the most delicate of
instruments. The taste she seemed to radiate was of the best chocolate
ice cream with raspberry sauce and whipped cream. Neenan was
aware of all of these sensual experiences but realized that they were
only a hint of the reality he had encountered.

"Both men and women in your world are metaphors for me. In
your case it seemed better to disclose at this time the womanly metaphor, since so much of your life and your salvation has been related
to women."

"Metaphors, metaphors." Maybe one shouldn't argue with God, but she seemed to enjoy it.

"How else can limited creatures know the unlimited?"

"I take your point. . . . You laugh a lot, don't you?"

"If you're God, you have to laugh."

She seemed to treasure that line, because her laugh after it seemed quite self-satisfied. If you were God, presumably you had every reason to be self-satisfied.

"Do you weep too?"

"One of the reasons I take particular delight in you, Ray, is that you are so very quick and clever with the right questions. Certainly I weep. Does not every parent weep when a beloved child suffers? At this moment I laugh with you and weep with those you have left behind."

"How can you do that?"

"It's one of my little tricks," she said with yet another rich laugh.

"You sound a little like Miriam. Or should I say, Miriam sounded a little like you?"

"Either way. We both are pleased. Her job, as you realized, was to reveal my maternal love."

"I understand. Well, I think I do."

"I rejoice that I finally possess you as I have always desired and weep for the temporary pain that my full possession of you causes your other lovers. I will wipe away their tears, that I promise you, because I desire them too."

"You want to possess me?"

"You have it wrong, Ray. I already possess you. And you of course possess me. Love, as a very wise human once said, is not so much the desire to possess as the desire to be possessed."

"You don't mind my asking all these questions?"

"Certainly not. You amuse me greatly."

"Twelve-year-old boy."

"Was she not a wonderful gift?"

"The best. We will be together again?"

"Certainly, Ray. Why should you need to ask? I create because I love stories, especially love stories. Like all romantics I delight in happy endings."

"You're a romantic?"

"What else do I seem?"

"You need us then?"

Neenan was tense, anxious, excited, something like his state on the wedding night with Annie. Was God as vulnerable as Annie?

"Only theologians who have read too much Greek philosophy ask that question. Is it not evident that I want my creatures, even more than they want me? That in my own way I am as vulnerable as your good wife was on your first night together?"

"I guess so."

There was a pause as though the Voice was sizing him up, preparing for the next phase of their conversation. Or perhaps merely giving him the impression that she was sizing him up.

"You noticed your parents when you came through the tunnel?"

"Yes . . . What has happened to them?"

"They are struggling through their purgatory. They are trying to understand where their love story went wrong and then to set it right. Purgatory, you see, is not a place distinct from this one, rather it is an activity in which humans engage as part of being here. It is most exciting and most painful in that they must accept their shame."

"You make them do that?"

"No. Rather I make it possible for them to do it, and of course they want to do it. I intervene to limit the amount of time they can expend on each encounter. Their pain is pleasurable — as was your impressive reconciliation with poor Estelle — but they must pursue reconciliation at a reasonable pace."

"My parents with me?"

"In due course. It will be easy for you and very difficult for them. However, the reconciliation you sought in vain on earth will come eventually."

"Wonderful!"

Another pause. "You were very responsive to my messengers' promptings."

"They're good people."

"Oh, yes. A little too intense at times."

What was she about to spring?

"It is most difficult to explain to you, Ray, how much I enjoy you. Those very characteristics that your wife and other women found appealing are very attractive to me. You are a human in which strength and tenderness are nicely combined, even if it required considerable effort toward the end of your life to work out the balance."

"Thank you."

Whose effort, he wondered, mine or yours?

"Unlike the seraphs I read thoughts. You are now wondering what I'm driving at?"

She was like Anna Maria, as well as Miriam. That was nice.

"You don't have to read my thoughts to know that."

"There is but one problem, you see."

Here it comes, he thought. "And that is?"

"You came too early!"

"Huh?"

"I will now have to explain how I tell my stories. It will be a little hard to understand, because you are not God. As time goes on, you will understand me better: that is one of the great delights of this place. But never perfectly. . . . Is this acceptable?"

"I'll make a virtue out of necessity and say that it is."

Neenan felt himself inundated by an intoxicating stream of love.

"I do love you, so much," she said with something like a sigh. Something like Anna Maria's sigh.

"I love you too, though it seems presumptuous to say that."

"Not at all. That's what you're supposed to do and say. Like all storytellers, you see, I am an empiricist, a pragmatist, I play it by ear as I tell my stories. Since I deprive no one of their freedom, my characters and the forces of nature in which they live may choose not to follow my most preferred scenario. Therefore I must fall back on other and less preferred scenarios. In the end I see that their freedom leads to my happy endings, but it often requires, how shall I say it, considerable dexterity on my part."

"No, I don't understand it, but I guess I'm not supposed to."

"You were not supposed to die in that gunfight."

"Oh, oh," he murmured.

"The fight activated a scenario that was far down on my list of preferences. The poor seraphs blame themselves because they love you so much. It was, however, patently not their fault."

"And not your fault either?"

"I do not deny people their freedom. I simply stand by with other scenarios to work my way around their freedom."

"I don't see how it makes any difference. I was going to die anyway."

The voice sighed loudly. "No, my beloved, as a point of fact you were not, not yet."

"But the seraphs . . ."

"Were warned to tell you that you should straighten out your life lest you die in three months. Perhaps they misunderstood. It is only very rarely that we establish such a scenario."

That was pretty thin, he thought. "Lest?"

"I admit that it was thin. Scenarios get thin sometimes. It was necessary to scare you in order that you might not die, as one very unpleasant but highly probable scenario would have worked out. The fear of the Lord is the beginning of wisdom, as you may have heard. We avoided that less than preferred scenario and seem to have stumbled into another. I know you cannot understand me, dearest one, but believe that all was done out of love for you and respect for the freedom of all involved."

Another thick wave of love embraced him.

"I love you too much," he said, "to argue with you."

"You will always argue with me, Ray. That is in your nature, the way I made it."

"All right, what's happening here?"

"When less preferred scenarios develop which lead to a death before the more preferred time, on occasion we give the subject a chance to return."

"I read the screenplay. Like the woman in it, I want to stay here with you. There's no one back on earth — if that's the right geography — that needs me like her family needed her."

"That's not altogether true."

"You're going to tell me who needs me?"

"Naturally. You noticed those two adolescent women with the blank faces at the side of your death bed."

"Yeah. Who were they?"

"The twin daughters Anna Maria is carrying in her womb. She does not know yet that she is pregnant. When she finds out, she will be very happy because they are the enduring result of the love between the two of you during the last days of your life, the result indeed of that lovely little incident on the beach."

"Oh." What do you say when God springs that on you? "Wonderful!" he said, testing the word and finding that it fit. "I wish I could be there to take care of them. Now I'll never know them . . . not on earth anyway."

"You need not worry. It will be an easy pregnancy for her and an easy childbirth. We will take good care of them. The seraphs—who, as you know, love 'offspring'—will dote on them. It is not essential that you return to be a father to them."

"If I'm not needed, then I don't want to go back."

"No one does. I said you were not essential. I did not say that it would not be a much more preferred scenario if you saw them to adulthood."

"That takes a long time these days."

"Oh, yes, Ray, it does. I would be with you all the time of course. Like I always have been. They will be extremely important young women. It would be most preferable for them to have a father present, especially one like you."

"I see," he said, not liking the idea at all. Sure he would love them. But couldn't he love them just as well from here? Would he not be even a better advocate here—wherever here is?

"It also would be preferable," the voice went on inexorably, "for you to be present to support your wife's growth and development as a person, a woman, and a writer, and your daughter's growth as an actress and as a wife, and your son's growth as a executive and as a husband and father."

"That's playing dirty."

Another delighted laugh. "I never promised I wouldn't do that in search of the best possible scenarios."

"I don't get this at all. If you'd asked me before I was shot whether I wanted to stay with them, I would have said yes. Now you have to talk me into it. What's happening?"

"You've found out, just like the woman in the screenplay, what comes after death. You remember that she never feared death again. Neither will you."

"Yeah, but . . ."

"All the other delights will have to wait several decades. And worse yet, you will have to struggle with two strong-minded and contentious young women, you will have to be a parent again. It doesn't look like much fun, does it?"

"From the point of view I'm in now, it certainly doesn't, especially since you say they'll be all right without me."

"And better with you," she said softly.

"Not much better."

"We would know that only at the end of the story, as the various scenarios unfold. And, by the way, if you return, your recovery will be rapid and complete. My little friends will see to that."

"Yeah," he said meekly.

"I have made the case for return, Ray, mostly because I will so enjoy the story if you go back. From your point of view that may seem selfish on my part."

"I'd have to know you a lot better than I do to make that judgment."

He was swept up in another amused divine hug. He didn't want to give those up.

"Now, I will be very serious, Ray: it is your free choice. I mean that. You are not by any means absolutely essential to the continuation of the story. I will love you no less. If you do not freely choose to go back, you will be no help to Gabrielle and Michelle. However, I will abide by your decision. Whatever you decide will please me."

"Bullshit!" he exclaimed.

The Voice thought that was very, very funny. Then she added more seriously, "If you go back, my beloved, I will miss you even more than you miss me. Nevertheless, you are completely free."

"You know better than that," he replied.

"What do you mean?" she asked, apparently greatly pleased by his disrespect.

"With love there is never complete freedom, my lover," he replied, as though he were talking to Anna Maria or Gabrielle or Michelle. "I know that as well as you do. The way we exercise our freedom is shaped by wishes of the ones we love. You'd like me to go back to take care of that mercurial Sicilian and those two little brats, all of whom we both adore. Since you are my lover and I yours, I will do it. Naturally. Of course."

He paused and then added the word that she was waiting to hear, just as he would have for Anna Maria.

"Joyously."

God hugged him again.

"Are you sure I will be back?"

"Do you think I could do without you?"

"I guess not."

"And whenever you wonder whether I am with you and waiting

for you, you need merely contemplate the wonderful metaphor of myself I created with you in mind and gave you as your wife."

"Metaphors everywhere," he sighed.

"Perhaps there will also be on occasion little shipments of raisin cookies."

Then he was whirling through space — or through somewhere. God did not waste time on long good-byes, did she?

Two pretty girl kids? They'd wear an old man out. Or maybe keep him young. He looked forward to meeting them. For the first time he was glad that he was going back. God did know best after all.

He felt another divine hug. Will those continue? I hope so.

Then Michael and Gaby were with him, carrying him, happy smiles on their faces. The angel brats were singing a hymn of joy.

"You'd better not try to change their names," the boss seraph warned him.

He spun downward toward Chicago, a city bright in anticipation of Christmas.

Then he was at the ceiling of the intensive care room.

Anna Maria and the woman doctor were sobbing in each other's arms. Everyone was weeping, except the twins, who had been returned to their mother's womb.

"I'm so sorry we lost him," the doctor said through her tears. "It was so terribly close."

Have I got a surprise for you.

He twisted back into his body. The various beepers in the room began to sound again, vigorous and reassuring.

"We've got him back," the doctor shouted triumphantly.

Better not take too much credit.

He opened his eyes and tried to manage a grin.

His wife's smiling, tearstained face filled his vision. He reached out and touched it gently. He thanked the Voice in the radiant cloud for her.

As a metaphor, she'd do just fine.